SORCERY & SACRIFICE

SORCERY
AND
STAGECRAFT

ONE

KRISTIN L. HAMBLIN

SORCERY AND STAGECRAFT

Kristin L. Hamblin – kristinlhamblin.com

Copyright © 2024 by Crown of Laurel Press, Owasso, OK

Cover Design by saintjupi3rgr4phic

Editing by Lisa Lee Editing

Map by Cartographybird Maps

Library of Congress Control Number: 2024902747

Paperback ISBN: 978-1-959230-06-9

For anyone who's ever dreamed of one day waking up with magic and being whisked away to a land of unicorns and fairies.

THE FAE REALM

EMBIDIAN SEA

TROLL
HIGHLANDS

EASTERN
BANKS

AMELYN
RIVER

OLDINGER
FORTRESS

ALBERRY

THE FAE
KINGDOM OF
ASENTIA

WESTWATER
LANDS

GOBLIN
KINGDOM

WESTLAND
GNOMES

DIATEM

LIRIAN
FOREST

UNICORN
SANCTUM

SOLICE

SPRITE
FOREST

THE HUMAN WORLD

CORDELIAN
OCEAN

MARSO
RIVER

PULTON

NORTHLAND
FOREST

TIMBERCROSS

FALLHOLD

HUNTERTON

KINGDOM OF
TAUNFALAN

RICCI
PLAINS

ALBERON

DEVSHIRE

PARNUVIAN
DESERT

CHAPTER 1

S he'd performed hundreds of times—almost since the day she was born—but Ricci Menowin's heart still raced as their caravan approached the town. Hunterton, the latest in a never-ending rotation. But tonight, she'd perform the lead role for the first time.

Her large, loud, smothering but still perfectly loving family had never trusted her before. Her rising nerves wouldn't let her forget this was her one shot to prove she could handle it. If she failed, there'd be a crowd of spectators waiting to throw rotten vegetables at her. Her family wouldn't get paid, she'd ruin their reputation, and her sister-in-law would be ready to take back the role she'd had for years now, sending Ricci to the background again.

No big deal.

Reins held loose in her hands, Ricci sat next to Papa on the driver's bench. The wagon's tottering jostled her bones as they passed wooden homes and shops. Plenty of townsfolk, some with heavy, fabric-draped baskets, still teemed the market stalls, which was good. Evening was not the best time to arrive to town, when coin ran low and folks ached to go home after a long, weary day.

Thankfully she didn't spot any other troupes on this end of the market. A group in the previous town had camped right next to them—and worse, they'd employed a magic wielder who drew the crowds—and coin—away. Mama wouldn't allow their troupe to do the same—not even potions for simple smoke effects.

Something bumped Ricci's back and she jumped.

"Might as well open this now," Mama said through the wagon's open window, voice muffled from inside. She leaned over Ricci's bunk with a rare smile, holding out a package wrapped in brown paper and tied with twine. "Happy birthday."

Papa chuckled and took the reins. Presents were rare indeed. Their family traveling troupe barely made enough coin to support everyone.

"Thank you, Mama." Ricci took the package and ripped into it. She gasped at the peek of shiny green material and tore faster. It was definitely a new costume of some kind, and much needed too. She'd outgrown her last dress months ago—the length becoming scandalous.

Ricci pinched the top and lifted it out of the paper remains. "Oh!"

The emerald-green fabric shimmered the full length of the gorgeous gown and down its long sleeves. The neck was rounded, and the chest was accented with gold piping in front of cream fabric forming a triangle down the front. She touched the slippery cloth with the tips of her fingers. Finally, a woman's dress instead of a girl's. Busty.

"You only turn sixteen once." Papa cleared his throat, and his mustache twitched. "Mama and Nora worked real hard on it."

Nora had been a great addition to their troupe since Ricci's oldest brother Lanny married her a few years ago. She was a wonderful seamstress, something Ricci would never be no matter how hard she tried.

"It's perfect for my new role." They'd yet to perform her brothers' latest creation, but had rehearsed it many times, and she knew all her lines by heart.

Mama took the dress and wrappings inside. Their two horses slowed in the street traffic, allowing Papa to scout a good place for their performance. They needed lots of space and lots of people. Ricci turned around in anticipation of what came next.

Sure enough, a drum banged behind them, and a moment later Nicholas appeared on the road—the youngest and most comedic of her three brothers. Even fourteen years younger than him, she was often the more mature one. He never took anything seriously, so court jester was a good role for him. His costume was green and purple, with an outrageous hat that had four points ending in tinkling silver bells hanging in front of his white-painted face.

People stopped to turn and stare, some smiling and pointing in delight.

"Hear ye, hear ye!" Nicholas called in his overly-loud voice. "Gather one and all, and feast your eyes on a marvelous show of love and adventure, comedy and tragedy. You have the privilege to witness the Magnificent Menowin Traveling Troupe!"

He banged his drum a few times, winking at Ricci as he passed.

She rolled her eyes, smiling.

Nicholas repeated his speech as they traveled the full length of the road. It wasn't a very large market, but it certainly wasn't the smallest they'd performed for. Some waved away the lure of Nicholas's entreaties, still others followed, likely wooed by the size of the caravan—four wagons deep, painted bright greens and florals that caught the eye. After three generations of frequenting the same markets, they were known for their engaging shows.

A group of girls Ricci's age walked together alongside the road, skirting around market stalls and laughing together. They stopped in front of a pair of grinning boys, striking in their trousers and vests. They looked so carefree, so comfortable with each other. Lifelong friends. What must it be like to grow up in one place? Maybe even live in a house where you could stretch out your arms and not touch both walls.

One of the boys looked up, meeting Ricci's eyes. His dusty-blond hair hung in curls to his chin. Ricci gave a small smile. He laughed and bent toward his friends, who whispered to each other. Ricci lowered her head. Heat burned her cheeks. Her life must look like a joke to them. They wouldn't think so little of her if she were famous, performing for the king himself. One day.

Papa led the horses into a semi-circle in a clearing just past the last market stall. "It's late, Ricci," he said. "The crowd won't wait forever. Best you go get ready." The wagon lurched to a stop.

Ricci nodded, biting down her embarrassment. As soon as she came of age, she could leave all the traveling behind. She'd prove to her family it was possible to earn a living without hopping from market to market.

"Forget about them. Family is all the love you need. Now go get ready," Papa said. Ricci crossed her arms, and he nudged her. "Use your gift, Ricika." Something her parents liked to tell her before a show to remind her to do a good job, that she was talented.

It didn't take as long for Papa to get ready. He usually played a scholar or wise man, with nothing more to do than don a black robe and maybe comb his mustache since he had no other hair. Ricci hurried inside where Mama, already dressed, held the new costume up. Ricci's heart fluttered as anticipation returned. She pushed ridiculous thoughts of meeting people her own age out of her mind and stripped off her plain, brown linen dress. Keeping her underclothes and skirts on, she stepped into the shiny costume.

Mama cinched up the back a little too tight, then sat Ricci down to re-braid her red hair, twisting it up, like a woman of high class would. Facing the tiny mirror, Ricci applied lipstick and powder, darker and more dramatic than she would in real life, so as not to look washed out from afar. The emerald dress drew out the gold flecks in her green eyes, and with her long neck exposed, she suddenly hoped those boys would be at the show.

Without the wagon's rustle, the murmurs of the gathering crowd grew more distinct. Her brothers, uncle, Papa, and cousins would be busy organizing their few props and tending to the horses. Nora, with her son Jace at her hip, would be readying their costumes. Aunt Roma would be arranging a makeshift backstage. Outside, Nicholas juggled and told tired jokes to warm up the crowd.

"Give me a lass with a nice ample... mind!
Let her touch be sweet as can be.
And after I'm fed, make her wild in... spirit!
Oh, to give me such glee.
No, I do not jest, give her nice supple... skills!
And may her whimsy be wild and free."
The crowd roared with laughter.

Ricci spun and glared at the window. "Oh, why does Nicholas have to sing such wretched tunes?"

"That one was rather horrible." Mama frowned as she moved to finish her own makeup. She would be playing the

5

role of the Evil Sorceress. The dark-burgundy gown swayed against her thin frame. "Your brother plays to the crowd. This one must be a little rowdier than some."

Ricci bit off her reply and shoved her stockinged feet into thin leather slippers. Yes, they had to play to the crowd, but why didn't it bother anyone else that it was done at the expense of women? *It's the way things are*, her mama and sister-in-law had said a hundred times.

Someone knocked on the door. "It's Nora," Ricci's sister-in-law called out before letting herself in. Even in her spinster dress of dull browns and creams, face smeared with soot to play the part of the Wise Lady, Nora couldn't hide her beauty. A scarf covered her head, but tell-tale golden curls still peeked out. Her son Jace wasn't with her.

Nora flashed the warm smile that had endeared everyone to her the moment Lanny brought her home. "Ricci, you look amazing. Closer to twenty than sixteen." She gave Ricci a loose hug that was her typical greeting when they were perfor-mance-ready. "Happy birthday."

"Thank you, Nora," Ricci said sincerely, unwilling to let resentment ruin this evening. Nora had had the perfect, stable life. Ricci still couldn't understand why she'd traded her charming home for Lanny and a life always on the move. "You did a wonderful job on the dress. I love it."

Nora started to reply, but Mama cut her off. "Are the boys ready? Uncle Patrick and Aunt Roma? The cousins?"

"All ready," Nora replied in a cheerful voice.

Ricci sat on Mama's bottom bunk, leaning back on her hands.

Without the time to build a proper stage, the grass would serve their needs. Lanny's wagon provided cover between sets. They performed this way often, when the crowd or time of day didn't justify the effort or expense of a proper platform.

"How are you feeling, Ricci?" Nora moved a small stool beside her. "Nervous for your big role?"

Ricci lifted an eyebrow. Nerves were the last thing she felt. She was born for this. She'd never had a part big enough to show what she could do, but acting was in her blood. Tonight would be different, her time to shine.

The emotions were already building like a rising bubble inside her as she rehearsed lines in her head. Her character, Princess Kasma, would fear for her life from the Evil Sorceress, she'd cry for her missing family, she'd love her rescuing hero fiercely. Ricci would make it the realest thing this backwoods rowdy crowd had ever seen.

She looked at Nora. "Just anxious to get on with things."

Outside, Papa's booming voice took over as he began the introduction. "Ladies and Gentlemen, lads and lasses, prepare yourselves for a tale of love and adventure..." The crowd cheered, and Ricci's heart leaped. "Of comedy and tragedy..."

"Places, ladies," Mama said. "Use your gift, Ricci."

Ricci started. Mama had never called her a lady before.

Her mama checked her makeup and tall, black wig once more before following Nora out the door. Ricci smoothed her dress. The crowd cheered when they caught a glimpse of her shiny costume, but she didn't look, simply hurried behind Lanny's wagon where the others already waited. She guessed there were about two dozen spectators. Hopefully they'd all stay for the whole thing. Townsfolk hardly ever paid if they left the show early. Never, in fact, which was why they kept their performances under an hour. A half-hour was best.

Ricci knew about the plays that went on for hours, performed for lords and kings. That was what she wanted to do someday—perform for an audience that valued the art of what they did, not just looking for cheap entertainment. And find people that would smile back, not laugh and whisper to their friends because, clearly, simple kindness was too much to bother with.

Nicholas had changed out of his jester costume to become a Sorceress's Servant. He waited behind his wagon with their middle brother, Bartley. Aunt Roma—Papa's sister—who'd be doing the sound effects, was with Jace behind Papa's wagon. Jace—Lanny and Nora's son—had played a good baby when he was younger, but at three, he was more likely to sit down and cry in the middle of a performance than to act out even the simplest parts.

Uncle Patrick glanced up as Ricci approached but didn't comment on her dress or special day. He was quiet like that. He loved her in his own way.

"... It is our pleasure to present to you, The Tale of Princess Kasma," Papa finished with a thundering voice. He took a place behind the wagon beside Ricci's much-older twin cousins, cheeks reddened from all the bluster.

The frantic clanging of a loud bell sent her family to sighing. Aunt Roma had let Jace help with the sound effects again. The bell was supposed to be long and steady, like the gong of a church. No matter. That was Ricci's cue. She took three deep breaths, pulled her shoulders back, raised her chin, and stepped out from around the wagon, hands clasped demurely in front of her.

Some of the crowd cheered. The show had finally begun. Several whistled and cat-called. Ricci ignored them. They didn't exist. She was Princess Kasma in a grand courtyard. Her blood sang, bathing her in warmth so fine as to prickle uncomfortably for a brief moment—it must be a hot day in Princess Kasma's court.

She imagined the courtly flowers in their sculpted pots. Smelled their sweet scent as a gentle breeze caressed her painted cheek. Felt the hard stone beneath her thin shoes and heard her steps echo off the castle walls behind her.

Listened as a tower bell clanged unusually in the distance.

She imagined the scene so hard, it felt real. Looked real, too, but foggy, as if in a cloud.

The crowd gasped. "It's magic."

A woman screamed.

Ricci didn't hear them. They didn't exist. "Oh, happiest of days are these, for I get to marry my true love on the morrow." She welcomed the joy that washed over her, lighting her smile and glistening her eyes. The crowd grew silent. "I'll never want for anything more, save that tomorrow arrive and I shall be married."

A gasp from behind let her know Nora had entered the scene, just as rehearsed—but Nora missed her line.

Ricci turned to see Nora as a wise old lady, golden curls still peeking from her headscarf, standing beside a hedge of perfectly pruned roses, mouth agape and eyes roving over the courtyard as if she'd never seen one and had no idea how she'd got there.

"Who are you?" Princess Kasma asked.

The old lady blinked, as if coming aware of herself. "I-I am no one of consequence." Her words were disjointed, confused, and lacking the old-lady rasp she should have for someone her age. "I overheard you're getting married tomorrow."

Princess Kasma smiled and twirled, green dress fluttering. "Yes! Aren't I the luckiest princess?"

"Allow an old lady to give some advice, if I may." The rasp was there, and her words were stronger now, more confident. She approached with a hunch. "Happiness comes in all forms. You must learn to look beyond the immediate moment, and think of others more than yourself." And with that, she was gone, disappearing behind the hedgerows.

With a flick of her wrist, Princess Kasma waved the advice away. "But I'm getting married." She took her leave between two thick trees with large purple leaves.

As soon as Ricci stepped off stage, the world turned back to normal. The crowd cheered manically behind her, a roar full of wonder. The grass returned beneath her feet, the temperature warmed, and her family smiled at her behind Lanny's wagon. All but Nora, who looked pale and leaned heavily against the wagon wheel.

"You did great, dear," Mama said. From their spots behind the wagon, they couldn't have watched the show, but they heard Ricci's lines and the crowd's reaction. Mama and Nicholas stepped out for their scene.

Ricci grinned. She'd never had so much fun. She had poured everything into those few, cliché lines.

Now Mama, the Evil Sorceress, laid out her plans to kill Princess Kasma and take her place to marry the prince so she could be queen. A crash sounded as Nicholas—the Sorceress's foolish servant—tripped over a prop table of fake potions. The crowd roared with laughter. Ricci chuckled, imagining her brother rolling dramatically in the grass.

"Fool," the Evil Sorceress said in a haughty, powerful voice. "Clean up this mess. The wedding is tomorrow, and there's no time to waste." Mama reappeared as she stepped off stage. Nicholas followed shortly after, dropping jars and vials in stumbling comedic haste.

Bartley, her second-oldest brother, stepped from behind his wagon wearing black tights and a dark blue vest with gold piping, hair pulled back in a low tail—his princely attire. The wedding scene. It was almost Ricci's turn again. Mama grabbed a veil from the prop chest and pinned it to Ricci's hair, folding it in a way to hide its many rips. Like most of the things needing replaced, they simply couldn't afford it. The sun was almost set, so the darkness would hide its shabbiness.

Ricci retrieved the smushed bundle of cloth flowers, smacking them against her palm in a futile effort to breathe new life into them.

"Here comes my fair bride now," Bartley said. Ricci used to shudder at the thought of having to play a love interest to one of her brothers.

She glanced at Nora, concerned she might be getting sick, but Nora had regained her color and no longer leaned against the wagon, though her brow creased with worry.

Ricci walked regally back on the stage, once again focusing all she had on putting herself in the moment. The crowd cheered for her. Prince Vamere smiled a dazzling smile, hand extended back to her. Heat prickled from Ricci's middle and over her skin once more, a staticky feel in the air like before a storm. The courtyard appeared before her eyes, foggy, as it had before.

The crowd gasped with delight. Prince Vamere's hand drooped. Papa was in front of him, the priest to marry them. Both of their mouths hung wide open, and they stared around the stone courtyard with its flowers and pale pink sky.

Pink? Ricci's imagination was getting away from her.

The distant gong sounded again—probably Jace in the sound effects—but Uncle Patrick covered it up with a somber wedding tune on the mandolin—Ricci's cue to walk to her husband-to-be.

The crowd was their witness to the blessed event.

Princess Kasma lifted her chin, smiling wide for her fiancé, and stepped lithely to the beat of the sweet music. This was the happiest moment of her life. Everything she'd ever wanted was about to come true. Prince Vamere met her gaze, and he shook himself. A slow attempt at a confident grin had replaced his confusion when she reached the front and he took her hand.

The priest cleared his throat. "We are gathered today, prince, princess, and poor humble peasants." He gestured toward the crowd who laughed. They, too, stared around the bright courtyard, eyes darting to the sound of chirping birds.

The priest continued. "Do you, Princess Kasma, take Prince Vamere to be your lawfully wedded husband?"

"I do," she said, voice loud and sure.

Prince Vamere flashed a loving smile.

"And do you, Prince Vamere, take Princess Kasma to be your lawfully wedded wife?"

Prince Vamere stared into her eyes. "I do."

"Oh no, you don't!" a voice shouted from out of sight.

The Sorceress entered the courtyard. Her deep burgundy gown and piled black hair sucked the light from around her. Behind her followed the hunched servant and two henchmen, swords drawn. The Sorceress gasped, stumbling backward with a hand over her heart. The henchmen caught her, looking equally surprised.

That was not what they'd rehearsed.

The courtyard flickered away for just a moment, revealing their green-painted wagons. Ricci focused, forcing her imagination into the story. The courtyard flickered back again.

Prince Vamere threw Princess Kasma behind him, pulling a ceremonial sword from its sheath. "You shall not have her!"

The henchmen recovered, and a violent duel erupted between them and Prince Vamere. Swords clashed until one by one, Prince Vamere felled the enemies.

"Save me, you fool!" the Evil Sorceress screamed to her servant.

The servant glanced comically from side to side, then ran for his life, arms in the air. The crowd laughed.

Prince Vamere faced his princess, smiling.

"Look out!" Princess Kasma cried.

He turned just in time to avoid being impaled by the Evil Sorceress. He blocked, then ran her through with his sword. She fell to the ground dead.

The crowd cheered, hands raised and clapping with everything they had. Prince Vamere and Princess Kasma held each other.

"The Wise Old Lady was right," Princess Kasma said. "Life is about more than just me. It's about us and our happily ever after."

As if it never was, the courtyard disappeared. Grass and the semi-circle of wagons replaced stone and hedgerows. The wedding guests became the motley crowd, cheering like they'd never cheered before. They pumped their fists in the air, barely holding the children back from rushing the impromptu stage. The adoration flowed over her, fueling her up for next time, though her racing heart had yet to calm. She'd given her best performance. Everything had felt so real this time, more real than ever before.

Too real.

Her family glanced warily at one another as they each emerged from their spots behind the wagons. Together, they formed a line across the stage and bowed or curtsied. Ricci looked up at the sound of coins plunking into their collection basket. Townsfolk dug deep into their pockets, throwing more than just a few coppers.

"Princess Kasma!" a tall skinny fellow yelled out, waving. Others took up the call.

Ricci looked to Papa.

Papa stepped forward. "Thank you for your generosity, fine people of Hunterton. Princess Kasma must retire for the evening, but please, tell your friends and neighbors. There will be three more performances tomorrow."

The crowd pushed closer. Lanny and Nicholas guarded the collection basket while Ricci and the rest of her family retreated to their wagons. The golden-orange evening had become the dark of night, with only their caravan lanterns and a spattering of street lights left. Inside, Ricci plopped down on a stool, grinning. What an evening! She turned her face up to her parents, waiting for the praise she'd earned.

They stood silent. Watching her. Mama worked her hands, all veins and knobby bones.

Papa met Mama's worried eyes, then moved to the window and drew the curtain aside. "Lanny has the basket," he said. "He's shaking hands with some of the last townspeople."

Papa should have stepped out to let them change by now, but he just stood there at the window.

"Was something wrong with my performance?" she asked. The crowd certainly didn't seem to think so.

"You didn't notice anything unusual?" Mama asked.

"You did wonderful," Papa said at the same time.

The royal courtyard had seemed real, but it was only in her head. She'd look like a crazy person if she asked if anyone else saw what she'd seen.

"Well, I thought it went great." Irritation coated her words. She'd given her best performance ever, maybe even the start of her ticket out of this way of life, and they hadn't even said how she'd done.

The door burst open. Lanny, eyes wide, hefted the coin basket.

"This is more than we make in a whole day of performing!" he said.

Ricci grinned. She *knew* she'd done something right.

All three turned their eyes to her. Lanny looked exultant. Mama and Papa looked worried.

Her parents had been much older when Ricci was born, putting an eighteen-year difference between her and her oldest brother, Lanny, which was probably why they all still treated her like a child. She'd always be the baby to them.

Well, let them judge her performance too harshly. Ricci didn't care. Fame meant money, money meant her family would be provided for, and then one day she'd be able to settle down and perform for the king.

CHAPTER 2

King Theron sat up on his cold, hard throne. His wings flared. "You feel it, don't you?" he said to his watching guard. They stood as still as stone, red eyes behind black armor.

Dust rained down from the stone walls and ceiling. Blistering winds battered the keep. More of his subjects shuffled into the throne room, heads tilted but silent. Wondering.

King Theron eased back down, wings tucked in. "Yes. After all this time." They watched him, hundreds now gathered. Torches cast shadows over their forms and the dark, windowless space. "Not much longer now. We will be ready."

"Yes, my king," they rumbled.

He flashed a wicked grin, exposing fangs. "A portal has opened."

CHAPTER 3

A distant bell sounded an alarm. *Gong gong gong.*

Lela Ashryn lifted her head from the herb garden, hands stilling in the dirt. Her long ears picked up the faint pinging—something she never thought to hear in her lifetime. Something that hadn't happened in centuries.

Panic washed over Lela's skin, pushing away the meager growth energy she'd used to tend the herbs.

The alarm meant only one thing. A portal had opened. The prophecy was being fulfilled.

Lela had read the stories. She'd listened when Mata taught her, over and over. Lifetimes had passed since the last portal between realms had closed, but the fae race hadn't forgotten what was promised if it ever opened again.

Death for their people.

Mata. She had to get home. Her mata was in danger. They all were.

Lela's hands shook as she stood, automatically dusting the knees of her leggings. She risked one more moment's hesitation and looked across the dirt road and beyond the field of green grass with white flowers. Her lifelong friend, Oren, stopped just inside his front door. From this distance, Lela could barely make out the anxious expression on his face.

He mouthed the word *go,* then hurried inside his family's two-story cottage and shut the door.

"Lelana!" Mata's dark hair flashed between the vegetation.

Lela sprinted through rows of evening primrose and echinacea, past turmeric, ginger, and many others. Mata was the healer for the surrounding area, and since she didn't possess any command over the energies, the herbs were everything. If they didn't thrive, their patients suffered.

Mata sighed with relief when she spotted Lela. "The alarms. Come." She turned toward their small cottage.

Pata. A spike of worry stole the rest of Lela's breath. What was Pata doing right now? Mobilizing the army to meet the threat? Moving to protect Prince Renic and the royal family?

Pata was King Sidian's general. He could take care of himself. Lela shoved her worries deep inside, though Mata had to be wondering too. The instinct to protect each other came with the bond of being family.

Lela rushed up the stone steps to the cottage's front door just as the evening sun burned through its last golden rays. The smell of baking bread replaced fresh-churned dirt. The familiar scent didn't ease Lela's racing heart or shattering nerves.

The bells still tolled, overriding all senses.

Mata had already lit the lanterns, bathing the space in the warm glow of a false comfort. The cottage was tall enough for a loft, with a ladder to where Lela slept, a single bedroom for Mata—Pata too, on the rare occasions he came home—a small kitchen, and the main living area where the patients were treated. Wounded hunters, injured farmers, and even the rare birthing mother.

19

Lela crossed the wood floor, sanded light from years of scrubbing it clean of blood. Mata, with her slender frame and youthful face, pressed against the front door like a fae barricade to the threat of the alarm tolling outside.

"It's really happening, isn't it, Mata?" Lela asked, breathing unsteadily from her sprint. Sage and garlic from the herbs hanging to dry in the doorway filled her nose.

"It is, Lelana." Mata rushed to the kitchen, and the sounds of banging pots filled the space. Of course, she'd already be preparing. Her mata never sat still.

The tolling of the gongs ceased. Lela held her breath.

Mata's clanging paused. "The portal is closed."

But the danger had not passed. Anything could be headed their way.

"We must gather in the town square," her mata called from the kitchen.

"Yes," Lela said simply, heading toward the ladder to the loft.

She knew the procedure. Meet at the town square in Diatem. Prepare in case of evacuation to the safe haven in Oldinger—an ancient fortress with the strongest protection energy. The town elders would tell them what to do. With hope, they'd have news, knowledge of what trouble Pata might be part of.

What trouble was coming for them.

Lela reached the top of her ladder when a knock at the door made her jump. She slid back down, but the door opened before she reached it. Oren's bright blue eyes met hers, and he smiled—a forced thing that didn't hide the fear in his eyes. Her troubles lessened and breathing came easier. But she couldn't return his smile.

"Oren." Her voice trembled, composure cracking. It was easy to pretend everything was alright when it was just Mata.

The lanterns illuminated his light blond hair as his smile slipped. He took two quick steps, reaching out as if to embrace her, but then stopped, patting her arm instead. "Don't worry, Le," he said.

She and Oren had grown up together, getting into trouble in the woods and angering their mothers. She'd been in love with him ever since becoming old enough to know what love was. Sometimes she sensed he felt the same, and sometimes it seemed all in her head, but he was careful around her. Custom dictated he couldn't court her until she turned eighteen, as he had just a few months ago. He was certainly free to court whomever he wished in the meantime.

Lela frowned.

"Is that Oren?" Mata called from the kitchen.

"Yes, Mata Ashryn," he said. "Mata sent me to see if you needed any help." Because they already had one male in their house to help with things. How nice it must have been to have both parents around when the world was coming to an end.

Mata made a disapproving tsk sound as Oren set down a packed bag.

Oren saw Lela watching it. "It didn't take me long to pack." He shrugged.

Oren was already dressed in travel clothes—a tight, hunter-green tunic with long sleeves, dark trousers, and leather boots laced up around his calves. His hair was in a tail lest it get snagged on a branch during a hasty retreat.

He strode for the kitchen. "Need more water from the well, Mata Ashryn?"

Lela ignored the rest of the conversation as Oren disappeared into the kitchen. She clasped her hands in a crushing grip. Maybe things would be better if Oren wasn't here.

But that wasn't true. If this turned into an escape for survival, Oren was definitely the one she wanted at her side.

He was strong, confident, handsome, and able to talk his way out of anything. Good with a bow, too. She'd be okay in a fight —her pata had seen to that on his rare visits home. But they'd be better together.

She climbed the ladder to her loft bedroom and yanked a sturdy, waterproof satchel from under her bed. Mata would bring most of what they needed, but Lela had her favorites she couldn't part with—mostly herbs for healing. She'd always wanted to be a healer, a true healer, using the energies. The powerful ones could make wounds go away as if they never were. But she only possessed meager skill in growing things. It was such a fragile balance, requiring complete concentration, and she'd never been very good at channeling the energies.

Lela tucked the herbs under some well-made travel clothes, a cloak for warmth, sturdy boots, and her basic healer's guide, and that was all it took before her pack ran out of room. Just enough space left to help carry some of the food and water. She lamented her books, tales of demons and heroes embellished from fae legend.

Maybe it would turn out to be a mistake and then all this worry would be for nothing.

Lela stared at the leaf collage Oren had made her, pinned to the wall, allowing herself ten more heartbeats to pretend the gongs had never tolled. He'd gathered the leaves last autumn, arranging them from biggest in back to smallest in front, in all the wonderful shades of scarlets and apricots. Something in his energy kept them from fading to brown.

Lela hurried into her travel clothes—thick sturdy leggings and a tunic that had cost a fortune in herbs for trade, but Mata had insisted were necessary. She'd never worn this set before. The journey to Diatem was not far enough to need sturdy travel clothes, but the journey after was uncertain. Would they be able to return home, or would they be directed elsewhere?

Lela braided her silver hair, grabbed the packed satchel, and hastened down the ladder. A flash of gold from her bookshelf caught her eye as she descended. The medal Pata had won for bravery fighting the Westland gnomes. He'd given it to Mata who'd given it to her. He said they made him brave, so it really belonged to them. Then just as quickly, he'd gone away again, off on another campaign.

Lela swallowed against a hard lump. She strived to be as brave as him.

Mata stuffed a few apples into a bulging bag and tied a sloshing waterskin to her belt beside a sheathed knife. "I've set out a meal. Eat quickly. Kamina will be waiting for us."

A bowl of porridge with fruit waited on the small, worn table. Lela's stomach rumbled, and she gulped it down. Kamina, Oren's mata, would leave them behind if they took too long. Lela finished and went to wash her bowl.

"Don't trouble yourself." Mata set Lela's waterskin and a knife for her on the counter. "Time to go." She turned, grabbed two packs, and headed out the door.

The wooden bowl clacked loudly as Lela dropped it. Her mata never allowed dishes to go unwashed. Never. Their home had to be clean and sanitary for their patients.

Lela grabbed the items, slung her satchel over her shoulder, and hurried outside to a dark, cool night. She shut the door tight behind her.

Her mata stood on the dirt road speaking in hushed tones with their neighbors, Oren and his parents, Kamina and Melovin. Each dressed in similar travel clothes, holding lanterns to light their way. They stood around Mata in a circle, leaning close, faces intent as they spoke too low for Lela to hear. They stopped as she drew near.

Mata turned to her. "Let's go."

Oren took Mata's extra bag and held back to walk by Lela's

side. No smoke rose from their chimneys now. Only the moons, Prisanthony and Pirus, and their lanterns lit the way. It was a two-hour walk to town, nothing difficult, but it was odd they weren't taking Oren's family's wagon. Perhaps they expected too much of a crowd for oxen.

Every word Oren didn't say and every movement he made filled Lela's entire awareness. None of those movements were to touch her, though her own hand had twitched to hold his several times. Apparently, that wasn't allowed since he came of age.

More and more fae joined them on the road as they passed unseen fields and through an outlying village. Conversations remained terse and hushed, not like a regular gathering to celebrate a marriage or meet for market. Then, people wore bright colors and laughter filled the road. Now it was all dark greens and browns, meant for blending in.

Fear and worry festered like an itch she couldn't scratch. The silence crushed her until she couldn't take it anymore. "Do you think we'll learn what's happened?" Her voice sounded loud in the dark. She turned to Oren and found him already looking at her, eyes creased with real worry.

He opened his mouth to speak, but whatever he meant to say was drowned out by the sudden clanging of the gongs. They chimed loud and long, closer this time. Lela's breath caught in her throat, and she reached out to Oren, grabbing his sleeve. His warm hand took hers as everyone on the road ran toward town.

The portal had opened again. Were the humans coming to destroy them?

Her heart beat in her ears as boots pounded over the road. They were only halfway to town—still a long way to go. Faster groups passed them, but no one yelled or pushed.

Lela's heart slowed after a few minutes, her panic

subsiding with no immediate danger, but then leaped again when she realized Oren still held her hand. The feel of his skin zinged over her palm and the sensitive tips of her fingers. She risked a glance at him. He dropped her hand without looking at her.

Cool air met her skin, which felt infinitely emptier. No one spoke for miles. Then, as if a summer rain had suddenly moved off, the gongs ceased tolling. Their parents immediately slowed to a walk, everyone panting and shifting their heavy bags.

No one seemed to want to speak, as if they were too wise and patient for mere curiosity. Maybe they were.

"Does that mean the portal is closed again?" Lela asked, huffing from their long run.

She might as well have been speaking to the wind. No one answered, attention remaining on the road ahead. Oren's lips thinned, but he stayed silent too.

So, now he was eighteen and too wise to speak? Of course, no one knew the answer to her question, not for sure, but that didn't mean it wasn't worth their time to say so, right?

She shook her head. Fae didn't waste time with things that served no purpose. That included excessive questions.

Lela shoved her irritation aside. She could only be who she was, even if that person asked pointless questions and longed to receive affection from a male who wouldn't give her any.

Not long after the gong ceased ringing, the road widened and the crowd thickened. Torches lit the way. Their pace was slowed some by those who'd chosen to bring horses and wagons, each packed with provisions.

Their nearby village was not big, but it didn't need to be. Most fae tended to their land, so the village houses belonged to the shopkeepers and town council members. Still, Lela usually loved visiting. A trip to the village meant a chance to barter with people over the price of her herbs, then barter with others for the things they didn't make on their own. Milk and butter, for one. They didn't own livestock, just chickens. If there was ever a surplus, Mata would give it to Lela, who'd spend it on books about healing herbs.

Now there was no market, no magic shows. Fae crowded into the square where a dais had been hastily built to the side. The press of bodies forced Lela close to her mata's back and Oren's side. He smelled of honeysuckle and tilled earth. He didn't seem to notice they breathed the same air.

The gongs chimed and then stopped once more before the council ascended the dais. The cries of children and murmur of elders hadn't stopped, but now a hush fell over the crowd, leaving only the whisper of clothing as bodies shifted.

The alderfae—the eldest elder among them, some say a couple thousand years old—dressed in a blue robe from neck to floor, stepped forward. Two councilmen flanked him wearing similar robes.

"Fae of Westwater, I commend you for gathering today. All these years, we'd hoped our efforts would prove fruitful, that these days would never come." He scanned the crowd, gray-streaked hair blowing loose in the breeze. "I will read the curse as transcribed from the original text.

"'You have eradicated the power of the Nether Realms, and driven us out of this world, sundering our peoples. Here now we issue this foretelling that no time or magic can desolate. And the prophecy shall be laid forth that a doorway will open once again, whence the doom of the fae will march through, and their people be laid waste through red flame and ash. And they shall be no more.'"

Goosebumps prickled along Lela's arms. She'd never heard the prophecy in full. Red flame and ash? That was how the demon world was described in children's stories. The prophecy was the reason portal opening had been outlawed, and any fae with the energy to create one had been persecuted to extinction long ago.

The crowd cried and pushed Lela closer to the dais. She cast an irritated look behind her and saw only dozens of panicked faces. It took some time before Alderfae Delmuth quieted the crowd again.

"Please, fae folk. We will divulge all we know, but we must act with caution and patience." He paused for emphasis. "Warriors have been dispatched across Westwater lands, but our last correspondence from King Sidian's emissaries indicates the portal has not been found. It is possible it's appearing at different places, making it hard to locate since the alarms ring all at once, regardless of where the portal is. The humans have not passed through."

A weight lifted from Lela's shoulders.

"What are we to do?" the voice of an elder shouted somewhere near the front of the crowd.

"The prophecy has come true!" a woman behind Lela added in a shrill voice.

"It's been over three thousand years since we rid ourselves of the humans and their destructive natures," Alderfae Delmuth said, speaking over breakout conversations. "They promised to come back, cursing us. We must prepare for what they'll send through the portal." He took a deep breath that made Lela's head jerk up at attention. "King Sidian has gifted the opportunity for every of-age brethren to join him in the preparations. Signup tables are already assembled in front of the council hall. It is only voluntary. For now."

Lela's heart plummeted into her stomach. Oren tensed beside her, his breathing coming faster. She could almost hear him working through this offer, the chance of a lifetime. Fae of age normally trained for years before allowed a trial to enter the king's armies. Once a member, you were a hero, no matter how long or what capacity you served. No door would be unopened, you would be looked at with honor, forever. But, it was a minimum commitment of five years. Only a small span of time, really, but not to Lela.

Five years was a big chunk of her life, much more than the months she thought she'd had left to wait for him. And this time, there was real danger, not just border skirmishes and embellished war stories. This time, she couldn't join him.

She clenched her fists. The offer hadn't been extended to females. And why not? Why did he get to go and not her? She'd go in a heartbeat. After serving her time, she'd have free access to the best energy training, advancing her meager skills to something greater. Pata couldn't ignore her if she was in his army.

Not that it mattered. She wasn't of age.

The alderfae was still talking, but Lela didn't hear a word.

She grabbed Oren's arm. The words begging him to stay died on her tongue. He'd always talked of joining one day, just not this soon.

Oren started out of deep concentration and turned, his blue eyes half hidden beneath his lowered brow. He'd never been so handsome, and he'd never looked at her as he did now —like he cared for her as more than a friend.

What if she never saw him again?

"You're going to do it, aren't you?" She grabbed his arm tighter, tight enough to hurt, but he didn't wince or pull away.

His eyes grew distant again. "Our kingdom needs people like me. It makes sense, Lela." He turned away, still pretending not to notice her bone-crushing grip as he ripped his arm from her.

He was right, of course, but she was too. She knew what

happened to people who joined the king's armies. Even if they survived, some didn't come back. Just like her pata.

Mata turned around with a relieved smile. The crowd around them dispersed. Lela had missed whatever the alderfae said.

"Ready to go home, Lelana?" Mata sounded elated.

"Home?" Lela stared over Mata's shoulder.

Oren pulled his parents aside. Their tense faces told Lela all she needed to know. They embraced their son, and then he stepped away, heading toward the council hall. He didn't look back.

"Lela?" Mata asked, following her gaze. Her smile turned into a frown of understanding. Mata's voice took on a sympathetic tone that made Lela want to run far away with hands over her ears. "He's of age. He's free to do what he wants."

Lela shifted her pack, holding herself back from rushing after Oren.

"Let's go home, my young one. There's herbs to tend." Mata, without waiting for Oren's parents, followed the crowd down the road that led out of town.

Lela forced her steps away from Oren. "Why are we returning home?" she asked, not really caring.

"You didn't hear? They haven't seen anything from the portal. We don't need to evacuate." There was an unspoken 'yet' at the end of her sentence.

Lela's boots dragged the ground with each step. Her mata tried to placate her, though they both knew Lela's melancholy had nothing to do with the threat of war. She'd planned her life out already. Since she couldn't go to a healing school, she'd be a small-town healer like her mata, with Oren by her side—and he didn't even care enough to stay for her.

Lela and her mata walked in silence the rest of the way home. Oren didn't follow.

CHAPTER 4

Ricci lounged in her tiny top bunk, nose practically to the colorful ceiling. The gentle rocking of the wagon lured her to drowsiness. Even after three days of travel, rest, and no shows, exhaustion prevailed. Their plays had yielded so much money, the family wanted to stay an extra day in Hunterton. Blessedly, Mama had reminded Papa that they'd miss market in Fallhold if they didn't move on, much to the disappointment of the growing crowd. Many had come to see them more than once, something that rarely happened before Ricci played lead.

She'd given it her all each time, bringing that sweet court-yard into view as if the setting was real instead of just a story her brothers had concocted. In fact, the storyline was so popular, they'd decided not to make many changes for the next town. Papa might have been content to perform in Hunterton forever, but the market moved on and so, too, should they. It was their way.

Obviously, something was off about the whole thing. It couldn't just be her acting that made the crowd go wild. They all seemed to see what she did, and it scared her. But nobody questioned it after that first performance. The fact that they *might* speak up scared her even more. If whatever was happening could make them famous, make people come to them, maybe the endless traveling could stop. So Ricci kept her silence.

Now, Papa led the caravan, as usual, while Mama and Nora sat on the edge of Mama's bunk, mending torn costumes. Crystal lanterns threw rainbow hues around their home, adding more layers of color over the already bright space as the wagon jostled side to side. It was stifling inside, but Ricci was still too tired to care. They'd arrive in Fallhold the next day, and the performances would start all over again. She couldn't wait, and needed all the rest she could get before then.

Mama and Papa must have been able to tell. They'd assigned her the easy tasks when they stopped each night— tending the fire and stirring the soup someone else prepared— while the others cared for the horses, chopped firewood, hunted for meat, and repaired wagon wheels. It was odd, but she certainly wasn't going to complain and end up with *more* duties.

The wagon slowed and pivoted, distracting Ricci from the yellow flower she'd painted on the ceiling when she was a child. She peered through the thin curtain out the window. They had stopped at a small clearing off the trail. Ricci closed the book she hadn't been reading and hopped down. Mama was the first outside, likely in a hurry to relieve her aching bladder. Ricci moved to follow, but Nora closed the door, cutting off the orange light of another sunset, and spun to face her.

Ricci reached around Nora for the door handle, earning a face full of blonde curls. "Excuse me."

"I thought they'd never leave you alone," Nora said,

unmoving. "No one seems willing to ask, so I will." Slightly taller than Ricci, she stared down at her. "How did you do it?"

Ricci blinked and swallowed. "Do what?" Would Nora make her stop? Would she take back the lead? Ricci wasn't even sure she was actively doing anything.

"What you did during the play. The courtyard." Nora studied her. "Do you truly not realize?"

Ricci glanced at the door. "Did I do something wrong in the courtyard scene?"

Nora gulped and glanced around, as if afraid someone was listening. "I saw it. Lanny saw it. We all saw it, even the audience. You did something. You made the scene real somehow. Even the trees looked different." She breathed deeply, waiting.

Ricci's heart sputtered a new rhythm as Nora confirmed out loud everything Ricci already knew. "I don't know what's happening," she whispered.

Nora grabbed Ricci's wrist, her palm slick with sweat. "The courtyard was real. A different place." Her grip tightened. "You transported us somehow." She lowered her voice. "You performed magic."

Ricci's breath caught. *Magic.* Her family didn't even speak of magic. "I know. I knew it couldn't be in my head. At first, I thought we were all just caught up in the performance. But it's just an illusion." She'd heard of people with the ability to create images of things not really there.

"Grass doesn't become stone no matter how much you imagine it. I felt it beneath my feet, for the Gods' sake. The flowers smelled sweet, until the play was over and they disappeared." Her voice rose. "It was real."

Ricci's whole body shook. She wasn't magical. Her parents and ancestors had no magic in their blood. Mama said magic was evil, something to stay away from, even if she was alone in her views.

Ricci fumbled for the stool behind her and sat hard. "Does Mama know?"

"I'm sure she suspects. Look, I know Mama's not keen on magic, but the rest of the world is." Nora placed a hand on Ricci's shoulder. "I think it's wonderful. You could become famous with your gift, like you always said you wanted."

Ricci looked up, shocked. With as much as they all avoided magic and any talk of it, she did not expect Nora to support her use of it. Guilt overwhelmed her as well. She'd always been jealous of Nora having the lead role, not encouraging as Nora was being now.

It was too much. Ricci jumped to her feet and bolted past Nora, through the door to the waiting woods. "Excuse me." She tossed the words over her shoulder.

Ricci ignored her family, already hard at work settling into their campsite for the night. She didn't look at them—though she felt more than one set of eyes on her back. Holding her simple dress against the catching pricks of the overgrown brush, she passed several trees before finding a thick, tall one. She rounded it and pressed her back against the rough bark, which bit through her linen sleeves as she fought to catch her breath.

The courtyard, with its singsong birds and warm breeze... it felt real, but she'd never imagined it actually was. An illusion, at most. Now that the truth was out there, it seemed insane to think she could ignore it.

But was the courtyard real, another place in the world that truly existed? Or was it something she formed from her imagination? Whatever she'd done, she couldn't do it again. What if the scene called for a ship in the ocean or a burning hell? Things could go very, very wrong. Her family could be hurt. Not to mention what would happen if the mage council found out.

Ricci couldn't play lead again. Nora could take her place.

The thought stabbed her lungs, bleeding the breath from them.

But what choice did she have?

She took care of her business and trudged back to the camp, steps heavy. The thought of not playing lead again opened an unfamiliar ache inside. Her role had brought such a sense of peace and release, like she was meant for it.

Nora's worried eyes caught hers first when Ricci stepped back into the clearing. She was already tossing vegetables into a pot over a fire, her son playing with sticks in the dirt by her feet. Darkness was falling, the roaring fire and caravan lanterns already bathing the space in soft glows. Crickets and frogs rivaled each other for the loudest sound, but at least the breeze was cool on her heated cheeks.

Nora mouthed, 'Are you okay?'

Ricci gave a slight shake of her head. She needed to speak to Papa. Her brothers were gone, likely hunting with the cousins, while her aunt and uncle gathered firewood at the tree line.

Mama wasn't in sight, probably preparing bread in the wagon, but Papa was by the horses. He'd unsaddled them and tied their leads to the trees near the parked wagons. He crouched, picking caked dirt and pebbles out of May's hooves. The horses swiveled their heads to watch her.

She took a shaky breath. "Papa, I think Nora should take the lead role at the next town." Her tone came out confident, though she felt anything but. Her chest ached. Giving up her lead, her dreams, was the hardest thing she'd ever done.

Papa's shiny head popped up, and he dropped May's hoof. His broad form rose as he turned, looking at her with stern eyes. "What foolishness has my daughter-in-law put in your head?"

"Don't you know?" she asked, rubbing a hand down May's dusty flank.

His stern composure cracked, and his shoulders drooped. He rubbed the bridge of his nose. "Mama had planned on talking to you tonight. I should have known that city-dweller would be the one to speak first."

"Papa, now is not the time for your prejudices. I should have been the one to speak first." Ricci barely kept her voice from shaking. Everyone had figured it out. She'd been fooling no one.

He stepped away from the horses, and Ricci followed. "At first, we didn't know what was happening, then we figured out it was you. You didn't seem to realize it, though, and it didn't bother or surprise you. I knew you'd come to us when you were ready."

"And?" she asked. "It's magic." The last word came out almost a whisper. The forbidden topic.

"Yes, it's magic." He put his big hands on her shoulders. "I see it as a unique way to fully become your character."

Ricci looked away, not sure if she wanted to hear more.

"Oh, but it is your way, Ricika. It's your own special way to play your role, and everyone loves you for it. You make it real. You transform us all." He smiled, reverence plain in his tone. "It's another one of your gifts."

None of it made any sense. Her whole life, Mama had said magic was something to stay away from. In truth, it had always fascinated her.

"Mama knew, and she was okay with this?" Ricci asked. "What about the danger?"

He cleared his throat. "That's what Mama wants to talk to you about. Once we figured out what was happening, she wanted to stop you immediately. The family convinced her to give you time." He scratched his mustache.

Ricci shook her head, trying to rid the heaviness of the past half hour. "Well, let's go talk to her." She stomped away from the half-formed protest on her papa's mouth. Putting off unpleasant tasks only spoiled the time it took building the courage to face them. Better to get them done and over. Papa's blessing didn't take away the danger or the uncertainties—it didn't mean she'd get to keep the lead—but some of the tightness in her chest unwound.

She wanted time to think, time to be alone, but there wasn't an alone when you were part of a troupe. No private room to escape to, no place to go where others would not see— unless her newfound magic made real places. Then she could create her own.

Her hands shook.

Mama met her at the wagon door, arms crossed with a spoon in her hand. "I heard what you and Papa said. We will discuss it at dinner." Her mouth was twisted, matching Ricci's attitude. "Go tend the soup."

Ricci threw up her hands and marched to the fire. Nora watched with wide eyes as Ricci snatched up the ladle and stirred the soup. She wisely didn't say a word.

Her brothers and cousins proudly returned with deer meat, which was cut up and cooked in the stew. Mama presented two perfectly brown loaves of bread, and Nora announced dinner. Mama cut into the bread, filling the chilly night air with a steamy, yeasty aroma, while Ricci ladled the soup, her mouth watering. She served herself last and joined her family, sitting beside Mama on one of the logs surrounding the deliciously warm fire. She ignored the curious glances.

The heat of the broth warmed her belly, but her troubles plagued her as she chewed through tender meat and soft carrots—a rare luxury. The crackling fire and familiar conversations comforted her.

Beside Mama, Papa set down his bowl and stood. The chewing stopped as everyone stared his way, faces solemn in the orange glow of the fire. Ricci swallowed a lump of stew-soaked bread, gone flavorless.

"It's time we address what we've all suspected." He looked across their group, from Nora and Lanny, and their son Jace who was busy refusing more stew, to Bartley and Nicholas, to Aunt Roma and Uncle Patrick and their sons Axis and Adam, and finally his eyes rested on Ricci.

She held his gaze, but more than anything she wanted to seek the comfort of bed and hide under her quilt.

"It's no secret now that Ricci can access magic," Papa said, tone emotionless but firm in the way of someone making a speech.

Ricci watched her family closely. They exchanged glances with one another—no surprise, just worry. Lanny looked at Ricci with concern. Maybe he was concerned for Jace.

"Ricci would like to make an announcement." Papa sat and leaned forward, expectant.

What? Ricci glared. It was Mama who had something to say. Ricci set her bowl down and rose slowly to her feet. Everyone stared at her, waiting, and though the feel of multiple pairs of eyes was nothing new, this time she wasn't acting. She would only be telling the truth.

She licked her lips. "So, it looks like Papa's right. I can do magic." Just saying it aloud felt surreal. She looked at Mama. "I haven't had much time to think about it, but it might be safer for everyone if I step down from the lead role. Nora can take my place." The words gutted her.

Her brothers stood at once. "Not a chance, Ricci. You were born for this," Lanny said, fists clenched.

"We've never made so much coin before," Nicholas said at the same time.

"You have to keep going," her twin cousins, Adam and Axis, said in unison.

Mama remained silent.

"It's her decision," Bartley, who usually kept quiet, said. "But for what it's worth, Ricci, I think it's the wrong one."

"You do?" They'd clearly had more time to think about this than she had.

Bartley shrugged, as if discarding his opinion even before stating it. "You've never been happier. The illusions, or whatever they are, aren't causing harm. I see no reason she shouldn't keep lead." He sat and stared at the dirt.

"And what happens when the setting isn't a sunny courtyard wedding?" Ricci asked, voice rising. "I have no idea how this works, or how I did what I did. But, what if the princess is taken to an evil place? What will my imagination conjure then?" She took a deep breath. "What if they aren't illusions, but real places." She said it as a statement and could see by the weighted looks in her family's posture that they hadn't thought that far.

Mama sat rigid and silent.

"Easy," Nicholas said brightly. "We won't write plays where you're in a setting anything less than pleasant or happy." He smiled at his cleverness.

Nicholas made it sound so easy, and his solution made sense.

Nora looked up. "I grew up near a community of mages. I've seen the awe and the horror magic can inspire." Ricci winced, and Nora offered a small smile. "But I don't believe that of you. I still think it's wonderful. We can make this work."

Lanny, who'd looked worried at what Nora might say, relaxed and nodded his agreement. "We can change the performance. We'll put Princess Kasma in a safer place than a strange courtyard."

"Let's vote," Papa said, nodding at the group. They always made big decisions through a family vote. "All in favor of Ricci keeping the lead?"

Hands shot into the air. Little Jace glanced at everyone then stuck his hand up, too. Excitement brushed Ricci's heart, but she didn't let it show. Could she really handle this? The lead could be hers. They'd be rich. Maybe even settle in one place for good.

"No," Mama said, cutting through the voices like a crack of the reins. She stood. "Magic is dangerous. Practicing without a permit, which we can't afford, is illegal." She put a hand on Papa's shoulder. "We say no, Ricika. It's not worth the risk."

"What?" Ricci shot to her feet, temper flaring at Mama's uncompromising resolve. "We've already voted. And what risk? We worked out how to make it safe. And maybe I could get a permit with the extra money we've made." She looked to the rest of the family for support, but they stared at the ground. No one wanted to cross Mama.

"Trust me. It is too dangerous, and I will not put you at risk. No more magic." Mama started to clean up, as if that was the final word. Ricci's acting career—her life, her dreams—halted before it'd begun, with vague and dodgy answers the only given reason.

"Papa?" Ricci asked.

"It's too dangerous," he said, then winced and looked away.

Ricci showed her back to the lot of them, heading toward the wagon. Mama didn't know about magic, so how could she know it was dangerous?

She swung around. "I'll control it," she announced. "I'll keep the lead, but I won't use magic."

Lies. She didn't know how to control it, and wouldn't if she could.

Ricci spun before Mama could respond and continued on to the wagon. Like Papa said, her magic was a gift. They always said to use her gift. The ticket to making her dreams come true. She wasn't stopping now.

CHAPTER 5

C allen Kealamin wiped a dust rag dipped in lemon oil carefully between the colored potion bottles on Master Marek's shelves, doing his best not to grumble. It'd taken him weeks to memorize what potions went where—all the pink, purple, green, and blue glass in various shapes with no obvious organization. Master Marek had been back for all of a day, and now the bottles were rearranged in a new, seemingly random order. But Gods forbid Callen try to sort them.

Master Marek was a genius, if obsessed with his work, but did he have to be so disorganized?

The room was dark and musty. It had to be. Too much light could damage certain concoctions. But being Master Marek's apprentice wasn't so bad. Sure, it came with all the usual scut work of cleaning, manning the shop, never having enough time to study as hard as Master Marek wanted him to, but it had its perks too. He didn't have to live under his parents' rule, Lord and Lady Kealamin, and be pampered every day like some infant. Thank the Gods magic had manifested in him young.

The bell rang downstairs—a customer through the front door. Master Marek was out, so Callen set down the rag, dusted off his hands, and descended the dark wood stairs to the shop below.

"Good afternoon, Mrs. Sardoma," Callen called out when he spotted her gray hair in its usual short curls pinned to her head. It had been a slow, uneventful day so far. It was nice to have a customer, even if it was Mrs. Sardoma.

She nodded, typical frown on her face, and went right to the basket of willow bark in the corner, plucking out a couple sheets and examining them. She bought bark about once a week to make tea for her arthritic bones. The bark was priced by the piece, so she always took a long time picking the freshest, biggest one.

Callen shook his head and straightened the bottles lining the room. Shelves wound the small shop, covered in baskets of herbs and teas, and potions corked tight and in dark vials to keep out the harmful light from the front windows.

Mrs. Sardoma laid her purchases on the counter, something of a satisfied smirk faint on her mouth.

Callen cut a strip of linen and wrapped her willow bark and lavender oil, tying it with a length of twine. "Five marks, please."

Mrs. Sardoma shoved her copper coins across the polished counter, exact change, and snatched up her package. She left without a word.

"Have a good day," Callen said to the door as it thunked closed.

He sighed and ran his fingers through his short hair. Master Marek had promised a lesson this evening, and it was the only thing making this slow afternoon bearable.

He'd been an apprentice for seven years, since he was ten.

In all that time, his parents hadn't come to visit. He was their dirty secret, and they were glad to be able to hide him so his accidental magic couldn't ruin his older brothers' and sisters' chances for suitable matches or political conquest. 'Magic is for peasants,' Father said, a belief shared by anyone with money.

Callen unclenched his jaw as two customers entered the shop—a man and a woman—the bell at the top of the door chiming. He nodded to them, not recognizing them. They got a lot of first-timers when market came to town with its exotic wares and eye-rolling troupe shows, especially because this was a stopping point on the way to Timbercross, where the mage council resided, and where lots of countryfolk went for magic licensing during market time.

"Let me know if you have any questions," Callen said.

Master Marek allowed Callen to organize the shop, so everything was labeled and in its proper place, but that didn't mean newcomers would know what they were looking at. It took a while to learn the difference between 'Pairswax' and 'Parspotion'. One was used to bandage deep cuts, the other to rid yourself of body hair. Both were big sellers Callen had to work up in large batches.

The door banged open, hitting a shelf of small mauve bottles labeled 'love potion'—actually just a simple brew that promoted euphoric feelings in the user. Master Marek walked in with a long stride. He smiled weakly at the customers. His billowing dark-purple robe swished as he moved through the shop and disappeared through the door and up the stairs, with a nod at Callen. His steps echoed up the wall, shaking the hanging dried herbs.

Callen winced. Master was in a mood.

The couple looked at him with wide eyes.

"I'm sorry about that," Callen said. "Help yourselves to a stick of enchanted peppermint candy. You'll find it restorative." He gestured to the glass jar on the counter filled with sticks of green and white, then pointed to the bell beside it. "Please ring if you need any assistance."

Callen took his time going upstairs. His master had put him in charge of the shop years ago. While other apprentices spent most of their time studying or practicing magic, Callen had this shop and the brief moments Master Marek wasn't too busy to train him. He wasn't going to screw it up.

Master Marek lounged in one of the matching brown armchairs, rubbing his forehead. His emerald and gold necklace lay askew on his chest, and his short, curly, peppered hair looked more matted than usual. Though he was only in his forties and mages were supposed to age slower, he looked much older—the stress of being a council member, perhaps. He owned a large estate on the edge of the next town, with servants and cooks to tend to his every need. Callen had no idea where he got his money. Inheritance, maybe. The shop certainly didn't make that much coin.

Callen went to the far side of the room as his eyes readjusted to the dimness, checking his potions. Each sat in pots of various sizes on counters or, for the larger cauldrons, on stands. Some sat stagnant, only requiring a stir now and then. Some brewed over constant, low heat to set the properties in place and ensure the proper melding.

Using a thick rag, he lifted the lid on one of the larger pots, holding his body away from the heat. Steam rose like a punch, bringing with it a foul tang. Today it smelled like cat urine. Yesterday, cow manure. It was a popular but harmless potion to use on your enemies to ruin dinner parties or such, named after the flower that gave it its foul odor: shista. Callen held his breath and gave it a quick stir with a nearby ladle. It was almost done.

"Put the lid on that wretched concoction," Master Marek bellowed. "Smells like feet."

Callen plunked the lid down. He moved to a sweeter-smelling pot, the one with the peppermint stick potion, opening it quickly. Its strong, shocking smell filled the space, overtaking the shista.

He finished stirring and turned around. Master Marek sat up, staring at him with a contemplative look.

"Don't grow up to be an idiot like my colleagues," he stated, then stood and paced around the room, dodging the various work tables, hands clasped behind his back.

"I won't." Callen suppressed a sigh. When his master was in one of his moods, he could go from patient and kind to irritable and short-tempered if the breeze blew the wrong way. It was the kinder moments that kept Callen from becoming too intimidated, though he probably should be. His master was one of the most powerful mages in the four kingdoms, even if he'd become known as something of a hermit in recent years.

Master Marek was a good mentor, but he was working on something big, bigger than pointless council meetings, he'd said. Callen's eyes flickered to the cauldron in the corner, set apart from the rest on a raised platform.

"How fairs the potion?" Master Marek asked. Callen wondered sometimes if his master read his mind.

Callen scratched the back of his neck. "I've brewed it exactly as you instructed, Master, procuring only the freshest ingredients and paying close attention to the timing. The color looks right this time, a flat teal with few bubbles. It's a clear day. If the instructions are correct, it will be ready tonight after the cast of the moon."

Master Marek nodded. Then he blinked a few times, and a

pleased smile spread on his lips. "Well done." A high commendation. Pride bloomed in Callen's chest. This was his fifth attempt at whatever potion Master Marek had in mind. The purpose had not been disclosed, and he didn't ask.

But he suspected.

"How about a lesson, and then shall we test it out?" Master Marek asked. "Swords this time."

Callen grinned and rushed to the stairs. "I'll close up shop." Swords were one of his favorites, ranking right up there with summoning the elements.

Master Marek grunted as Callen flew down the stairs. The couple was gone, not having bought anything, and the peppermint stick jar was empty. Callen gritted his teeth as he locked up and closed the curtains, surveying the stock. At least nothing else had been taken, and he already had peppermint potion brewing. And they'd left the jar.

He entered his living quarters through a door behind the counter, grabbing a cloak. He left out the back to find his master already waiting. Their shop was one of many lining the dusty road of Fallhold, a small stop on the way to the city of Timbercross where his family and master resided.

With pursed lips, his master headed to the building behind the shop which served only one purpose—magic practice.

Inside the building's cool darkness, Master Marek lifted his hand and the wall sconces lit up around the room. Mounted weapons decorated the walls, though they never used them. Wood chips covered the floor and scented the air with musty pine. Their purpose was to soften the landing when he got thrown on his rear. They did not.

Master Marek stopped halfway across the room and turned to face Callen, feet slightly apart and hands out in front. Callen copied him, as he copied him in everything in these rare training sessions. He'd need every skill and more to pass the Magery test in a couple years.

"Have you been practicing?" Master Marek asked.

Callen suppressed a wince. There was only one thing Master Marek ever asked him to work on outside their sessions and bookwork, and it wasn't sparring.

Teleportation.

His master's life's work was to find a way to cross the kingdom or the seas in an instant. The discovery would bridge the magical community and allow for shared knowledge. Of course, the fact that his master would be famous and remembered for all time didn't hurt, either.

"I have, but I'm no closer than last time. The gift of the Nether Realms escapes me." As it did every mage in recorded history. A power that supposedly allowed one to teleport to other parts of the world. Maybe even other realms.

Truly, at this point, Master Marek must have been testing Callen's endurance and patience, because no one possessed the power to teleport. But, if Master Marek wanted to test him, Callen would win this contest. He wouldn't be caught whining or not giving his all.

Master Marek sighed with deep disappointment. "Maybe the potion will prove effective."

Where I am not, Callen thought, but pushed the bitterness away as Master Marek raised his arm.

"Form your blade," Master Marek said as his own appeared, a harmless wooden sword that still left purple bruises where it met its mark.

Callen focused, pulling the magic to him—like water from his own personal well. The magic warmed him, waiting to be shaped and unleashed. It was a second heartbeat pulsing even faster than his own.

Callen gave it a tiny mental push, and a wooden practice

sword formed in his waiting hand. He smiled with pride and glanced over to his master. It had taken him a long time to learn to channel it into actually doing something productive and not just flying out of control, breaking random mirrors and furniture like it had at his parents' house.

Sword raised and ready, Master Marek charged. He drew from magic to give his aging body strength. Callen jumped back, pivoting his weapon to block. With a sharp whack, their swords met, the force vibrating down his hand and hurting his bones. His master clearly had aided the blow with magical strength.

Callen fed magic into his speed and ducked the next hit, swinging low at Master Marek's legs—and met flesh. His wide eyes met Master Marek's furious glare before he registered the sword swooping toward his head. He leaped back, pushing magic into the movement, but the sword clocked him in the temple. Pain exploded in his skull. The room spun, a blur of brown walls and windows, green and blue from the forest and sky outside. He fell heavily on his rear.

Master Marek's sigh was unmistakable, echoing over the throb of his heart in his ears. A slight whoosh sounded as his master's sword vanished.

"I think you're actually getting worse," Master Marek said. "At least at swordplay. Your potion making is doing quite well. If you'd spend even a fraction of your time on this, you could be great one day." He leaned down and gave Callen's shoulder a reassuring squeeze. "You have time. You're already well ahead of most of your peers."

"Yes, Master." Callen didn't bother saying what he really thought; that Master would pitch a fit if he didn't keep the shop going. That it wasn't swordplay he needed to be great at, not really. It was the use of magic in the swordplay.

"Shall we check on the potion?"

Callen used a quick pain relief spell to temper his pounding head and pushed to his feet. "Not yet."

Master Marek graced him with a smile, and they both summoned their practice swords again. They sparred until the sun had almost set, and though Callen ached from head to toe —as usual—it had been a productive session. His speed and strength magic had improved.

Master Marek allowed time for a meal at the tavern across the street, his treat, but only because the moon was not yet high enough in the sky to reach the potion. Callen ate his roast chicken, fresh bread, and apple tarte with relish. Expending magic always left him hungry. He barely downed the rest of his ale before Master Marek hurried him out the door. It was time to test the potion.

The food turned leaden in Callen's stomach. It had been a pleasant afternoon, but it could all go bad if another batch of potion failed. And it would. Master Marek was determined to teleport, and if he couldn't do it through magic, he'd do it through potions.

The potions room was dark but for the glow of some of the uncovered brews and vials, which let off different colors depending on their components. Using the dregs of his magic, Callen lit the lamps, casting everything in gentle orange light. The scent of peppermint hung heavily in the air, stinging his nose.

He felt Master Marek's gaze as he grabbed a black glass vial from a crate of empties, uncorked it, and put a funnel in the top. On the dais in the corner, he lifted the lid from the meticulously-crafted brew. A subtle sour smell wafted up. Callen pulled aside the shades, and moonlight slanted into the room. It hit the bubbling, teal potion. Callen drew in a breath. Too many heartbeats went by and nothing happened. Then, starting from the center and spreading out, the liquid turned a lighter green, giving off a faint glow.

Callen hurried to swing the cauldron off the low flame. It had actually worked, just as Master Marek's instructions said it would. There could be no doubt he'd followed every step exactly right this time. Now they had to test it. Using the funnel, Callen ladled some of the steaming liquid into the vial and stoppered it, not a drop spilled or wasted. The green glow showed through the black glass as he turned toward his master.

Master Marek held out long bony fingers, face expressionless as Callen placed the warm vial in his waiting hand.

"Very well done," he said with a breath of relief. Master Marek was never generous with his compliments, but Callen liked that. His parents had always been overly generous with theirs—especially in front of company—making them feel forced and ingenuine. "You must forgive my grumpiness, apprentice—the fiend in me likes to rear its head sometimes." He chuckled. "I haven't been myself since my wife died."

Master Marek's wife had been gone almost as long as Callen had been alive. But maybe no amount of time was enough to recover from the loss of true love. He used that excuse a lot in his grouchier moods. At least he had an excuse. Callen could have a plaque made above his father's study that said, 'Because I said so'.

"Shall we test it?" His master's eyes gleamed with suppressed joy, though his mouth didn't smile. Only a potion for teleportation could make him this excited.

Callen nodded eagerly and rushed to the sitting area in the middle of the workshop. Once he'd removed the rug and table and pushed back the furniture, they had a sizeable area to work with. Master Marek stepped forward, velvet mage robe rustling over the bare floorboards, and unstopped the bottle.

The potion had already cooled enough not to give off any steam.

Callen held his breath once more. *Please work. Please work.*

If his master found the right brew, the search would be over. No more leaving for weeks at a time. Callen would finally have his undivided attention. He'd finally be trained to become a full mage.

Master Marek raised the bottle high out from him and tipped it ever so slightly. The smallest drop of glowing green spilled over the rim of the black glass and hit the floor with a plop. Quick as a wink, Master Marek recorked the bottle and stepped back, eyes locked onto the tiny spot on the floor.

Nothing happened. *Come on,* Callen pleaded. Master Marek let out a long, slow sigh. Callen was afraid to meet his disappointed gaze. Another failed attempt. Master Marek would leave again, and the lessons would be over for a while.

Callen shoved his hands in his pockets and turned away. Master Marek gasped, and Callen spun back around. The spot, dark now where it soaked into the wood, fizzled. Tiny bubbles rose and popped, and thin mists of steam swirled.

"It's working!" Callen said.

Master Marek leaned forward, mouth going slack.

His master hadn't believed Callen could do it, but he *did.*

The steam turned to smoke as the fizzing mass went black and sunk into the wood floor. The noise grew faint as it disappeared deeper into the wood, then stopped altogether.

"Huh?" Callen rushed forward and peered into the copper mark-sized hole.

Master Marek put fists on his hips and glared at the ceiling. "Congratulations, Callen. You've created acid." He grabbed the satchel with his things from the coat hook by the backdoor. "Because of your failure, I must go and find another recipe.

Don't burn down the shop while I'm gone." He left before Callen could even reply.

Callen unclenched his fists, biting down his resentment. He'd worked so hard. It wasn't his fault it had failed.

Acid? He pushed his fingers roughly through his hair. This was as close as they'd ever gotten. Of course his master was upset. To come so far and still fail. All those carefully procured ingredients? All those ridiculous steps had led to creating acid? Where was the portal? Where had the acid gone?

Callen bent and put his face to the floor, sticking his eye over the new hole. He could barely make out his quarters below from the moonlight in the window. His room! Callen rushed down the stairs, pulling small motes of magic from his well. He pivoted at the bottom and burst into his living quarters. Using magic to light the lamps, brighter than the workshop above, he scanned the ceiling until spotting the tiny hole, right above his desk.

"Oh no," he murmured, rushing to where his precious spell books and notes were spread across the surface. A smoking hole had burned straight through his copy of *Deannon's Binding, From Magic to Application*.

Groaning, he flipped through the pages. The hole grew bigger the further back he went, eradicating essential words and instruction. Master Marek would be so angry. These books were rare! Callen tossed the book on his desk chair, then noticed the hole through the papers on his desk. He shuffled them aside. The hole went into the dark-stained wood. He crouched to the floor. The acid potion had burned a hole straight through.

Callen sat back, palms on his forehead. He shouldn't be surprised. At least this potion had yielded something with an actual use. But if he couldn't prove himself, he'd never be allowed to take the tests and become a full mage. Or even move on to something other than potion making. Worst of all, he'd prove his father right—that he was nothing more than a disappointment. A failure.

He shook himself and looked at the hole. He could bottle the rest and sell it for two silver broams—*For Your Enemies* or *For Daring Escapes*. If it sold well, he could get more ingredients and try again. He needed to go to market anyway. Maybe he'd make enough money to replace his ruined spell books without Master Marek ever knowing. And maybe next time the potion would work.

CHAPTER 6

The next morning, Ricci dressed for their first performance in the town of Fallhold. Mama tried to make small talk, but Ricci replied with one-word answers, and soon they readied in silence.

What Mama says goes, so there would be no arguing with her, or even getting a real answer from her. She said her piece, put a stop to the vote, and that was that, so Ricci would just have to *prove* she could handle keeping the lead and using magic. If she could prove there was no danger, what would be Mama's objection—at least, once she got over her rage at being disobeyed?

Mama had let her keep the lead. She thought Ricci could control it—turn the magic on and off like a lantern light. She was in for a surprise. Ricci had no idea how it worked.

Her family cast sympathetic looks as they took their places behind the wagons. Papa wouldn't meet her eyes, but his guilt was plain.

The crowd was thick for this time of the morning. Good. Nicholas had done well to draw them in.

Ricci breathed deeply, trying to relax and focus on her role —and not the hundreds of ways this idea might fail. She only hoped the magic would work, now that she knew it was real.

The bell rang, signaling her cue. She walked out onto the wooden platform her brothers had built and thought of peaceful nature and flowers. A warmth entered her belly and seemed to flow out of her. As she delivered her lines, a faded field slowly expanded outward from her, shaping itself until it was all around them, the audience too. The grass was long and flowing, the wind almost cold. The crowd gasped in wonder, then applauded like mad.

Relieved, Ricci smiled, truly happy. This was what she was meant to do.

Nora as the Wise Old Lady entered the stage. Her mouth opened in surprise. But then she shrugged and smiled before moving on with the play. Nora had given her approval.

Papa was the only one who didn't forgive her. He stared hard, frowning as he acted the priest to marry Princess Kasma and the prince. But he didn't stop her or the play.

Then it was Mama's turn to take the stage as the Evil Sorceress. Ironic she'd play the part of someone who practices magic.

When she stepped onto the wooden planks and took in the surroundings, her jaw clamped shut with an audible snap. Ricci continued on as Princess Kasma, ignoring her mama's ire. Mama had no choice but to keep going, glaring daggers and giving the worst performance of her career.

The audience didn't notice. They were manic, cheering even for the quiet parts. Except for one person. A girl around Ricci's age stood at the back of the crowd, taller than those around her. She looked confused and out of place in leggings instead of a dress. Those strange gongs rang like last time. But when Ricci looked again, she was gone.

Ricci wanted the play to never end, so of course it went by as if it was the shortest thing they'd ever performed.

When it was over, coins rained down on the stage as they bowed, and not just coppers. Tears stung Ricci's eyes at the generosity. She'd really given the townspeople something beautiful. How could Mama expect her to stop?

When they were almost back to the wagon, Mama grabbed Ricci by the upper arm and squeezed. Ricci gaped, too stunned to resist as Mama pulled her inside. She closed the door behind her, locking everyone else out.

So it was going to be like that, was it?

Ricci already had her hands on her hips by the time Mama turned to face her.

The tears in Mama's eyes stopped her cold.

"I told you no for a reason," Mama said, hands upraised. "Why didn't you listen?"

"I don't understand," Ricci said, all the heat she'd planned to put in the words gone. "There was no danger. The crowd loved it."

"And when word spreads of what you can do, what then?"

"We'll make more money?" Ricci said slowly. Was this a trick question?

Mama threw up her arms. "You need to trust me."

"I do trust you, and I'm asking you to trust me." Ricci softened her voice. "I can do this. There is no danger, and think of all the money we can make." She hoped beyond hope that her mama couldn't sense the lie. She had no clue if she could do this, but it was worth it to find out, if it solved all of their problems.

Mama shook her head, worried eyes gazing out the window. But she didn't say no.

"Please, Mama." Ricci took her hands. "Let me do this. If anything bad happens, or you start to see something dangerous about it, then I'll stop. I won't play lead anymore." The words were hard to say, but they were true. If there truly was danger, as Mama seemed to believe, she wouldn't put her family at risk. But there was no danger.

Time ticked by in silence. Mama shook her head.

"If you're worried about endangering the family," Ricci said in a rush, "I could set up my own show nearby. I'm sure Lanny could write me a safe script." It was a horrible plan, one that just popped into her head, but she'd do it if that was what it took. "I could travel separate from you all."

Mama's mouth fell open. "No." She swallowed hard, then wrung her hands. Agonizing moments ticked by. Someone barged in, but quickly retreated. "Okay, Ricika." Her body straightened, and she pointed her finger. "But if I see danger, then you stop."

"Yes! I promise." Ricci hugged her mama hard.

She'd won this small victory. Now she'd have to figure out how the magic worked so she wouldn't prove herself a liar— that magic wasn't dangerous.

CHAPTER 7

A week after the town meeting, Lela still jumped every time the gongs rang. She hadn't unpacked her bag, and kept her travel clothes ready, just in case. There'd been no word from Pata, but that was no surprise. If he knew more than the alderfae, he probably couldn't say.

There'd also been no danger. Whatever group was responsible for opening the portal, they hadn't invaded, and they hadn't attacked.

The sun cast its morning rays on Lela's hunched shoulders. Kneeling in the garden, she inhaled the pungent scent of basil drifting on the breeze. She dug bare fingers through the cool, loose dirt, feeling grit and pebble slide over her skin. She channeled the energies, coaxing new vines to sprout a few inches before moving on to a new patch.

Forget forget forget.

She gripped a handful of dirt, then shoved it back in the ground, tilling the small area for new planting. Even these simple actions, which normally brought joy, couldn't distract her from what would happen today.

Oren was leaving.

He'd returned the morning after the town meeting, his parents wearing proud smiles as they passed down the road by Lela's hiding spot. Well, she hadn't really been hiding among the rows of dill and sage. And she certainly hadn't been waiting for him to come home, either. She'd merely been harvesting the herbs and chose not to show herself.

That hadn't stopped Oren from looking straight toward her with a confused expression on his face, like he could sense her. He'd looked back once more from his front door before going inside.

Lela hadn't seen him since. She wouldn't ruin his time with his family or humiliate herself by begging him to stay.

Instead, she'd thrown herself into her work, urging new plantings to bud into prominent sprouts, clipping herbs and hanging them to dry or milking them of their useful nectars. He hadn't come to see her, and so of course she wouldn't go see him. But it had been lonely. There was no one else their age for miles. Mata baked travel bread and cookies, but shook her head when Lela found excuses not to deliver them across the road.

What could she say? He had to know how she felt, though she'd never spoken it before—that wasn't allowed—a custom so old it was law. And knowing how she felt hadn't kept him from signing himself away—an irreversible action. Maybe he'd meet someone of age, someone he could be with and not see as a child.

Moisture leaked down her face, and she wiped it away with a finger, smearing dirt on her cheek and not caring. She sat back on her heels and stared at the mess she'd made of her neatly lined rows. She missed the days when they could tease and play freely, like the time he hid her trowel and wouldn't give it back until she promised to be his servant for a day. He'd ordered her to bring him tea, and she'd given him a cup of mud instead. The whole thing had ended in a mud fight that ruined their clothes and made both their matas furious. Lela smiled.

The crunch of rocks underfoot made her head swivel.

"Good morning," Oren said, a guilty look on his face and a heavy pack on his back.

Lela's heart stuttered. She stuck her hands back into the already over-tilled dirt. "Mata's inside." She silently pleaded he wouldn't comment on her useless tilling or the mess she'd made in her anger.

Oren sighed, and the sound made her wince.

"I'm not here for her, Lela." He stepped closer, voice somber. "Would you look at me?"

She pulled her hands from the dirt, wiping them on her already filthy leggings, and turned her face up to him. Her eyes narrowed, giving away her hurt. This might be the last time she ever saw him. Why couldn't she just be nice?

A slow smile formed on his face. Then laughter burst from his closed lips. *Laughter!*

She shot to her feet, hands on her hips. "I'm glad you find this all so funny, Oren." The anger in her words wiped the humor from his face.

He was leaving and didn't even care. Worst of all, she couldn't follow him. Only males could join. She couldn't check on her pata or protect Mata. He was leaving, and she was staying to do nothing but wait for the humans to destroy them. She wanted to scream.

He raised his hands, eyes wide with shock. "No, no." He stepped close enough to nearly breathe the same air. "Here." He reached up and wiped a callused thumb across her cheek. The abrasive grit reminded her she'd smudged dirt on her face. She must look like she felt—ragged inside and out.

A careful smile re-formed on his face, and his thumb lingered on her skin. Warmth blossomed in her cheeks.

Oren dropped his hand and took a half step back. "I'm leaving now. I wanted to say goodbye."

"Thank you for finding the time." She stared at the yellow hollyhocks crowding the wooden perimeter fence. They served no purpose, except that they were beautiful and she loved them.

"I should have come sooner. I just…" He didn't finish whatever he'd meant to say. "Anyway, it's not forever. Five years isn't so long."

No, not so very long, unless he stayed longer or found his mate and never came back. Or died on some distant battlefield. Or in some distant realm.

Lela had always believed in the elders' stories of other realms, and now they had been proven. "I'll see you in five years then, if I'm still here when you come back."

Something like hurt flashed in his eyes, but it was gone before Lela could be sure. He smiled. "Maybe you'll have your own adventure, just like we always said, and we'll see each other at the end."

"Yeah." She huffed at her own foolishness. Their final moments, and she was *wasting* them. She faced him fully, looking him in the eye. "Good luck on your adventure, Oren. I've always cherished our friendship. I'll… I'll miss you while you're gone."

"I… me too, Lela." He stepped close and embraced her in a tight hug.

Her arms automatically wrapped around him, slipping beneath his pack to rest against his warm back. She lay her head against his neck and breathed him in, one last time. Tilled earth and honeysuckle. His heart pulsed beneath her. He let the hug last a few moments longer than friends—she was sure of it—before he let go.

She pulled a chain from her pocket and held it up. A small glass vial hung at the end containing crushed dried lavender, a smell he'd once said reminded him of her. "In case you find yourself needing to remember home."

Color touched his cheeks, and he took the chain gingerly in his hands. "Thank you." His words were soft. "Be safe." He turned and left the herb garden. The sound of his steps was long gone before Lela managed to stop crying. Had he seen her tears?

"Lelana?" Mata called from the direction of the house.

Oh, great. Mata couldn't see she'd cried over this male. Lela cleared her throat. "Going for a walk!" she called and dashed out of the garden toward the field at the back of the house.

This time of year, the land was a sprawling green dotted with wildflowers and surrounded by trees of brilliant, bright color. It gave an incredible view from the hills beyond. Her legs sought those hills. She and Oren had spent countless summer days climbing them, seeking the seclusion on the other side where their parents couldn't see them swing from trees or throw rocks in the small hidden pond. It was the perfect place now to escape her pain.

Her desperate run slowed to a fast walk halfway to the hills. They were never as close as they looked. She climbed up the side of the first hill, weaving around the sparse trees, and already felt lighter. Oren would be back. And she wouldn't pine for him while he was gone, just as he clearly wouldn't be pining for her. He hadn't even given her a goodbye gift.

Her legs burned as she crested the tallest hill, then her shins ached as she made her way down. There were a few small mounds, and then the clear pond they loved to swim in so much reflecting lilac hues, and beyond, a beautiful field with more flowers than even the one by her house.

In the time it took her to reach the pond, the sun had shifted in the sky, bringing a different, higher-pitched cadence of insects than the low buzzing closer to home. The insect noises and occasional rustle of the trees, the scuffle of her leather boots over grass and dirt—she let it all consume her.

Lela sat in a dry patch of dirt at the water's edge, folding her knees and studying the clear lilac perfection, the serene way the insects jumped and floated over the surface. Oren had discovered this pond and the flower field beyond, a secret place they'd told no one else about. They'd even seen unicorns on a few occasions.

A strange feeling, like static in the air, made the hair on her bare arms stick up. A faint metallic taste coated her tongue. Outside the cool shade of the trees and further into the meadow, a shimmering wall appeared. It stood as wide as her cottage and reached toward the sky, distorting the air like a large heat wave.

Lela stood slowly. Her energy senses tingled, yet it hadn't come from her. She stepped around the pond, Oren's voice in the back of her head. *You don't know what this is. Don't go near it.* She ignored him.

This didn't feel dangerous. Some strange phenomenon of the air, perhaps? Five-petaled blossoms of red and purple brushed against her leggings as she waded through the field, one careful step at a time. She'd wanted a distraction, and here it was. What could this be?

The shimmering wall didn't change as she approached, unlike a mirage that disappears upon approach. Only now she could tell it wasn't a wall of heat distortion. This had depth.

Like looking through several panes of thick glass, the trees were still on the other side. The staticky, energy feel buzzed around her, but she still sensed no danger. She reached out a careful hand and stroked the edge of the mirage. Her fingers passed as if through air, becoming distorted as well. There was no pain, just a strange tingling. She stuck her whole arm through. Still nothing, except perhaps a rise in temperature.

"Hmm," she murmured. What was on the other side? Oren would tell her to walk away. Well, he wasn't here.

She breathed in deep, held her breath, and stepped through.

The field faded, though not completely. Lela's mouth dropped open as the sky turned a pale shade of blue. Cheering people, their backs to her, replaced the expanse of green. They stood in front of a wooden platform wearing strange clothing. Loose pants and shirts with strings hanging from them. Dresses the colors of pale flowers. No one wore dresses, except royalty or for the binding ceremony. Everything was opaque, like through a thick fog. Lela rubbed her eyes, as if that would make this place disappear.

The people stared at the platform, a stage, where a girl wearing an emerald-green gown spoke to a male.

"We've walked too long, wandered too far, Prince Vamere," the girl said, facing the crowd. "They'll think something happened between us and we'll be forced to marry." She batted her eyes and turned to face the male.

Lela gasped. The girl... Her ears! Her ears had no point. Lela's eyes darted to the audience, focusing on the features she'd ignored before. They were shorter, and fatter, with rounded ears, and round faces lacking any sharp angles.

Humans.

Gongs chimed across the field, audible even this far from home.

The girl looked up suddenly, as if she'd heard. They locked eyes.

Lela stumbled backward, out of the mirage. She tripped over her boots and fell onto flowers and tall grass. The mirage shimmered in front, all signs of the humans gone.

The gongs raged. Lela scrambled away from the mirage just as it disappeared, taking the feel of energy with it. No, not a mirage.

A portal.

Lela shot to her feet, ripping at the grass in haste, and launched into a sprint toward home. This was the danger they'd been warned about. These humans would be their doom, somehow. Trees blurred by, and the hills came and went.

The rounded, smiling faces hadn't seemed dangerous, but that didn't matter now. That girl. The energy seemed to come from her. Was she a powerful wizard seeking to destroy them? She must be, if she was the one who opened the portal. But she looked so young, no older than Lela herself.

"Lela!" Mata shouted from the back of their cottage.

Lela put on another burst of speed, gongs mixing with the sound of her panting breaths. She took her mata's outstretched hand, and they hurried into the house. Lela collapsed in a heap to the floor.

"Too far, Lelana," Mata reprimanded, hand over her chest. "You should not have gone so far away."

"I'm sorry," Lela puffed, trying to regain her breath. "I'm sorry."

"The danger can come at any moment, young one." Her tone was gentle, and Lela was reminded of why. Oren had left this afternoon. Mata must think she was upset because of him. "I won't have you leave me like my sister." Mata's sister had gone away when Lela was just a baby. No one had heard from her since, and Mata thought the worst.

"Mata, listen." Lela stood and squared her shoulders. "We must write to Pata immediately." She took a shaking breath. "I found the portal."

CHAPTER 8

L ist in hand, coins in his pocket, Callen closed up shop early and sauntered down the street. He wasn't the only one heading to market. Helga, the Cedar Inn owner's wife, stepped out her door almost at the same time, empty basket in hand. Many people visited market every day it was in town, stocking up on hard-to-come-by supplies or seeking better prices.

Callen doubted he'd find everything on his list, but he had to try. Master Marek couldn't move on with Callen's training until they found a potion that worked.

His shoes scuffled over the road, the dirt packed tight from all the recent travelers, newcomers who'd made the shop a lot of money these past couple market days. The sun shone low, warming his back as he headed east. After only a few blocks, the stench of horse manure accompanied the shouts of peddlers.

"Fresh fish!" one called.

"Try my wife's preserves," another offered, but Callen ignored them.

Fallhold had no regulations where the vendors set up, so long as the road stayed clear for carts. One could find a spice market right next to a gold merchant. Callen had his usuals—the rare herb dealers—and they liked to set up just north of the market fountain.

Callen made his way there at an increasingly slow pace due to the number of people milling from stall to stall, women and men already overburdened with wares, or young people just looking for the perfect place to spend their few precious coins. The scents of roasted nuts and cinnamon made his mouth water. He'd have to find that stand once he'd purchased his ingredients. Sugared almonds were one of his favorites, and hard to come by.

The market square was the most crowded of all the avenues he'd crossed, as usual. Children laughed and splashed each other in the fountain that bubbled a fine stream in the middle of the cobbled area. Temporary stalls lined every inch of useable space surrounding it, pouring into the branching alleys. Horses clopped through, eyes wide and ears back from the noise and mayhem of a lively market. A lone mandolin player plucked in a corner, collecting coins, the sound nearly drowned out by the cacophony of voices.

Callen spotted the cream-colored canopy of his favored merchant immediately and made his way over, ignoring the calls of the shopkeepers and the stares of the pretty girls beside the fountain.

Beneath the canopy, arranged on makeshift shelves and tables, was a mini herbalist shop. Herbs and ingredients lined the small area, sitting loose in baskets or sealed in glass and wooden jars.

"Callen," an old man exclaimed. He hopped off his stool, seeming happy to see a familiar face. "What'll it be today?"

"Theo, it's good to see you again." Callen handed his list to the squat, graying shopkeep who scanned it and assembled what he found into Callen's basket. Theo had been running this stand longer than Callen had been coming to market.

"Saria's been asking of ya." Theo set a measured amount of dried catstail into the basket. "I ought to bring her to market with me next month."

"That's okay," Callen said quickly, dropping a satchel of an odd-smelling herb he'd been examining. "I wouldn't want to trouble her."

Saria, Theo's granddaughter, was the same age as Callen, but not his type. As a rule, he didn't court much. Marriage at a young age was something his parents always had in mind for him, since he served them no other purpose as the youngest of six. Anytime anyone stepped even close to pressuring him, he backed away as far as he could.

"Hmm, probably for the best," Theo mumbled. "She met a new fellow over in Timbercross anyway."

Callen felt Theo's eyes on him, but he didn't look up. A basket and his list shot in front of his face.

"Found it all but the agoron oil. Sold out this morning," Theo said. "Next time bring me a real challenge."

Callen nodded his thanks, taking the items and reaching for his coins. It hadn't been complicated this time, but he really needed that oil to brew Master Marek's potion again.

"Want to special order the agoron?" Theo asked, an eager look in his crinkled eyes.

Agoron oil was usually easy to find, and Theo charged a fortune for special orders.

"No, thank you." Callen handed over the agreed upon amount of marks, pocketing the rest.

Theo took it without fuss. "Hey, since you have some coin left over, you ought to visit the troupes. There's a big green one set up to the east, along the main thoroughfare. They've a pretty girl playing the lead, and people say she puts on quite the show."

Callen smiled and said he would, though he had no intention of doing so. Those shows were a clichéd waste of time. The annoying thing now was that Callen would have to spend precious time traveling the market, finding another vendor for the oil. But it was worth it. If he could perfect the potion, this next batch might work.

Callen bid Theo farewell and stepped out from the shade of the tent. The warm sun was nice after the cool air under the tent. The pack of bodies in the square had grown thicker as evening neared, bright dresses and dusty tunics squeezing their way past each other. Callen pressed into the throng, holding his basket close.

To go south, where he'd had luck last month, meant cutting across the busiest space around the fountain in the middle of the square. He turned sideways to edge through the flow of bodies, but a towering man with arms as thick as tree trunks barreled into him, pushing Callen against the fountain. His knees banged on the concrete edge. He rubbed at the throbbing pain. The crowd gave him no reprieve as the flow ushered him east instead of south. He allowed the mass to carry him the wrong direction, looking for a way to cut through to where he wanted to go, but there was none. Eventually, he made it to the eastern edge of the square and almost knocked over a man banging a big drum and wearing a ridiculous purple costume.

The man—a jester—smiled wide, the sound of the drum vibrating Callen's skull. "Hear ye, hear ye!" he called in a voice as loud as the drum. "Prepare to feast your eyes on the lovely Lady Ricci, in a show of true love and adventure, comedy and tragedy. Follow me to witness the Magnificent Menowin Traveling Troupe!"

The jester's drumming and obnoxious proclamations bounced off the wooden storefronts lining the road as he continued east, now with a large following. Callen rolled his eyes. The troupes were an inevitable part of a busy market. Where there were townsfolk with coin, there'd be cheap entertainment to take it.

Callen shook his head and maneuvered around the square to the southern tents and market stalls. For the next hour, he scoured the market—avoiding the east where the jester had gone—but had no luck finding the necessary oil—just vendors who'd be more than happy to special order it for him.

His feet ached despite his sturdy boots, and dust caked the hem of his robes. He munched on a stick of savory roast chicken and salty potato cubes, washing it down with ale before admitting defeat. The east side of market wasn't known for selling what he needed—mostly blacksmiths, armories, and cobblers took those spots—but it was the only place he hadn't visited. He did not want to have to come back tomorrow, or be forced to give Theo four times what agoron oil should cost.

The crowd had thinned some, probably thanks to the heat, so it took little time to pass the storefronts and reach the market stalls—and of course, the traveling troupes.

The pointy hat of the jester stuck up above the heads of the marketgoers, and his drum banged over the constant conversations and shouts from shopkeepers. Another show must have been starting. Sure enough, further down the road, a band of wagons in bright greens and blues with swirls of gold wrapped around the back of a raised platform. A big man wearing priest's robes made some kind of announcement. The crowd surrounding the stage was so thick, Callen had to step off the road to go around them. He'd never seen so many people that eager for another cheap play.

KRISTIN L. HAMBLIN

He hopped over a ditch streaming with reeking human and animal refuse, then finally pushed past the troupe. He exhaled in relief when he spotted a market stall with a pestle and mortar sign just down the road. Closer, he saw it was a wagon which opened to reveal the shopkeeper's wares. An old woman with wispy hair eyed him eagerly as he approached. He took a moment to make sure his basket was covered. His apprentice mage robes would be enough to tell her not to try to cheat him, but it was better if she couldn't guess what potion he was making and hike up the prices in anticipation.

"Welcome to my humble shop, young mage." She flashed a crooked-tooth smile to accompany her attempt at flattery. Apprentices weren't considered mages until they went through the trials and certified as such. "What can I help you find?"

Callen eyed her wares—herbs that were overdried and thin, meaning the plants weren't healthy to begin with, bottles of potions where the liquid ingredients had split into separate levels. It took special care to transport weather-sensitive potions, and these hadn't been given that kind of care. Luckily, all he needed was an oil, and she had a good stock.

He picked up the clear vial, uncorked it, and inhaled. It was pure, undiluted by water. "I'll give you two broams for this."

The woman chortled. "Twenty."

Callen started, nearly dropping the vial. He could do almost two special orders through Theo with that kind of coin. He hastily put it back. It'd be a waste to counter; he'd never get her down to a reasonable five broams. "I don't need it after all."

"Wait!" She lifted an arm, her loose sleeve sliding down to reveal thinness and wrinkles. "Fifteen, then. That damned troupe has kept all the business away."

Callen's lips thinned. "Four. And how would a traveling troupe keep business from an apothecary?"

The woman's eyes narrowed. "Twelve. Customers take one

72

look at that stage, and they forget what they came for. They don't make it this far down the road before that redhead steals them away."

Callen looked to the stage, but all he saw was the crowd. "Five. What makes this redhead so special?"

The crowd around the stage erupted into cheers.

She clenched her teeth. "Ten, but that's as low as I go. They say she makes you see things, like you're really in the play alongside her."

Callen snorted and crossed his arms. Troupes couldn't afford an illusionist, let alone the permit for one. Besides, they weren't very common. "Six."

"No, young mage, I will not."

He weighed her words and the fact that no other customer had come close to approaching her during their haggling. And the fact that he didn't have time to wait for a special order. The potion had to be finished before his master returned. "I'm willing to pay seven broams and keep you in mind for my next market visit, but if you will not accept, you'll never see me again."

She watched him, then shifted her gaze to the full shelves of her wagon. "Fine," she growled. Under her breath, she added grumbling, "Might as well give the lot away."

Callen grabbed the oil and handed her the exact amount of coin. Seven broams was only slightly better than a special order. The woman's continued grumbling faded to the background as he turned to the stage, intrigued. An illusionist was not too many steps down from a mage. He could spare a few minutes to watch a play on his way back to the shop.

With his basket of wares and the thickness of the crowd, it took a lot of maneuvering—and a lot of dirty looks and cursing —to get close enough to see even the very tops of the actors' heads. There was no redhead though. Currently on stage was the same bigger man as before, this time in what was clearly meant to be a knight's outfit, as well as two more men in knight's outfits—long tunics tied with red belts over tight leggings, with fake swords in their hands and dented metal helms on their heads.

"We told his majesty we'd find his bride, and we must not fail!" The tallest knight raised his sword in the air with gusto. "We will rescue her from her doom or die trying."

The other two shouted, "For king and country!" Then the trio hurried off the stage.

The crowd burst into applause. Callen sighed. Another predictable story of a princess in trouble. He started to leave.

"Shhh," someone nearby said. "She's coming next." The man turned to a couple beside him, eyes alight with excitement. "I've seen this play four times so far."

"That's nothing," a woman two rows behind said. "My husband and I have followed Lady Ricci for two towns already. We came all the way from Hunterton. And my sister saw her very first play!"

Callen raised an eyebrow. These people were crazy. No traveling troupe was good enough to have a following. If they were that good, they'd be working in Devshire for King Willmot himself.

The boasting died out suddenly, and Callen whipped his focus ahead. A girl around his age stepped onto the stage. She pinched the lengths of a shiny green gown, held up in front of her, as regal as any queen. With her chin high, red hair tumbled around her face in graceful waves. Heavy makeup hid what was probably true natural beauty, but that was typical of these traveling troupes.

It didn't stop the crowd from drawing a collective breath as she opened her mouth to speak her lines.

"I mustn't fear. My prince will come for me. The Wizard

Harlen may think he can woo me with false fields of beautiful wildflowers and songbirds, but this is merely a mirage. A prison. My heart is not so easily won." Her voice was sweet as spun sugar, melodious as a summer song, with words sure in their deliverance, even if tawdry.

He wished he could be as sure of anything as this girl was sure her prince would rescue her.

She bent down slowly, reaching for something with a small smile on her face. Callen stood on the balls of his feet, craning around the person in front of him, but there was nothing but raw wood planks and empty air below her fingertips.

The girl's smile grew, then Callen gasped. There *was* a flower there. A whole field of red and purple wildflowers, soft stalks of grass waving lazily in a breeze much cooler than the hot spring day he'd just been standing in. A sweet floral fragrance wafted over his heated skin.

The sky turned pink.

Callen's basket slipped from his fingers.

Magic.

Giant oaks—or something like them—rustled where the troupe's wagons stood, though their image was distorted, as if they were only half there, as if in a haze. Instead of green, their leaves radiated with every color of the rainbow.

How was she doing this? She must be a strong illusionist indeed. Callen had only ever heard of simple things, like making a single rabbit scamper across the table and disappear into the air.

The girl plucked a red poppy and brought the bloom to her face. The crowd—he'd nearly forgotten them—ahhed as she nuzzled the soft petals against her cheek.

Callen shook his head. Powerful indeed. His feet were immovable stones as the play continued. The prince and his knights found the girl in the field. She was so happy to see them, falling into the arms of her betrothed. The men didn't break character, standing in the middle of a wildflower meadow that hadn't existed minutes before.

The play took an expected turn when the evil wizard appeared and challenged the prince to a duel. What Callen hadn't expected, however, was for the prince to lose. The girl held her dying prince in her arms and wept openly. Callen found his eyes tearing too. The way the actors made the audience feel part of the moment, and the images to go with it. Everything felt so real.

When Princess Kasma escaped and the play ended, the image disappeared, bringing the hot sun back. The crowd burst into applause amongst sniffling and noses blowing. Callen had expected a typical happily ever after, and instead had watched a tragedy that still had his breaths coming faster than they should have.

The actors took the stage, and Callen's gaze stayed locked on the girl—Lady Ricci—as she bowed, eyes shiny with tears and a wavering smile. She looked distressed, like she was still locked in the throes of grieving for her lost beloved. It was a play. Nothing more. Except, it *was* more, somehow.

She was one of the first to leave, though she had to know the applause was all for her. Coins plinked like rain onto the stage as the knights scrambled to collect their takings.

The crowd remained, chanting for Lady Ricci, until the jester returned, banging his drum to quiet them down. Callen recognized him now as one of the prince's knights.

"We hope you enjoyed the Adventures of Princess Kasma. Lady Ricci and the rest of the Magnificent Menowin Traveling Troupe will return for our final performances tomorrow before following the market to Timbercross." He gave a deep bow and a final bang of his drum before exiting the stage and disappearing inside a bright green wagon.

Callen hastened to pick up his basket, thanking the Gods none of the contents spilled, as the crowd reluctantly dispersed. Several lingered as if hoping it was some cruel joke and there actually would be another performance today.

The sun dipped lower in the sky. Callen scratched his neck. The girl must have a unique skill in casting illusions, though that only explained the visual part. Had he only imagined the smells of the flowers and the coolness of the breeze? He'd watched little of these traveling shows, because they were all the same. Except this one. This one had been much, much different. It was almost as if they'd been transported to a different place.

And that girl... She'd seemed so sad at the end, even after the play was over. The other actors were too busy collecting their money to notice. She clearly needed comfort. And her magic had been incredible. Where had she trained?

An irrational need to see her smile filled him, and his feet moved before he could think better of it. He rounded the stage, heading toward the wagon she'd escaped to.

What are you doing, Callen? She's a performer. An especially good one. She didn't actually lose her prince.

The sound of weeping came from behind the wagons, within the brush and scraggly trees. He barreled ahead, going around them. All the actors must have gone inside. All but one. Even her weeping was melodic and pure.

He followed a trampled path through the brush and into the thicket. A stray ray of sun glinted off her shiny dress, catching his attention just steps into the foliage. She sat at the base of a thick shade tree, knees drawn and head in her hands.

Callen slowed his approach. What was he doing? A twig snapped beneath his boots, and he winced as she looked up and gasped.

Callen held up his hands as she scrambled to her feet.

"Sorry! Sorry. I don't know what I'm doing. I just... I heard you crying. I wanted to see if you were okay."

She wiped at her face, smearing the thick makeup, and stared at him with guarded eyes. This was the real her, not the actress, and she was all the more endearing.

"I'm fine." She bit her lip and sniffled once. "I get very deep into my roles and sometimes need a moment to compose myself." She eyed the path behind him.

He backed up, clearing the way for her while nodding. That made sense. "I'm very sorry to disturb you then. I didn't mean to scare you." Good Gods, this was not going well. He was frightening her like some predator, stalking her alone in the woods. "I'm Callen Kealamin. I'm an apprentice mage to Master Marek of the high council. I work at the potions shop back in town." He flashed a smile he hoped would put her at ease. "We have the best peppermint sticks around."

Her eyes widened, and she nodded, sidestepping to the path out.

"Is there anything I can do to help?" He backed further into the woods to help her not feel nervous. "Your performance was amazing. I've never seen such skilled acting. Normally I avoid watching these kinds of things, uh, but I was pleasantly surprised." He shoved one hand in his pocket and tightened the grip on the basket with the other, heat creeping up his neck.

"Thank you." The girl backed to the opening in the brush. In a moment, she'd be gone.

"How did you do it?" he asked quickly. "Your magic is very strong."

Her mouth gaped. "I didn't do anything. You saw what you wanted to see. Good day." The flash of her green dress disappeared around a tree, and he was left alone.

"Well, that couldn't have gone any worse." He kicked a loose rock, sending it shooting into the bushes.

Maybe he could find time tomorrow to come back and see the show one last time. Master Marek wouldn't notice his absence. Something about her, this Lady Ricci and her magic, begged to be unraveled. Who was she when she wasn't Princess Kasma? How did her magic work? He looked forward to unlocking the mystery.

CHAPTER 9

Ricci slammed the wagon door behind her, startling her parents from counting the day's coins. "A mage," she said, struggling to regain her breath. "A mage sought me out. He asked how I was able to cast my illusions."

She stared at their wide eyes, willing them to speak. How could she have been so careless? A mage in the audience! She never should have been on stage while a mage stood watching. He'd turn her in. She'd be arrested for using magic without a permit. They hadn't saved up enough to get one yet.

They were doomed.

Papa scratched the back of his neck and stared at Mama, waiting for her to have all the answers. Mama didn't notice. She watched the door as if waiting for the mage to blast it apart. Ricci held her breath, mind racing for a way to fix this. If Mama suspected danger, she'd never let Ricci act again.

The thought had crossed her mind to keep it to herself, but this affected them all. The mage council could close down their troupe for good.

Finally, Mama looked up. "I'm sorry, Ricika. I shouldn't have agreed to let you practice magic."

The instant the words left Mama's lips, the pain took Ricci's breath away, opening a raw ache within. To stop practicing magic meant to stop acting, as they went hand-in-hand now. She couldn't give up her dream.

Papa opened his mouth to speak, then stopped as if changing his mind, then opened it again. "I've counted it all twice." He jangled a handful of coins. "We can afford a permit now."

"Oh, yes," Ricci said, spirits lifted.

Mama's frown was immediate. "She hasn't been to school or been trained. Besides, permits cost more than you think—enough to feed the family for a month."

Papa smiled wide, lifting the basket.

"But Mama," Ricci said. "Timbercross is only two days away. There's a mage council there, right?"

Mama scooped up Papa's new boots and a rag, dipping it into a new jar of polish. "That doesn't change what's done. You've been seen."

Papa scooped the coins into a leather pouch. "Ricci doesn't need the magery test, only a permit for illusions. Shouldn't require any training."

Mama's rag swished as it trailed over Papa's big-as-barrels shoes. "The Harland Troupe's mage had to study for years."

"He's not a mage. He studied to learn tricks, sleight-of-hand and the like." Ricci leaned against the door, feigning an ease she didn't feel. They were ganging up on Mama, and the only reason it was working was because Mama was allowing it.

Papa leaned back on his stool. "A farmer with the special knack to calm his animals, or a peddler who can lift twice his weight in supplies. These small things don't matter to the council—they're simple and won't become any more than they are—but the council is happy to charge for the permit. More money for wars and such."

"And we have enough?" Ricci asked. Their take was sizable today. Very sizable.

"Trust me, it's enough." Papa laughed.

"Well, then let's hurry and get this permit," Mama said as if that had been her idea all along. "I don't want to fret about some stray mage looking for a reward."

A reward? Ricci didn't think the boy meant to turn her in for a reward. Otherwise, why approach her? The image of his gray-blue eyes creased in concern behind wisps of onyx hair flashed in her mind.

The tension eased from Ricci's shoulders. If the mage didn't report her, she'd be safe. And once she got the permit, she could cast her illusions without worry.

Papa cleared his throat. "All you have to do is demonstrate your talent like you do on stage, then the council will examine your magic and grant you a permit."

Ricci's mouth popped open. "They have to examine me?" Mages made her nervous anyway, but to have such important people as the council examine something she barely under-stood did not sound like the best idea. "What if they don't like what I can do?" She didn't ask what she really feared—what if it was more than a simple illusion?

"No, love. They'll be entranced as we all are," Papa said.

Mama nodded. "Just have something good in mind before you go. It'll help you feel less nervous."

She didn't have a choice. Her family needed her to get this permit. What she could do helped them all.

Mama's polishing slowed. "Mmm," she mumbled to herself.

Ricci and Papa stared at her.

"We'll have to cancel tomorrow's shows if a mage is sniffing around," Mama said.

"I agree. I don't want to do any more shows until I'm licensed," Ricci said.

Papa stood. "Good idea. I'll have Lanny post a notice. We'll leave a day early, and that will give us time for Ricci to be seen by the council before Timbercross market." He winked at Ricci on his way out of the wagon.

Ricci remained silent, mind hammering that she'd just lost a day to prepare for whatever the council might want her to do. At least that mage, handsome as he was, wouldn't be able to turn them in if they were gone. He might have been just an apprentice, but he was an apprentice to someone that might cause them trouble. The sooner they left, the better.

"I'll change and go practice something to show the council." Ricci grabbed for the laces at the back of her birthday dress.

A warm hand assisted her frantic movements. "I want you to wear this when you see the council."

Ricci turned around to Mama's tight smile. "Why does it matter what I wear?"

Mama smoothed Ricci's wild hair back. "Let your costume be part of your illusion. If you show them a troupe girl ready to put on a great show, that's all they'll see." She dropped her hand, and the rare tenderness was gone as quick as it'd come. "Besides, it's the nicest thing you own, and first impressions are important."

Ricci left the wagon in a daze, wearing her plain linen dress, and returned to her temporary retreat in the woods. She'd found it their first day of Fallhold market—secluded amongst the trees, shade from the sun, a fallen log to sit upon —her own private sanctuary. Time to herself was rare, being part of a troupe. That young mage had taken even that from her. Who knew if he might come back to find her? But it was the only option she had.

She sighed and perched on the log. Things had grown so complicated since her birthday. What she needed was peace and tranquility. The fragrant field of wildflowers sprung to her mind. Yes, it would be the perfect thing to show the mage council. What young girl didn't like flowers and beautiful things? They'd only see it for the illusion it probably was.

She shook out her arms and forced a smile to her face. Happy. Joyful. Love. She closed her eyes and imagined herself in that field full of flowers, resting on a log like this one. Two deep breaths later, the warmth in her chest let her know the magic had surfaced. The rustle of leaves shifted, the sound coming from further away instead of above. The wind changed direction, blowing stronger and cooler. A sweet scent filled her nose, and her smile turned genuine as true peace wiped away all anxiety.

Ricci opened her eyes.

The scraggly trees had turned hazy, mixing with a meadow of wildflowers. She'd never cast an illusion alone before. There was always an audience, even if just her family. Tall grass and colored blossoms tickled her ankles, and the sun burned in the sky just where she'd left it, though there were more clouds now.

Ricci gasped. The sky was pink again, like the pale shade of a beautiful sunset, except the sun wasn't setting. She hadn't imagined that. How could she? But it was the most beautiful thing she'd ever seen.

Ricci reached down and plucked a red, four-petaled bloom and inhaled its musky, sweet scent. It was real, just like the one on stage. As real as the cool wind now blowing in her hair. The fuzzy softness of the flower's stem as she spun it between her fingers was undeniable. She let out an elated laugh, then stood and twirled in breathless excitement.

This place she'd created was real.

Ricci laughed again, throwing her arms out wide. She'd never had this before. Ever. Totally alone, free to do whatever she pleased, be whoever she wanted to be, and no one to expect anything of her. This place was hers, and she embraced it. The log she'd sat on faded, becoming almost transparent. More flowers and grass became visible within, as if the log wasn't there at all. As if *it* was the illusion and not this place.

Her grin widened. This field could be as real as she wanted it to be.

Her field of vision expanded to include the nearby trees—thick trunks topped with billowing leaves. Large leaves no longer the familiar green, but heaped with color. A tree with blue leaves that faded to pink on one side and over to lavender on another. Another with leaves fluttering in the breeze in shades of the sea that faded to yellow. *So beautiful.*

A gasp rang out behind her. Ricci spun, arms curling protectively inward. Her heart beat fast under her hands. Had the mage followed her here? But the gasp—she was sure that was what it was—sounded female.

She reached back with her foot, feeling for the log, never taking her eyes off the trees. When her foot found nothing but grass, she risked a glance down. The log was gone.

Distant gongs rang out, like the frantic chime of a bell tower. Blood pounded in her ears. This couldn't be a simple field and nothing else. What lay beyond the picturesque meadow? Places with towers ringing out warning bells. Where was she? What had she done?

She had to get out of there. Now.

Ricci glanced back to the tree line and screamed. Her

scream mixed with the frantic gongs still raging in the background.

A girl. Long silver hair, a rugged brown tunic with straps and pockets all over, and tight leggings beneath boots laced up her calves. The girl tensed, but she wore a calm expression of curiosity. She'd seen that hair before, half obscured by a crowd. Sharp cheekbones. Pointed ears.

Ricci's vision swam. The instinct to run willed her legs to move, but they wouldn't budge. She was caught in a dream. The wind blew the girl's hair back from her shoulders, further highlighting her unusual ears. Like the fae in children's stories.

Ricci squeezed her eyes shut. *Go away, go away, go away. Make this all go away. I want to go home.*

"Why have you come here?" the girl called out with an odd accent.

Ricci didn't open her eyes, but that didn't stop the pounding of the girl's boots as she ran toward her, or the gongs still ringing from afar. *How do I get back?*

"What do you want with us?"

Ricci took three deep breaths, forcing them to be slow while her heart tried to burst from her chest. She opened her eyes.

"Wait!" The girl reached for her, desperation on her face.

Ricci gasped. Warmth burst within her.

Then it was gone.

The warm air returned, the trees were green, and the sky was blue again. The log scraped against the back of her legs. Ricci collapsed onto it, sobbing into her hands. She was back. The girl and the colorful meadow had been real. It wasn't her imagination. It was a real place with real people.

How would she ever convince the council it was just an illusion? How could she ever go back there again?

CHAPTER 10

Lela stumbled over the spot where the human girl had disappeared. She'd been so close. Mata would absolutely kill her if she found out she'd returned to the flower meadow. But her people needed answers. Maybe if she could capture the portal opener herself, this torture would end.

The girl had been so happy, spinning and enjoying the flowers, then scared witless when she'd realized she was not alone. She'd become clearer, less like a mirage and more real the longer she'd stayed. Did that mean she'd crossed all the way into their world?

Then the girl just vanished. But not without a trace. Lela reached down and snatched up the flower she'd dropped, stem snapped off at the bottom. She twirled it in her fingers. The breeze shifted with no memory of the previous disruption.

There was something about the girl... more than her unique energy. She radiated innocence and naivety. It was almost as if she didn't know what she was doing.

That didn't mean she meant them no harm. She was human—not to be trusted.

The gongs abruptly stopped, and Lela took off for home. Her feet pounded over dirt, mind racing. Mata would be furious if she didn't find a good excuse for her absence during an alarm—maybe even then. Pata had written back. He said to stay put and tell no one else where the portal was. He was coming home to investigate. Finally. After three years.

He'd been around more while she was growing up, training her to fight or taking her to the castle where he reported to the king. Now he was practically a stranger, but he loved her and Mata, and they'd missed him fiercely.

They needed to be rid of this constant state of fear—the gongs going off and never knowing if this time meant their doom. If she could unravel the mystery, she'd be hailed a hero. And if she could do it before Pata arrived, she'd make her family proud.

Oren would stop seeing her as a child. So many doors would be open to her.

The portal opener would be back. If the king wouldn't allow Lela to help by joining the army, this was something she *could* do. And she didn't need anyone's help to do it. There was no reason to wait, not with the answers so close. She would discover what the whole kingdom was looking for—knowledge of what was coming next.

All she needed was to find the human girl.

CHAPTER 11

Callen backed into the shop, two hands wrapped around his basket of goods. It had taken entirely too long to find all the supplies, but the detour had been worth it. The play was more than he'd ever thought it could be. All because of *her*. He hadn't been able to shake her from his mind the entire walk home. Her performance. Her beauty. Her sadness.

Her magic.

Technically, it was illegal without a permit. He hadn't seen one posted, but he wouldn't report her. And he wouldn't ruin the chance to see her perform again in the morning. Maybe he could learn her trick. There was definitely something unusual about it. It was more than seeing what she wanted the audience to see. Callen felt what she'd wanted him to feel too, as if physically transformed to a different place.

The basket slipped from his fingers, landing hard on the counter. Could it be? Was she creating new places?

A shuffling came from above, followed by a faint cough.

Callen froze. Master Marek was long gone. No one else should be upstairs.

Robbers.

The potions were highly valuable, and dangerous if moved. Robbers wouldn't know which ones were safe to handle. The whole place could burn to the ground with one wrong spill. The sound of furniture scraping against the floor spurred Callen to action. He grabbed a vial of Peppersting off the shelf. Also Thoroughsleep, a colorless gas made to knock someone unconscious. Robbers wouldn't steal his hard work. His apprenticeship depended on it.

Silent as he could, he opened the door to the darkness above and crept up the steps. At the top, a quick peek showed one pair of dusty boots near his most precious brews. The robber was alone. Several lids banged as the robber rummaged through the stock, likely trying to figure out which was most valuable. Callen's heart beat against his ribs. He pointed the stopper on the Thoroughsleep high up and away from him and pulled, releasing it into the room. A quick burst of magic sent the gas floating away from him and toward the robber.

A few breaths later, surprised garble preceded a loud bang as the robber fell, knocking over an unlit oil lamp to shatter on the floor. Callen gripped the Peppersting and pulled more magic up to light the lamps. He crept up the last of the steps. Orange light draped over the lower half of a thin, unconscious figure. He wore purple robes stitched with the mage council insignia.

Oh, Gods. Master Marek.

Callen rushed to his side. "Master."

He shook his master's shoulder, and his head jiggled back and forth. No bleeding, and his master still breathed. But he'd fallen hard.

Callen raked his hands through his hair. He was in deep

trouble. "What have I done? You weren't supposed to come back." His master could be out for hours with Thoroughsleep.

Callen jerked back. He should leave, pretend he hadn't been the one to incapacitate a long-standing member of the mage council, someone who could single-handedly ruin Callen's life—and his family's life, and their friends' families' lives—if he woke up that livid.

He moved away, slowed, then stopped. No. It wasn't right to leave him like this, even if he lost his apprenticeship because of it.

"Master—"

His master roared to consciousness, arms flailing. He rolled to his feet faster than an acrobat. Callen jumped, his back hitting the railing beside the stairs. He sensed the pull of magic as his disoriented master's head whipped back and forth, seeking the assailant. He must have called magic before falling unconscious. That was the only way he could have awoken so quickly.

Callen held up his hands, though they'd do nothing against an attack. He didn't dare summon his own magic. "It's okay! It's only me." He still held the Peppersting and quickly shoved it into his pocket. "I just got back from market. Are you all right?"

Master Marek narrowed his eyes. His jerky movements slowed, finally realizing there was no danger. "Just returned? How did I get on the ground, Callen Kealamin?" His tone was full of suspicion, and he never called Callen anything but 'apprentice'.

The wood railing pressed into Callen's back. "I thought an intruder was stealing the potions. I'm truly sorry." No matter what, it was better he told the truth. Master Marek would have it anyway, through spells or potions of his own making. Callen had learned that the hard way early on. "It's Thoroughsleep."

He lowered his gaze under the heat of his master's glare. "I thought you left town."

Master Marek took a long breath through his nose. His readied magic lessened, then disappeared. Callen peeked up, stomach dropping at the expression on his master's face. He wasn't angry, he was resigned, lips set in a frown and eyes soft.

"You're almost more trouble than you're worth, Callen. Almost. Your father really wanted you to become my apprentice, and the high lord usually gets what he wants."

Sweat beaded across Callen's forehead. His apprenticeship couldn't be in jeopardy. He'd worked so hard.

And what did Father have to do with any of this?

"I'll work harder. I can be an apprentice worthy of your name."

His master shook his head and turned away. "You've yet to create a potion that does as I wish. Only failures, explosions, and holes in the woodwork." His voice rose in volume, and he slammed his fist on the table. "I need that potion!"

His roar shook the nearby vials. Callen winced and took a shaky breath.

Master Marek rarely showed this side of himself. He could terminate the apprenticeship for any reason and at any time. No matter how angry his master was with him, Callen couldn't let that happen. He would not go back to his family a failure as he'd failed everything else in their eyes. Back to their rules, expectations, and constant disappointment in him? No. Becoming a mage was his dream. He had to find a way to create a teleport so his master would complete his training. He had to prove he was meant to be here.

Whatever the cost.

"You want the power of the Nether Realms, right?" Callen blurted.

Master Marek's eyes widened in alarm, then turned greedy. Covetous.

"I mean, like teleport?" He spoke fast as an idea formed. "What about an alternate reality? I saw someone at market today. A girl—part of a traveling troupe—who can make people see things. Real things. Flowers of all different colors. They even smell real. Maybe she can help us." Callen trailed off as his master's expression went from captivated to bored.

"Don't waste my time, Callen. Brew the potions. That's your role. And I have mine." He hastened with a slight limp toward the outside door, grabbing a bulging bag that clinked with the sound of potion bottles. "I'll be in Timbercross. I'll send instructions." The door slammed behind him.

Callen collapsed into the nearest armchair, rubbing his eyes. He shouldn't have mentioned the girl. She was the first thing he thought of to save himself from being a disappointment in his master's eyes. He'd meant to protect her. It could mean big trouble to practice without a permit, and he hadn't hesitated.

Guilt creased his brow. His master hadn't seemed to care. Maybe it'd be okay.

But what if she *could* lead him to the secret of teleporting? What she did was more than simple illusions, really. Maybe she was actually opening portals to new places. What else could explain the change in temperature? Nothing would esteem Callen more than solving the riddle plaguing Master Marek. His life's goal. And a noble one—if they could travel across the world and back with a simple spell, all sorts of problems might be solved. And not just bridging the mage community, as his master said, but things like hunger and war.

The next morning, Callen didn't even bother opening the shop. He simply washed, dressed, and headed to town. He didn't notice the townspeople wore downtrodden faces until he came upon the empty field and the simple notice stuck to a pole in the dirt.

Magnificent Menowin Traveling Troupe has moved to Timbercross.

Callen's hometown.

His face turned as downtrodden as the townspeople's. He had to see her one more time. There was no choice but to go.

CHAPTER 12

T he day it took to reach Timbercross passed in turmoil, Ricci fidgeting in her bunk as she scrambled for a way to fool the mages. Her family had nearly arrived, and she was still no closer to solving the problem. All she could think about was the girl from the meadow.

Ricci had opened a gateway to another world.

And now she'd run out of time to form a plan to face the mage council. She'd never convince them it was only an illusion. If anything, every time she used the magic, it only became stronger. The ability to open portals wasn't supposed to exist. It's not like the mage council would just grant a permit and send her on her way. No, if they discovered what she was really capable of, nothing would be the same. She had to keep it secret.

The wagon lurched to a stop. Ricci glanced out the window. Stars twinkling in the night sky outlined Papa on the driver's bench, reining the horses. Timbercross would be the first big city Ricci performed her lead role. Or, would have been, if she didn't need a permit first. Since becoming Lady

Ricci, it'd only been small towns—practice runs for the real show.

Ricci jerked at a loud bang, elbow sending her small collection of worn books tumbling. Lanny burst inside.

"I got it, Mama," he exclaimed, waving a paper around and grinning at Ricci.

Ricci's head tilted sideways with a feeling of dread at the way Lanny looked at her.

"Oh, good, son. That's good." Mama turned up the lantern, finished putting on her boots, then took the paper.

Lanny flashed a grin and left as swiftly as he'd come.

"What's that, Mama?" In the weak light, Ricci caught the flicker of a blue crest at the top of the page before Mama turned.

"Papa was worried it might take some time to see the mage council, so he sent Lanny ahead. The Gods know we can't afford to put our shows on hold long." Mama sighed, then looked at her with concern.

Ricci jumped from her bunk, landing with a loud thump. She swallowed hard. "What did Lanny find out?" Her fingernails dug into her palms.

"On market days, the mage council opens their doors to anyone seeking a permit. They have spots all day long. Lanny signed you up for a morning slot. You'll head out at daybreak." Mama tapped the letter on the counter. "There will probably be a line, but I suspect you'll get that permit just fine."

Ricci's breath exploded out in a rush. She dropped to her parents' bed. Daybreak?

Mama went to help with chores—apparently not noticing she'd left her daughter in a state of full-blown panic.

"What am I going to do?" Ricci whispered. She dropped her head in her hands.

After chores, which Ricci barely remembered doing, and dinner, which she didn't touch, it was late. Very late. The moon had already set, and Ricci lay in her bunk, desperately trying to sleep. The cacophony of crickets and Papa's soft snores couldn't drown out her heart pounding in her ears. They were going to discover her secret. The mage council would stare down from the rafters, scores of them watching her every move, and when she transported herself to another place, they would know. They'd never let her act again.

She tossed and turned until the sky turned the faintest blue. Papa shuffled out of bed as if a clock had struck the hour.

"Ricci," he whispered, trying not to wake Mama. "Time to go." Clothes rustled, and jars clinked as he went about readying for their journey.

Ricci couldn't tear her wide, aching eyes from the wooden ceiling. She was doomed.

"Ricci," Papa said a little louder.

She forced herself to dress, donning her costume as Mama had suggested. They left, amazingly, without waking her. Ricci shook her head when Papa handed her a trail biscuit. She was going to be sick any moment, and a dry, tasteless biscuit would just stick in her throat and block whatever might come up.

Outside, dew coated each blade of grass and each wagon as her family slumbered in deep, peaceful, unharried sleep. Their boots crunched loudly on the dirt road. Some early-rising merchants waved or nodded as they passed. The first rays of sun bathed the sandstone buildings lining the street as they delved deeper into Timbercross. Horses pulling carts and servants carrying baskets crowded the roads. The aroma of fresh-baked bread mingled with the stench of human refuse.

How Papa knew where he was going, Ricci had no idea. Their troupe came to Timbercross twice a year and camped in the same spot each time, never quite making it to the heart of the city.

Though, it was undeniable when they arrived at the mage council. It stood taller and fancier than the surrounding buildings, with tall marble columns. A fountain bubbled out front, purely for decoration and not for washing, with a marble statue of a man, naked but for a loin cloth, with flexed muscles and sightless eyes. What this had to do with magic, Ricci couldn't guess, but it definitely spoke of power and influence.

They followed several others to the back of the building, where a line already formed in front of double doors carved with fancy flourishes and set with a blue-painted crest. Ricci shuddered and silently took her place beside Papa in the line. She guessed they were mostly farmers who'd traveled far and wide to be here, given their dirt-stained clothes, some alone and some with a companion, but a wide range of ages all quietly chatting. Her skin felt too tight, her breaths too shallow. With great effort, she resisted counting how many people stood ahead of her. Her turn would come either way.

A bell tower chimed nearby, then a lock clicked and the doors opened, splitting the blue crest in half. Several more people lined up behind them, pinning them in.

Despite their early arrival and Lanny securing them a morning spot, it still took two agonizing hours before they reached the front of the line. Some people exited holding papers and looking relieved, but not everyone. Most of them looked disappointed, heads hanging as they rejoined their companions. More people went home empty-handed than received a license.

Papa gripped her shoulders, probably worried she would bolt any moment. True, so true.

"Next," a young man in navy-blue mage robes called out, turning back inside without looking at her.

Ricci went to take a step, but her leg didn't budge. She couldn't do this. They would see the truth right through her.

"You'll do fine." Papa kissed her cheek and handed her the letter Lanny had brought back, along with a large, jangling pouch. It weighed down her arm, heavier than it looked. "Use your gifts."

Ricci stumbled into the building, blinking as her eyes adjusted to the sudden darkness. The cooler air kissed the sweat on the back of her neck. She put the strap of the coin pouch over her shoulder and chest, gripping the leather with slick palms as she followed the young mage down a long corridor.

Another mage passed by going the other way, followed by a middle-aged man in plain clothes. The man watched the floor, crestfallen. Ricci saw no paper in his hands. Would she share the same fate?

At least he was walking out of here and not being thrown in prison. What if they had the power to hear her thoughts? They would read her guilt like a children's story and pick out every time she'd broken the law practicing magic without a permit.

Her mage stopped so abruptly, Ricci nearly ran into him. He opened a simple door. "In there."

Ricci swallowed and stepped into a small room. A woman mage smiled up at her from behind a desk. The space was empty besides a few wooden chairs around the perimeter, two of which were occupied by commoners writing on parchment. At least, she assumed they were commoners, as they wore street clothes and not mage robes.

The door closed behind her, making her jump.

"Hello." The woman took Lanny's letter without looking at

it. "Fill out a form and return it to me." She offered a piece of parchment and a pencil.

Ricci stepped forward, knees wobbling, and took the paper. It shook in her fingers. The chair at the side of the room creaked as she perched on the edge.

Name - Ricika Menowin

Birthplace - The back of a wagon somewhere in the Ricci plains

Town of Residence - The same wagon

Ability - Illusion

And possibly opening a doorway to another world.

Oh, Gods. What if they really could read her mind? She glanced up at the woman, who smiled at her.

Ricci quickly signed at the bottom and gave her the paper. "Do I pay now?"

"No, you only pay if approved for the permit. I'll summon you when it's your turn."

She returned to her seat and watched as the two people before her went, and two more took their places, filling out their papers with far, far less awkwardness than Ricci displayed. Everyone seemed to belong here and know exactly what to do. Except for her.

The door behind the desk opened as each applicant took their turn. Ricci strained to see a hint of what might be waiting for her, but all she saw was blackness. The commoners didn't return to the waiting room.

"Ricika Menowin," the woman called, standing and holding Ricci's paper to her. "Just through there."

The woman nodded in encouragement, but Ricci couldn't

muster a polite response. She took the paper and walked to her destiny.

Inside, windows offered little light as the navy curtains were closed tight, and tall ceilings, at least double the height of the waiting room, made the room feel cavernous. Three mages sat busily writing at separate desks—not the hundreds she'd built up in her mind. The mage in the center held out his hand without looking up.

It took several heartbeats for Ricci to realize he wanted her paper. "Oh." She rushed it over to him.

He peered at it through wire-framed glasses. "An illusionist?" His voice held mockery, and also a promise of swift punishment if one were to challenge his authority. "And what would you do if we permitted you to practice illusion magic?"

I can open portals, she screamed in her head. She waited for a reaction, but nothing. They couldn't read her mind.

"Miss Menowin?"

"I—" Her voice came out a croak. She cleared her throat. "I'm a principal actor in the Magnificent Menowin Traveling Troupe. My small, small ability can make it seem there's a field of flowers or a stone courtyard instead of a stage." She put her actress smile on, but it wavered. "It delights the crowd."

The two mages on the outside watched the one in the middle, whom Ricci now noticed was quite a bit older than the others.

The elder mage examined her, finally noticing her fancy dress. "A troupe performer?"

Ricci gave her best Princess Kasma curtsy. She was playing a role, and she only just now realized it. Mama had been right. If they saw her as nothing more than a young, simple street performer, they'd be less likely to see more than she wanted them to.

The set of the elder mage's mouth made it clear he had little respect for traveling troupes.

"Very well." He put down his glasses. "Let's have it."

Oh, Gods. Now was the hard part. She had to show them something or they wouldn't grant her a permit. Could she even cast under this kind of pressure? And could she keep it from going too far and taking her to a different place?

She took a shaky breath and closed her eyes, trying to forget where she was, what was at stake, who sat in front of her. She focused on the flower field, the place she'd seen the most thanks to all her Princess Kasma roles.

Flowers. Red and purple, flowing in the breeze. Grass swaying gently underfoot. Breathe, just breathe.

Ricci peeked through her eyelids. A sigh of relief came at the sight of pink sky and bright colors. The mages still sat in front of her, staring around and then scribbling in their notes, half-faded within her illusion of the sunny field. She felt it now —the magic didn't want to be held half in and half out of these two places. It pushed her to continue, to make the other world the reality. She clenched her fists against the strain. She couldn't let that happen.

Something slammed into her from behind, knocking her onto the grassy ground. Air burst from her lungs as her face met dirt. Her tenuous hold on the magic slipped. The opaqueness disappeared. She sucked in deep lungfuls of air, now fully in the other world.

In a panic, Ricci pushed herself up. The mages were gone, only grass and rainbow trees where there were once walls.

"No, no, no, no." She grappled for the magic to take her back.

Firm hands grabbed her arms from behind. "You can't go yet," an accented, feminine voice said. "I need answers."

Ricci jerked, pulling against her attacker, but the grip held firm. "Let me go! I have to get back. You don't understand."

The gongs began pealing from a distance.

"No." Her attacker spun her around so they faced each other. "You came to my world. I will have answers."

The fae girl! Up close, her fierce hazel eyes stared Ricci down, her pale, angular face pinched with worry. Long, silver hair was tucked behind her most distinct feature of all—her long ears.

Ricci gaped. Seeing her up close made it so real.

"Why have you come here?" The fae girl shook her.

Ricci blinked. "I don't know how I came to be... wherever I am. Please. Let me go." She had to get back. What did the mages think about her disappearance? She pulled against the girl's iron grip. "They'll throw me in prison." How long had she been gone? She told them she was an illusionist. They'd know she lied.

"Who will throw you in prison? Why are you here?"

Ricci thrashed. "The mages—if I don't go back now." She had to get away.

The grip loosened. "You mean the wizards? They cursed us. Are you with them?" Her tone turned angry.

"Me, working with the mages? No!" Ricci pulled again.

"If you're not a wizard, then what are you?" The fae girl looked utterly confused, her grip loosening still. "What harm will you bring us?"

"Harm?" This girl was crazy. "I'm just me, Ricci. I wouldn't harm anyone."

"Ricci? My world is in danger, and you're the cause. I need answers." All anger had fizzled out of the fae girl. She seemed only desperate now. Scared.

"I can't help you. Now let go!" She ripped out of the stunned girl's grip.

103

Navy curtains. Tall ceilings. Scribbling mages.

Quicker than she expected, the wide-eyed fae girl disappeared, and Ricci stood once again in the mage council room. She could barely see in the darkness after the midday sun of the flower field.

The three mages had stood from their chairs, mouths gaping.

She was back. Her heart raced, pounding in her ears. She smoothed her dress with shaking hands, fingers meeting grass and dirt. She was covered in it.

Ricci dropped her arms at once and pushed her shoulders back. Time for her most convincing role yet. She laughed, a delighted thing that she'd practiced over and over until it reeked of "fine lady." The sound filled the silent room, and the mages jumped.

"I forgot to mention I can make myself invisible as part of my illusion." She gave them a knowing smile, as if it was all part of the show, as if they'd played right into her hands. "The crowds love that one most of all. It's very convenient for comedic timing, too."

The younger mages looked to the elder, who took a slow seat, scrutinizing her every inch of the way down to his chair. The younger mages followed suit.

"You expect us to believe you forgot?" the elder mage accused, eyes narrowed. "Or were you trying to hide it?"

Ricci's breath caught. "No, never. I'm a performer. I was putting on a show, to demonstrate how I entertain my audience." She fixed her plastered smile. "Do I pass?" Her pulse raced, almost visibly ticking the glittering green dress.

"You disappeared for minutes, Miss Menowin. Minutes," the elder mage said. "We have a busy day with lots of others to examine. Why did you not answer when we called?"

"Well, if I move at all, even to talk, I am revealed. I wanted to show you how long I can stay invisible." Her smile wavered.

The elder mage scribbled more notes. An eternity passed before he looked up. "The ability to turn invisible is a powerful illusion. Where did you train to learn such control?"

Her heart skipped a bit. "I didn't train. I, um, practiced on my own."

The mages' heads shot up. "You performed magic without a permit?" Their stern expressions judged her.

Her composure cracked. "I'm sorry. I know I shouldn't have, but I couldn't help it. It comes to me like breathing, without having to think about it. Please forgive me." She clasped her hands to keep them from shaking. "I need a permit so I won't be breaking any laws. I'll pay whatever the cost."

The elder mage scribbled more notes. "We appreciate your honesty. We can't have commoners performing magic as they please. It would be chaos." He melted red wax onto her paper and pressed a stamp into it. The mage's crest. "You will be fined for practicing without a permit. But," he held the paper in the air, "you've been approved."

Ricci's grin was immediate—this ordeal could finally be over—and she took the paper. Even in her hands, it didn't feel real.

"Miss Menowin, you have a real gift for illusion. If you ever tire of acting, consider applying to one of the mage schools. It's not too late, you know." He waved her to a door behind them.

"Thank you so much." She hurried through in case they changed their minds.

She couldn't believe her luck. A man sat at another desk, and he took her paper and flipped it over to the back. A bunch of writing was already printed there, and he filled in the rest including the date, then had her sign. He looked at her funny when grass rained down on the paper, but she shoved her money at him, and he didn't comment.

It took every coin in her pouch, but she would have happily paid it twice over to never have to go through this again. Nothing could touch her.

The urge to run out of this place was as strong as when she arrived, but finally, Ricci stepped back into the blinding afternoon sun, squinting. Papa came to her at once.

She held the permit high and proud. "We did it, Papa!"

"Ah, that's outstanding. Never had a doubt." He hugged her. "What is that on your face? Dirt?" He drew a handkerchief from his pocket and rubbed her cheek, dirtying the cloth.

Ricci gasped. Her face, too?

The fae girl had tackled her hard. But maybe the mages hadn't noticed—it was dark in the room. No one had said anything. She was still safe.

"Let's go home and have a rest. Shows start in the morn," Papa said. "We'll have a celebration feast. I'm starving."

That's right. But how could she go back to the flower meadow?

They traveled home through the busy streets, Ricci watching behind her the whole way. All the relief and excitement of securing the permit was gone. The fae girl could have killed her if she'd wanted, but she hadn't. That beautiful world, what could it be in danger from? Certainly not Ricci. That didn't make any sense.

Ricci fretted as they walked, barely seeing their surroundings. The fae girl said she wanted answers. She wasn't going to let Ricci be. She might be waiting even now for her to return. But maybe Ricci could convince the girl she truly wasn't a threat. Then the girl would leave her alone, and she could keep performing.

CHAPTER 13

Lela lay in the field of flowers, arms behind her head like a pillow. White clouds drifted lazily overhead, mocking the thoughts tumbling in her head. She'd been so close to getting answers from the human. The gongs had ceased their frantic pealing mere minutes after the girl, Ricci, had disappeared. Several hours had passed since then, and the human hadn't returned.

Lela had no doubt that was what she was—human. She'd read about them growing up. Slow, weak, dim-witted. One of her favorite stories was the battle between fae and humans, good and evil. Long ago, humans and fae lived together, but then the humans, ever breeding and multiplying, got greedy. They demanded more land and resources, more than they really needed. They hurt the land in their consumption-driven frenzy. The wonderous fae king Gaeleath battled them in a hundred-year war, one even humans and their rapid breeding couldn't outlive. Good defeated evil, and the humans were driven out of this world. The human wizards managed to cast one spell before they left. A curse.

The prophecy.

Whenever the portal should open again, that would be the end of days for the fae. Such was the conviction and hate of the humans, the faes did not forget the warning, even as the centuries passed.

But this Ricci had no knowledge of the prophecy. In fact, it seemed the wizards were against her, if they meant to lock her in prison.

Lela had waited since morning to see if Ricci would return, but now evening approached. A whole day gone without tending the herbs. And worse, Lela hadn't returned home at the ringing of the gongs this morning. Mata would lock her in the house and hide the key.

In truth, the gongs had rung off and on often for weeks and nothing had happened. Even Mata merely gasped and shook her head before resuming chopping vegetables or making poultices. Ricci could have enacted whatever evil the humans had in store, but hadn't. Did she truly mean no harm?

Lela stood, dusting dirt off her bottom. Her boots dragged as she moped away from the field. Still no answers, and Pata would be home any day. At the edge of the trees, she stopped cold, sensing it. Like the static build of a coming storm. Huge amounts of energy. Certainly more energy than Lela was capable of. She whipped around and found the human, Ricci, half-faded as if not completely in the fae world. The girl had improved—before, all Lela could see was a mirage from this far away.

Ricci stared with wide eyes, arms raised as if to fend off an attack. Lela raised hers as well, to show she was unarmed, not daring to take a step closer or risk frightening the human. Ricci wore a plain linen dress, much less gaudy than before, with long sleeves and a hem down to her ankles. Her red hair was braided, hanging over her shoulder. They studied each other for several long moments.

Lela swallowed. "You came back." Ricci jumped at her cold tone. "I won't hurt you."

"Is your world truly in danger?" Ricci glanced side to side, as if fearing an attack.

Truly, Lela considered it. "Yes. From you."

"I'm no danger." The gongs rang out from the town, shifting Ricci's unblinking stare. "What is that?"

"That's you," Lela said. "Portal magic is outlawed. Our world is warded to detect it and sound the gongs. When you close the portal, the gongs stop."

Ricci held her breath for a moment, then closed her eyes. Lela sensed an increase in the energy, and Ricci became fully visible.

"It takes a little while for them to stop." Lela slowly stepped closer. If Ricci moved suddenly or attacked, Lela had a knife, freshly sharpened and coated with poison of her own making. "Why did you come back?"

Ricci shrugged. "I'm not really sure. But, you said your world was in danger. This is such a beautiful world. If I can help by answering some questions, what's the harm in that?" She shook her head. "I shouldn't have come."

"Wait!" Lela stretched out her hand. Humans were selfish creatures, only looking out for themselves, no better than the evil, mythical demons. But this human wanted to help, and they needed answers. "You can call me Lela. That's very impressive, what you can do. No one's been able to open a portal in centuries."

The gongs ceased ringing.

Ricci brushed non-existent dust off her skirt, taking in her surroundings. "I'm not even sure how I do it. It just comes to me."

So how would this human bring down their world? "Is your mata a mage? Or is your mata or pata a leader in the human army?" Lela held her breath.

"What's a pata?" Ricci's eyebrows scrunched together.

"Oh, um, the one who sired you."

"My papa? No. We're actors. We travel the lands bringing joy through our performances." Her tone sounded offended, or maybe defensive. "And what about you? Is your papa a leader in your... fae army?"

Lela flinched. Why was the human asking about their army? But, maybe it was good if the humans knew they had a powerful force ready to defend them. "My pata is a general for King Sidian. He commands a powerful army. I'm an herbalist. I tend the herbs on the farm and help Mata. She's a healer."

Ricci didn't react to the news of an army, as if she didn't care or it wasn't important to her.

"What do you know of my kind?" Lela asked.

"Nothing," Ricci said. "Fae are made-up creatures for story-books." She put a finger to her chin. "Like unicorns or demons."

Lela stared at her. "You don't have unicorns in the human world?"

Ricci's eyes widened.

"Never mind. What happened after you left this morning?" Lela asked. "No one threw you in prison." It came out more accusatory than she'd meant.

Ricci's shoulders unclenched. "I was in the middle of an important trial. If they learned I could come here, who knows what the mage council would have done to me."

"So, you are a wizard?" Lela's hand twitched to her sheath.

"No. I only have this one ability—to open portals, apparently. But I had to show it to them in order to buy the permit."

"You need permission to practice the energies? And you

have to pay for the privilege?" *Ridiculous.* "It's not like that here."

Ricci shrugged. "Maybe it shouldn't be, but that's the way it is. But I never meant to scare you or make the gongs ring. And I do not mean you or your people any harm. I just want to continue acting." She finally stopped staring at the ground and met Lela's gaze.

There was something about this human girl. She should be scared of Ricci, but she wasn't. It was like looking into the eyes of someone she'd known her whole life.

But still, Lela hesitated. Here was a human, which history said was evil and had been banished. Her very presence meant disaster. She'd shown much courage, or much stupidity, returning to a foreign world after being attacked by a stranger. She didn't even have a weapon to defend herself.

"The humans cursed us with a prophecy that says the beginning of our world's demise starts with a portal being opened. Your coming here means my people eventually perish." She leaned closer. "How many worlds have you visited?"

Ricci rocked back. "Are there other worlds? And what do you mean, perish? I haven't done anything. I wouldn't do anything. I swear it."

"Then why are you here?"

It took Ricci a long moment to respond. "At first, I wanted to entertain my audience and support my family. I still want those things, but I also need escape." She paced, clunky steps trampling the flowers. "My roles in the plays, they consume me. I'm angry when there's hate, weeping when there's tragedy, and I live in a wagon, constantly surrounded by my family or an audience. I have no friends. No permanence in my life. This place," she gestured to the field, "this world gives me

peace, and happiness. And solitude—until you came along."
She smiled hesitantly.

Lela wanted to return the smile, and her heart clenched for
Ricci and her sadness. "I believe you mean us no harm, Ricci.
But I cannot believe that this won't still end badly for my
people." Ricci felt like an old friend, and there was no energy in
the air to say she was being charmed to feel that way.

"Then let me help. My magic keeps bringing me here, so
maybe if I tell you about myself, you'll see no harm will come
from me." Ricci sat in the grass, patting the grass beside her.

Lela stayed where she was. Guilt washed over her at the
hurt in Ricci's eyes. What was it about this human that made
her feel she could trust her, that she had nothing to fear
from her?

A soft tinkling carried to Lela's ears on the wind. Laughter.
She glanced sharply toward the tree line where flittering
movement drew her gaze.

Ricci shot to her feet. "What is that?" She squinted, jaw
dropping. "Is that a fairy?"

Lela grinned. "A sprite. They never stray this far from their
forest." Reverence overtook her tone as the little sprite, barely
visible except for the occasional glint off her iridescent wings
and flower-petal dress, perched on a branch and watched
them. Watched Ricci.

It was time to hear the human out. "Tell me about your
family and your connection to the wizards."

Ricci nodded, still eyeing the sprite, so they sat in the grass
across from each other. For the next couple of hours, Ricci
shared without reserve. She spoke of her parents and brothers.
Of her performances as Princess Kasma marrying the handsome prince. How the ability to open portals had come to her,
and her fear of the wizards discovering her gift.

The more Ricci shared, the more Lela couldn't help but

share in return. It'd been so long since she'd had someone to talk to. She told Ricci of her family, shocking Ricci with how differently families worked in her world. They spoke of their favorite things to do—they both loved reading—and boys they liked. Ricci hadn't had a chance to meet many boys, but Lela told her all about Oren. Too much, probably.

"You'll see him again. It sounds like it's meant to be." Ricci scooted close and tentatively patted her hand.

Lela almost didn't mind. It felt nice. Though she still waited for their demise to come through a portal any moment.

"What's it like to be a... fae?" Ricci struggled with using that word. "I mean, what will you be when you grow up?"

"I want to be a healer, but not like my mata. She uses herbs and bandages. I want to learn to do it with the energies." Lela sat forward in her excitement.

"You mean magic? Can you do that? Learn to use magic in different ways? I thought you were only gifted magic to do specific things."

"Magic is for children. The energies of the earth are what we channel to do the extraordinary. And if you can use them to do one thing, why can't you use them for something else? But, it takes a strong channeler to learn to shape it to different uses. And there's a small window of time. By the age of eighteen, which I'll be soon, a fae has as much ability as they ever will. Most believe you can't learn to rechannel the energies anymore after that." Lela sighed. "I don't have much energy. If I had more, Pata would have sent me to train at Gemiara, a school for the energies." She forced a smile. "But that was not to be my gift."

"I want to be a famous actress, performing on stage in one city in a home without wheels." Ricci gasped. "Gods, how long have I been here?" She shot to her feet. "They'll be looking for me."

Lela rose as well, torn over how to feel. She'd actually enjoyed this closeness, even the beginning of a friendship, but Ricci was *human*. A quick look toward the trees told her the sprite was gone. A rare, but special visit."I still don't know where the threat will come from. I still have so many questions."

"Well," Ricci said. "I'll be back. Tomorrow actually. We've got a full day of shows."

Lela shook her head. "No, Ricci, you can't come back. The gongs. I know now that you mean well, but no one else does." And maybe if Ricci stayed away, so too would the danger.

"Performing is how I feed my family." Ricci's form faded. "I'll prove that you can trust me."

"I'm serious, Ricci—"

"I won't hurt anyone. I promise." She smiled and was gone.

Lela stared at the empty spot, waiting for the gongs. They didn't sound. The portal was opened and closed too fast to be detected.

Pata would arrive any day, and as much as Lela longed for his return—that he'd come back and they could be a family again—nerves filled her belly. He was a stranger. She'd barely seen him a handful of times for a handful of weeks her whole life. What would happen when he found Ricci? Would he hurt her? Capture her?

She rubbed her face, then dropped her hands and swallowed against the revulsion working its way up her throat. She disgusted herself. Ricci's safety could never be more important than her own people's.

Lela sprinted for home and whatever punishment awaited her.

Mata had been furious, sick with worry. She made Lela work late into the night with nothing but the moons to light the garden as she finished the chores she hadn't touched during the day. The next day, disappointment was the only thing Lela felt as the gongs chimed off and on. Ricci hadn't listened. Did she not believe the danger was real?

Mata ran Lela ragged doing both of their chores as punishment. Sweat dripped down her brow as she swept the front porch. Mata had decided the entire house needed a good cleaning. Lela was too nervous to be upset. Besides, she'd earned it.

A low rumbling like distant thunder had her scanning the skies—clear pink and spring crisp. She leaned the broom against the wall and stepped into the bright green of the garden. The rumbling grew louder, closer and constant.

Mata called from just inside the door, words tense. "Lelana, come."

"What is that?" Lela backtracked to the house, eyes on the road. She could almost place it.

"Your pata arrives." Mata's face took on an excited, youthful look. Fae mated for life, and he was her love.

Lela's heart sped. "Can't I greet him?" It'd been nearly a year since she'd last seen Pata. He'd been dealing with a border skirmish against invading trolls.

"Not this time, young one." Mata smoothed Lela's hair, which she'd chosen to wear down and loose, except for one thin braid with beads at the end. She rushed off to the kitchen where the scents of a small feast wafted—pheasant roasted with dried herbs, fresh rosemary bread, and strawberry lavender cake, from what Lela could smell.

Lela stood there, arms crossed. Why wouldn't she be allowed to go outside? She stepped to the window and peeked out. The rumbling grew louder. The coarse wood of the window sill vibrated beneath her hands.

"Horses." That was what that noise was. Lots of horses parading down the road. Hundreds, thousands of them? "Mata, Pata isn't alone." Lela knew what Mata would say even as she spoke.

"The legion comes to meet the threat to our people," Mata said quietly from the kitchen. She was afraid.

Fire and fury, she had to warn Ricci.

"I'll be right back," Lela said before charging out the door.

"Lelana, wait!" Mata called, but Lela slammed the door behind her.

Dust rose in plumes down the road, though the warriors weren't yet visible through the trees. Lela snuck around the far side of the house and burst into a sprint toward the hills that led to the flower meadow. She didn't know what to hope for; that Ricci would appear one more time so Lela could warn her, or that ... It was too much to hope that she'd suddenly decided to stay away. The need to protect Ricci was overwhelming.

"Lelana." The deep voice behind her stopped her short. Pata.

She turned. He sat astride his unicorn, Bromlin, near the back of the house. A layer of dust stuck to the sweat on the black steed, its sides puffing and obsidian horn shining with every movement. The magnificent creature never ceased to take Lela's breath away. Unicorns were rarely domesticated.

Pata wore a black leather uniform etched in silver, bow slung across his back and a sword at his hip. More weapons were hidden beneath his leathers. He looked exactly as she'd last seen him, unsmiling, still young with no signs of his hundred and twenty years.

"Pata." Lela gave a slight bow of respect. She tried to hide her panting and the urge to look behind her shoulder.

He stared beyond her, as if sensing her thoughts. "Where were you going?"

"I thought I might see the army better from the hills." Lela walked back to him, trying to act as casually as possible. The instinct to lie for Ricci had been instantaneous. Without even thinking about it, she'd protected her. What was wrong with her? Her skin crawled with the need to rub away the guilt. She couldn't choose a human over her own kind.

"I've missed you, Pata." Lela stopped far enough away not to make the unicorn nervous.

Pata smiled. "Ah, my young one, it's been a long time. You've grown so much."

Was that regret she saw in his eyes? But no, it was gone. "Mata has missed you, too," she said.

Pata's eyes lit up, and he swung down from Bromlin. "I will greet her." He handed Lela the reins, and then his long strides carried him into the house.

Lela smiled. As cold as he might be, there was no denying his love for her mata. Careful of the unicorn's horn—a rare beauty, lent from King Sidian himself, and ridden with Bromlin's permission—she let him smell her hand, then led him to the small barn. They kept no animals in the barn; it was solely used to shelter Bromlin when Pata returned home. Out of respect for her parents' privacy, she took her time tending to Bromlin, brushing him down and giving him fresh hay and water. She even inspected his hoofs for rocks or clumped dirt.

The gongs didn't ring the whole time.

The sun had set by the time she left the barn. She stumbled at the sight of hundreds of campfires scattering the field and hills. They stood out like beacons in the night, accentuating the movement of a thousand or more fae warriors. The noise of them—their horses, conversation, clinking of plates and swords—overtook the normal nighttime noises Lela loved.

She walked faster at the thought that Oren might be

among them, but no. He wouldn't be trained enough for action yet.

She'd never seen an army assembled before, and now they camped in her backyard. And they were here for one purpose. To stop Ricci. Harmless, innocent Ricci.

Lela scanned the distant hills. Scouts already patrolled them. She hadn't even said a word to Pata about where the portal was being opened, but she hadn't needed to. She'd given it away, enough that he knew the general direction.

There was nothing Lela could do to warn Ricci.

She finally made her way inside, stomach rumbling. Mata and Pata sat at the kitchen table, hand in hand, plates full and untouched.

"Lelana," Mata said. "Come and eat."

Lela piled her plate with the food Mata spent all day preparing. She never cooked like this when Pata was gone.

Lela's mouth watered. But food could wait. "Why bring the warriors, Pata?"

He stared at her, because he knew she knew the answer. "Lela, your mata says you've been going to the portal, disappearing behind the hills every day, disobeying my wishes. Who do you go to see?"

Lela grabbed her fork and took a bite of roasted mushrooms dripping with garlic and butter. Pata hadn't even tried to tiptoe to the heart of the matter. He'd plunged right in. She couldn't lie—what would that accomplish? Only truth would win.

"Her name is Ricci. She's a human, and she means no harm." Her chin jutted. Ricci had been to their world several times, never once presenting a threat. She was kind, with no connections to the wizards that had cursed the fae.

Mata gasped, fork clanging to her plate. She turned wide eyes to Pata.

He stared at Lela, frown growing deeper beneath disapproving eyes. "Means no harm?"

"She's my age, and she's like a friend." The words were true, impossible, but true. "She can help us discover where the real threat is."

He stood, chair tumbling backward. "Friend? Have you lost your senses? You know," he stepped around the table and loomed over her, "you *know* what that portal means. And you befriended her?"

Lela had never seen him lose his composure, not once. But she didn't flinch from his anger, its heat mere inches from her face. "She's just a girl, Pata. Not an evil wizard." Her voice remained surprisingly steady and calm despite her thundering heart. "I can tell you anything you want to know, and you'll see she's not a threat. Or come with me to the portal and meet her. Alone," she added. "You'll see."

Pata stood back, studying her. He righted his chair and resumed eating, gesturing for her to do the same. She took small bites of the now tasteless food, not daring to meet Mata's eyes.

"Alright," he said. "Tell me everything."

She set down her knife and fork, and told him everything.

CHAPTER 14

Ricci's family didn't question her when she returned to camp, either about where she'd been or the smile on her face. The first day of shows in Timbercross had gone wonderfully. The crowd ate it up, growing larger as time went on.

Despite the stress of it all, everything was going perfectly. Lela was everything she'd ever hoped to find in a friend. Kind, devoted to her family, a good listener. And the best part was, it didn't matter that Ricci's family would pack up and move to a new town in a few days. Lela would always be a portal away, no matter where Ricci was.

She'd show Lela she was in control of her magic, and that she would never use her portals to harm anyone.

As Ricci ate the celebration feast her Papa had promised, she celebrated more than just getting her permit; she celebrated maybe finally having a friend.

CHAPTER 15

It took Callen three agonizing days to finish brewing the potions and close up shop, and only because he started even before receiving permission. He'd made a safe gamble—it was only the second time in seven years he'd asked for leave. All his master needed to know was that he was going to market in Timbercross, and hopefully by the time Callen returned, he'd be that much closer to solving the riddle of the Nether Realms. He left out the part about pursuing the girl from the traveling troupe.

Stepping out of the coach and into Timbercross's balmy night air felt like he'd never left. Callen reached into his pocket and tipped the driver.

The driver's eyes went wide. "Thank ya kindly, M'Lord."

Callen eyed the coin and winced. He'd given an entire silver broam. He'd been in his hometown for all of five minutes, and already accidentally fallen back into the role of a noble's son. He'd have to be more careful.

With a hearty wave from the driver, the coach left him at

the station. Callen ambled his way to market street, following the stench of fish.

Timbercross was a booming riverport town, importing and exporting goods by boat, so market day was really every day here, but twice a year the town exploded—fall harvest and spring festival. Sandstone buildings glinted in the lantern light while people moved about all hours of the day.

The inn's sign swung in the gentle breeze.

River's Edge Tavern

Well-lit on the outside, lanterns blazed and candles burned in the windows, even at this late hour. Several patrons entered and exited, not wearing anything too fine but definitely not a ragged bunch. And it was about as far away from his parents' estate as he could get. Perfect.

The inside was crowded, with bodies overflowing every table. Several people sat in front of the bar at the long counter, sipping mugs of ale or hunkered over steaming plates of mouthwatering meat and butter-slathered vegetables.

A few of them looked his way, eyeing his black robes— king's law forbade him from removing them in public, a way to identify mages at all times. He stepped to the counter, not paying them any heed.

"What'll it be?" the innkeeper asked from behind a scraggly black beard.

"Ale, please." Callen sat on a stool, not bothering to unshoulder his bags. "Innkeeper," he said as the man poured his drink from the tap. "Have you heard of the Magnificent Menowin Traveling Troupe?"

The innkeeper set the ale in front of him. "So, you're one of them—those followers of theirs." He smirked. "They're just one block over." He laughed and turned his back to the counter.

One of those? "I'm not one of their followers." He sipped his drink.

"No? You're here, ain't ye?" The innkeeper poured a pint for another customer.

Callen's lips thinned. He gulped his ale. "Are there any rooms available?"

The innkeeper chuckled. "Rooms are hard to come by during market. Not cheap neither." He glanced down at Callen's apprentice robes. "I have one, but it's for those that can pay. Rich folk. Sorry, kid. Better luck far away from market." He turned in dismissal.

It would be so easy to use his name, Lord Callen Kealamin, son of High Lord Cameron Kealamin III. Instead, he slid a gold coin across the bar, one of the precious few from his parents. "Is that rich enough?"

The innkeeper's mouth parted behind his beard. "Of course, M'Lord. Might have started with that." The coin vanished as if it had never been. "I recognize you now. I knows who you are, M'Lord." At Callen's frown, he added, "I won't say nothin'."

"Good. I'd like a hot meal and a hot bath in my room as well." Callen slid off his stool.

"I'll see to it, M'Lord." The innkeeper nodded and handed Callen a brass key. "The only door at the top of the stairs."

Callen turned for the stairs, hoping his burning cheeks weren't obvious in the dim room. Yes, he was a son of the richest family in Timbercross, but he hated using his name to gain favors.

"M'Lord?" The innkeeper stopped him. "First show's at eight bells."

Callen dipped his head in thanks and headed upstairs. The

room was on the third floor, twice the size he expected. He lit a couple lamps. Heavy velvet curtains framed picture windows that looked out on the street. In the distance, lights marked the slow curve of the Marso River. Callen set down his bags and slumped onto the four-poster bed.

He'd gone through a lot of trouble to get here. Mostly to help Master Marek discover a way to teleport, but also to help himself as well. The mage tests were the most important thing.

Eight bells? He'd be there at six.

Six bells chimed from somewhere down the street as Callen blearily walked one block over. Breakfast had been hasty, griddle cakes and eggs at the bar before he headed out, yawning. The sounds of market greeted him even before he rounded the corner. The sun was barely up, and already shopkeepers peddled their wares. Customers stepped around stalls bursting with fruits and vegetables, smoked meats, or colorful linens. It'd be madness later. Well, more madness.

A juggler with a white-painted face performed in the middle of the road, and Callen hurried to him.

"Come one, come all to witness the amazing Dorian the Magician. Just follow the crowd!" The juggler tossed all three balls into the air and then caught them neatly in his pocket. He finished by flourishing toward the single wagon behind him, painted a deep purple.

Callen's shoulders drooped. The crowd, however, did not head where the juggler pointed. They whispered excitedly amongst themselves, hurrying further down the street. Callen followed them, craning to see a flash of the green wagons.

The crowd merged with an even bigger group, and sure

enough, four green wagons lined the back of a small clearing. A temporary stage stood in front, much more impressive than before, raised a few feet off the ground and complete with curtains blocking the view of what lay behind. The crowd had to know it was much too early for a show, yet here they were already eagerly waiting.

Eight bells was too long to wait. He had to talk to her and see what she knew.

Callen forced his way through the horde, aiming to go around the stage.

Someone shoved him from behind. "I've waited all night for this spot. Get your own!"

Callen's magic rose from his core, a defensive habit, but he shoved it down. "Official mage business."

The man, a peasant in dingy clothes, backed away, hands raised. "Sorry."

Callen kept going, getting dirty looks. Apprentices didn't command as much respect as a full mage, but no one else tried to touch him. He finally reached the caravan behind the stage, but no one was outside. They were probably all preparing for the show. Or sleeping, as he should be, instead of creeping up to her wagon like a perfect stalker.

He wasn't even sure which wagon was hers. A paper with a blue crest had been painted with lacquer and nailed to the side of the first wagon. A permit. He stepped closer.

Ricika Menowin. To practice the magic of illusion only as it pertains to performing.

Had he missed seeing this before? But no, it was dated only recently. Perhaps the girl, Ricci, couldn't help after all. She must have been a powerful illusionist to have fooled him. Though, with Master Marek always on the hunt for a way to teleport, perhaps it wasn't so unusual that Callen had seen what he'd wanted.

"Just great." He scrubbed his face. All this way for nothing.

"We're legal now. You have nothing on us."

Callen jumped. Ricci stood at the wagon door in a home-spun dress that skimmed her bare collarbones. Her red hair was unbound and tumbling over her shoulders. His mouth dropped open. She was a completely different person without all the makeup. Gorgeous.

"What, did you think you might turn us in for a reward?" She stepped off the narrow porch, brow set, looking pissed.

He shook his head to clear it. "There must be some kind of misunderstanding. I never intended to turn you in. I'm an apprentice, not even a full mage." Is that why she'd been so nervous before?

"Then what are you doing here?" She leveled her gaze at him.

"Ricci, who's there?" An older woman's muffled voice sounded within the wagon.

"No one, Mama. He's just leaving," Ricci called back.

"Good. We have a show to prepare for," Mama said.

Ricci stared at him, arms crossed.

He felt ridiculous. "Gods, I'm sorry. I saw your performance in Fallhold, and you were amazing. It was so real, the way you cast that illusion. I experienced things that shouldn't have been." He rubbed the back of his neck. "I thought maybe you could help me. You have a real gift."

Ricci uncrossed her arms. Some of the guardedness left her eyes. "I do?"

"Yes!" He chuckled at his own excitement—at his need to please her. "I've never seen such a talent. If you weren't so good at acting, I mean, if it wasn't clearly where you're meant to be, I'd suggest joining a mage school and maybe becoming an apprentice."

Ricci smiled, and it warmed him.

"Callen, right?" she asked. "You still haven't said why you are here. You need my help?"

She'd remembered his name. "Right," he said. "I did, but now I guess I'm just another crazed fan." What other explanation could he give, now that he had written proof her power was only illusion and not, in fact, the gift of the Nether Realms? "I'm here on an errand for my master." A white lie to cover the fact he was clearly losing it. "I didn't like how we parted before. You were so sad, and I didn't help any. I wanted to make sure you're okay."

"Things are better now." She got a distant look, like she was remembering something.

"I'm glad," he said, putting as much honesty and meaning as he could into two simple words.

She looked down, thick lashes sweeping her pink cheeks above a faint smile. "Sorry if I seemed... off before. I thought you were going to report me."

"Believe me, the fault is entirely mine. I probably seemed off, too." Callen chuckled. "Would you like to have breakfast with me?" The words rushed out before remembering he'd already had breakfast. "That is, if you have time. And if you're hungry." He rubbed the back of his neck.

Ricci's cheeks reddened, and she glanced behind her. "I'd like that. But I have a show." She frowned, looking regretful, and not the fake kind that meant she was glad for the excuse.

"Right, of course. Another time then." Callen backed away, shoulders drooping. There would never be another time. Now that she couldn't help him with his task for Master Marek, he'd return home. Ricci's troupe would move on to the next town, and they'd never get another chance to see each other. But it was for the best. If she couldn't help him, she was a distraction. "Good luck with the show." He turned.

"Wait," she called. "I'll be right back."

His breath caught as she disappeared into the wagon. He was going to regret this.

Minutes later, she returned carrying a basket, closing the door against loud protests from inside. "I have time for a quick picnic nearby." She held up the basket. "A fan brought us these pastries."

He grinned. "That's perfect." He took the basket as she stepped down from the wagon, offering his arm.

Her feather-light touch occupied all thoughts as she led him to a patch of rocks within eyesight of the wagons. The Marso River trickled somewhere through the trees in the distance. With the basket between them, Ricci offered him a buttery pastry with orange filling and a shiny sugar glaze, taking one for herself as well.

He bit into it, the sweet tartness exploding over his tongue in amazing contrast to the flaky crunch of the crust. "Mmm, so good."

Ricci laughed and took a smaller, more dignified bite. "So you're studying to become a full mage?"

He wiped his mouth with the back of his hand, chewing fast and swallowing hard. "That's right. Once I pass the mage tests, I can do anything I want. But I'd like most to work with the council and take on an apprentice myself one day." And be a much better teacher than his father and Master Marek. "And you? Do you always want to be a traveling actress?"

She wrinkled her nose in the most endearing way. "I'm hoping my... illusion magic attracts the king's attention. If I can secure an invitation to perform for him, then maybe I won't have to travel anymore."

He didn't miss the way she stumbled over calling it illusion magic. "Your illusion is amazing. How do you do it?" At her raised eyebrows, Callen lifted his apprentice robes. "Always trying to learn new things and impress my master."

"I'm not sure exactly how it works." She brushed crumbs from her dress, not meeting his eyes.

"That's okay. That's not really what I'm trying to learn anyway. Before I read your permit, I thought you might be able to help me, like I said. Most of my time is spent trying to find a way to open—"

"Ricci!" someone shouted.

Ricci startled. "That's Mama. I have to go." She gathered the basket. "Will you come to the show?" Her gaze lingered on him, drawing a pleasant heat to the surface of his skin.

"Wouldn't miss it." His words were soft, surprising him. Her smile turned wider as he took her arm for the short walk back to the wagon. They hadn't had enough time. When would they get another chance to talk? "Can I see you again?" he blurted. "Maybe tonight, after you're done performing?" Ugh, what was he doing?

She paused at the door, and her eyes lit up. "I have a break after the first show. I'll meet you back here?" Her gaze dipped to his lips as he nodded, then she turned the knob and went inside.

Unable to contain his grin, Callen made his way back to the waiting crowd in front of the stage. It had grown considerably. He squeezed down the middle until he found a place nearly at the front. Time slipped by quickly, especially as the appearance of the jester got the crowd roaring with laughter.

"There once was a maiden fair,
Except for her chin covered in hair.
In exchange for a kiss, she'd grant you a wish,
But of her breath, beware!"

Callen bounced on his toes as the curtains parted, and the crowd cheered when Ricci took to the stage, nearly drowning out her lines. She was beautiful in her green dress which hugged her curves. He saw and heard enough to guess it was the same play as before.

The prince told Princess Kasma to meet him outside his castle so they could run away together. Ricci stood alone on stage. "Now where is that handsome prince of mine?" She twirled, sending her skirts billowing. "At least it's a beautiful spring day. There's nothing more precious than the first blooms of a new season."

Ricci closed her eyes and leaned down. There was a collective gasp as the stage's raw wood become a transparent field of grass. Callen stared, stunned, caught in the beauty of the world. He felt what Princess Kasma felt, seeing what she saw.

Ricci smiled and reached for a red bloom. It plucked right into her fingers as if real. The cool breeze blew, pushing away the scent and heat of unwashed bodies, replacing them with trees and nature. How was she doing that? The crowd applauded like mad.

"My love is as tender as these new petals." Ricci inhaled the scent, eyes closed with a smile of bliss. Then she opened them and met his stare.

Callen's heart skipped a beat. His lips spread in a slow smile.

Her cheeks turned pink, but she didn't look away.

A tall figure dressed in dark leather, sword in hand, loomed behind her. He had long hair and an angular face. Callen didn't remember this character, but then he'd missed the beginning of the last play. Odd, though. He looked faded, like the grass, half there and half not. His sword was real.

"Prince, oh Prince?" Ricci pouted, glancing side to side.

Dread twisted Callen's insides. His magic lurched. Something was wrong.

The man raised his sword. Ricci didn't turn around. Was this part of the play? The crowd fell silent in suspense. The man reached for her, perfect calm on his face.

"Ricci!" Callen cried out, pointing.

She spun and gasped. True surprise. The man lunged, grabbing her around the waist with one arm.

Callen didn't think. He jumped onto the stage, gathering his magic. The audience cheered.

The man pulled her back against him and held his sword to Ricci's throat. "Close the portal. Take us to my realm. Or I'll end you here and now."

Her eyes locked onto Callen's. Fear. Desperation. Her throat bobbed as she swallowed, and she flinched. Blood trickled from her neck.

Callen's teeth mashed. Lightning pooled in his hands, forming into balls.

"Do it," the man snarled, eyes on Callen's quick-growing spell.

She cried out. Static filled the air.

Ricci disappeared. She was gone, the man with her.

Callen's magic stumbled to a halt, lightning dissipating into the air. The crowd roared their approval.

Her family gaped in horror, pouring onto the stage.

This wasn't part of the show. Ricci had teleported. She'd *teleported*.

Where had she gone?

CHAPTER 16

Cold steel bit into Ricci's neck as Callen and her family disappeared completely. The fae man's grip around her chest crushed her lungs. An army of warriors dressed in black and silver on horseback surrounded her, thick as a forest. Pointed ears, bows drawn and aimed at her heart. She shook, trying to hold in her hysterics—it wouldn't help. Each movement redrew the sword across her stinging neck.

He would have killed her if she hadn't closed the portal.

"Pata!" A scream wrenched Ricci back to awareness.

Lela. She'd told the fae where to find her.

Lela struggled, two soldiers holding her back by the arms. "You're hurting her!"

Tears streamed down Ricci's cheeks, mouth trembling. Lela was the only one who knew where Ricci would appear.

The sword lowered, and the grip around her middle eased. Ricci took a gasping breath, vision swimming as blood rushed back through her body.

Someone wrenched her arms behind her back, and she

cried out. Manacles clasped around her wrists, cold at first, then burning. Oh, Gods, they burned! Ricci screamed and fell to her knees.

"Pata!" Lela pleaded. "Stop, please!"

Ricci bucked, sure her wrists were on fire.

The man, Lela's father, grabbed her before she landed face-down in the grass. He hauled her to her feet. "Iron plated in gold spelled to prevent you from using the energies," he said, voice low and steady. Emotionless. Lela yelled, and he turned. "Release my daughter."

Lela rushed up, panting, but Ricci barely noticed. There was only pain and the constant stream of tears in her eyes.

"Don't do this, Pata. She won't harm anyone." Lela's cool hands cupped Ricci's sticky cheeks. Ricci breathed easier, just for a moment. "I'm sorry, Ricci. I told you to stay away." Lela kissed her brow, and the pain in her wrists ebbed to almost nothing.

"Lock her up," Lela's father said, ignoring her.

Ricci met Lela's pleading eyes. "What are they going to do to me?"

Lela bit her lip and shook her head, gaze going to her father. "I don't know." Tears slipped down her face.

Rough hands grabbed Ricci under her arms and hauled her backward. They dragged her across the field, slippers falling off one at a time. The soldiers watched, then on some silent command, they formed lines and followed, leaving Lela and her father behind. The captors crested a hill, wrenching her shoulders, and she involuntarily yelped. It was nothing compared to the pain when they'd put the manacles on her wrists.

They reached a garden of fragrant herbs that the soldiers trampled on their way to the road. The smell of horses and the clang of metal were the only warnings she got before being tossed into a wagon, landing hard on her right shoulder. She whimpered and righted herself, huddling in the corner, arms still locked behind her back. An empty bucket sat in the corner. Small, barred windows let in scant light. She didn't dare try to look outside. She didn't need to. The horses clopping onto the road meant she was surrounded.

She should have listened to Lela. She told her to stay away, but Ricci never thought Lela would have her captured. Why would she do this? What did the fae think she would do? Their prophecy was about someone else. Please, Gods, she had to get home.

Ricci squeezed her eyes tight, concentrating. The stage, fresh cut pine, a cheering crowd. Her family, eyes full of love.

Light flashed from behind her. Pain like fire seared her wrists. She bit her lip against the scream, falling to her side and panting.

Ricci lost track of time as she struggled to remain conscious. The pain faded little by agonizing little. Eventually, she realized they were moving, wagon wheels bumping over a rutted road, and horses on all sides. She sat up when the pain faded enough to be bearable, but her shoulders *ached*. She leaned against the wall to support each shoulder one at a time against the pull of the manacles.

An insistent bladder had her staring at the empty bucket. They had to stop soon and allow her to relieve herself. She moved to the door, feeling around for a latch. There were no seams or hinges, and no handle of any kind. No way out.

Hours passed, and the sun slanted low through the bars of the window. They weren't stopping. She didn't have a choice. She scooted back to the bucket, then gathered her dress as best she could with her hands locked behind her. Without being able to see, she squatted, thankful when the urine splashed into the bucket.

The wagon dipped. Ricci stumbled, bumping over the bucket. Urine spilled, rolling in every direction over the wagon floor, soaking into her fine, glittery, emerald dress.

She burst into tears, crying in earnest for the first time. What was going to happen to her? Where were they taking her? She'd trusted Lela—she was supposed to be her first friend. And what about Callen? No one had ever looked at her like he had when he'd jumped on that stage. Like he would do anything to protect her. And her family—what must they be thinking?

Ricci sobbed against the splintery floor until her tears ran dry.

Night fell, sending Ricci to shivering with the cold. Each shudder sent a fresh wave of agony up her arms. Her dry, cracked lips rubbed against each other as she whispered prayers to the Gods she'd never prayed to before.

The wagon rolled to a stop. The door flew open, flooding the inside with even colder air. Ricci didn't move.

"She's fouled herself," a rough male voice said.

Ricci didn't struggle as she was hauled out of the wagon and held upright. She stared at the ground, lantern-lit and crawling with black boots.

A heavy presence stepped in front of her. The general.

Someone else grabbed her wrists and unlocked one of the manacles. A hiss escaped as her arms hung free at her sides. Needles of pain bloomed over her skin. Before she could rub her blistered wrists, her hands were recuffed in front of her. The manacles were a bright gold with vines of thorns etched into them. Her shoulders screamed.

"Now that you've learned what happens when you attempt to open a portal, I doubt you'll try again," Lela's father said. "If you do, sore wrists will be the least of your concerns, human."

Ricci glared up at him. He looked younger than Lanny,

scandalously too young to be the father of a girl her age. He met her gaze with cool indifference. The dozen fae encircling them showed no emotion either, except for the one holding the lantern. He sneered when her gaze flicked his way.

The general walked on without another word. Two soldiers hauled her back into the wagon, where a small cup of water and a bowl of something like porridge sat waiting. Ricci lunged for the water, nearly tipping it, and drained every drop. The porridge was bland, oats and water and nothing else, but she ate every morsel, scraping the last bits with her fingers since they hadn't given her a spoon. Even with her hands bound together, the freedom of movement was glorious.

The sounds of crackling fires made her ache for warmth. For home. Mama and Papa would be sick with worry, with no answers and no idea she wasn't even in their world anymore.

Ricci drew her soiled skirt closer, locking in every ounce of heat she could. Eventually, she shivered herself into oblivion.

CHAPTER 17

As the warriors dragged Ricci away from the flower field, Lela watched, eyes stinging and guilt burning every breath she took.

Lela felt her pata's gaze but couldn't even look at him as they trailed behind the entire *army* it took to imprison one young human. He'd explained it; he had orders. The portal opener posed a threat. Their people were at risk. But that couldn't erase how *wrong* this felt.

"You lied to me." She crossed her arms.

Pata stared straight ahead. "I only agreed to listen, and it was clear the human has deceived you." He raised his hand when she started to speak. "It's hard when you're young. Everything is emotional. Everything holds attachment. With age comes wisdom and experience. Control."

Silence stretched on. Ricci hadn't deceived her; everything within her said she could be trusted. Her body *screamed* with the need to protect Ricci, even as it made no sense. Pata's visit had gone all wrong.

Lela gaped as the warriors marched right through her carefully cultivated herbs—the straightest path to the road. "Pata, my garden—"

"Oren sends his regards," he said.

Lela's heart jumped. New recruits weren't allowed to write or contact anyone—part of their full-immersion training. Pata shouldn't have said anything. This was a peace offering.

"Oh?" She pointlessly pretended indifference.

Pata's mouth quirked into almost a smile. "He's excelling at training. One of the best at weapons and endurance."

"Good." Another well-trained warrior to protect the fae against a defenseless human.

They reached home, and Pata held the backdoor for her. "Take care of Mata. She needs you." He placed a callused hand against her face.

He was always so good at guessing exactly what she was thinking. As much as she needed this embrace, she resented it. He'd deceived her. He hadn't really listened, only let her talk while he went ahead with what he'd already planned to do.

"Don't hurt her, Pata. Ask your questions, but set her free. You owe me that. Promise me." Please let her be okay.

"I can't promise you, young one. You know that." His words stirred unease in her soul.

He left, not bothering to follow her inside. Lela rushed to the front window, gripping the sill with white knuckles.

With the efficiency of decades of training, the warriors rode away, Ricci's prison wagon surrounded on all sides.

Mata put her hands on Lela's shoulders. "You did well, Lelana. Our world is safer for your sacrifice."

Lela could only nod, throat tight. She knew that. The prophecy was rooted in deep fear, enough that portal magic was outlawed and warded. She tried not to think about what Ricci was going through. Scared, alone, betrayed in a foreign world.

She hugged her mata tight, inhaling the scent of rosemary. "The warriors trampled my herbs. I'm going to see about the damage."

Mata smiled, but her eyes crinkled with pity. "Yes, that will be good for you."

Lela took a couple honey biscuits from the kitchen counter, then headed to the garden. Road dust clouded the air from the warriors' passage. Pungent scents—basil and coriander—drifted with the breeze, the strong smell only herbs crushed underfoot could make. When she was lost in the tall rows of heather and berries, when she was sure Mata no longer watched her, she doubled back and climbed the trellis to her bedroom window.

Quietly, she slipped inside and lifted the bag that had been carefully packed since the day of the first gong. Mata banged around in the kitchen. Lela pulled the honey biscuits from her pockets and added them to her rations, then snuck back out of her room as she'd done countless times to play with Oren after dark.

If she couldn't convince Pata not to take Ricci, then she'd have to rescue her. There was no other choice. Resisting the need to protect her would be like resisting the chance to save Mata if she were in harm's way. No choice at all.

With one last look at home, Mata safely inside, Lela took to the road. Her slow speed chafed, as she was on foot and the warriors on horseback, and they'd had a head start. She'd never catch up, but Pata had taken her to the king's castle in Alberry a few times, so she knew the way.

The days running the fields and hills with Oren had kept her fit for the long trek, but when night fell and forced her to rest, her bruised feet radiated pain. Her spirit was bruised too. She'd never left Mata before, and she'd never dared defy her parents. If she succeeded, she would break both their hearts in the name of what she felt was right—which might not even be right at all.

Lela ate one of the honey biscuits, a handful of berries she'd collected on the road, and some dried meat, washed down with tepid water from her waterskin. Bone-tired, she fell asleep by the light of the moons.

CHAPTER 18

Before the sun had risen, the wagon jolted forward, startling Ricci awake. No food or water awaited her. Her stomach growled. Thirst clouded everything—every thought of her family or escape. No one spoke to her, and they didn't stop again until nightfall. The wagon door opened, and she braced to be pulled outside, eager for fresh air and to stretch her legs, but that didn't happen. The same meager portions of water and porridge were left. Someone dumped the waste bucket, and then the door was shut up tight again.

Thus began a pattern that lasted for days, though how many, Ricci couldn't be sure. They blended together in a repetition of not enough water, even less food, and aching cold. Days were nicer, when the sun came through the windows and warmed her skin. It rained once, but the bars were too close together to stick out her hand and catch any water. She stuck out her fingers instead, licking up each precious drop.

Ricci used the abundance of time to plot her escape. The general kept the key to her manacles hanging from his belt. Shiny and gold, like a beacon of hope. All she needed was a split moment to grab the key. She wouldn't even have to run far, just long enough to unlock the manacles and portal out of there. Home.

At some point, the wagon stopped bumping over ruts. The road's surface smoothed out. The horses' clip-clops became more defined. When Ricci peeked out, she saw houses and—except for the colorful trees and pink sky—almost convinced herself she was in her own world, a world where they didn't treat young girls like criminals, and even the criminals weren't treated this badly. Then the soldiers appeared, lining shoulder to shoulder on each side of the road. Townspeople—no, fae—stood behind them, huddling against each other and staring at the wagon in fear. Children, though not very many, clung to mothers, pointing, while fathers shielded them. The soldiers were there to protect the fae.

From her.

Ricci hunched down, hiding from their fear and accusations. The sway of the wagon and her weakness from lack of food lured her toward sleep. She was just dozing off when they rolled to a stop. Her eyes widened. Boots approached, and the wagon door opened. Her whole body tensed. The general watched as she was hauled out. The key sparkled at his waist. She gaped at the sight behind him—an enormous castle made of gray stone. It rose higher than she could see, even craning her neck.

A wooden door flanked by guards opened in the castle wall, showing black beyond. The general turned toward it. Ricci didn't hesitate. She lunged.

The guard yelled as Ricci slipped from his relaxed grip. Ricci sprang for the key as the general turned toward the commotion. Arms wrapped around her waist, dragging her to the ground. She blinked, and the tip of a sword filled her vision.

"Unwise," the general said.

"Let me go." Ricci's voice cracked. She'd been so close.

The guards dragged her inside the castle into the blackness. It smelled of crumbling decay and dust. Lanterns lit a cold hallway. They took her down winding stairs until her bare feet stung from slapping and scraping against the rough stone. At the bottom, the room widened into an open space with cells around the perimeter. Torches showed where mold grew on the stone walls and floor. They led her to an open cell already flanked by guards. Rough hands shoved her in. She stumbled, weak, to the hard ground. They did not remove her manacles.

The bars closed with a slam, and a lock clicked. The general stood in front of her.

Ricci grabbed the bars. "Why am I here?" she pleaded. "When can I go home?"

Silence. He wouldn't give her answers. Like Lela said, to him, she was the downfall of their world. He didn't offer a single piece of information before he turned and walked away, taking the guards with him.

She ran her bound hands along the door and walls, looking for weaknesses, anything she could use to escape. She shook the door and tried lifting it. Nothing.

Exhausted, she sat and grabbed her knees, huddling in the corner of her prison. How had it come to this? This couldn't be real. There had to be a way to escape this nightmare.

They left her there alone. For how long, Ricci didn't know. The torches burned out, bleeding to darkness. There was no window to let in the light. As her eyes adjusted to the pitch black, she realized it wasn't completely dark. Faint light glowed from the stairs where torches further up must still have been lit.

She shivered, mind forming a plan. They couldn't keep her

in this cell forever. Hopefully. And when they let her out, she'd do whatever it took to get home.

Something scuttled, claws scraping across the stone floor. Ricci shuddered. Who knew what foul creatures this strange world held?

Footsteps echoed down the staircase. Ricci could barely see from the corner where she huddled, but she didn't dare move closer. Two guards carrying torches stepped aside to flank the stairway. More guards streamed into the open dungeon before a woman stepped from behind them and approached Ricci's cell.

Like the others, her face was blank of emotion. Her long ears showed prominently below her pinned-up hazelnut hair. She wore a dress made of a dark material—torchlight showed it might be red—which hung weightless around her tall, slim figure.

Ricci shoved backward as far as she could, stones digging into her back and scraping her arms. The woman knelt to eye level, dress billowing out behind her. She sniffed, and her hand flicked as if she might cover her nose against the stench, but then didn't.

Ricci couldn't look away. This was the first fae besides Lela she'd seen up close that wasn't a soldier. She looked royal. Would she help? "Water, please, ma'am. Water."

The woman tilted her head. "Has she been given no water?" she asked without looking away. "Fetch some." A guard left, but he didn't hurry. "She'll need to be cleaned up before questioning. See to it." The woman stood. "Such a fragile thing you are, human. So fascinating to see one up close after all this time."

Her words were unfeeling, but the woman's eyes were full of guilt. Maybe sympathy. They kept falling to the manacles at Ricci's wrists, then her soiled clothes.

"Lady Sarafine," a guard said. "I will escort you out."

The fae woman, Lady Sarafine, nodded. "Yes. Don't take very long. The court is waiting." She pivoted, throwing the scent of musky perfume toward Ricci.

Questioning? This could be her way to prove her innocence. Maybe she could convince them, like she had Lela.

Water came in the form of a freezing cold bath. When the guards opened the door to deposit it in her cell, there were too many of them to make a break for it. They relocked the door and at least had the decency to put up a ragged curtain. Ricci stuck her face in the water, gulping frantic mouthfuls. It tasted mildewy and metallic, like old pipes. It was magnificent.

When she'd had her fill, she stared at her cuffed wrists and debated skipping the bath. But after countless days of travel in the same urine-stained dress, she welcomed the chance to be clean. With difficulty, she managed to wriggle her dress and underclothes over her head, but they wouldn't go past her wrists. She stepped awkwardly into the bath which came up to her knees. She shivered, lowering herself down into the water. Her toe kicked a scrub brush and a slimy bar of soap. She did the best she could on her hair and body until something slid under the curtain. She jumped.

"Put it on," came the simple command.

Teeth chattering, she stepped out of the tub. Her precious birthday dress Mama and Nora had spent countless hours making was now ruined and hanging from her arms. There was no towel and no way to pick up the new garment without soaking it.

"Hurry up. We're removing the curtain."

Ricci squeaked and snatched up the scratchy thing on the floor. The garment looked like a large potato sack with short sleeves. The neck was wide enough to step into, and she pulled it up over her chest just in time for the curtain to be ripped away. There was no way to get her bound wrists into the sleeves, especially with her sodden clothes still hanging from her arms.

Her cheeks burned. No one but Mama had seen her so undressed.

The guard frowned at her, as if it was her fault she wasn't fully clothed.

"I need the key to her binders," the guard said. He watched the floor.

The two behind him exchanged glances. "Only General Ashryn has the key, sir," said one. Uncertainty colored his tone, like he feared giving the wrong answer.

Her guard blinked slowly, then pinched the bridge of his nose. "Take her to the council."

Dressed like this? "You can't possibly mean for me—"

They moved to grab her.

"Wait." The lead guard pulled a sharp-looking knife from its sheath.

Ricci gasped and backed away.

He grabbed her arm, fingers digging into bone. "Be still, *human*." He took her dripping green dress and underclothes, and cut through them cleanly. They splatted in tatters to the floor.

Heartache ripped through her. The guards gave her no time to dwell on the ruins of the dress. Ricci gripped the new garment to her chest, arms and shoulders bare as they led her back up the stairs. She stumbled trying to keep up with their grueling pace. Up, up, up, they went. Ricci panted for breath, shivering wet. She counted each door they passed, trying to learn the way out for when she escaped. Finally, they left the stairwell and turned through a door flanked by more guards.

This hallway was beautiful—just as she'd read in fictional stories of the fae. Even as her mind jumped to the worst conclusions about what came next, she couldn't deny it. Open and bright with sconces interspaced on the walls. Polished marble floors, cool and smooth on her weary feet. The high ceiling was beamed in dark wood, and night had fallen outside the tall windows. Paintings of landscapes blurred by as they led her further along. She searched every hall for a way out, but they were each as endless as the next.

Ricci balked when they entered an open doorway. She'd never seen a more enormous room. Two dozen fae in robes and dresses of fine make, like what royalty or nobles wore, sat behind tiered tables around the perimeter. She recognized Lady Sarafine and the general among them. Lined up between Ricci and the noble fae—guarding them, she realized—were soldiers like the ones that had taken her. Their bows rested slack at their sides but with arrows nocked.

The guards brought her to the middle of the room and shoved her hard to the floor. Her knees cracked against the marble. She cried out, the sound echoing around the room. Her dripping wet hair stuck to her face as she clung to her garment with her bound hands and tried not to weep in front of all these important fae.

They murmured amongst themselves, but Ricci kept her eyes on the white-marbled floor. Thin black swirling lines blurred in her vision. The chain on her manacles clinked with her shivering.

What part should she play? Should she act weak and defenseless, or strong and defiant? Did she even have the strength to play a part? And would it matter? They'd still consider her a threat either way. It wasn't in her to be strong now, so it didn't matter. Papa always said honesty was best, and since she'd done nothing wrong, maybe honesty would set her free.

"Well, give the poor creature a blanket or something," a female fae said from across the room in that strange fae accent.

There was a rustling sound, then someone approached and dropped a red shawl over her shoulders. She gripped the edges close, not realizing how so very cold she had been.

A gavel pounded against wood, and the murmuring ceased. "We have called court to learn of the threat posed by the portal opener. The prophecy, as was the final act of hate by the humans leaving our realm, states that our peoples' demise will follow the opening of the portal."

Ricci risked a peek through her matted hair as the speaker continued. He stood behind the centermost table directly across from her. Long black hair was tied behind his head, and a royal blue tunic shimmered subtly with embroidered silk. She couldn't deny his beauty—all the faes' beauty. This one wore a simple silver circlet at his brow.

He turned his gaze right to her. "We will have our answers, and your cooperation. The prophecy will be stopped no matter the means."

Fear coiled tight in her gut.

"Proceed, General Ashryn."

He sat, and the general stepped forward, bowing.

"Thank you, Prince Renic." General Ashryn paced in front of Ricci. "What is your name, human?"

Oh, Gods. How could she be expected to speak? She opened her mouth, but nothing came out.

He stopped pacing. "You will answer me, or I will make the binders the least of your worries."

Ricci nodded.

"What is your name, and where do you come from?"

"My name is Ricci Menowin, and I come from Timbercross, in the kingdom of Taunfalan." Her voice was barely a whisper, but still loud enough for the fae, apparently. Their murmurings roused with her first utterance.

"How old are you?"

"Sixteen," she said.

Their volume increased until the gavel banged again, quieting them.

"Who is your mata and pata?" Prince Renic asked, to a chorus of whispers and the wide eyes of the general. "Are they human?"

"My parents? Of course they are human."

The prince slumped down and looked away, seeming to lose all interest in the proceedings. But was that disappointment in his eyes?

General Ashryn resumed pacing. "How do the humans plan on infiltrating and destroying us?"

Ricci gaped. "Humans—we know nothing of fae. Nothing of portals or other places like ours. There is no plan to attack or destroy. I'm just a simple girl. I promise I never meant to cause any harm." She met Lela's father's scrutinizing gaze.

"How many others can open portals?" he asked as if she hadn't spoken.

The questions went on like this. Ricci's voice went hoarse, but no one offered her water. To conserve energy, she gave one-word answers as often as she could.

"What kind of weaponry do the human armies use?" the general asked with no signs of tiredness.

Her vision spotted. "Um... I don't... I don't know."

"This is going nowhere, General," Prince Renic said. "Let her rest."

Ricci nearly sobbed as the general waved an annoyed hand at the guards to take her away. She hadn't convinced them of anything. They weren't going to let her go home.

Back in her cell, the general unlocked one of the manacles

to allow her to put her arms through the sleeves of her new dress, like a nightgown made of scrub brush. She considered running but lacked the strength.

"I'm no threat," she pleaded as he locked her cell door. "Let me go, and I'll never return. I promise."

He ignored her.

Porridge, water, and a half-rotten apple slid through the bars. They let her keep the expensive shawl. Her torn birthday dress was gone.

CHAPTER 19

The days wore on as Lela passed through small towns of hobble homes and scant shops, through sweeping countryside and farmland, forests as colorful as the one by her home, always heading north. She cursed the rain when it soaked her through, boots sucking into mud. When she reached the town that marked the halfway point, she spent valuable coin to stay at an inn where she washed her clothes and restocked supplies. By the time she got to Alberry, she was three days behind the warriors, and only because she bartered some of her precious herbs to ride in an onion merchant's wagon part of the way.

News of the portal opener came easy. From the crowded taverns to people gathered in the streets, Ricci's capture dominated every conversation. But they didn't believe the danger had passed. Fear and worry remained.

"The portal has been opened, so what happens to the portal opener matters not," the townspeople repeated to each other.

At a tavern near the castle, Lela sipped her cider and

listened to *everything*. Rumor said a special session of court, with the elders and Prince Renic himself, had convened to question Ricci, but so far nothing useful had been divulged. It was also said the court thought she was lying and planned to torture her. Whether this was true, Lela couldn't know for sure. But she was out of time.

Her travel clothes reeked of horses and onions, she could run into her pata at any moment, but none of that mattered with Ricci's life in jeopardy.

Lela paid for her light meal of crusty bread smeared with soft cheese—a bit of basil would have drastically improved the flavor—then headed to her last stop. The army barracks. Of any location in town, that was where she was most familiar. Her mata took her there to visit Pata when he was between campaigns but couldn't return home. Lela had done most of her training here. Maybe Pata wanted her to join one day.

The crunch of grit under her boots was lost with the passing carts and horses and the birds chirping in the intermittent trees, their leaves not as vibrant in color as those at home. As she approached the wall surrounding the army barracks, the sounds changed to the shouts of the training warriors running their courses or practicing weapons.

A squad of recruits marched by in near-perfect formation. Lela couldn't help but search them for Oren, disappointment flooding her when he wasn't there.

Lela went over the plan as she walked. All she had to do was get inside, and then she knew her way around the barracks well enough to reach the castle. She'd pose as a maid, find Ricci, and free her.

Lela absently scanned the new recruits on the battlements and surrounding area for Oren. There sure were a lot of them around. The draft had brought in many.

Few other citizens traveled the gravel trail, and the eyes of the guards on top of the wall seemed to see right through her confident strides, searing her skin. She kept her head down. A thousand things could go wrong before making it inside. The last thing she wanted was to use her pata's name to gain entrance and completely change her plan, but she would if she had to.

She slowed near the gates flanked by two young guards in the standard black and silver uniform. A hand clamped down on her shoulder and spun her around. Her muscles coiled.

Oren's big, blue eyes stared right into hers. "What in the valley are you doing here?"

Her mouth popped open, and warmth flooded her cheeks. He was as beautiful as she remembered, except now his lean frame exhibited more muscles, and his unruly hair had been trimmed, combed, and pulled back in a low tail. The leather uniform fit him perfectly.

But what was that onion smell? *Oh, stars. It's me.*

"Lela?" He shook her. "The portal opener is here, in Alberry, and you decide *now* is the time to visit me? You know it's not allowed. Does your pata know you're here?"

She stepped back from his grip, shoulders drooping. "Why are you here? I thought you'd be training." At least he was alone.

"I am training. I'm on sentry duty. My partner is just over there—don't look. He and at least a dozen other guards are watching us, wondering what kind of trouble you're making. You shouldn't have come to see me."

"I'm not here to see *you*, Oren." The world didn't revolve around him—just her world. "Wait, you can help me." He could get her into the barracks. He might even know exactly where Ricci was kept. If she could convince him, she'd rescue Ricci much faster. "Pata doesn't know I'm here, and it has to stay that way."

"What?" he hissed, grabbing her arm. "You've lost your mind."

"Oren. Stop. You're making your friends nervous." She couldn't see them since her back was to the castle, but their rising voices confirmed it was true. They were coming. "Tell them I'm your sister, and our mata is dying."

"Everything okay, Oren?"

Lela glanced back to see another young warrior stepping slowly toward them.

"All good, Zem. This one was just leaving," Oren called out. To her, he whispered, "Go home, Lela. Go home where you'll be safe." He turned and walked away from her to his sentry partner. Zem glanced between them, then backed away like prey not wanting to call attention to itself.

Lela crossed her arms. She hadn't come all this way to be told what to do. She already had two parents. "Fine. I'll leave. But I'm planning something and could really use your help. I passed an inn on the way here, Quiet Tree. I'll be there one night, and then I move without you." She turned from the approaching guards, not looking to see if Oren watched her. Things would be easier with his help, but she didn't need it. Not if he was going to be a stubborn ass about it.

One night. That was all she'd wait.

Not two hours later, Lela sat at a table at the inn snacking on fried mushrooms. She'd picked a table in a dark corner of an already dimly lit space. Sparse light leaked through grubby, garbled panes of glass that set the tone for the rest of the inn.

Oren strode in wearing regular clothes—pants, a long-sleeved shirt, and a vest. A chain hung from his neck with a vial of crushed lavender. She smiled. He'd kept her gift.

He plunked himself down in a chair and pulled the plate over, eating her food.

"Can I help you?" she asked, irritated and secretly relieved he'd come. The mushrooms were a luxury she shouldn't have splurged for.

"I thought it was my help you needed." He popped another mushroom into his mouth, eyes crinkling. "What's all this nonsense you were going on about?"

"So you're going to be nice now?" Lela snatched back the plate and looked around. The room was mostly empty, but she lowered her voice to a whisper anyway. "How are you here?"

"I used your idea. I told Zem you're my sister, that Mata is sick." He took a generous gulp of her tea. "Ugh, you always use too much sugar." He smacked his mouth. "Of course he didn't believe me. He thinks you're my mate, so he's covering for me. But I don't have much time."

Lela lowered her voice even more, ignoring how that word made her heart jump. "I need your help to free Ricci, the portal opener."

Oren spat out tea in a spray. "That's not funny. I'm risking a lot to be here."

Lela wiped her face. "I'm serious. She's innocent. She's just a girl who doesn't know what she's doing or how to control her energy."

"You're mad." Oren shook his head.

She leaned closer. "Yes, the portal was opened. Yes, the prophecy is real, but our doom will not come from *her*." She took a breath. "She's innocent, and they are torturing her, and she's paying the price for someone else's corruption."

"It doesn't matter if it comes from her. She is the cause. She is the source. Can't you see that?"

"No," she said simply. It was Pata all over again.

He raked his fingers through his hair. "You could have jeopardized everything I've worked for here, Lela. But I'm not even angry about that, because it's nothing compared to your recklessness. Traveling alone in a time such as this? How could you put yourself in danger? What about your mata?"

The words fought their way through her clenched teeth. "*What about Mata*? She's perfectly safe!" She threw up her arms. A few people looked their way. Lela lowered her voice again, scooting her chair closer. "It's Ricci who needs our help. If you don't want to give it, fine. Just tell me where they are keeping her. Tell me how to get to her."

Oren opened his mouth, ready to interrupt, probably to tell her how stupid and unsafe she was being again.

Lela held up her hand. "I love you." She gasped—the traitorous words had slipped right out her mouth. But she needed him to understand, to *listen* to her. She needed him to know the truth before he dismissed her one more time. "We've known each other our whole lives, but this is more than that. More than mere friendship." Her lips trembled as he watched her with wide, baring eyes. "I love you like my soul isn't whole when we're not together. I love you like I'll never know happiness again because you don't feel the same about me." Her shoulders slumped under the weight of her foolishness. "Please trust me and help me do the right thing."

Oren's features softened, and his cheeks turned red.

Oh, stars, he was embarrassed for her.

"Or don't help me," she said, exasperated, standing to leave. "I'm saving Ricci either way."

He took her hand, urging her back down. "You *are* mad." His voice came out low and gravelly, gentle. He sat silent, staring. Weighing. Deciding.

She wouldn't ask again.

Oren sighed. "I must be mad, too." He squeezed her hand, then let go and stood, chair scraping back. "I'll do what I can."

Lela leaped from her chair and hugged him.

They didn't hug like this back at home, but she was so grateful he'd decided to help. She couldn't resist melting into him. His heat and the familiar sweet scent of honeysuckle comforted her. When he stepped back, his soft face slid over hers, almost like a caress.

She straightened, nearly dizzy. The embrace had been rain to a droughted soul. It was almost enough to forgive that she'd confessed her undying love, and he hadn't returned it. She hadn't really expected him to.

He glanced around the room. No one was paying them any attention. "I'll help, because I can see you're determined no matter what. But this is wrong."

"You're doing the right thing, Oren. I wouldn't ask otherwise."

"We'll see. I'll be back." He grabbed her last mushroom, chuckling at her outraged face. "Make sure to order a bath." His chuckle became a laugh as he left the inn.

Lela's eyes landed on the empty plate, just the right size to connect with the back of his infuriating head.

But she couldn't stay angry. Oren was going to help her. He could save so much time if he found where Ricci was kept. And he would—she trusted that.

Lela took his advice and washed the onion scent off in the public bathhouse, luxuriating in warmth and cleanliness and cursing Oren in equal measures. She rented the loft in the barn —the only space her coin would fetch—and waited.

CHAPTER 20

Callen stared, skin gone cold, at the spot where Ricci and the strange man had just disappeared. All that remained was the flower she'd held, the pretty red foreign thing. Numb, Callen picked it up. It was real as real could be, not a prop. It also wasn't like any flower he'd seen.

None of it was an illusion. Ricci had the gift of the Nether Realms.

The curtain closed behind him, muffling the cheering crowd. The other actors—Ricci's family—rushed to him.

The biggest and oldest of them reached him first, nearly bowling him over. "Where has she gone? What have you done with my daughter, mage?" he demanded, gut and bushy mustache invading Callen's space.

"That man, he took her," one of the male actors said.

"I knew this day would come. I just knew it," a woman wailed. "Our baby, our gift from the Gods has been taken from us." She clung to the mustache man's sleeve. Her face contorted into despair. "You said this wouldn't happen. She's ours forever."

They all talked over each other, jostling Callen. The mustache man glared daggers at him, and the crowd roared for the next scene to start.

"It wasn't me," Callen shouted. "But I will do everything in my power to bring her back." She was the key to all his problems. And she was in mortal danger.

The cheering turned to boos, then the curtain jerked as things were thrown at it. Rotten apples flew from underneath.

Mustache man glanced at the apprentice robes, then wiped a tear from his eye. "I must calm the crowd. Please, go with my wife to the wagon. I beg you to help us."

The wife, a weeping mess who must have been Ricci's mom, silently led the way offstage to the lead wagon. Callen wracked his brain harder with each step. What could he possibly do? The gift of the Nether Realms was supposed to be lost, which was why Master Marek sought out a potion instead. So how could Callen possibly figure out who took Ricci or where she went?

Ricci's mom let him in, and he got his first glimpse of the inside. A bunk bed took up the space at the far end, and they'd managed to cram an entire house in between, with a kitchen, a writing desk, cabinets and closets and nooks for storage. The bright, gaudy colors and glittering crystal lanterns actually made it inviting. It reminded him of his disorganized shelves of colorful potions.

Ricci's mom pulled out a small stool next to a tiny table that folded down from the wall and gestured for him to sit. "You have magic. My Ricci has magic. You can help her."

Callen gave a tight smile. "I will do my best." How was he ever going to find her?

"No!" She slammed her hand on the table, making him jump. "You will help her." She sobbed anew. "I don't know how to help her. She didn't come from me." She grabbed the neckline of her dress and tugged.

Callen fumbled the handkerchief out of his pocket. The woman was in shock, clearly.

She took it but didn't use it, only twisted and wrung it with her hands, as if desperate to put them to use doing something, anything.

"We found her. As a baby. I don't know anything about her magic." She met Callen's eyes as tears streamed down her face. "Her mother held her in her arms, dying on the side of the road. We stopped, and she died. Ricci was only hours old. I was too old to have another child by then, but I'd always wanted a daughter." She sniffled. "Ricci Plains. That's where we found her, and why we named her so. Her mother's only words were to keep her safe. She wouldn't even tell us Ricci's full name. Only her first name. It had magic ties, she said. We made a promise to keep her safe. And we broke that promise." Ricci's mother sobbed even louder.

Callen patted her back awkwardly, thoughts on Ricci. What had happened to her birth mother? And magical ties? That would explain where Ricci got her gift, if she was from a magical family.

She took a shuddering breath. "Her given name is Oriana. I never told her any of this. I was supposed to keep her safe."

Beautiful. "I will go to my master, and we will find her. In the meantime, put up posters and make it known she's been kidnapped." Maybe the place they went was nearby. With her fame, it could lead to something.

When they told Ricci's father the plan, he handed Callen a piece of parchment and a sack of coins. "This is where we'll be, following the market, searching for her, doing everything we can. Please, find us or send word when you know something."

Callen tried to hand back the coins.

"Keep the coins for my daughter. She may need them to get home." He grabbed Callen in a bone-crushing hug.

The rest of the family waited outside the wagon looking ready to do battle, brows drawn and fists clenched.

"I will do my best to find her," Callen said again. It didn't ease their worry, but they let him pass, some even thanking him, so he hurried to find a carriage.

Thank the Gods Master Marek had gone to Timbercross. There were only two places he could be. Since it was still morning, he'd most likely be away from his mansion and in the heart of the city at the mage building. The building housed the council and apprentices, conducted permit testing, and held classes.

Two brown horses and a no-nonsense driver propelled the open carriage. The driver didn't speak as they headed toward the mage building, allowing Callen plenty of time to ponder his stupidity. He'd promised the impossible. He'd spent years trying to do the one thing Ricci had done effortlessly, and he was no closer to accomplishing that goal.

And what if she'd gone to another realm? No one would ever be able to find her. But her magic was everything he and his master had worked to find for years. If it was in his small power to help, he must. The thought of what Ricci might be going through made him sick.

When Callen reached the mage district, the buildings shifted from rough sandstone to smooth rock. The roads were cleaner, shrubbery tended, and a general feeling of wealth took over the scenery. Even the smell was better, leaving behind the stench of refuse for clean air.

Mages hadn't been persecuted in decades, ridding the need to live separately from commoners, but it was convenient to be near like-minded people. Mages bought supplies at mage-specific stores and sent their children to mage schools.

Callen hadn't gone to a mage school, not because his parents couldn't afford it, but because becoming an apprentice to a member of the council was the more prestigious route.

Callen paid the driver and stared up at the mage building. At four stories tall, it towered above the surrounding shops and businesses. Smooth gray stone covered every facet, with windows lining each level and stars carved in relief at the corners. He entered the echoing marble foyer and climbed a staircase to the second floor, knocking at the last door on the right. Master Marek's office.

"Go away," a gruff voice said, muffled through the door.

Callen entered. Master Marek sat behind a large desk shuffling through papers, looking grumpy. His master's moods were unpredictable.

"Callen," he said with true surprise, cheering. "You're supposed to be on leave. Well, since you're here, organize these papers. I'm late for my meeting with the council."

Callen grabbed the loose papers—potion recipes, mostly—and sorted them. "I need your help, Master. It is most urgent. But you can gain from this as well."

"I've done you enough favors," he said, taking the papers and shoving them in a bag, scrambling them again. "Since your leave is over, please get back to the shop and tend my potions."

"I saw someone open a portal," Callen blurted.

Master Marek dropped the bag. It tipped over, spilling papers across the smooth floor. He rounded the desk and into Callen's face. "Say that again. And do not speak if it's not true." His voice rang with power, eagerness alight in his eyes.

"I saw someone open a portal. It's true."

He pulled Callen into a chair, then scooted another one close. "Tell me everything."

"I went to the market this morning—"

"Stop!" His master held up a hand, blinking like the sun

was in his eyes, though the curtain was closed. "Don't say another word, Callen. Leave now."

Huh? "But someone needs my help."

Master Marek's eyebrows dipped in anger again. "Then speak," he commanded.

Callen spoke quickly. "I stopped to watch one of the traveling troupes. There was a girl on stage." He hesitated. Ricci had performed illegal magic. But she was in danger.

Would his master remember Callen mentioned her before?

Master Marek shook him by the shoulders. "What about the girl? Speak!"

Callen told him every detail of Ricci's disappearance, changing one minor thing. "The man muttered something, like a spell, then took her with him."

His master's eyes went wide. "The man. Did he have pointed ears?"

What? "Pointed ears?" Callen shook his head. He hadn't been looking at the man at all. He'd been watching Ricci stand terrified with a sword to her throat. "I don't know. I don't think so."

Master Marek slumped back in his seat. "You've done well, my apprentice. We'll find this man. It will be a simple tracing spell." He flashed a rare smile. "You can return to the shop."

"I promised the girl's family I would see her safe. I want to help." Callen spoke with conviction, pushing past the tendency to second-guess his every word and action when it came to his master.

Master Marek nodded. "Very well. But say nothing of this to anyone, especially anyone on the council."

"I'm afraid it will be common knowledge. A lot of townsfolk saw her disappear."

Master Marek scowled. "Then we must hurry. Grab my bag."

Callen scrambled for the bag and the scattered papers.

"Leave those. The potions are useless to me now. Only the mysterious portal opener matters."

Bottles clinked around the inside of the bag as Callen lugged it. In no time, they were in his master's private coach headed back to Ricci's stage.

Callen's heart raced. What if the tracing spell revealed Ricci was actually the portal opener and not the man, as Callen implied?

Screams filled the air as they neared. People rushed down the street, running in the opposite direction. Callen stuck his head through the window. Smoke billowed on the horizon.

"Hurry Master, something's happened."

They urged the driver, but it was slow-going against the opposite flow of traffic. The smoke thickened, and the crowds increased, bringing their progress to a standstill.

Callen hopped out of the coach, unable to wait another moment. He took off at a run, swerving around people, parked carts, and carriages. His boots slapped over paving stones. Finally, he saw the flames.

The stage was on fire.

Had the kidnapper returned for the rest of Ricci's family? Was Ricci here?

Callen dodged the bucket brigade that fruitlessly tossed water on the inferno. It evaporated before even touching the ten-foot flames. His breath rushed out as he spotted the green wagons, horses harnessed and struggling to get away.

He sprinted to the lead wagon. Its wheel was stuck in the mud. The men, including Ricci's father, dug with shovels, frantically trying to free it before the heat could damage the wagon or harm the horses.

"Stand back," Callen yelled. He called his magic to him, drawing it up from the well within. It was full, thanks to not making any potions recently. It warmed his core, sweat beading on his brow as he channeled it.

Ricci's family jumped back in surprise as the wagon wheel slowly lifted from the ground. They cheered when it cleared the mud. Ricci's brothers pulled the horses until the wagon was safely free.

Callen stumbled, hands on his knees. A loud roar and an ear-splitting hissing noise had him spinning around. Master Marek had arrived. He'd put the fire out in a matter of moments. Smoke rose from the remains.

"Foolish apprentice," his master said. "Helping the peasants instead of helping me. What if the fire burned the magical traces away?"

Callen's spirits sank. Master Marek was right.

Ricci's dad approached, removing his hat and running a hand over his bald head. "We canceled our remaining shows, and the fans went crazy. Started booing and ripping apart the stage. If someone hadn't started that fire, they would have come for us next." He replaced his hat, cheeks red and puffing. "Can you really find my Ricci?"

His master shot Callen a look that said he didn't care one peppermint stick about helping this family. "Keep everyone back while my apprentice and I cast our spells."

The words were for show. Master Marek had never taught Callen how to cast a tracing spell, but it was beyond him anyway. Tracing magic was difficult for any mage, but tracing magic to a different realm, well, it had never been done before. And the way the stage looked, it would be even more challenging. There wasn't much Callen could do except keep out of the way.

Master Marek stepped onto the black husk of a stage, not bothering to hitch his robes, though he did step carefully, minding the weakest boards. He must have been using a spell to keep stray embers from singeing his robes.

Callen followed, lifting his robes like women's skirts lest he catch fire. His boots crushed glowing-red embers as he watched where he stepped. He bumped into his master's shoulder.

Master Marek gave him a look. "Lead the way, if you please. Take me to where you saw them disappear."

Callen took two steps to the left and gestured to the ground —the stage was not that big. "Here."

"Watch closely." Master Marek took the bag from Callen and rummaged inside until he produced a vial of clear liquid. *Insiffadus Peroxilous*, the label read. The cork unstoppered with a pop, and he splashed half the contents over the stage.

Nothing happened except some faint sizzling where the potion met the dying embers. But some potions didn't activate without the intention behind the magic that came from the mage.

Callen took a few steps back as his master closed his eyes. Even with the leftover heat from the raging fire, Callen felt the immense power behind his master's intention. So much raw magic. Callen's own well was a thimble by comparison. Like a wave washing over the potion and bringing its purpose to life, his master shaped the spell to his bidding.

The potion bubbled and hissed, stretched and moved like slime, over the warped stage, seeking its prey—the portal opener. It was a power Callen would take years to master. A branch of the liquid slime shot toward his foot, and he hopped backward. It stretched out, thinner and thinner, and then it snapped back into itself, becoming a round blob over a single point—where Callen had last seen Ricci.

"Yes," Master Marek said, rushing to the blob. His brow unfurrowed. "Can you see it Callen? Link your magic to mine."

Callen called upon his magic eagerly. His master never let them link before. He must have been truly happy to finally have a lead. Callen reached out, sending a tether to catch the edge of invisible magic connected to the potion blob. The strength of his master's power rocked him backward.

"Easy. Steady now. Hold on to it." Master Marek's encouraging words bolstered him.

Callen took a deep breath and followed the magic to the potion. He shaped his own magic, giving it intent. *Find Ricci.*

After a moment of dizzy concentration, he gasped. He *felt* her. She was scared. No, more than that. Terrified and in pain. He looked up to find his master watching him.

"What do you see, boy?" Master Marek asked carefully.

"See? I don't see anything." Callen closed his eyes, trying to see with his magic. He pulled even more from the well within him, focusing harder to force it to his will. A castle made of stone, ancient looking. Torches. "I see a dungeon."

"Good!" Master seemed pleased. "What else?"

Callen strained, pushing himself to the limits of his ability. His head swam, forcing him to open his eyes and reorient his vision. "Nothing but blackness."

Master Marek cut off his magic, severing Callen's tie to the other end of the tracing potion. It was like suddenly losing a limb, but without the pain. The ground rushed up, and he collapsed, panting. His master's magic had been supporting him. He'd thought he'd been doing it all on his own.

"Even with my aid, I didn't expect you to see anything. Maybe you have a gift after all," Master Marek said casually as he strolled toward the edge of the stage. "The trace found the girl, so the man you spoke of must be near her. She is indeed in a dungeon, but she's not within our reach." He paced back as Callen struggled to sit up. "She's in another realm. The realm of the fae." His mouth curved up.

Callen's jaw fell slack. The fae were a fairy tale. Children's stories. A race no one believed really existed in a world that never really was. The gift of the Nether Realms was thought to take you to a different place in *this* world. But his master wouldn't lie. "So the man who took her, he wasn't human?"

"No."

"How do we get her back?" Callen pushed to his feet, body shaking as his magic well slowly replenished.

"We can't." Master Marek shrugged his boney shoulders. "But he took her for a reason, and he may return again." He left the stage, not a hint of soot on his impeccable purple robe, while Callen looked like he'd been rolling in mud with the pigs. "We can only wait. In the meantime, I'll have your things sent to your parents' so you can be close when I need you."

Sitting and waiting for something to happen was unacceptable—especially at his parents'. He'd find a way to reach her through the trace. Perhaps a potion.

Hang on, Ricci.

CHAPTER 21

Ricci lay on the hard floor of her cell, counting her breaths. The torches had long burned out, leaving only darkness. Someone always relit them eventually. Different fae coming and going. To stare and to point. To laugh or sneer. She only looked long enough to see if the nice fae lady would come back.

She never did.

Days or hours could have passed since her first questioning. She didn't know. They'd questioned her two more times since then, the same questions. She told them what they wanted to hear, giving made-up military details, but she could never confess to what they were really after—that the humans were planning a war with the fae. They couldn't believe it wasn't true.

Sleep came and went, but there was no way of knowing if it was day or night. There was no water left for tears, and her wrists bled from too many unsuccessful attempts at removing the manacles. The scuttling of small creatures in the corners of the room no longer bothered her except that they were a reminder this place and these horrors were real and not going away. Maybe the fae rats knew how much time passed.

Voices sounded from up the stairs. A door slammed. Ricci scuttled away and huddled in the back corner of her cell. Boots trudged, and torchlight flooded the room. Ricci shielded her eyes. The light pained.

Someone stomped to her door, but she didn't look to see who. She held her bony knees to her chest, rocking back and forth.

"You have until tomorrow," a deep voice said. The general. "If you haven't told us what we need to know by then, we start using these."

Ricci finally looked up. Two men held trays of instruments, the kind you'd see in a traveling physician's bag. Their jagged edges gleamed in the torchlight. Her entire body trembled.

"These will hurt you in ways you can't imagine, and then you'll tell us everything." The general shuffled closer. Speaking softer, he said, "Don't let it come to that. Confess."

Her jagged nails bit into her palms. The general wasn't lying. If she didn't find something to say—whatever they needed to hear—he'd torture her.

"Why did you open the portal into our world?" he asked.

Ricci tried to speak, but her chattering teeth locked together, refusing to open. Her body shook beyond her control.

Her chest tightened. "I'm a scout for the human army."

"How many others like you are there?" His voice rose.

"There are no others. Now let me go." Her throat burned, the words hoarse. "We won't attack. You're too powerful."

The general sighed as if truly regretful. "One day, young human. One more day is all you have left to tell us how the humans plan to invade our world." He took a torch and replaced the extinguished one beside her cell.

She buried her face in the scratchy dress and did not peek

until they'd been gone for a long while. When she did, the glinting of torture tools shined over her. He'd left them in front of her cell for her to see and fear. She could do a lot of damage with one of those. She scrambled to the bars, reaching a leg far as possible. Out of reach.

Her body went limp. She'd tried everything to escape— digging at the stone with her empty bowl, pleading with the guards, searching the bars for weaknesses. Nothing.

Would she ever see her family again? What about Callen? No one had ever looked at her the way he had as they'd shared orange pastries. She'd been so nervous, yet completely at ease with him at the same time. She wanted more of that, more time to know him and share about herself in return.

He'd jumped on stage to save her. His magic had been so strong before she was forced to close the portal.

But she'd never see him or her family while she still wore these manacles, locked in this cell. When that kind fae woman came back, Ricci was prepared to do whatever she could to get her to help.

And in case that wouldn't work, she used every quiet, lonely moment to craft answers for the general's next round of questions. The truth hadn't saved her. Now she would give them what they wanted to hear. Dates, locations and sizes, anything they wanted until they let her go.

CHAPTER 22

After a miserable night in the barn's loft, Lela awoke to someone shoving her shoulder.

"This is a good look for you." Oren's irritating voice jarred her further from sleep. He backed to the top of the loft ladder.

"Good morning to you, too." Lela blearily rose out of her itchy nest in the hay, balling her fists.

Oren burst out laughing. He covered his mouth. His guard uniform accentuated his muscles in the most glorious way.

"What in the valley is so funny?" The sun through the loft window showed it was barely dawn.

"Nothing." He struggled to compose himself and ended up sputtering with another round of laughter.

Lela couldn't help but smile even though she wasn't in on his secret. He hardly ever laughed so freely since he came of age. It was as if he'd hit a magic number that meant he had to be serious all the time.

"Tell me," she said, laughing with him now.

"Your hair." He doubled over, unable to finish the sentence.

Lela's hand shot to her head. Her smile vanished. Hay stuck out in every direction, as if a brood of chickens made a nest while she slept. Several nests.

"Oh no." She frantically plucked at the hay, shaking her head and ripping out hair in the process. "It's stuck."

Oren only laughed harder, turning her plucking into a red-hazed frenzy. She finally grabbed a brush from her pack and ripped through her locks until the hay and hair stopped raining down. There was a time she wouldn't have cared a lick how she looked in front of Oren. Now that it mattered, she always seemed to be in disarray.

Oren managed to contain himself by the time she tied her hair into a low tail. His cheeks were bright, eyes shining, when she turned around. Her anger dissipated as he held her gaze.

"You missed one." With a soft touch, he slowly tucked her hair behind her ears, fingers grazing her sensitive skin. He held up the piece of hay and cleared his throat. "I volunteered to work patrol through the night. It's the only way I could think to find what you are looking for."

"Thank you," Lela said with feeling. He'd always wanted to be a part of this army, and he risked everything by helping her.

He stepped closer, and her heart skipped.

"I know where she is," he said, voice low. "I saw her."

"Is she okay? Where is she?" The questions tumbled out.

"I was patrolling the dungeon when your pata walked by with a group. I left my post and followed behind them. They went right to her." He ran a rough hand through his hair.

"The dungeons." Lela covered her mouth, shaking her head. "How could they do this? She's my age. She's innocent and helpless." Guilt tore through her. If only Pata had listened. "We have to save her. You have to help me."

"We can't trust her. She's the *portal opener*."

"I understand how you feel, Oren. We've been taught since

birth to fear her and what she can do. But you saw her. She's no threat to us." Lela took Oren's hand. Butterflies traveled from her fingers and danced in her middle.

He gave a soft gasp, looking at their hands. "You shouldn't look at me that way." But he didn't let go.

"Trust me. Even if you don't trust Ricci, trust me." She stared up at him, beseeching. "Sometimes you have to question everything you think you know to be true. The things we've been taught to fear and hate might be just the opposite." She swore his gaze flicked to her mouth, but then he stepped away, gently pulling his hand from hers.

"I trust you. But I also trust in the prophecy. Something bad is coming."

Lela could accept that. She'd have to. "Okay. Let's make a plan."

"I can get you to her, but I don't have a key."

She sighed, running her hand over her hair and scowling when she found more hay. "So how do we get one?" Pata would have one, but there was no way she could get close to him.

Oren shook his head. "She's locked in a cell, and the binders she wears take a special key. Your pata keeps it with him at all times."

"Any chance you could steal it from him?" Lela peeked cautiously only to meet his indignant frown. "Yeah, I figured you'd say that." She kicked at loose hay. "Well, what about someone else, someone who might be able to get close enough to him besides us? Is there anyone who might be sympathetic to Ricci's treatment?"

Oren rolled his eyes, then they widened. "Actually, there is someone."

"Who?" Hope sent her heart to skittering.

"Lady Sarafine. She gave Ricci her own cloak for warmth. I couldn't believe it except I saw the cloak myself."

Lady Sarafine lived in the palace. Her father claimed a large parcel of land to the north that shared a border with the trolls. Years ago, she'd won Prince Renic's hand in a competition called the Strife. They were engaged but had yet to marry. Rumors said he loved someone else. King Sidian was aging, and furious with the delay—the crown can't be passed down until the prince has his own heir. Either way, Lady Sarafine might be able to get close to Pata.

"You have to find her. See if you can trust her. We must have those keys," Lela said.

Oren met her gaze, wary. "This could all go so, so badly. You know that, right?"

"I know. I'm sorry for all I'm asking. I know it's too much. There's just no other way. If you've changed your mind, I understand." She wouldn't hold it against him. This was bigger than anything either of them had ever done, with the biggest consequences if it went wrong. They'd see it as treason. The punishment was death.

Oren's hands formed fists. "No, I'm in."

Lela smiled, gratitude filled her in such abundance it welled in her eyes. "Okay."

They spent the last of Oren's time going over the rough plan, but then he had to go.

"Meet me at sunset at the castle bridge. I can get you in the castle. And hopefully Lady Sarafine will give me the keys." He stepped down the loft ladder, pausing before disappearing. "Ricci doesn't look well, Lela. It's cold down there. Her uneaten food was covered in mold. Her teeth chattered like maybe she had a fever. I heard your pata speaking. They plan to torture her for information tomorrow." Disgust flickered over his face.

"The way they're treating her is wrong." Then he climbed down and was gone.

CHAPTER 23

L ela tried to prepare by resting—which she couldn't— and eating—which she had to force each bite. Her body was a bundle of nerves and fear. She was about to commit the biggest crime, second to opening the portal herself. Everything she'd been taught went against their plan, but everything she *knew* said it was the rightest thing she'd ever do.

What was the worth of her life if she didn't choose to do the right thing when it was within her power to do so? She'd reported Ricci before meeting her, and it was a mistake she couldn't live with.

Lela dressed in her newly-washed travel wear. The dark color and sturdy material would undoubtedly come in handy before the night was over. She stowed her pack in the barn—it was too big for a rescue mission—but stuffed her pockets with provisions in case they had to flee.

Alberry was the biggest city in the kingdom, so it was only natural to see people about even after dark. Long shadows bent and swayed from torches lining the gravel path as she headed to the bridge. Wide, with stone columns and wooden rails, it was a good meeting spot and the only way across Amelyn River to the castle.

Oren stood in the light of one of the torches flanking the bridge, like a halo behind his chiseled face, leaning casually against a column.

"You rock-head," she hissed. "This is a secret mission." She tugged him into the shadows off the road.

"Now you're the one being obvious," he said. "I'm off duty. On leave for the night. I need to be seen outside the castle, so the more people, the better."

"Oh." Heat flooded her cheeks, and she was glad of the dark. "What about the no-contact policy?"

"No one knows you. You could be just a girl I met." He shrugged. "This is a good spot, anyway. Ready?" Lela knew him too well to miss that he disguised his nerves as eagerness.

"I'm ready," she said. "Wait, did you get the key?"

He glanced back at the empty road. "I'll tell you on the way." He grabbed her hand and pulled her into a run.

Lela had only a moment to appreciate how he'd been the one to take her hand this time before they were flying down the hill toward the river. Thick piles of leaves exploded as they scrambled down the dark hill. Their passage was so loud, it might as well have been an alarm. But no one shouted. No one spotted them.

Moonlight lit the way as her eyes adjusted to the dark. Prisanthony and Pirus were in full force tonight. Their light glinted off the river ahead, which flowed swiftly and smoothly, and wide as wide can be.

"You didn't mention we wouldn't use the bridge. How in the valley's name are we going to cross that?" she panted.

Oren didn't answer, but when they reached the bottom of

the hill, he darted to a pillar. She squinted at the small boat tied along the bank.

"You've been busy," she said, impressed.

"This is always here. The guards use it to smuggle their mates in." He paused, and his eyes widened as if he realized what he'd implied about her. Suddenly untying the rope took all his focus. "We'll secure it on the other side and use it to make our escape if all goes well." He gestured her inside, and she complied, grabbing one of the oars.

The water splashed as her oar cut through the water. "And Lady Sarafine?"

"I found her," Oren said. "She said she needed time to get the key but she'd have it by tonight."

Lela's rowing faltered. "That sounds so suspicious. Do you trust her?" Maybe this was too big a risk to take.

He rubbed his neck. "I pretended to deliver her a letter—it was actually for your pata. When she noticed the mistake, I said how the letter must be about the portal opener and how they plan to torture her."

"And?" Lela's knuckles ached from gripping the oar so tightly.

"She casually asked about the human, so I told her the truth. She was irate to hear of Ricci's treatment—a reaction most would hide. So I felt her out some more. She grew suspicious of me, like she was nervous I'd report her for sympathizing with the human. So I told her our plan."

Lela's gasp echoed off the stone bridge above them. They'd nearly made it to the other side. "I knew you'd have to, but..." She willed her thumping heart to calm. So much risk.

"I know. The things I do for you." He shook his head, like he couldn't believe it himself, then grinned. "She was shocked at first, but then she locked her door and offered to help. She took the general's letter and planned to use it to get near the key."

Lela took a deep breath. "I want to hope she can be trusted, but this doesn't feel right. We have to find another way. Maybe I can use my energies to grow a vine and pick the lock." The boat ran aground, and Lela jumped out, avoiding the water. Yes, they were desperate, and yes, they were short on time, but could they trust a *lady* of the court?

"That will work for her cell, but not the spelled manacles. We need that key." Oren splashed into the shallow water, tied off the boat, then led her up the shore until they were away from the main castle gate. "This is the hard part."

She followed his gaze up the hill to the base of the castle, where impenetrable walls and dozens of guards stood in their way.

Lela nodded. She was ready.

Oren rubbed the back of his neck. "Er, we'll have to act like mates, in case we're seen."

Lela's mouth curved into a grin, reveling in his embarrassment and using it to keep the fear at bay. "How do mates act?" She batted her eyelashes. "I'm not of age, so I don't know what love is."

Oren rolled his eyes. "Come on." He took her arm, and they trudged up the hill to the castle.

It all looked the same—just one endless, dark, towering wall of stone with jutting turrets—but Oren seemed to be heading in a specific direction, so she kept quiet and allowed him to lead.

Their boots shuffled over grass and dirt, the noise easily covered by the gurgling river. Insects chirped, fleeing the diving bats that darted across a sky full of stars. Lela and Oren followed the wall as it seemed to curve, though it was hard to tell.

Oren stopped and pushed her against the wall. Hands on either side of her face, he grinned a predatory grin.

"What in the valley are you—?"

"Sorry about this." His lips crushed her mouth, and his body pressed against hers. Lela's eyes went wide. Her arms automatically wrapped around him—she'd longed for this. And then she noticed the torchlight. Someone was on the wall above them. Watching them.

No! This couldn't be her first kiss. Stars, was Oren really this bad of a kisser? Like a fish gasping for air out of water. Still, the butterflies roared deafeningly in her ears. He kept moving his head side to side. Should she move hers too? *Ugh.* She was just standing there. Like a statue.

Oren abruptly pulled away. He took her arm and pulled her along. Not a word. Not a glance. Their onlooker must have moved on. She roughly wiped spit from her mouth.

That had gone so badly. How many times had she dreamed of kissing him, having his arms around her?

"You're really bad at that," she said. Not like she'd been much better, but still.

He snorted. "That wasn't a kiss. That was an act. When I kiss you properly, you'll know it."

Her core thrummed and melted.

Fine, so that didn't count. Done.

Did he mean to one day kiss her properly, then?

Ugh, *focus.* Ricci needed them. They were no help to her if caught and hung for treason for daydreaming about the perfect first kiss.

Oren stopped and knocked on the wall. Lela noticed the outline of a doorway just as it opened, and a menacing guard stuck his head out.

The guard wordlessly looked them over, examining Lela from head to toe. Oren pulled her closer. The guard moved aside to let them in. The small room was dimly lit, with scant furniture, but they didn't stay long. They quickly passed from room to hall to room. Lela became dizzyingly lost. Whatever guards they passed gave them a quick glance and then ignored them.

"I thought we weren't supposed to be seen in the castle," she dared to whisper as they passed through an empty hall-way. "Won't you be recognized?"

"I haven't been training that long," he said. He opened a door and led her through it. "Still better not to be seen."

The room had a single bed, a chair, and nothing more. A faint scent of mildew and staleness blanketed the air.

Oren closed the door behind him. His cheeks blazed red.

Lela's jaw hung in surprise. "I'm your mate." Oh, stars, that didn't come out right. "I mean, that's why we're in here. To pretend so the guards won't question my being here."

"Yes." Oren backed into the corner, as far away as possible. As if she might get the wrong idea. "It's already late. We shouldn't have to wait long. Just long enough to make it believable." He coughed and looked away.

Lela sat on the edge of the chair, having no idea how long 'long enough' would be. Neither of them touched the bed. Silence stretched on between them.

"When are we meeting Lady Sarafine?" she asked to break the tension.

Oren jumped at the loudness after so much quiet. "Soon. After we meet her, we'll go see Ricci." He looked away. "Some of the guards accept bribes, you know, to see the human."

Lela gaped, aghast. Nausea washed over her. Ricci was nothing but a freak show to them. Did her pata know about this?

"I'm sorry, Lela. None of us have ever seen a human before. We're just curious, that's all."

Lela shot to her feet. "You?"

Oren stepped toward her, hands raised. "No, of course not."

She shook her head, lip curled. "No, but you still justified their behavior. She's alone and scared, and you treat her like a wild animal." She held her stomach.

"Not me, okay?" Oren seized her hand. "I know her life matters."

Lela nodded and slowly sat back down again, pulling away from him. She couldn't expect him to understand completely. It was clear he didn't trust Ricci, the portal opener. But he was still here.

He straightened. "It's almost time. Are you ready?"

Nerves jangled around her heart. They had no choice. She'd wronged Ricci. Now maybe she could make it right. "Let's go save her."

CHAPTER 24

Oren took Lela's hand and led her out of the room. The hall was dark and empty. He dropped her hand.

Lela's lips thinned.

On silent feet, they made their way down the dim hall. Ahead of them, a guard turned the corner into their hall. Oren and Lela jumped into a darkened doorway, her heart skittering. The guard's head turned toward them as he passed. She pulled Oren to her, his body flush against hers, stone digging into her back. The guard passed without slowing.

"Quick thinking," Oren whispered. "It's best we aren't seen by too many people."

"Uh-huh." Lela's heart drummed to a new rhythm, his nearness claiming her.

"Let's go." He stepped away.

They wound through another maze of hallways and endless staircases, following their plan of pretending to make out in dark corners whenever they encountered any guards. If only they didn't have to pretend.

Eventually, he pulled her through a curtain and into an alcove so dark she couldn't see a thing. Oren stiffened at her side. A rustling sounded in front of them.

"How many guards are waiting to imprison me?" Lady Sarafine said, just a voice in the darkness.

"We're alone," Lela replied, finding her courage. "Are you?"

A jangle of a key ring. "Yes, but the human won't be for much longer. Hurry."

Oren grabbed it. "Thank you. Wait, there's only one." He tensed.

Lela grabbed his arm, tugging him back a step. "It's a trap." Her heart thundered in her ears.

"Shh, wait." Lady Sarafine stepped out of the shadows, hands up. Her thin, red dress pooled at her ankles, complimenting her elegant updo. "I couldn't get the key to her cell. It wasn't with the gold key. I tried, I promise."

Oren examined the gold key in his hand. "This is the real one."

"How much time do we have?" Lela asked. It would be faster to use the energies to pick the lock.

"Not enough to find a key to the girl's cell," Lady Sarafine said. "But I can help you." She glanced around nervously.

Lela watched her. "We don't need your help. And how would you get the key now if you couldn't before?" She narrowed her eyes. "Why are you really helping us?" This female would be the next queen. Why would she risk everything, unless she wasn't risking anything?

Lady Sarafine raised her chin. "I can't get the key, but I can portal you into Ricci's cell."

Oren and Lela gasped.

She was a portal opener.

"How is that possible?" Lela couldn't believe it. They'd been hunted into extinction since the prophecy.

"I'm done denying my gift." Lady Sarafine set her shoulders. "We don't have much time."

Relief and gratitude prickled Lela's eyes.

"She's right." Oren's voice rang hollow. Lela couldn't imagine what he was thinking.

"Can you portal us from here?" Lela asked.

Lady Sarafine shifted her stance. "I don't know how strong I'll be."

"Then we'll go to her." Oren led them from the alcove, and no guards waited with crossbows. They set off, hurrying. They left the more decorated part of the castle and crossed through a simple courtyard, empty of any shrubbery or statues, and entered a new door. There were more guards in this part of the castle. Lady Sarafine took the lead, and no one questioned their presence. Oren wrapped his arm around Lela, keeping her close. Keeping up the façade.

Lela could only hope her pata wasn't out strolling the halls. She was dying to ask Oren why in the valley couldn't they have found a secret passage or something, but she held her tongue. It wasn't worth being overheard.

Oren approached a guard at a desk, wordlessly passing him a shimmering jewel and pulling Lela closer.

"That won't be necessary," Lady Sarafine said, handing back Oren's payment. She faced the guard. "We wish to view the human."

The guard's lips thinned, but he nodded and gestured toward an open doorway.

They passed through and down another hall lined with cells, all the way to the very end where they descended yet another winding staircase. The unmistakable coughing of someone very sick echoed even up to the top of the stairs. Fae didn't sicken easily.

Lela pushed passed Lady Sarafine.

"What if someone is down there? Keep with our story." Oren reached for her, but she didn't slow, taking the stairs two at a time, winding down and down.

They finally hit the bottom where the endless coughing was. No one else stood in the antechamber lined with barred cells. The putrid scent of sickness slapped her in the face. Torture instruments lay on trays on display in front of the only cell lit with torches.

Lela ran, then gasped at the horror.

CHAPTER 25

Callen wiped the soot and ash from his robes as best he could before hopping into the carriage with his master. He'd explained what they could to Ricci's family—that the tracing spell had worked, but that they couldn't follow where Ricci had gone. Her mother had teared up, but then the family started into a frenzy of dismantling camp, determined to find her.

Master Marek had kept quiet, not mentioning anything about Ricci being in another realm, for which Callen was grateful. It would only worry them more when apparently nothing could be done.

Except that Callen didn't accept that. There was no way he could sit by and do nothing while Ricci was in danger.

The carriage bumped along, wheels grinding gravel behind the clopping of the horses' hooves. A cool breeze blew through the open windows, ruffling Callen's hair.

"Master, what if we found a way to use the trace as a kind of tether, a way to stream our magic into their world? Maybe we could transport ourselves that way, somehow, or maybe use magic to help Ricci." So many things became possible with magic, and there were so many things Callen didn't know yet. Maybe he'd find that one thing that would trigger an idea or a yes from his master.

"Won't work." Master Marek didn't look at him. "There is no way to reach another realm without a portal. For a lifetime, I've tried."

Callen sighed. That was the third idea his master had declined since they'd left the market. It was a stretch, of course. Callen had collected the blob of trace potion carefully into an empty glass jar he'd found in his master's bag, though his master said it was useless and not to bother. But when Callen opened his magic, he still felt Ricci on the other side—like a teasing caress, the warmth coming close but not quite touching his skin. She was still alive, and he wouldn't give up on her.

He was still wracking his brain for new ideas when they stopped in front of the mage building.

Master Marek grabbed his wrist. "Your leave is over. Your personal belongings will be removed from the inn to your father's where you may sleep, but you will accompany me in my tasks here. And you will say nothing of the teleporter." He squeezed hard, then let go. "This is the discovery of the ages, but we don't have proof yet. The pair of us will be taken for fools if we spout off our mouths now."

He'd stay anywhere but his father's estate. "I won't say anything." *Unless saying something will help Ricci.*

"Good. Your future as a mage depends on it. Let's go. I am very late to a council meeting."

Callen spoke fast. "They might discuss the teleporter. They might even have new details. If I accompany you, I can use the information to be of better help." He held his breath. Anything might be vital to help find Ricci. The discovery of a way to open portals wasn't as important as her safety.

His master gave the barest of nods, and they hurried to the council room deep in the heart of the mage building. Normally, apprentices weren't invited until they were much further along in their apprenticeship. Master Marek was rewarding him for finding proof of the teleporter. Excitement had him outpacing his master.

Junior mages opened the doors, exchanging glances as Callen followed his master in. Callen had always been fascinated by what went on in this secret room. They walked through a dark hall which finally opened into an imposing room with a checkered floor encircled by tiered seating full of mages. So much power held in one room. He'd never seen so many gathered in one place and couldn't help but stare. In purple robes, the council sat in the front row with the high master in white. All the others in the room wore blue. Callen was the only apprentice, his black robe a clear sign he didn't belong. Even that couldn't ruin this moment for him.

The mages cast him irritated looks as he took a seat on the second row, just behind his master. They'd interrupted the speaker in the middle of talking about a proposed amendment to rule such-and-such which would alleviate the need for such-and-such permission when aid was needed during a crisis in the kingdom. Or something. He tried to pay attention, but he was too busy wondering if they would talk about Ricci.

The speaker stumbled over a few more sentences before he drew to an awkward close, unnerved by the interruption. Another mage took a spot in the middle of the circle. Callen recognized him as Master Finch, one of the leaders of the mage council.

"Thank you, Master Banton. We will put the matter to a vote at the next meeting. Now that Master Marek has arrived, we can speak to the rumors of an occurrence in the market this morning."

Muttering rippled up and down the tiers. Callen gripped his knees. How much of what they heard would point to Ricci as the one to cast the spell, and not the man in black? The council would take over her life if they knew the truth. If she ever came back.

"Master Tuttleston?" Finch gestured beside him in invitation. Another mage on the leadership council stood and joined him.

"Yes, we're all glad you could finally join us." Tuttleston pressed his lips into a line. "What we've heard—from many sources at this point—is that a portal has indeed been opened. The gift of the Nether Realms is real." He smiled as the room erupted into conversation. "And I have discovered the portal opener."

Master Marek tensed.

Callen's brow creased.

Tuttleston took a piece of parchment from inside his robes and held it up. "A girl by the name of Ricika Menowin applied at this very building and was approved for a magic permit. That permit granted her permission to perform illusions for her traveling troupe." He tucked the paper away. "This morning, she disappeared and hasn't returned."

"That only proves what we already know," Callen said, somehow having found his way to his feet. All eyes swiveled to him. "That she's a powerful illusionist."

"Sit down," Master Marek hissed.

"You dare interrupt your betters?" Tuttleston asked.

"I was there this morning. It wasn't Ricci who cast the spell. It was the man who took her to another place." Callen prayed they'd believe him.

Was it only this morning?

191

Tuttleston and Finch's eyes landed on Master Marek. "And when were you going to tell us your own apprentice was an eyewitness to the event?" The gloating flowed off Tuttleston like a stench.

Right, Callen wasn't supposed to mention anything. To anyone. He slowly took his seat, wishing he could hide beneath it. Standing there, speaking to the council, was something Callen had only dreamed of one day being important and powerful enough to do. Except the circumstances were all wrong. He should be in a place of honor as a full mage, not someone to be ignored.

Callen didn't look up as his master took a place in the middle of the circle. "While you were busy taking credit for my discovery, I was busy discovering it." He circled the room, looking each mage in the eye as he spoke, taking true command of the room, unlike the previous two speakers. "My apprentice and I are investigating the source of the magic. When we find the portal opener, the council will be the first to know."

Nose in the air, Tuttleston took his seat. The meeting droned on for a while longer, but there was no more mention of portals. If anyone was capable of finding a way to help Ricci, it would be this room full of the world's most powerful mages. Callen itched to speak again, to convince them Ricci wasn't the portal opener. The words waited for the right moment, but the moment never came. He was in enough trouble as it was.

Afterward, he silently followed his master back to the office. Inside, he shut the door softly. Maybe if his master forgot he existed—which clearly a softly closing door could accomplish—he wouldn't get in trouble.

When Callen turned back around, Master Marek was right there, in his face. Rage burned in his eyes. Callen jumped, back hitting the door.

"You brainless imbecile," he roared. "I told you to say nothing at all. Nothing!" He stomped to his desk. "You told them everything. Let them think the girl is the portal opener if they want to. There was no need to give them any more information than they already had. None!"

"I'm sorry, Master. You're right." But he'd do it again if his outburst convinced the council Ricci wasn't the portal opener.

Callen understood his master's possessive need to claim this discovery, but now that everyone knew about it, why not work together? He kept his lips shut tight.

Someone knocked on the door. Callen spun to answer it, grateful for the interruption.

A young page held out a note. Callen took it, but his master snatched it out of his hand.

"Ha! You've been summoned for an interview with High Master Aldridge," he sneered on the name, "to testify of your first-hand account of the portal opening. Alone." He lit the letter on fire with magic in his palm, and it burned up in moments. His master turned over his hand, letting the black ash dust the polished floor. "Remember, apprentice. This is my discovery."

"I know, Master." Callen fumbled for the door, afraid to turn his back lest he end up in flames as well. He'd never spoken directly to the high master, but his nerves couldn't be stretched any thinner.

He hurried down the hall back to the council room. Only one mage remained, High Master Aldridge, head of the council. Though it was hard to tell how old he was—the ones with the most magic tended to age a bit slower—he was the youngest ever to hold the position. It was a source of contention for Master Marek, who'd been a close second in the vote, and was even younger than Aldridge—though you couldn't tell by looking at him. The high master held the position until their death.

"Callen, take a place in the center." He smiled beneath dark eyebrows and black hair parted sleekly down the middle. "The discovery of a portal opener is big news in our circle, as you know. The ability has never been seen before, at least not that the history books would have you believe. But our own sources have long memories."

"Yes, High Master." Callen's master had hinted as much whenever Callen questioned the practicality of attempting to brew a portal-opening potion.

High Master Aldridge leaned forward. The sleeves of his white robe spilled over the table in front of him. "Tell me what you witnessed this morning."

Callen took a deep breath, bracing himself to not say more than he should, and recounted his version of the story just as he had to Master Marek, keenly aware of the magical intent he felt in the room. Like a faint hum buzzing his insides, but only when he thought of it. The high master cast some kind of spell as Callen spoke, but he couldn't tell what it was for. He had his suspicions, though. Truth finding.

He slowed his words, careful not to rush as his nerves jolted. If the high master detected a lie, everything Callen had worked for would be in jeopardy. They could strip him of his apprenticeship.

The magic ratcheted as he reached the part about the man appearing on stage. Everything he'd said so far had been the truth, but the magic sensed the lie he'd formed in his mind, even before it left his lips. It prodded against him like a fox ready to pounce. Sweat beaded his upper lip.

"The man had a sword. Ricci didn't see him." How was he going to tell the lie? Words became sparse as his focus split into two directions. "I sensed something was wrong. I cried out to warn her." Callen called up his magic, easing back a bit when the high master's brow furrowed. "He grabbed her from behind and put a sword to her throat." Callen slowly shaped the magic to form a barrier of protection, something he'd only studied until now. "I readied lightning to strike him. The audience thought it was part of the show." The vibrating pressure of the high master's magic vanished. "Then the man closed the portal. They disappeared, blood trickling down her throat." He stared without seeing as the horror and helplessness of that moment consumed him.

The heaviness of the magic lifted from the room, and the breath rushed from him. Had it worked?

"I was weighing your words for truthfulness, if you're curious to know, and I sensed something interesting." High Master Aldridge folded his hands.

"What's that?" Callen gulped.

"You care for the girl."

Relief rushed over him as heat brushed his cheeks. He'd lied under truth magic—to the *high master*. "I'm not sure."

"Perhaps your head has not caught up to your heart, but it matters not. You do care for her."

They barely knew each other, but Callen did care for her. From the instant she'd locked eyes with him in her moment of peril, it became more than just finding the girl with the gift of the Nether Realms. Even more than his lifelong dream of becoming a mage.

Callen raised his chin. "Yes, I do. And I want to help her. There has to be a way to bring her back."

High Master Aldridge stood. "But how? Only this fae can transport from realm to realm." He gave a warm smile that Callen couldn't interpret. Perhaps he was just humoring a young apprentice—if there was a way, the high master would know of it.

"Master Marek said it was impossible," Callen said, shoulders hunching.

"Nothing is impossible. I want to hear what ideas you have. The minds of youth, they are free from our prejudice and rules. Free to think in ways that we simply cannot." He nodded his encouragement. "Please."

Callen blinked. He'd never expected the head of the council to be so kind. Wise, yes, but not kind and patient, unlike Master Marek who was so cross all the time.

Callen finally returned the smile. "If we can trace the magic to this other world, then maybe we can do other things with that link, too."

"Yes, Callen. Good." The high master clapped. "So you've traced the magic to the portal opener in the other realm then." He raised an eyebrow.

Callen's mouth parted. Did the high master know he'd lied? Or had he already suspected Ricci was the portal opener? And if he did? He seemed kind, but would he use Ricci for her gift, or tell others who might do the same?

"Yes, I traced the magic to the portal opener," Callen said.

"The portal opener being Ricci, right?" High Master Aldridge winked. "Don't worry, apprentice. It's right that the council should know."

Callen's heart thundered as he quickly weighed his options. Did the high master really know he'd lied, or was he trying to trap him? If he lost his apprenticeship, he'd be no help to Ricci and he might be her only chance. But if he stuck to the lie and the high master believed him, they'd be trying to track the wrong person, and what good would that do?

"Yes, it's Ricci. I'm sorry. I suppose it's too much to ask that we keep it between us?" Callen asked.

"For now," the high master said carefully. His smile was

long gone, but he didn't seem angry over the lie. "Yes. Let's not tell anyone just yet."

Callen's shoulders slumped. He was just bumbling his way through life, aiming for these high goals and failing at every one of them.

Master Marek was going to kill him—if the high master didn't get to it first. "My master and I performed the tracing spell at the stage. That's the real reason we were late to the meeting." But he'd left the tracing potion blob in the bag in Master Marek's office. "Can an active tracing spell do more than trace when it's between realms?" His words hung hopeful in the air between them.

The high master stepped toward the exit. "Maybe? We know so little about the gift of the Nether Realms, but nothing is impossible. Let's find your girl." He smiled.

A weight lifted off Callen's shoulders, just a bit. The high master wanted to help, though it seemed impossible that the head of their order would bother. Why would he? But Callen would take it. It was the best shot he had.

CHAPTER 26

The manacles clinked, cutting against Ricci's festering wrists as she sipped the last drops of mildewed water. Grit crunched between her teeth, and she was glad it was too dark to see inside the tiny cup. At least they still bothered to give her any liquid at all.

But, of course, a dead prisoner couldn't give them their answers. Not that she could either. She knew nothing of her gift—curse—other than that she could perform it. The more ill she became, the more humorous the situation was. *They* feared *her*. Somehow, her ability made her a threat. Maybe she'd jump at them next time they came and see what they did.

Ricci laughed mirthlessly, which dissolved into a wet, wracking cough. When it finally subsided, her lungs burned. She lay on the cool stones, and they poked her cheek as she pressed her feverish skin into them.

Three pairs of legs stood at her cell door.

She pushed up and crawled back to her corner.

"Ricci," someone sobbed, bending down to the ground. She reached for her through the bars. "I'm so sorry. Please be okay."

Ricci peeked from behind her knees. The fae girl stretched her hand even further, face shadowed by torchlight. The fae boy beside her wore a sickened expression that crinkled his bright blue eyes. Behind them, Lady Sarafine wrung her hands, glancing back and forth at the stairs.

"Ricci, it's me. We're going to save you." The girl's long silver hair slipped over her shoulder as she reached.

"Lela." Ricci's voice croaked out, hoarse from her illness. Hope bloomed like sunshine.

"Yes." Lela smiled through her tears. "And this is my friend, Oren."

Oren stopped just before putting his hand on Lela. "We have to hurry. Lady Sarafine, portal us in."

Was this a trick? Were they even really standing here?

"I've never done it before," Lady Sarafine said, her cool confidence broken. "Only seen it done. But I'll try."

None of what they were saying made any sense. Ricci focused on Lela. "You betrayed me." A weighty statement of fact that had replayed in her mind a hundred times, but it came out with less heat than she'd put behind it because of her weakness.

"I didn't mean to," Lela said, sobbing. "When I reported the portal opening, I didn't know you. But I'm here now, trying to fix it."

Ricci coughed, holding her chest to contain the pain. Lela had come for her.

Oren's gaze flicked to Lela. "You are fixing it. You're here." His tone changed. "Do it now, my lady."

His brief glance told Ricci everything she needed to know. This handsome fae would crawl over hot coals for Lela if she asked.

Her addled mind thought of Callen jumping on the stage.

Lady Sarafine took a deep breath, and the air buzzed with the feel of magic. The forms of the three fae turned hazy.

Ricci gaped. Lady Sarafine could open portals.

Ricci shot up, room spinning dangerously fast. "Close it fast. The gongs."

Lady Sarafine's eyes went wide, then scrunched in concentration. The fae disappeared from in front of the cell and reappeared inside.

Lela threw herself to Ricci. "I'll make it right. I promise." She wrapped warm arms around her and gasped. "Oren, she's burning up." She held a hand to Ricci's forehead.

"Burning up? It's so cold in here." Ricci shivered. She couldn't stop staring at Lady Sarafine. This was real. Another portal opener. She was being rescued.

"Why would you help me?" Ricci asked.

"For your mata. She helped me once when I didn't deserve it."

Ricci gasped, blinking. "How do you know my mama?"

"You look like her." Lady Sarafine glanced up, brow creasing. "You look like him, too."

"How do you know my parents?"

"There's no time. Hurry," Oren said, watching the stairs.

"Here." Lela handed Ricci a waterskin.

The slosh of water took over all thought. Ricci snatched it and drank deeply of the cool, clean liquid. It flowed over her dry tongue and throat. The worst of the achiness eased from her joints and limbs.

Lela tugged it away before Ricci was ready. "Not too much all at once. There's yarrow and willow in there." She handed Ricci something green and leafy. "Eat that."

Ricci didn't care what it was. It was fresh and edible. She stuffed it in her mouth and chewed.

Oren produced a single key from within his guard uniform. Ricci dared to hope it was the right key.

"It's thrumming," Lela said.

Ricci felt... something—now that Lela mentioned it. Some kind of power that tied it to the manacles somehow.

"How did you get this?" Ricci asked. "The general had this key." Lela's father.

Oren gestured behind him as he reached for the manacles.

"Lady Sarafine." Ricci owed gratitude to the strange fae all over again. Would Mama remember helping her? "Thank you."

Lady Sarafine gave a small nod. "Our gifts are powerful. They were once celebrated. They should be so again."

The first manacle hissed and then clicked open. The weight dropped off Ricci's wrist like a ton of stone. Ricci and Lela gasped. Oren winced.

Her wrist was raw and oozing. Ricci had almost forgotten the pain, but the fresh air sent it stinging. Tendrils of red traveled up her arm.

Lady Sarafine turned away.

"This is bad, Ricci." Lela immediately rummaged in her pockets for more supplies. She lathered on ingredients that burned, then cooled. She kissed Ricci's brow as Oren unlocked the other manacle. The metal slipped off, and Oren caught it before it clanged to the floor.

Like a great boulder had been removed, a crushing weight lifted off Ricci. She immediately took a deep, filling breath. Strength trickled back into her. Depression loosened its devastating grip. She hadn't realized how badly the manacles' magic had affected her until now that it was gone.

Footsteps sounded from up the stairwell.

Ricci froze.

"They can't find an empty cell." Oren stepped over to Lady

Sarafine, pocketing the key. "Get us out of here. Ricci, use your portal once we're gone."

Lela squeezed her arm. "Wait as long as you can. Give us a head start."

"Hurry." Lady Sarafine and Oren had already turned hazy.

Lela rushed to them, and they disappeared, reappearing outside the cell. Panic seized Ricci's throat. She was alone again, locked inside the cell. She stretched her arms, reminding herself she could. *Breathe.*

"Time's up, my lady," the guard called from the bottom of the stairs.

Ricci silently slid the manacles back around her wrists, being careful not to latch them. She slunk back to her corner.

"Did you enjoy the show?" The guard looked Lela up and down.

Ricci couldn't see Lela's expression, but Oren hurried her along, saying, "It's not every day you get to see a human."

Ricci shuddered. She'd seen fae come and go, but she'd hidden in her corner, ignoring them outside of how she might use them to escape.

The guard followed behind as the three of them ascended the stairs.

Then Ricci was alone.

No, not alone. They'd given her a gift. Her freedom. She slipped the manacles back off her wrists and reached for her magic, pulling it toward her like an old friend.

But something was wrong. The magic didn't fill her like before. Gone was the depth she remembered. Like drawing water from a well, hauling a heavy bucket, only to find the barest of drops at the bottom.

The manacles had drained her. How long would it take to build back up enough to get her home? But Lela had said to wait. She and Oren needed time. Time to get away, time to cover their tracks.

How much time was enough?

Ricci huddled in her shawl, wishing for more of Lela's warmth and kindness. Lela hadn't betrayed her after all.

After a few minutes, she tested her magic again. There was barely anything there—just a sliver.

A portal wouldn't open. How much time before the general made good on his promise?

CHAPTER 27

After Lady Sarafine left them without a word, Lela and Oren hurried away from Ricci's cell and back into the main castle as quick as they could, hiding in the shadows and stopping to fake-kiss when necessary. Any minute now, Ricci would open a portal. The alarm would sound, and there'd be no escaping.

Lela's stomach roiled at the haunting images of Ricci and the state they'd found her in. Injured. Starving. Sick. Under-dressed with no blankets or bedding of any kind. Put on display like some kind of wild beast—worse.

Her own pata! How could he treat anyone this way, even a prisoner? It sickened Lela to her very core. Her vision swam with red.

"Hurry," Oren said as she followed him through empty hallways and winding staircases.

It was still dark outside, no hint of sunrise through the windows they passed. The shadows aided their escape.

They turned a corner, and the sound of several voices

flooded the hall. Oren pulled Lela into an alcove behind a curtain just in time.

"What if she won't give us anything new?" someone asked.

"Then you know what we have to do."

Pata. She stepped to the curtain and peeked out. Pata walked ahead of the group, expression stern and set. Two of the men behind him weren't guards.

Lela gasped. Torturers.

Pata went to torture Ricci. And she hadn't left yet.

A strong hand clamped around her arm. Oren dragged her into the shadows, covering her mouth just as Pata jerked to a stop, turning toward her.

She held her breath.

"General?" someone asked.

Lela's heart pounded. Had he seen her?

"It's nothing," Pata said.

Their footsteps trailed away.

"Let go," Lela whispered behind Oren's hand. She squirmed in his firm grip.

"Do you promise to stay quiet and hidden?" he said, irritated.

Lela bit his hand. He squeaked and let go, shaking his arm.

"I was being quiet. I wasn't going to do anything," she hissed, though it'd surely crossed her mind.

"Didn't look that way to me," Oren retorted, eyes narrowed. "We have to go."

"My own Pata is about to torture my friend for information she doesn't have to give!" And she couldn't do a thing about it. Attempting to stop him would only create more problems.

Oren waved his hands, urging her to be quiet, though she hadn't raised her voice above a whisper. "She'll open a portal any minute, and we must be gone when she does." He checked the hall, then left without waiting for her.

Lela gritted her teeth and followed. They ran through the remainder of the castle, the surroundings looking more familiar as they approached the secret door in the outside wall. The same burly guard that let them in opened the door to let them out with a lopsided smirk and a wink at Oren. Lela rolled her eyes.

Oren grabbed her waist for show, but something was missing this time. There had been a hint of warmth when he'd touched her before, but now it'd gone cold.

He didn't speak as they jogged their way back to the bridge. The boat waited where they'd left it. Oren untied it without looking at her.

"What's wrong?" she finally asked. She knew him too well to overlook his behavior.

He looked at her like she'd lost her mind. "We just released a human who's supposed to be the most dangerous enemy our world has ever known. We haven't even escaped yet. There's a very slim chance we don't get caught anyway. And you ask what's wrong? Get in the boat."

Her lips thinned. She stood her ground. "All that was true before, but you would still look at me. Why won't you now?"

"You bit me," he muttered.

Of all the things to be upset about? "Ha! Wasn't the first time. Probably won't be the last."

That should have made him smile, but instead, he said, "You're such a child."

Her face burned like he'd slapped her. She put a hand on her cheek to ease the phantom pain.

Oren studied her, gaze dipping to her lips parted in hurt, and his eyes softened. "I don't give a fig about my life," he said, "but you might have been seen. I couldn't stand to see you hurt. How can you be so reckless?"

"Oh." Understanding chased the pain away. He didn't care

that she'd bitten him. He didn't care that she'd dragged him into her foolish plan. He cared about *her*.

Their eyes locked. Her heart skipped. Shivers danced over her skin and into her chest when he didn't look away. The moons cast light over his perfect features, the fullness of his mouth, the set of his jaw. Time could freeze and she'd be happy for eternity, locked here in this moment with him.

The gongs rang, the sound slamming into them at this close range.

They weren't the gongs of a portal being opened. They were an alarm—a call to arms.

CHAPTER 28

The magic wouldn't come. A portal wouldn't open. Tears slid down Ricci's cheeks as she stared at her upturned, bleeding wrists. "Why isn't it working?" Panic rose into her throat, choking her.

The stomping of boots sent her scrambling for the manacles. She slipped them on, praying to the Gods that they had to be latched to work.

The general and his two torturers approached, along with a few guards. His downturned eyes and the set of his mouth made him look almost regretful. "Time's up."

The torturers stepped forward, and Ricci understood. They were here for her.

She plunged into her magic. *Work work work.* It came to her call, but nothing happened.

The general cocked his head. Could he sense what she was doing? Was that something fae could do?

"Do you have anything you'd like to tell us?" he asked.

Work, please work. Sweat poured down Ricci's face.

The general nodded to the torturers. They bent down to collect their shiny instruments.

"Open it," he said.

Two of the guards unlocked her cell door.

"Bring her." His dark command was the axe on the chopping block.

The guards hauled her out of the tiny cell, and she struggled to keep the manacles from slipping off. No one noticed in this dim light that they weren't latched. They shoved her, and Ricci cried out in pain as her knees cracked against the stone floor.

One of the torturers dangled a metal device in the shape of a boot in front of her.

"This is called a foot press," the torturer said. He opened its hinges, and the inside was covered in thin spikes.

Ricci shook uncontrollably.

The guards tightened their grip on her arms while the torturer grabbed her bare foot. She kicked violently, but they squeezed her to the point of pain.

The torturer smiled. "This tightens slowly until either you give us answers, or your bones are pulverized."

A guttural moan escaped her lips. She thrashed, no longer caring if her manacles gave her away. *Work, damn you!*

The general watched on, arms crossed over his chest, as the torturer fit the device over her foot.

She kicked, and spikes buried into her skin.

Ricci stilled her thrashing and screamed.

"We haven't even started yet," the torturer said.

"All we want is the truth, and then this can stop," the general said.

She pleaded with her magic, digging with all her might for every last scrap. *Help me!*

A warmth broke through her primal fear, like a scarce ray of sunshine amid a raging storm. It wasn't her magic. It was a person.

Callen?

Her fear cleared away, just for an instant. Her magic hadn't abandoned her.

The torturer turned the crank, tightening the piece that would crush her foot.

Ricci gritted her teeth and glared at the general. "I will not be your prisoner."

He tracked the movement as she twisted her wrists, letting the manacles clatter to the ground.

Her well was full enough. She drew from it. *Home. Callen.* Quicker than ever before, the room went opaque, overlapping with a different room in a different world.

The guards dropped her, quaking in fear.

"Stop her!" the general yelled.

With a burst of concentration, he was gone. The dungeon and the darkness and the torturers and the horror disappeared.

She squinted into the bright light of the new room, clean and fresh, wood and marble.

Callen stood in front of her, eyes wide. "Ricci." He bent down to her, and she collapsed, sobbing, into his arms.

She was home. She was safe.

CHAPTER 29

The call-to-arms rang out like a building storm.

Heart pounding, Lela jumped into the boat. Oren shoved off the shore hard before hopping in, giving them a fast start. Shouting rose above the rushing water, loud in the briefest of pauses between the ear-splitting gongs.

Had Pata noticed the missing key? Ricci hadn't opened a portal yet. Had she been discovered?

"We have to go back, Oren." Lela stopped rowing. "We have to help her."

Oren glanced at the castle battlements, now teeming with soldiers. "There's nothing more we can do for her."

Lela continued rowing, guilt burning her insides. She should have stopped her pata, delayed him somehow.

Before they reached the other side, warriors with torches streamed out of the castle gates. Lela's heart sped tenfold.

Oren grabbed her hand as they ran aground. "This is where we part ways. Keep to the shadows. Don't let yourself be seen by anyone. Leave town now and go straight home."

His commands chafed, but she didn't argue. If he got

caught, he had an alibi. If she got caught, Pata would know, and both she and Oren would suffer. "What will you do?"

"I'm just a warrior out on leave, racing to get back to my post." He smirked, then grabbed her in a tight hug.

She melted into him, but he let go too soon.

"Good luck," he said, then dashed away, leaving her cold and alone in the shadows. At the top of the hill, he joined another group of warriors racing across the bridge back toward the castle.

She prayed to the stars he'd be okay. That they both would.

CHAPTER 30

Ricci had never felt such comfort in her life. She stretched her legs and reached with her arms and still couldn't touch the edge of the bed. Soft sheets caressed her skin. The mattress pillowed around her, cocooning her aching body in a warm cloud. The air smelled of lemon and laundered linens. Unpolluted. Clean.

This was not her bed, nor was this a cell in a dark dungeon. The room oozed luxury, with thick, heavy draperies and a fireplace glinting with gold gilding and marble. The flames cast plenty of light in the otherwise dark room. It was sometime in the middle of the night.

Was this a fever dream?

Her wrists and calf were bandaged, and she wore a soft cotton nightgown.

"You're awake." Relief coated Callen's voice.

Ricci squeaked, pulling the covers to her chin. Callen sat in an armchair beside the bed. He poured her a glass of water. Tangled thoughts of this boy and where she was mixed around in her head. How did she get into this nightgown?

She seized the glass from his hand, drinking in big eager gulps that dripped off her chin until the glass was drained.

Callen accepted it back, anguish on his face. "You were gone three weeks," he said. "I did everything I could to find you."

She met his eyes, heat touching her cheeks.

He didn't refill her glass but instead passed her a bowl of broth. "It's cold now," he said apologetically.

She didn't bother with a spoon, gulping it from the bowl as she had the water. Delicious.

"Where am I?" She settled back against the pillows again.

"You're in the high master's house. High Master Aldridge of the mage council. We didn't know what to do when you arrived, so sick. We thought it best to bring you here. The physician saw you this morning. He said you're dehydrated and malnourished, but whoever salved your wrists must have a real talent for healing. The infection was gangrenous, but it's healing. Your coughing is subsiding too. And your fever broke while you slept."

"What about my family?"

"Your family has been sent word. They traveled on with the market, not knowing where you might be, but they are coming back now. They spread posters in every town trying to find you." He rubbed his hands together. "How could they have guessed you weren't in any town in Taunfalan?"

Ricci stared at the thick embroidered comforter, trying to take in his words. Her family was safe. She was safe. Callen was taking care of her. Lela had saved her.

"You found me, didn't you?" she asked. "How?"

"My master, Master Marek, is a very powerful mage. He formed a tracing spell."

She was grateful to this Master Marek.

"But I didn't sense anyone else," she said. "Only you. It was you I came back to."

Had that come out too strong? Her gaze shot to Callen, but he looked down at the bed, a slight smile on his lips.

"Yes, I was working on a way to follow the trace to come get you. The high master helped me with that part, for weeks. We never actually got it to work, so we were both surprised when you appeared." He chuckled. "I sensed you as well. You were frightened. I couldn't know what might be happening to you over there." He hesitated. "What are they like?"

Ricci shuddered. "They're soulless monsters with no morals." Guilt followed her hasty words. Not all of them were bad.

He reached and patted her hand, grief etched in his every feature. "I felt something was wrong on that stage. I *felt* it! But I waited to act until it was too late. When I saw him hold that sword to your throat." He shook his head, jaw clenched.

Ricci touched her long-healed neck where the blade had nicked her. "You couldn't have stopped him. He had an entire army waiting to take me." She squeezed her eyes, fruitlessly trying to drive out the memories that tore at her.

"Do you want to talk about it?" he asked, tentatively.

"No." Her hands trembled. "I want to forget that place ever existed. I'm going home to the way things used to be before this curse ever befell me." What once had been a blessing— earning money for her family, the key to her dream of performing for the king—now meant only pain.

"I know you've been through hell, but there's something I need to tell you," he said. "Portal opening," he began, as if he wasn't sure how to word what he wanted to say. "It's a rare gift. As in, you're the only one. In centuries. Even then, High Master Aldridge says no human could do it, that we relied on the fae."

She thought of Lady Sarafine. "I met a fae who can."

He raised an eyebrow. "I convinced most of the council that the soldier performed the magic, but the high master knows the truth. And even if he didn't, you're the only person to ever cross into another realm."

Ricci nodded, wondering what he was leading to. Whatever it was made her heart speed up. "He is a general, actually. Why tell them it was him?"

He rubbed the back of his neck, grimacing. "If others find out the truth, they will use you for your gift." He paused. "There will be an inquisition before you're allowed to go. They will question what you saw, what you know."

"What?" She threw the covers off and slid to the edge of the bed. Not another inquiry. "They cannot keep me here against my will." She stood, and the room spun. "Where are my clothes?" Right. The linen sack and an elegant, filthy shawl were long gone. She stumbled.

"Whoa." Callen held out his arms to steady her. "I don't mean now. When you're well. Please, lay down. No one is forcing you to stay. You need to rest."

Ricci eased herself onto the bed—not because his words assured her, but because strength failed her.

Callen lowered his arms slowly, as if making sure she wasn't going to pass out first. Gratitude washed over her. He didn't owe her anything. Yet he was still helping her. He'd been on her mind the whole time she'd been gone.

"I don't agree to be questioned. I've had enough of that." Her voice wobbled. "Besides, what will they want to know?" The thought made her hands tremble. "I wish this curse had never come to me." The soft words were laced with pain and loathing. "I'll give it back to whichever God thought they'd play some cruel joke."

Callen sat in his chair, eyes never leaving her face, as if

afraid she might disappear again. The fire cast shadows over his face, showing stubble. "I wish you wouldn't see your magic as a curse. I know it's only brought you misery, but think of all the good it can bring as well. There is so much we can learn from people of another world. So much we can study and apply here to better our lives and our future. This could answer so many questions about what's out there, and why we haven't been able to accomplish this before. You could learn to go to other worlds besides theirs and ours." He shook his head. "See it that way, as a gift."

He was only curious, so she considered that there might be truth in what he said, but she didn't see it. She kept coming back to his use of the word 'people'. They weren't people. They were monsters.

"You don't understand, Callen." Her eyelids drooped, but she forced them open wide, sitting up. "Humans cursed them. We promised the end of their world if we ever found a way back to them. We don't remember because it was so long ago, but the fae live a long time. Some of them were around when this happened. And then I go and accidentally stumble into their backyard."

Callen watched her, fascinated. This must have been the first he'd heard any of this, or anything about the fae. Of course it was.

"They don't trust us. Me. They don't trust me. And I can't ever go back." She relaxed back into the pillows. "They have a special alarm. Magic designed just for me. And it alerts them if I open a portal there. I can't ever go back." She could almost feel the disappointment radiating off him.

A thought occurred to her. "What if the council asks how I got here? They'd never believe the soldier brought me back."

Callen rubbed his neck. "Umm. Well, how did you manage to get back?"

"I had help." She hoped Lela was okay.

"Staying as close to the truth as possible is best."

"I could say someone I befriended brought me back. Maybe they just wanted to learn about humans." It was weak, but hopefully believable.

Callen nodded. "It might work. Now, enough planning. Let's talk about something good. Tell me about your family." He smiled. "Your parents seem like nice people. Your dad sure gives good hugs."

Ricci brightened. "He gave you a hug?" She chuckled. "Gods, I miss them." What she wouldn't give for one of Papa's hugs right now. Her eyes welled.

"He nearly collapsed my lungs. They were ready to take on the world when you disappeared. Are all those men your siblings? I have a lot of siblings too." He moved to sit beside her on the bed.

Ricci smiled, touched. It was so easy to be herself around him. He'd known just when to change the conversation to put her at ease. "Just three of them. The loudest, slobbiest ones."

They swapped older-sibling stories, laughing until Ricci couldn't keep her eyes open anymore. Callen kissed her hand before he left. The thrilling feel of his lips followed into her dreams.

CHAPTER 31

The sun had risen when Ricci next woke. The room was empty, the fire burned out. She stretched, and the achiness was gone. Her head didn't spin, chest no longer tight, and breathing came easy. Her health was almost back to normal. But she'd never be the same. Her time in the dungeon wrapped around her like a second, dark skin. It brought stinging tears to her eyes and uncontrollable shaking whenever she thought of it. And every thought led back to that wretched place.

Someone knocked at the door.

She marveled at the courtesy. No one knocked at home, and if they did, they never waited for an answer.

The person knocked again.

"Come in," she called.

The door opened, and she sat up in surprise. This was not the attractive apprentice she'd come to look forward to. He was a middle-aged man with a warm smile, black, parted hair, and crisp, white robes.

"You're looking much better today," he said, closing the door and taking Callen's armchair.

She'd never met this man before, yet he acted as if they were lifelong friends. She didn't trust him.

He chuckled. "I was there when you teleported from the fae world." His smile disappeared. "You were very ill. They didn't treat you well over there, did they." A statement instead of a question.

"No," she answered anyway, hate and disgust behind the single word.

He shook his head. "I'm High Master Aldridge, head of the mage council."

"Oh, this is your house," she said with a bit of surprise. She should have guessed.

"Yes, and you're a welcome guest as long as you need. I must say, I'm excited to finally meet you properly. Your abilities are extraordinary. The entire magical community is abuzz with news about the portal opener. Someone finally exists who can bridge between worlds." He shook his head, amazement etched into his lined face and shining eyes.

Ricci stared at the covers wishing she could crawl under them and hide forever.

"Don't worry. Only two of us know that the portal opener is you."

She studied him, and he winked. What was his game? Why help her? Was he one of the people Callen had warned her about? Someone to use her for her gift?

"Callen told me what you said about this supposed curse we put on the fae so long ago. It's not true. There is no magic that can curse an entire realm to its doom. But, of course, a species with such long memories will believe in all kinds of lore and prophecies. You can see why they would react the way they did."

It did seem far-fetched that she could be the sole cause of their demise.

"Why are you telling me all this?" The words came out ruder than intended—he was helping her recover, after all—but none of that mattered. This was the mages' world, and she didn't belong in it. She was going home and never looking back.

"Your inquisition is today, and you need to be armed with as much knowledge as possible."

She gasped.

"Now, now. It will be alright. I will help you. You must answer their questions truthfully, but do nothing to lead them to believe you're the portal opener. It was all the soldier in black—the general. It's the only way you'll be free to return to your normal life."

She blinked up at him. Could his help be genuine?

He smiled kindly again, patting her hand. "Yes, I do want to help you. The way some would use you, after everything you've been through, is no life for anyone, especially a girl your age. If we can convince them, fully, that you're not the portal opener, then you'll be free to go. And you can come back when and if you're ever ready to share your gift with the world."

"Thank you," she said softly. She wanted to believe him—what he promised sounded so easy—but she didn't. He was the head of the council. His goals served the mages. "But what if I refuse this inquisition? The fae questioned me relentlessly. I'm not ready to live through that again." She hid her trembling hands in her lap.

"You've been through a lot. But I'm afraid it will only arouse more suspicion if you refuse. This is the chance to clear your name." He squeezed her hand. "Now let's get you dressed." He pulled a cord by her bed, and the door immediately opened, letting in a handful of female servants. "Ready her for the inquisition, please," he said, standing. He left with a parting smile.

Ricci watched after him. She could leave now without even getting out of bed. But she wouldn't touch her magic ever again. If this was what it took to be done and put this horror behind her, so be it.

Ricci and the servants—four in all—stared at each other for half a breath before the servants flitted into action. In no time, she was soaking in a bathtub nearly as big as her home. The bubbly, warm, rose petal-scented water lured her to sleep before the servants burst in and began scrubbing every part of her. Her cheeks blazed, but she didn't stop their ministrations. Gods knew she needed this after her weeks of captivity. They had to empty the tub and refill it when the water became too gray from her filth.

Warm towels went around her body and hair, and the bliss uncoiled the last of her tense muscles. She dressed in what they had picked out for her—a sky-blue dress with long sleeves and thin lace over the top half—the nicest dress she'd ever worn that wasn't a costume.

She dared a glance at her reflection in the long mirror beside the wardrobe. Her mouth fell open. Her cheekbones were pronounced, a dark hollowness under her eyes. Her waist was tinier, face so much paler. Breasts nearly non-existent.

Still, her red hair bound up this way made her look like a lady. The fine dress fit perfectly. It was odd, seeing her entire body at one time. They didn't have such a large, fancy mirror back home. She looked less gangly than she'd expected, but too skinny.

A knock startled her away. "Come in," she said, feeling like an imposter in her fine attire, admitting guests as if she was someone important.

The door opened, revealing Callen. Excitement sparked

through her heart. He looked toward the empty bed first, but then moved on, searching. He froze when he saw her. His lips popped open.

"Wow," he said. "You look beautiful."

Pleasant heat crept up her neck.

He closed the door behind him. "Are you feeling better?"

"I'm on the mend," she said, sitting with the reminder of her fatigue. "Thanks to you." His genuine concern and unyielding care eased her spirit.

"It was the least I could do." He smiled warmly, then straightened. "Right, I'm here to collect you. It is time."

Time for the inquisition. Her knees trembled. She'd gone over what to say and what to avoid saying, but that didn't make this feel any less like what she was forced to do in the fae world. She might be properly dressed and fed this time, but it was just a scenery change.

Almost done. Just this one more thing.

"You'll be fine. No one will hurt you. And I'll be there the whole time."

"You will?"

He nodded. Somehow knowing he'd be there, that he'd protect her, helped.

Only Callen accompanied her on the carriage ride to the mage building. The only thing able to distract her from the mounting fear was Callen—the feel of his gaze as she stared out the window, or the way their knees brushed when the road became bumpy. Nerves chased away the creeping exhaustion.

They stopped at a tall building that Ricci recognized from her magic permit test, but this was the front, all formal columns and marble, instead of the back with its plainer façade and lines of people. Callen helped her down from the carriage, his hand warm and sure. They stood on the stone walkway, a warm breeze tickling the back of her bare neck.

"I'm sorry about everything, Callen." Something compelled her to apologize before they were no longer alone. At his curious look, she went on. "I've never trusted magic or mages. When we first met, I thought you would turn me over and endanger me and my family. I was hostile and maybe even cruel."

"No, don't you worry about any of that now." He took her hand.

"But now, I'm not myself. I don't trust anyone anymore. The high master has been nothing but kind, but I can't help but think he'll turn against me. And it doesn't make any sense!" She shook her head, confused and frustrated. Exhaustion weighed on her like a smothering blanket. It was fine to pretend she'd be fine while she was safe and warm in that bed with Callen's constant attentiveness. Now she was stepping back into a nightmare, and she was not okay.

"Steady now." Callen put his hands on her shoulders. He waited until she met his eyes. "You have every right to feel these things. My parents disowned me. My own family wanted nothing to do with me when they found out I had magic and wouldn't go into politics like my father. I thought I'd never forgive them. They realized the error of their ways and chose to support me, but it took a long time for the hurt to go away." He squeezed her shoulders. "Gods, that's nothing like what you've gone through. Nothing. But what I mean is that you need to give yourself time to heal. Pace yourself. You'll trust when you're ready, and I'll still be here waiting."

He was right. She could be stronger than this experience, with time. She lifted her chin and wrapped her arms around him. He held her tightly until she sighed and let go. Together, they entered the building where High Master Aldridge awaited them.

"Go on in, Callen. Everyone is already assembled. I'll accompany Ricci into the council room."

Callen hesitated but then did as told. Master Aldridge led her in a different direction, stopping outside a set of double doors.

"Remember," he said. "It was the fae general. Not you. Whatever else they ask you, that is the one thing you must stick with."

"You won't be asking the questions?" She had counted on him steering the questions away from ones that would be tricky to answer.

"I'm sorry, no. A panel was assembled by a vote. But I'll be in there. Wait for my call."

When he left, Ricci leaned against the wall, letting it support her weight. Voices of the most powerful men and women in the world pitched around the room as they waited to scrutinize her, judge her, and decide her fate. Weariness sent her head spinning. She wasn't ready for this much excitement.

Ricci straightened and took three deep breaths. She pushed her shoulders back and raised her chin. She was no longer Ricci, portal opener. Her new role was Ricci, the victim of an atrocious kidnapping by the fae monsters. She was born to act, and this was the role of a lifetime. For her life.

CHAPTER 32

At High Master Aldridge's bidding, Callen reluctantly left Ricci and headed toward the council session. Her pain—what she'd been through, and what she had yet to endure—hung like a fog around him.

Gods, he couldn't believe he'd compared his family trouble to her own experience. He had never been tested the way she had in his entire life. His was a life of privilege, a traipse through a field of dreams and good fortune, compared to hers.

Ricci's return had complicated everything at the mage building. Every mage in the council—no, the city—wanted to speak to the girl that had visited another realm. Luckily, the high master had kept them at bay.

It was exactly as Callen had thought. The ones who suspected her of being the portal opener no longer saw her as a person but as a tool to be wielded in their favor. He might have been able to help Ricci escape when she'd reappeared, but a scribe and the high master had been in the room.

It took him many days to come to terms with that reaction —to help her leave instead of turning her over to his master.

Her ability was the answer to all his problems, his ticket to Master Marek finally training him for the mage tests, but he hadn't even considered any of that. His only thought had been to help her get away.

In the weeks that she'd been gone, he'd never stopped trying to find a way to reach her. Fortunately, that served his goals *and* his master's, so Master Marek allowed it, and High Master Aldridge helped with the trickier spells.

Of course, his master was furious Callen hadn't told him immediately that Ricci was back. Callen protested that he couldn't go against the wishes of the head of the council, but he wasn't sure his master believed him. While Ricci recovered, his master had been the lead voice in favor of her being the portal opener.

This need to protect her, to save her from anything that might cause her harm, was blinding. Like he'd been given a potion of the purest, most potent kind that made him unable to see anything but her and her needs. His own petty concerns had drifted to the back of his awareness, and it was the most freeing experience he'd ever known. To finally find someone, and to put their needs before his own, to even want to put someone else first... his lungs filled easier, and he could conquer the world.

As long as he was with her, he was on the right path.

And yet he couldn't tell her any of it. He couldn't tell her she'd become his purpose.

Ricci didn't trust anyone. Those words drove like a dagger to the hilt into his heart. But he didn't blame her. Look what magic had brought her.

And now she'd face the mage council alone, unprepared, and ill.

He'd almost won over the council. But then she'd come back, and the general hadn't come with her. Why would the general take her away and then simply send her back without word or reason?

He'd tried to satisfy everyone's curiosity so they wouldn't question her, but there was no getting around this inquisition. There was no law to keep her with the council, but if the high master thought she might be dangerous without learning more control, they could find a way.

Still, Callen had to protect Ricci, which mattered so much more than any of his own problems. He'd find a way to fix things with Master Marek once it was all over. Opening portals, connecting the mage community across the world, and being remembered forever might have been his master's life-long dream, and Callen was more than willing to help, so long as that didn't endanger Ricci.

Callen entered the council room as the mages took their seats all along the tiers. Master Marek stared coldly before sitting at a special table within the circle arranged for him and the other seven panelists. These were the people who'd be questioning Ricci.

Callen took the chair normally designated for his master since every other seat was full—some even stood in the alcoves. They were as curious as Callen about this other world —the world of the fae.

High Master Aldridge, white robe like his own personal spotlight, entered the circle center. "I call to order this formal inquisition of Ricci Menowin, that we may further our knowledge of the event in which a portal to another world was opened." He stared gravely around the room. "Before she enters, I remind you that no law has been broken. No crime has been committed. We are not a jury, nor this young girl our accused. We only wish to gather answers and information, with which we will decide what to do in continued meetings." He waited as heads nodded.

Some of the tension flowed out of the room, and Callen relaxed ever so slightly. These mages had come for blood, but the high master keenly reminded them that was not what they'd get today. Hopefully the panelists listened.

High Master Aldridge nodded toward the hall he'd come from, and Ricci entered the circle. Whispers circled the room, but everything faded to the beat of Callen's heart thrumming in his ears, and each step she took to the middle, head held high, looking so confident under the scrutiny of so many important and powerful mages. Mages whom she didn't trust —and feared.

Pride bloomed in his chest. She caught his eye before staring down the panel, and he nearly whooped out loud.

"Ricci Menowin, is it?" Master Marek began, tone condescending while he looked down his nose at her.

Callen wanted to throttle him for speaking to her so.

"Tell us what happened the day you went to the fae world."

CHAPTER 33

Eight mages sat at a table, watching Ricci intently. She knew how to read a crowd. These were her obstacles. This was who she must play to. She caught a brief glimpse of Callen seated behind them, and her heart fluttered.

One of the oldest sneered at her, stern face plastered between gray hair and a lean frame. "Ricci Menowin, is it?" he said.

Here was her biggest opposition. He didn't give a name— no way to know who he was—but he'd already decided her guilt.

"Tell us what happened the day you went to the fae world." He said it like a proclamation, as if he knew her own words would condemn her.

He didn't know anything.

She looked him dead in the eye. "My family makes our living by traveling from town to town, performing our one-of-a-kind show." She broke away from his penetrating gaze and walked the stage, eyes sweeping across the crowd. "I performed the role of

Princess Kasma that day in Timbercross. I cast one of my illusions —which this council licensed me for—and was in the height of my performance when the fae monster appeared behind me." She didn't have to fake the shudder that rippled through her.

Muttering scattered around the mages. Someone fidgeted in their seat—Callen.

"I'd never been so afraid," she continued, now locking eyes with Callen. "He held a sword to my throat." Her hand drifted absently to her neck where a pink line still remained. "He cut me." The words were near whispers, and anguish tore across Callen's face.

She took a trembling breath. "Callen tried to save me, but the general's magic was too strong. He transported me to his world."

Callen broke eye contact first, looking down in what appeared to be shame. Ricci paced back in front of the panel, watching the lead master. His expression was blank, almost calculating. He hadn't been moved by her emotional story.

"What happened once you arrived in the fae world?" he asked. "And leave out the frivolous details this time, hmm?"

She nearly scowled but managed to nod meekly instead. "They took me to their castle, locked me away, questioned me, and starved me near to death."

Angry murmurs rose around the room, but they quieted when the lead speaker raised his hand.

"What did they want to know?" he asked.

Oh no. Ricci's heart picked up as her nerves finally reared their ugly head. She couldn't tell them what the fae monsters wanted to know. Not everything. She focused on Callen's plan —the general was the portal opener. Not her.

"They asked about humans. How advanced we are."

The head mage did not look convinced.

"They asked about our armies, how big they are and what special abilities we might have."

His eyes widened at this, and angry outbursts rose around the room.

"You see?" the sneering mage said, voice rising above the throng. "They mean to battle us and destroy us humans."

High Master Aldridge banged a gavel on a table. "Order, please." After a moment, everyone quieted. "Master Marek, you will not speculate. Our purpose is to acquire facts only."

Callen's master? Why would he be so cruel?

The lead speaker, Marek, didn't reply. He simply went on as if the high master hadn't spoken.

"If it is as you say, and the general is the one with the power to open portals, how did you manage to escape?"

This was the question she'd dreaded. There were no half-lies to tell here. She prayed they wouldn't sense her dishonesty through magical means.

"I befriended a young fae while I was there," she said, voice loud and sure. "She unlocked my cell door. She transported me back."

More gasps and conversation.

Master Marek's mouth hung slightly open. "You mean to say that portal opening is common there?" He sounded incredulous.

"I don't know. I didn't meet anyone else. This girl was the general's daughter." She swayed but didn't falter. Gods, if only they'd give her a chair. Or end the questioning so she could go to bed and sleep for an age.

Heads nodded around the room. They believed her, or were starting to.

Master Marek seemed to realize it as well, eyes narrowing as he watched the room. "You've brought a lot of useful information before the council today, Miss Menowin. I only have a simple request that may speed things along."

Behind him, Callen tilted his head, curious with a hint of worry.

Ricci could read this mage. He had one final card up his sleeve.

"There must be a reason this general chose you, of all people. He could have picked anyone from our world, any number of humans were in the vicinity. Why not take my apprentice instead, who's clearly a more powerful mage than yourself?"

Ricci held her breath. She hadn't thought of an answer to this obvious question. Why would she be targeted for the kidnapping and not anyone else? "I'm not sure."

"No? I have a theory. It was your active use of magic he was attracted to. You did say you performed an illusion at the time he arrived." Marek smiled, but it wasn't kind.

"That could be it," she said, muscles relaxing.

Callen narrowed his eyes.

"I agree. Please demonstrate this illusion for us so we may understand what might have drawn him to you."

In the moment it took to register his words, Ricci's heart slammed into her ribcage. A cold sweat erupted over her body. Her fingertips went numb.

No. She couldn't, wouldn't open another portal to that monstrous place. Never.

Never never never.

Hands gripping the armrests, Callen looked ready to jump out of his chair.

The high master rapped his gavel against the wood. "I must object, Master Marek." His loud voice found its way through her panic, easing her back from the edge just a bit. "Miss Menowin is still recovering from her trying ordeal.

Asking her to perform magic at this time would simply be cruel."

"Hear, hear," Callen said, a lone voice in the crowded room.

"A small illusion won't take much," Marek said. "She's used to performing it multiple times a day. I feel it's important in our search for the portal opener."

She would not, ever, do this thing.

"As the high master says, I am much too weary to perform for you now." Her voice shook, adding to her claim. "If the panel has no further need of me, I will retire." She'd used those words in a play once, acting a fine lady.

Marek briefly whispered to the other mages on the panel. "The panel, who has the final say in what questions are important and what will be discussed here today, insists. The magical community, our world, depends on solving this mystery, and we cannot delay. You will perform. Now."

The high master sat back down, outnumbered, sorrow plain on his face.

Ricci shook her head, struggling to contain her gasping breaths. "I will not." Numbing tingles traveled up her arm.

Cries of surprise came from the mages.

Master Marek stepped from behind the table, closer to her. "You will, or be imprisoned for contempt."

Imprisoned? She couldn't go back to a cell, locked up with no light or air, worrying her family all over again. *Oh, Gods.*

"You can do it, Ricci," Callen said. The conviction in his voice did nothing for her fear, but it gave her strength. She could be brave and strong enough not to cross completely over. She'd done it for the permit test, after all.

"Very well," she said, finding her voice again. "If it will put this matter to rest." *I can't. I won't. I can't. I won't.*

But she had to.

234

If they learned the truth, they'd make her do it again. And again and again.

With timid hands, Ricci dipped into her magic, siphoning as little as possible for her task. The warmth spread upward, like a crack in the dam, too eager to come to her call.

"Show me the field of flowers everyone was so fond of when you took your test," Marek said.

Ricci's hold on the magic slipped, allowing more to come than needed. She squeezed her eyes shut and thought of flowers. *Not Lela's flowers, please. Anything but that.*

Collective oohs and aahs came over the crowd. It was working. Her eyes refused to open and see. There were too many nightmares associated with these once-peaceful flowers.

Marek's voice sounded right in her ear, making her jump. "Beautiful. It's so real, I can almost smell them." He inhaled deeply, and she stepped away without opening her eyes. "So sweet. I can almost feel the wind." As he said that, Ricci felt it too. "And the blooms are so near, it's as if I could pick one."

The sound of a stem breaking caused her eyes to fly open. The field of flowers was more real than the council room now. Marek stood before her, faded, smirking, holding a perfect red blossom.

The gongs alarmed from far away. Marek turned toward the sound.

"No!" she shouted, slamming the portal closed.

She stood beside Marek in the council room, the flower still in his fingertips.

The room exploded into chaos.

Mages cried out, standing and pointing. "Portal opener!"

Some left their seats entirely, making their way toward the circle. Callen vaulted over the front row, hurrying to her side. He pulled her to him, glaring at anyone who dared approach.

Marek watched it all with amusement.

"Order!" boomed the high master's voice, magically carried throughout the room.

Everyone drew to a standstill.

"This interrogation, I mean inquisition, has now come to a close. Please leave immediately." He came to stand on Ricci's other side.

"Let us be gone, apprentice," Marek said, watching Callen's every move as the rest of the mages reluctantly filed out of the room.

The high master remained.

Callen shifted his weight, indecisive.

"Go, Callen. I'll be alright," Ricci said. He couldn't lose his apprenticeship because of her, though his concern warmed her.

"It's alright," Marek said, and his eyes turned kind. "Stay. Help Miss Menowin recover from her ordeal." He turned to her with a small smile. "I do apologize for the necessity of treating you so harshly. I needed to draw out the truth of the matter, and my long years have taught me to be direct when in front of this group."

Was that the reason for his shortness? Either way, it didn't matter. Everyone knew the truth.

"I understand, Master," Callen said when she didn't reply.

"I'm sure you're worried about what will happen, Miss Menowin, now that your secret is out." Marek patted her arm in sympathy. "I think I might have an idea that will help. The two of you come visit me in the morning at my residence, and we'll discuss it."

"Yes, Master," Callen said.

Ricci said nothing. She didn't trust this man, whatever his reasons for treating her cruelly. He'd tricked her into revealing her true ability.

High Master Aldridge cleared his throat. "Only if you want

to, Miss Menowin. I must stay and sort this out, Callen, but please escort her back to my estate."

Ricci didn't trust him either. His kindness couldn't be genuine. She leaned heavily on Callen as they left the council building, surprised she was allowed to leave at all. He helped her into the carriage where she rested her head against the hard wall.

When it was just her and Callen, she spoke without lifting her head. "Why didn't they detain me for being a portal opener, or for lying about it?"

"It's not a crime to be a portal opener," he said as the carriage jolted to a start. "Though I suppose it is a crime not to be licensed. That's what High Master Aldridge and the council will sort out. I wouldn't be surprised if they issued the permit based on your performance today alone. There were certainly enough witnesses."

"Then why the interrogation?" She threw up her hands. "Why question me if I did nothing wrong?"

Callen asked permission with his eyes before taking her hand. "With this discovery, where you've been, what you've seen, it was only natural. And now, knowing what you can do, you'll be a tool to them." He squeezed. "I'll do everything I can not to let that happen."

It didn't matter. She'd never open one again. There was no possible purpose it could serve except to put her in danger.

"Marek sure knew what he was doing," she said bitterly.

"I'm afraid he played on your weariness, Ricci. He described things so you'd see them too, which shaped the intent of your magic without you realizing it. I'm sorry. I didn't think to warn you because he wasn't supposed to ask you. The high master forbade it." He shifted on the cushioned seat. "You have to understand that finding a way to open portals has been his life's work. Now he's found that it can be done but in a way he can't control. He can't open a portal without you. It frustrates him that his discovery would manifest in this way. He's not that bad, not as bad as he seemed today, anyway."

Ricci closed her eyes to the gentle sway of the carriage. It had all been too much for her weak body and mind. She didn't care about his reasons. She didn't trust him. By forcing out the truth, he'd ruined her life. What would the council do to her when she refused to ever open a portal again?

CHAPTER 34

The sun breached the horizon as Lela reached the inn to gather her stowed bag. Lingering risked discovery. She had to trust that Ricci escaped. Her pack was where she'd left it under a pile of boards beside the barn, all ready to go. She hefted it onto her back and headed toward home. She would tell Mata that she'd come to visit Oren, then left when the gongs started ringing.

They'd ceased ringing shortly after Oren left her at the bridge. That hadn't stopped the town from descending into chaos. Lanterns were lit in every window, people taking to the streets out of fear and curiosity. Husbands and wives huddled together on doorsteps as warriors hurried past toward the castle.

Lela was the only one going the wrong way, and it earned her a fair share of curious looks. Her dark clothes suddenly didn't conceal her as she'd intended, so she kept to the alleys as much as possible. Adrenaline still ran through her veins, keeping weariness at bay. It'd been a day since she'd last slept, and she'd feel it later when the walking took its toll. Maybe she'd get lucky and get a ride with a merchant leaving town.

There was less traffic on the road as she walked further from the drama unfolding behind her. The rumbling of hoof-beats up ahead had her scanning the horizon. A company of the king's warriors rode at break-neck speed, heading toward her—heading toward the castle. She stepped off the road—either that or be trampled—pressing against the storefront of some shop. They thundered by, kicking up dust, an entire company of men and women hurrying to answer the call of the gongs.

She'd done this, caused all this panic.

The pounding hooves rattled the shop's windows.

A hand slammed down on her shoulder, and she was dragged backward. Her heart jumped into her throat. Instincts took over as she kicked and tore. They rounded a corner and stopped in a narrow alley. The attacker spun her around.

"Pata!" The fight left her.

He stared down at her, face stern and completely readable. He knew she was involved.

"What are you doing so far from home, young one?" He didn't blink. Blood welled on his hand.

Lela shifted her pack where it'd slipped, buying time. Maybe she could convince him somehow, if her story was believable enough. "I thought things were safe since you caught the portal opener." She stared at the ground. "I wanted to see Oren."

"And did you see him?"

Lela froze. If she said yes, Oren would be in trouble for breaking the rules of his training. If she said no, he'd catch her lie if the guards said they saw them together.

"Only briefly," she said, forcing regret into her voice. "He sent me away. And then the alarm sounded. Something's

happened, hasn't it? That's why I'm returning home to Mata."
Stars above, this wasn't going to work.

His stern composure broke, revealing disappointment. "I trusted you, daughter, and yet you don't trust me. You lie. I saw you in the corridor last night. I know you were there with Oren."

Lela's heart pounded in her ears. She could run for it. What would he do to her? He was her pata, but he'd also mistreated an innocent girl. She didn't know who he was or what he was capable of, not really.

"If you knew I was there, why didn't you say something?" Her tone came out defensive. Panicking, her mind raced in a maze of dead ends.

He lunged and grabbed her upper arms, fingers wrapping completely around them. "What have you done, child?"

She flinched.

"I thought you were there for frivolous reasons, to chase after your indifferent boyfriend. And then the portal opener disappeared in front of my very eyes." His grip tightened to nearly bone-crushing, then he let go. Blood rushed back into her arms.

Her mouth parted as she backed up a step. More than anything she'd done, more than anything her pata might have done, this reaction scared her the most. He never showed emotion, always kept tight control of what he was thinking and feeling.

"I didn't do anything," she replied weakly. "I need to go home to Mata."

"You should never have left!" he shouted.

Lela's eyes widened.

"Too many guards saw you together. Maybe that wouldn't have mattered, except all of faedom knows where the portal opener came from. If someone suspects she was aided in any way, you'll be at the top of a nearly non-existent list of accused. How did you even acquire my key?" He shook his head. "I don't want to know. Return it. Now." He held out his hand.

"I don't have it," she said, voice shaking.

His chin lifted. "Oren has already been apprehended for questioning." The breath whooshed out of Lela. "The guard reported he was the last to visit the human. Him and his mate." Pata stared. "They'll find the key, and he'll be hung a traitor."

Blood turned to ice in her veins. Her body hung heavy. "No! Please, you can't do that, Pata. You wouldn't allow that." Panic seized her throat. Her mind cast about—how could she save him?

Pata stepped toward her and gently caressed her cheek. His eyes turned glassy. "Oh, my young one. Why didn't you listen? Now I have no choice."

She didn't have time to scream before his strong arms grabbed her. He dragged her through the narrow alley. She kicked and scratched, pulling and tugging. Guards on horseback waited for them at the end.

He'd known the whole time she was involved. She was going to die for this, and he didn't even care.

"Don't do this, Pata. Please."

She thrashed, trying to break free, but his grip around her chest was iron.

Wait. He held around her chest, not the middle like he'd taught—not her center of gravity, which would make her much easier to control.

They edged closer to the waiting guards, who watched on without a flicker of emotion. Pata's unicorn, Bromlin, stood beside them, empty and ready to receive its prisoner.

She used the wall to kick off hard.

Pata's grip slipped. This was her moment. She dropped like

a rock to the ground, letting her dead weight drag him off balance, just like he'd taught her. He pitched forward clumsily, letting go on instinct to catch his fall.

She exploded from her crouch, leaping into a full-on sprint toward his awaiting unicorn.

The guards shouted in surprise, drawing their swords. None of them reached for the energies, a rare stroke of luck that Pata would be accompanied by warriors without energy.

Lela plunged into her own, drawing it up in bulk as she reached the horse. *Grow*, she thought.

Vines shot out of the ground close to the guards, sending a thrill of satisfaction through her. Small vines, but good enough. Their horses spooked, rearing and shying away from their masters' commands.

Lela flew into the saddle. "Yah," she called, gripping the reins.

"Get her!" Pata shouted.

Bromlin took off with lightning speed, only moments to spare. Three guards raced after her. The wind whipped at her hair, and the pack bounced awkwardly on her back.

The sure-footed unicorn followed her commands almost intuitively, and she weaved in and out between buildings, rounding corners. Lela galloped through small courtyards, backtracking through skinny alleyways. She slowly gained enough lead to outpace her pursuers, the sound of them galloping somewhere behind her.

Lela used her precious advantage to turn one final corner and onto the open road. She gave Bromlin his lead, and that was all the encouragement he needed. A descendant of the wild mares some still said were touched by starlight, Bromlin shot forward. He knew the way home. Letting the stirrups support her weight, Lela lifted out of the saddle and leaned forward to aid their speed. The guards broke from between buildings and gave chase, but she had too much of a head start. Their army-issued horses were no match for her pata's rare unicorn.

"Oren," she breathed.

Their relentless pursuit left no opening for her to turn around and go back for him. Her eyes stung. He couldn't die. There couldn't be a world without him in it.

The landscape whipped by. Buildings at first, with people just a blur in her vision, then colorful trees and fields. When Lela was certain they no longer followed, she slowed the unicorn to a trot, then a walk, cooling him down. Air puffed loudly through his mouth and nose as he regained his breath.

She brought him to a stop, watching the empty road behind her. "You've done well, Bromlin." She patted his sweaty neck.

Oren. Surely he dumped the key to Ricci's binders somewhere. He would have known they'd question him since they were seen in the castle. Pata wouldn't allow him to be killed, right?

A shadow spread over her heart, making her chest tight. Pata knew. The guards knew. Everyone else would know soon enough. She was a traitor to her own kind.

He had been ready to arrest his own daughter, even knowing the punishment for the crime. He'd tortured Ricci. What else was he capable of? She didn't know him at all. But then, he'd been absent most of her life. Other young ones had both parents while they grew up. What was a couple decades in the life of a fae? But the king couldn't spare his general, and Mata wouldn't leave her home village to raise a child on the road, following Pata into danger on his endless campaigns.

She had to go back and free Oren. There must be something she could do even with the warriors on high alert everywhere.

But Pata would expect her to do just that. Thank the valley Ricci got away.

Bromlin stomped beneath her. She cocked her head to the side at the sound of hoofbeats. Riders approaching—fast.

She urged him on, his ears flicked back. He sensed his rider's indecision. Even as warriors pursued her, the need to go back was all-consuming. Things would die down in a few days. She'd use the time to plan how to help Oren.

Every step Bromlin took brought Lela closer to and further from home.

CHAPTER 35

Callen dressed in the room across the hall from Ricci's, which High Master Aldridge had kindly allowed him to stay in these past several weeks. The mage community seemed to understand he was looking after Ricci. He hadn't gone to his father's, not even to collect the belongings Master Marek had sent there from the inn.

Luckily, the mages—all of whom could destroy Callen on his best day—hadn't approached Ricci. The high master had something to do with that.

Someone knocked on his door, entering without being asked. "A message from Master Marek," the scribe said, holding out a letter.

Callen took it, staring down the scribe as she left. There would no doubt be a horrible lecture to sit through once they were alone again. After all, he'd opposed his master in an open council session.

He snapped the wax seal and read.

To My Apprentice,

I look forward to seeing you and Miss Menowin at my home at ten o'clock. Refreshments will be served.

Master Marek

Callen let his arm drop, releasing a long sigh. He'd never been to his master's estate before. At least Ricci would be there with him. Master Marek couldn't yell in front of her. Probably.

His master had more than one reason to yell, given that the shop had been closed too long now, the precious potions spoiled. Though, he was probably too preoccupied to care about the shop. Callen hadn't been much of an apprentice lately, but now that the inquisition was over, he could remedy that. There had to be some way to help Ricci and not fall behind on his studies for the magery test.

Callen took a quick bite of toast and a sip of tepid tea before heading to Ricci's room. Hopefully she'd rested.

The plan to hide her ability had gone all wrong. She should have been fleeing the city, labeled nothing but a harmless victim of circumstance. Now everyone knew what she could do, and his master would want her to stay. They wouldn't care that she'd lived through traumatizing hell, or that she was a performer just trying to get back to her family.

No. Even now, the kings and leaders of the world were likely plotting how to use her gift for their own gain. And even if all that wasn't true, things would still be much more difficult for her now. She probably hadn't realized it yet, but her acting days were over. The audience wouldn't trust what she could do again, knowing they weren't caught up in the story, or seeing some mere illusion, but being taken to a different world. A dangerous world.

His shoulders sagged with sadness for her and the heartache she'd feel when she realized.

He knocked on her door, entering with her quiet, "Come in."

His heart skipped a beat when she looked up from the writing desk. She'd dressed in lilac this time. Her pinned hair —red curls just waiting for the opportunity to burst from their bindings—highlighted her long, smooth neck. The soft skin of her bare collarbone.

"Did you need something?" she asked with a small smile.

He entered the room and cleared his throat. "We need to leave soon." He looked into her eyes, transfixed. How could she have gone through so much and still find the strength to smile?

Her smile grew. He'd been staring.

"Sorry!" He left, quickly closing the door and hiding his blazing cheeks.

Ricci's muffled laughter took him by such surprise.

"Callen?" she called from her room.

He flung open the door. "Yes?"

All hints of her laughter were gone. "I don't want to see your master. I'm not a prisoner, right? I want to go home. My family should be here by now. Or close." She watched him.

"Of course you're not a prisoner. My master just wants to talk with you, that's all."

"And then I can leave?" She tilted her head.

Honestly, he didn't know.

"It will be okay," he said. "You'll see."

Near the appointed hour, they rode in Master Marek's personal carriage, stopping at the foot of the staircase leading to his grand estate. One would think the property would be smaller than Master Aldridge's since he outranked him, but not so. Only a glance proved his master lived a more luxurious life, from the manicured lawn and gardens, to the size of the house, secured with a gate warded with magic against anyone who wished him ill.

The grandeur became even more sensational once inside, with a servant to show them to a dining room it took nearly ten minutes of walking to reach. Ricci barely uttered a word, simply gaped at the high ceilings, commissioned artwork, and crown moldings. The functionality of each room they crossed changed as wildly as the décor, from deep purple for a portrait room to a red as crimson as Ricci's hair for a sitting room.

The dining room was a refreshing change, with large windows bathing the room in sunlight, and mint-green walls that only added to the opulence rather than take away. They sat as directed, on opposite sides of a long table covered in a white cloth and trays of delicious-smelling food. His master was not yet present.

Callen's stomach rumbled.

Ricci gawked at the various dishes and numerous utensils. "I don't know how to be fancy like this," she said.

"Don't worry. My master won't mind. Just follow what I do." He'd grown up with this; ten-course meals and more forks than food. Though this was fancier than 'refreshments will be served.'

"Oh, good, you're here," Master Marek said, smiling as he entered the room. A servant tucked in his chair. He reached out without looking, grabbing the first thing he touched—the apple out of the pig's mouth. No one ate the apple. "Please, help yourselves." His master was in a good mood today.

Callen picked out some of his favorites—candied walnuts, finger sandwiches with ham, and thick wedges of cheese. Ricci chose fresh fruit, slices of meat on crispy bread, and roasted vegetables. His master ignored the rest of the food.

Callen dug in while Ricci took slow nibbles from her plate, peeking at Master Marek occasionally.

"Ricci, do you mind if I call you that?" he asked, then continued without waiting for a reply. "I wanted to apologize again for my directness yesterday. You do understand why I had to, don't you?"

Ricci met Callen's eyes. "I suppose I understand your reasoning. Callen said your work has been to open a portal." She straightened, setting down her fork with a speared carrot. "But I wish you had allowed me my privacy. It should be my business what my magic can do, and my business to tell whom I want."

"Oh, but it is not only your business," Master Marek said. "We've seen what can happen when your magic goes unchecked. Bad fae generals kidnap little girls."

Ricci frowned.

Callen swallowed hard. "Master…"

"You're upset," Master Marek said. "But I can help you."

"That's true," Callen said, smiling as the heaviness lifted from the room. "My master can teach you to control your magic and how to avoid using it when performing." He hadn't thought of that until now. If she only learned some control, maybe she could still act after all.

Skepticism was written in her narrowed eyes.

His master nodded slowly. "If you agree to stay here and help me learn what I can about the fae world and portal opening, I, in turn, would be more than happy to help you learn control."

Ricci crossed her arms. "For how long? My family needs me."

His master was a good teacher when he wanted to be. All the pieces fit together. His master would learn from Ricci, she would learn control, and then Callen could one day take the mage tests. And he'd get to see her.

"Ricci, learning from Master Marek would save you unnecessary heartache. You won't have to give up what you love." Callen nodded his encouragement.

Master Marek took a sip of wine, ignoring Callen. "You're welcome to stay as long as it takes. Your family, is there no one else who has this ability, or any magic at all?" He leaned forward, watching for her answer.

"No," she said.

Of course no one in her family had magic. They weren't her blood relatives.

"Master," Callen said. "Ricci's mother told me something that might help us with her magic."

"What did she tell you?" they asked at the same time. Master Marek with eagerness, Ricci with curiosity.

"Your birth name." If they found her blood relatives, maybe someone else already knew all about how to control portal opening.

"What do you mean, my birth name?" she asked.

Callen blinked, then his eyes widened. Oh, Gods, Ricci didn't know she was adopted. It wasn't his place to say anything.

Master Marek slowly stood, chair scraping backward. "Ricci Menowin is not her true name?"

Callen glanced between them, deciding who to answer first. Heat flushed over his skin. "Your mother told me Ricci isn't the name you were born with."

"What is her true name?" His master's voice was low and flat, as if trying not to spook a caged animal.

Callen glanced at Ricci. With a stricken expression mixed between dismay and curiosity, she nodded for him to go on.

Master Marek sat hard in his chair, his voice rough and gravelly. "It doesn't matter. You have to go."

At the same time, Callen said, "Oriana."

Ricci put her hands against her face. "Why name me one thing but call me another?"

Master Marek's quiet chuckles drew Callen's attention. "Red hair." His laughter grew until Callen worried his master had come unhinged. "Oriana," he said slowly, staring down at Ricci. He called up his magic, like a zing in the air.

Callen shot to his feet. What was the threat? His mouth didn't have time to form a question before their meal exploded off the table. Pieces hung suspended in midair, the force of the magic momentarily stronger than the hold of gravity. They fell. Ricci screamed.

Callen's magic roiled up from his well. He scanned the windows. Were they being attacked? "Master, what—?"

Master Marek's magic slammed Ricci to the wall, knocking her into a portrait that crashed to the floor.

"Callen!" Ricci screamed.

Callen's mouth dropped open. "What are you doing?" he shouted. His master's magic threw him back in his chair, pinning him as if a great beast sat on his chest.

Ricci and Callen strained against their holds. Master Marek ignored them, slowly pacing toward Ricci. Where were the servants? Why was no one coming to check on the noise?

"Oriana," Master Marek said again, emphasizing each syllable.

She whimpered.

"Let her go!" Callen shaped his magic, shoving it like an invisible battering ram again his master's.

"I thought you didn't survive," Master Marek said, looking her over as if seeing her for the first time. "I heard you died along with your mother, still inside her womb."

Fear filled Ricci's eyes for the first time. "You're mad. My mama lives."

Master Marek turned toward Callen. "Tell me what else you learned, apprentice. No more keeping secrets from your master."

"I'm not telling you anything." Callen panted, unable to breathe with the weight on his chest. He focused his magic, pushing against the bulk. Like blowing breath on a mountain.

His master pointed at Ricci. "You will tell me."

What was happening? Why would his master do these things? What did that name mean to him?

Master Marek leaped over to Ricci. She screamed.

"Stop! Okay." Callen took a shallow breath. "Ricci, I'm so sorry. Your mother told me they aren't your birth parents. They found you on the side of the road. Your birth mother was dying. She asked your family to take care of you."

Tears streamed down Ricci's disbelieving face. "Why are you doing this?"

Callen didn't know who she was talking to.

"Oh, Oriana. There's so much you don't know. We're going to accomplish many things together," Master Marek said. "Now open a portal for me."

"Never," she spat.

"Open it, or I'll steal all the air from your lungs." Master Marek's magic flickered as he shaped the intent of an untapped source.

Ricci's eyes went wide. Her mouth opened and closed like a fish out of water.

"Stop this!" Callen screamed. He thrashed against the invisible bindings, plunging deeper into his well of magic.

Ricci's skin turned white.

"Open a portal. Now," Master Marek said. He released her air, and she gasped and coughed in gulping bursts, cheeks going red.

"No," she sobbed.

Callen's fury flashed white hot. He was supposed to protect her, and here she was, trapped again. He'd trusted his master.

"I can force you, you know," Master Marek said casually. "There's a place I need you to take me."

Callen pushed against the magic, a fist against the mountain this time.

His master stole her air again. She grabbed at her throat, body pinned against the wall.

Callen reached, deeper than he'd ever gone, grabbing great armfuls of everything that made him who he was and who he would become. The hold on him twitched.

Master Marek spun around. "Almost impressive. But you can't break free."

Callen didn't need to break free.

With a final push, Callen sent the dining table crashing over. It hit his master at the knees sending him sprawling to the ground. Ricci dropped to the floor, coughing and gasping for air.

"Portal out, Ricci!" Callen yelled.

Desperation filled her face, but she didn't hesitate. Her magic spiked with an almost visual glow. A buzz-like static filled the air.

Master Marek pushed to his knees. Ricci turned hazy. He lunged, catching her by the wrist, turning hazy as well.

His master smirked. "Got you."

Ricci yanked, throwing Marek off balance. They crashed to

the ground, but he didn't let go. They struggled, coming back to their feet.

Master Marek secured her wrist with both hands. "You're not leaving."

Ricci reared her arm back and punched him right in the face. He fell as she wrenched her arm from his grip. Ricci's wide eyes met Callen's, then she disappeared.

"No!" Master Marek struggled to his feet, rounding on Callen. Face full of fury, he cut off Callen's air.

"You've spent half your life helping me find a way to make a portal, and when we find it, you let her go?" he roared.

Callen's lungs burned with the need to breathe. Air would not come. He pushed his magic uselessly against the barrage. Black spots bloomed in his vision. His head sagged, but his chest stayed pinned to the chair under the weight of the spell.

His master released the magic. "You will hear what I have to say."

Sweet lungfuls of air made him cough and gasp.

"Did you ever wonder the real reason I taught you to be so good at potions and neglected the rest of your training?" His master circled him, stepping over broken plates and bits of food.

Callen gaped. "You never intended to prepare me for the tests." He'd thought his failure was due to his lack of talent or maybe lack of power, that if he worked hard enough he could prove he was ready. It had become just another thing he fell short of in his life—a weak son and a weak mage.

No. His master had wasted Callen's apprenticeship finding a way to open portals.

"But you taught me other things sometimes." Callen couldn't believe this. It was like his master had become a different person.

"That was weakness." His master tossed his head. "Letting

my softer side through." He smiled cruelly. "This is your punishment for letting her go. Your entire mage life you've been my tool. You'll continue to be so now. I saw the looks you two shared."

"It won't work—she doesn't feel that way about me."

His master stopped. "Ricci will be back."

"Why are you doing this? I've only ever served you. I trusted you." His master might have been hard on him, but he was never cruel. This couldn't be happening.

"You'll find out." His master called up his magic.

"No!" Callen broke free of his bonds and lunged.

Master Marek backhanded the air with a casual flick of his wrist. Callen went sprawling.

The world slipped away.

CHAPTER 36

Lela and Bromlin plodded slowly on. The strong unicorn's head hung low despite resting off the side of the road every night. He'd done far better than any horse could have managed. More than once, she was forced to dismount and ease Bromlin through thick brush to avoid warriors on the road.

The ever-present shadow of worry deepened as she neared home. What should have been a happy occasion—freeing Ricci and coming home to Mata—felt all wrong. Oren was in trouble, and Lela herself was a wanted criminal being sought for imprisonment by her own pata. And she'd only be home long enough to pack provisions. To stay was to risk being caught.

Bromlin sped when the farm came into sight, recognizing rest and eager to find food. Lela sighed with relief, long and hard. Her stomach rumbled. Mata always had something fresh for her to munch on.

The gongs alarmed in the distant town. Lela gasped.

"Yah!" She snapped the reins, and Bromlin thundered forward.

Ricci had opened a portal. But where? Had Pata lied about her escaping before? Maybe she was still locked in the castle, struggling to get free. Maybe she'd escaped this time. Instinct had Lela leading Bromlin toward the flower meadow. Had Ricci come here? It was the one place she always came back to. If there was any possibility, this time Lela would be there for her friend.

Lela urged Bromlin on. Cutting through the familiar forest of brilliant colors in all different hues, it was easy to navigate, even at their break-neck speed. Just before she crested the hill at the back of their land, the gongs stopped. The portal had closed.

It didn't matter. She had to know. Bromlin stumbled up the hill, and Lela reined him to a stop. She couldn't push him any further without injuring him. She hopped off the saddle and left him puffing as she sprinted, cresting the hill and down. Past the lilac pond she and Oren had spent so many summers exploring, and through the colorful trees surrounding the flower field.

A violet shape huddled in the center of the field. Lela couldn't make out what it was. Then she heard sobbing. She ran.

Ricci lay curled in a ball, a voluminous violet dress sprawled all around her—clothing not from the fae world. Tears streamed down her dirt-stained face. Lela wrapped her arms around her.

"Shhh, it's okay. You're safe." Lela squeezed Ricci's bony frame.

"Callen," Ricci managed to sob out. "He's in trouble."

"Who's Callen? I thought you were the one in trouble. You escaped the castle?"

"What?" Ricci sniffled. "Yes, I escaped. Thanks to you and your friend."

"Oren."

"Right." Ricci sat up, drying her face on her sleeve. "There's a mage in my world who wants to use me. He almost killed me to make me open a portal. Callen, he's my friend. He helped me get away, but now he's in danger."

"And you came here," Lela said. They'd just saved her from danger, and now she was in danger all over again. "Couldn't you have gone somewhere in your own world?"

"I don't know. I've never tried. Besides the mage council building, I've only opened portals to your world, to your land. I had to act quickly."

Lela nodded. "My friend, Oren, he's in trouble too. My pata saw me leaving. He figured out we were involved and caught Oren. I got away, but they're looking for me."

Ricci gestured around the field. "But this is your home. Won't they know to look here?"

"Yes. We can't stay long." Lela stared at her hands, raw from riding, then glanced at Ricci. "Your wounds are almost gone." She took Ricci's hand, turning it over to examine her wrist. The sores were nothing but angry pink marks.

"Yes, our physician—healer—said whatever salve you put on worked like a miracle. And my cough is better too."

A twig snapped. Both girls jumped, staring at the source of the sound.

Mata stood at the edge of the field, hands over her mouth. "Lelana. What have you done?" Her voice came out with a quiver, more emotion than Lela had ever seen. She'd broken her mata's heart.

Lela stood and ran to her mata, hugging her tight. "It's okay. She's not dangerous."

"She's the portal opener." Mata pulled away, eyes dry. She studied Lela for a long moment. Lela resisted the urge to squirm.

Mata sighed. "No matter what, you're firstly my daughter. I trust you." She glanced up. "You're both exhausted. Bring her in for something to eat. She can sleep here tonight, then we'll decide what to do." Mata flicked Lela's chin, then turned and headed back.

Lela couldn't contain her smile. She'd expected anger and blame but had been met with love and acceptance. She'd known her mata loved her, of course, but she'd never expressed it in such a profound way. She held her hand out to Ricci. "It's okay." They could spare the time to gather supplies—but they couldn't stay the night.

Ricci didn't look convinced but came anyway.

"Bromlin is in the stables. He came trotting up, riderless." Mata cast a look over her shoulder.

Lela looked down, abashed. Bromlin deserved more respect than that.

"You're very brave," Lela said quietly to Ricci as they walked together. Mata's unhurried pace chafed. Every delay risked capture.

Ricci struggled to hold up her dress from snagging on the ground and brush. "No. You're brave. You defied your people to rescue me. I couldn't do that. I'm just a cowering, weepy mess all the time. I fear everything now. I trust no one."

"You have a right to want to crawl in a hole and never come out. And yet here you are, taking the hard steps and making the right choices to carry on." She squeezed Ricci's hand.

"I need to go back. I have to save Callen." Ricci grabbed Lela's arm.

"You've barely recovered from your last ordeal." Lela lowered her voice as Mata watched from the doorway. Ricci couldn't know fae had better hearing than humans. "You need food and rest. And we need provisions. We can spare one night." No, they couldn't, but Mata didn't need to know that.

Fae would always choose their mates first. Mata was morally bound to tell Pata where to find the human, and Lela didn't hold that against her.

Ricci lapsed into silence. Lela ignored the herb garden and the damage from the army's passing. The smell of home enveloped her in peace. Baking bread, drying herbs, musty hay-stuffed beds. She'd missed all of it.

The clacks of wooden plates on the table pulled Lela to the kitchen after dumping her pack. Ricci followed right in her shadow, glancing nervously around the humble cottage.

"It's only me and Mata here," Lela said, motioning Ricci to sit at the table.

"Just you two?" Ricci perched on the edge of her chair.

Lela grabbed a knapsack from a hook and began stuffing it with fruit and jars of food. "Pata is always at the castle, working for the king. My aunt, Mata's half-sister, came to see us when I was just a baby. She left before I was old enough to remember her. I have a brother too, but he's much older than me and lives his own life elsewhere."

Mata set two biscuits slathered in whipped honey butter from their beehives on each of their plates, along with two cups of warm goat's milk. Saliva filled Lela's mouth.

"How old is your brother?" Ricci asked, swiping a stray smear of honey butter off the side of her plate. She tested it on the tip of her tongue, then moaned.

Lela smiled and filled a waterskin. "Sixty-eight."

Ricci's eyes widened, and she stole a glance at Mata. "That's elderly in my world."

"So short!" Lela finally sat, provisions packed and ready.

Mata sat fried mushroom caps filled with melted cheese and roast quail in front of them, Lela's favorite. Was she feeling guilty for what she must do to her own daughter? Ricci sniffed the food, trying it hesitantly, then ate with a frenzy.

"This is amazing," Ricci said. "Thank you."

Mata nodded but didn't say anything back. In fact, she hadn't spoken to Ricci at all, not a word, just stared at her overly long.

"Most things come from our farm," Lela said to fill the silence. "We only have to trade for a few provisions, like clothing." Stars, this food was good.

"So, what do you do here?" Ricci asked.

"My favorite thing is to tend the herbs. I speak their language." Lela watched Mata sneak out of the kitchen without a word. So unlike her.

"What does that mean?"

"It means I know what they need just by looking or touching them. I can also coax them to grow." Especially when her life was in danger, it seemed.

"That's right, you know herbs. That's how you knew so much about healing me." Ricci patted her hand. "Thank you for that, and for everything. I only survived because of you."

Lela smiled, focusing her attention away from Mata. The warmth of Ricci's words filled a small hole. The weight of everything else had her eyes drooping—she'd gone too long without enough sleep—though she kept her ears attuned to the road, listening for approaching warriors. "Let me show you where we'll sleep tonight."

Ricci nodded, and after finishing their meal, they climbed the ladder to the loft. Lela had missed her room.

"Sorry it's so small," Lela said. Her eye caught Pata's golden medal he'd won for bravery, and her stomach twisted. She nearly threw it over the railing.

"It's not. You're lucky. I've always wanted my own room." Ricci examined the various décor and objects on the window ledge and bookshelf. "You have a lot of books." She pulled out a red one, eyes widening at the image of a demon on the cover, face split by a wide, evil grin.

"That's just children's stories. Mata used to read them to me, though she'd always skip the tales of the demon king." Because the story of the demon king wasn't a story at all. "I read them when she wasn't looking." Lela smiled at the memory.

Ricci shoved the book back and turned to her. "What's going to happen to us?"

"Ricci." Lela pulled her down beside her on the bed and lowered her voice to the barest of whispers. Lela had been avoiding this moment, when she had to admit how much trouble she was in. "You can leave when you need to. They are coming for me. My pata will come here. Soon." To condemn his own daughter. The words should make her cower in fear, but they didn't. She had to be strong for Ricci. "We can't stay here tonight."

"The general?" Ricci's voice rose in pitch. She took a deep breath. "You're in trouble for helping *me*. It should be my turn to help you."

"You wouldn't have needed my help if I hadn't told my pata where to find you."

"They would have found me eventually, even without your help. At first, I didn't know it was real, that a world could be so beautiful. I thought it all an illusion I created. Then I didn't want to stop. You warned me, and I didn't listen." Her shoulders bowed.

"Try to hold on to the beauty you remember when the bad memories creep in. We really are a peaceful, kind people. It's the dark ones like my pata that have hardened your heart against us." It wrenched Lela's heart to say so about her pata, but he was not the fae she thought he was. Her eyes stung.

"Not you." Ricci took her arm. "And I want to help you."

"What about Callen? Doesn't he need your help?"

Her face dropped. "Yes," she whispered. "If he's still alive."

Her sadness turned Lela's thoughts to Oren. His sloppy kiss flashed into her mind. She had to keep looking forward or risk falling apart. "Well, then we have to rescue him, like we did you. And then you'll help me find Oren." If he was found guilty, they'd still need a tribunal to declare his sentence. They'd carry it out publicly to make an example of him. All that would take time. Lela shuddered.

"We?" Ricci blinked at her. "You'd come back with me?"

"Of course. You're my friend. And besides, it will be too dangerous to stay here." Lela yawned. "But first, sleep. The energies can't function without proper rest. In the morning, we'll make our plans to rescue your Callen and then Oren." She lowered her voice. "We will leave when my mata is asleep. She cannot know where or when we will go."

Ricci nodded, gaze darting to the ladder.

Lela tipped her head back to see the sunset through her skylight above—a unique pane of glass that provided light for the indoor herbs in the planters along the loft rail. It was going to be a long night.

"We leave after dark."

CHAPTER 37

Friendship and conversation warmed Ricci's soul, even if it was just to buy time for the sun to set. Even if too many horrible, dangerous, reality-shattering things hung above their heads. She paced the room to keep from falling asleep, a room as big as her entire wagon. Lela's home was perfect, smelling of lavender and not shaking to and fro. Ricci stretched out her arms and didn't touch the walls.

She'd stay here forever, except for three important things: her family would arrive at the capital for her any day, she was a wanted criminal in this world, and Callen was in trouble.

She refused to believe what Callen said about her mama. Her family would have told her if she'd been adopted. Only Mama could clear it up.

"It's almost time to go," Lela whispered, glancing out the window at the dark sky. "Mata will be asleep soon."

"She doesn't trust me," Ricci said, examining a pink crystal on Lela's shelf. She'd noticed how Lela's mom avoided talking to her, the way she stared. But, it was the same as all the other fae she'd seen.

Lela sat on the bed, packed bags at her feet. "Believe me, I'm trying to convince her. It's especially hard because her grandmata was alive when humans lived here. She'd been in love with a human, you know. My mata heard firsthand how things had been, the potency of the energies behind the human's parting curse. They said the energy of it reached even the outlying villages, giving pause to even those without the mastery to feel such a thing."

Ricci crossed her arms. It wasn't fair that because of what she could do, she now embodied everything that was bad about the human race in the minds of the fae.

"If the magic was so powerful, why has nothing bad happened?" Ricci asked.

Lela shrugged. "Maybe the curse was just words, and the energies were a distraction. Or maybe the energies are slow to act. We've come to think of it more as a prophecy. That's how younger generations feel, anyway. If something bad is going to happen, I know it won't be from you. You wouldn't do anything to hurt us. But that doesn't mean it won't happen. You could have initiated something from your very first portal."

The front door burst open, making Ricci jump. Lela rushed to the ladder. She gasped and ran back to the packs. The stomping of boots sounded from below.

"He's here," Lela rasped, slinging packs over her shoulder.

The stuff of Ricci's nightmares stepped into the house, slamming the door behind him.

"Come on!" Lela pulled so hard Ricci stumbled toward the window.

"Wait, daughter," the general's baritone voice rattled the air. The ladder shook with his assent.

Ricci squeezed to Lela's side as she threw open the window.

266

"Stop." The general sprung into Lela's loft.

Lela froze, one leg out the window. His gray eyes shot to Ricci. Expressionless. Cold.

Her mind floated somewhere above her body, looking down and not present. This fae man had taken her from her family. Cut her. Starved her. Questioned her until she was a weeping mess, near death from sickness.

She shook uncontrollably.

"The army is not far behind me," he said. "Use the back-door. Horses are waiting for you."

"You expect me to trust you?" Lela stepped in front of Ricci. "You brought this army for me, just like you brought it for my friend. You captured Oren and tried to do the same to me. Is he still alive?" she asked, then shook her head. "Ricci, now!" She tugged her.

Now, what? What did Lela want her to do?

"I helped you escape the town," he said, blocking the ladder. "Oren is safe. I found him an alibi."

"Lies!" Lela said.

Hoofbeats thundered on the dirt road. Wagon wheels squealed. Ricci knew what she had to do—what Lela wanted. They'd never capture her again. She gripped Lela's arm, reaching for her magic.

The general lunged for them, but his hand slipped right through her. Faster than she'd ever done, they portaled back to the human world. Ricci closed it before hearing the gongs, panting with the effort.

The room was dark and dirty with dimly lit candelabras spaced apart on the rock walls. It smelled of dirt and mildew.

"Where have you brought us?" Lela asked.

"I've never seen this place in my life," Ricci whispered back. She didn't know why she whispered, but there was a dark, ominous feel to this dwelling that told her she should.

"Why would we come here?" Lela stepped away and looked around.

The rattling of chains brought Ricci's gaze to a dark hallway. Her heart sped. "Who's there?" she asked, no longer whispering.

"Ricci?"

"Callen!" Ricci and Lela rushed toward his voice.

Callen sat on the ground, wrists above his head in chains anchored to the wall. He pushed to his knees, gaping at Lela. "Ricci," he spoke fast. "It's a trap. Get out now. He's waiting for you."

"We'll go, but we're taking you with us," Ricci said. "Where's the key?" She reached for his chains.

"No, don't!" Callen jerked back. "The iron burns and blocks your magic." He tilted his wrists, and Ricci gasped at their screaming raw redness. "Marek has the key, and he'll be here any moment. Go!"

"One fae leaves, and two return," a voice said behind them.

Ricci and Lela spun around. Marek walked toward them, a crooked smile on his face.

Ricci reached for her magic, grabbing Lela's arm.

"Uh-uh." Marek held up his hand, then clenched it into a fist.

Callen's screams filled the hall. He writhed and twitched, body hanging from his wrists and tears streaming down his face.

"Stop!" Ricci shrieked.

Lela whipped a knife from her sheath and lunged. Marek dropped his hold on Callen, eyes going wide at the speed of Lela's attack. He couldn't call up another spell before she reached him. He twisted, and the knife aimed for his heart sliced his shoulder. Blood flowed, staining his robe. Lela stumbled past him. In the heartbeats it took her to reorient, he pulled a pair of manacles out from his robes.

Golden manacles, etched with vines of thorns.

"Lela!" Ricci rushed toward them.

Marek flicked his wrist toward Ricci without looking. The impact of an invisible boulder slammed into her. She flew backward, body crumpling on the stone floor. Pain burst over her body. White flashed in her eyes. Callen cried out beside her, straining against his chains.

Lela screamed. Ricci pushed to her elbows. The knife was gone. Lela was pinned against the wall with invisible magic, one manacle already in place. Ricci knew that agony well, the burning that stole your magic away. Marek reached for her other hand. Once latched, Lela would be under his control, unable to escape.

Ricci called for her magic. Lela had to go home. It was the only way to save her. The room around Ricci turned opaque, but Lela wasn't part of it.

Vines shot between the stones in the ground, reaching for Marek's legs. He blinked, and they burst into flames, quickly turning to ash.

There was no time. Ricci strained, trying to recenter the magic around Lela. It wouldn't move. Like it couldn't exist separate from Ricci.

The other manacle clicked around Lela's wrist. Lela glared daggers, helpless as he secured the manacles to a chain like Callen's. He released his magic hold on her. She dropped to her feet and kicked, nearly toppling him before he stumbled backward, eyes wide.

He turned to Ricci and raised his hand. "If you leave, I'll kill them both."

"Go, Ricci. Don't listen to him." Callen sat mere feet from

where she'd landed. Even with the opaqueness of her half-open portal, fear was plain in his eyes.

"No?" Marek crossed closer to her, hands raised. "How about I kill your family?"

Ricci froze, her portal fading.

"He's lying," Callen said.

"Don't test my resolve, Oriana. They trust me. They know I helped find you. Getting close to them would be easy."

Ricci looked into Callen's face and saw the truth of Marek's words written in his anguish.

"Why are you doing this?" she sobbed.

"I will claim what's mine, as I claim you, Oriana. You're mine too."

What did that mean? Ricci's portal dropped, magic spent. She shook her head against the spinning in the room.

"He's raving mad," Lela called out from across the room. "Leave, Ricci, before it's too late. Bring my pata here."

The general? Never. She couldn't risk her friends and family. Ricci struggled to her feet.

Marek nodded. "That's right. Don't listen to the fae girl." He sneered. "Long ears, just like your mother."

"I don't have long ears. My mama doesn't have long ears." Her voice shook.

"Callen left that part of the story out," Marek said. "Your mother was fae."

Ricci gaped. It couldn't be true. They were the words of a madman. "Let Callen and Lela go. Leave my family alone, and I'll do whatever you want."

"You don't believe me. But surely you must have doubted. You look nothing like them. You're too young for your so-called mother to have conceived you. And you carry magic, unlike the rest of them. Your mother told Callen all about it."

"But I look nothing like the fae." Ricci looked over.

Callen shook his head. "Your mother never told me anything about your birth mother, except that she died trying to protect you."

"Mama would have told me," Ricci said. "They don't lie to me."

Marek glanced at his bleeding shoulder. "Fenity was wise to keep you in the human world. The fae would never have accepted who you are." He stepped closer. "A fae with two powerful lineages. Your mother a fae with an ability shunned by her own kind, and your father a powerful sorcerer." He lifted his chin.

"You?" She shook her head slowly, thoughts going to Papa. He was her father, his warm, enveloping hugs and kind smile. The way he acquiesced to Mama's authority. "What happened to my mother?"

From his robe, Marek pulled a pair of plain iron manacles connected to a chain. "Your mother wanted to keep you from me. The poison didn't work as quickly as I would have liked. I thought she was dead, but she fled on foot, too weak to use magic."

Ricci was going to be sick.

"I'm sorry, Ricci," Callen said. "Leave now!"

"Go, Ricci!" Lela said.

"Hold out your wrists," Marek said to Ricci. He held the manacles in front of him.

Ricci backed away, tugging at her magic.

Marek took a deep breath. The words came slow and snapped her reality in two. "Oriana Stormbrook."

Pain like fire flashed on the sides of Ricci's face. She fell to the ground, thrashing and covering her ears. The agony ended abruptly, gone as if it never was.

But Marek quickly latched the manacles on. Ricci gasped, bracing for more pain.

Nothing happened—there was no burning agony like before.

"I thought so," Marek said with a look of satisfaction.

What was happening?

Using the chain like a lead rope, he pulled her to the wall and hooked it to one of the rings halfway between Lela and Callen, arms locked above her head. The rattling was so loud in her ears. Sounds were clearer. The dripping of water down the hall echoed loudly to her dizzy head.

Ricci didn't speak, numb. Lela and Callen's concern and shock radiated from both sides.

"Iron doesn't affect fae," Marek said. "Only the spelled manacles do, but those drain your magic. And we can't have that." He studied the three of them. "It'll be some time before your magic is restored after your failed rescue attempt. I'll have food brought to you." He turned to Callen. "Not you or the other fae."

No one said a word as he left, locking the door behind him.

"Ricci, your ears." Callen stared at her with wide eyes.

"What about them?" She couldn't touch them with her hands locked above her head, but she rubbed them against her arm, checking for injury.

She stilled. They were different. They were long.

Like the fae.

"What has he done to me?" Her voice shook.

"He revealed your true form." Lela's proclamation filled the space, disbelieving and weighty. "He must have placed a spell to disguise you from the humans when you were a baby. Fenity Stormbrook was my aunt. But a portal hadn't been opened in centuries. Anyone with the ability had been persecuted to death. No one ever could do what you do. If they had, the gongs would have alarmed and we'd know about it."

Ricci's voice came out hollow. She was that person floating

above her body again. "They didn't alarm when I left with you. If it's fast enough, they don't have time to detect the portal." The words came automatically, but Ricci barely heard herself say them. Her mind was too busy flying in a million directions.

Lela nodded. "So you weren't the one to trigger the prophecy. Fenity was, when she opened the first portal." She paused. "Your birth mata was my mata's half-sister. No one knew she could make portals. She must have hidden it in fear for her life."

"Then that would make you my cousin." Ricci couldn't believe it. Couldn't believe any of this madness. And yet, she'd gone right to Lela when she'd opened the portals. A friendship had bloomed almost from the start.

Her fingertips prickled as the blood rushed from her arms. The iron dug painfully into her bones.

"We're cousins." Lela's lips thinned in determination. "We'll find a way through this. Together."

Ricci tried to return her confidence and failed. She was imprisoned again, only this time her friends were with her, being used against her, her family was in danger, and she wouldn't be able to talk her way out of it. There was no answer she could give to spare any of them.

"It'll be okay, Ricci," Callen said. "We'll figure something out."

Ricci wiped her wet face on her tingling arm, wincing when she grazed the tip of her long ear.

Sometime later, the door creaked open and a servant entered carrying a plate of something steaming.

Ricci glared as he set it down beside her. "How could you work for someone like him?" she accused.

He unchained one of her wrists. The sensation of thousands of needles sticking her at once had her gasping in pain.

273

He left without a word. Ricci glanced at the food. Some kind of fish and a small loaf of bread.

"Why feed me?" she asked

Callen fixated on her plate. "Your magic is stronger if you're fed and rested."

"Have they fed you?" Ricci could guess the answer.

"Eat," he said. "There's no guarantee he will feed you again."

Feeling returned to her arm. She grabbed the bread and stuck it in her chained hand, then used her free hand to pull chunks off it.

"Catch it in your mouth," she said.

"What? No. That's your food. You need it more than I do."

Ricci hurled a piece of bread. It hit Callen in the chest and dropped to the ground.

"Ricci, don't waste it."

"Then catch it." She threw another. He ducked for it, but it hit his chin.

She threw a third piece, and it landed in his mouth.

"Good work," Lela said.

"Are you hungry?" Ricci asked her.

"No. Callen's right. If you mean to be manipulated by the wizard, then you must have sustenance or you might break."

Ricci continued to throw food toward Callen, but when he refused to eat any more, she stopped and didn't touch the plate. The last thing on her mind was hunger.

Fear, shame, guilt—those were her constant companions as they sat silent in near darkness, awaiting an unknown fate. How had everything gone so wrong? Her beautiful illusions had opened portals of nightmares, endangering everyone she loved. There was no one to blame but her own carelessness. If anything Marek said was true, then she was the daughter of a psychopath who murdered her birth mother. Her adoptive parents had lied to protect her. She'd barely met Callen and Lela, and they were already the most loyal and caring friends she'd ever known. And now Lela was family.

"I'm sorry. Neither of you would be here if it wasn't for me. I don't know what's going to happen. I wish I could keep you safe."

"It's not your fault, Ricci," Callen said. "We'll be okay."

"Look at me," Lela said. "You don't have the time or energy to wallow. This mess belongs to the wizard. We're in this together. And I'd do it again if it allowed us to meet."

Ricci nodded, and warmth chased away some of the darkness.

They all jumped as the door opened and Marek entered. Ricci pressed against the wall. He glanced at the food. "Starving yourself isn't going to save you. I am prepared to go to whatever lengths to accomplish my goal."

He paced over to Callen and kicked him in the stomach. Callen curled in on himself as much as his chained arms would allow, gasping and coughing.

Ricci cried out. "Don't hurt him."

"He ate your food. Ready to comply?" Marek asked. "Open a portal, but not to the fae world. I'm long overdue for a meeting."

"What other world is there?"

"Imagine barren wasteland, black rock, flowing lava, and ash-filled red sky." He unfolded a piece of parchment from his pocket. A painting with a red sky, black mountain range, and an old fortress. "Take us here." He pocketed the paper and unchained Callen from the wall. Callen's arms fell heavy to his middle where he'd been kicked. "My apprentice will be coming with me. You will use him to find us and open a portal in two hours, or I will kill him." He leaned close to Callen's ear. "If you try to escape, you'll be stuck in a world where nightmares are real."

"Don't do this, Ricci," Lela said. Her eyes were wide with true terror. "Please, I beg you. I've heard of this place. I promise you. It is worth my life, Callen's life, and even your own life not to open a portal there."

"That's enough of your lies." Marek reached into the air. The force of the spell slammed into Lela. With nowhere to go, her body cracked against the wall, and she went limp.

"Lela!" Ricci cried.

Callen pulled against Marek's hold, but then he held a knife to Ricci's throat, stilling Callen instantaneously. Lela's knife.

"Don't do it, Ricci," Callen said.

Marek pushed, and the blade bit into Ricci's neck. She couldn't help her whimper. "You may throw your own life away so casually, Oriana, but what of your family? Your mama, papa, brothers, aunt and uncle, sister-in-law, and precious baby nephew? Are you willing to throw their lives away too?"

Ricci couldn't speak for the knife at her throat, but he was right. There was nothing Callen or Lela could say to make her sacrifice her family. She closed her eyes and pictured the vile world he described. She pictured heat and blackness, fire and brimstone. She reached with her magic and opened a portal. Even only half in, the heat was overwhelming, whipping at her hair and stealing the air from her lungs.

Marek smiled. "Let's make it one hour, shall we?" He removed the knife and pointed it at Callen. They stepped a pace away, becoming as opaque as the world around them.

Callen locked eyes with her, sweat already beading his brow. He didn't want to go.

"I'm sorry," she whispered. She closed the portal, and they

disappeared. "Lela!" she called out. "Lela, wake up." *Please be okay. Please be okay.*

Lela moaned, but her eyes stayed closed, head hanging between her raised arms.

Tears stung Ricci's eyes, but there was no room for it. She'd just sent a maniac and the boy she cared about to an unknown, evil world. Every thread in her concentration had to be spent tracking him as best she could, making sure he stayed alive. What could Marek want with such a world? And what could make Lela so terrified of it?

CHAPTER 38

The heat hit Callen in the face like an open flame. He instantly broke into a sweat, noticing with some satisfaction that Marek did too. Not *Master* Marek, not anymore.

"Don't look at me like that, my young apprentice." Marek gazed toward the horizon. "This was always the goal."

Callen said nothing, disgusted for ever wanting to be like the insane man in front of him. He wiped the sweat off his brow with his apprentice robe, wishing for a long drink of cold water.

They stood on some kind of dirt road, barely detectable at just a shade smoother than the rockier ground on either side of it. Red. Red was the only way to describe the world around him. The sky glowed red, casting a red tint over the barren mountains and boulders around them. The only plant life was the burned-out husks of trees. Ash drifted down from the hazy sky.

Marek shoved him ahead, and he trudged down the rough road. The iron rubbed raw against his open sores, and his magic wouldn't come to his call. They wouldn't last an hour in this heat without water.

But maybe he didn't have to. If he caught Marek off guard, he could tackle him. Steal the knife and be rid of him. But not with Marek at his back. He'd have to be patient.

Their path slowly veered to the right, and eventually, a stone building appeared at the base of a cliff—a fort of some kind. Torn flags whipped in the blistering wind, and riders came to meet them. At first, Callen couldn't make out anything but black shapes. Then they approached, and Callen backed in fear, bumping into Marek. The horses had red eyes and bodies so thin they were skeletons with skin, but strong as they pounded up, not weak or sickly. The riders were worse. Layers of overlapping black metal armor hid all but their hands and faces, but it was enough. Callen's skin prickled with fear and warning. Their eyes were depthless, black on black in their sockets. No hair or lips, only teeth and fangs. And they gave off the scent of death—rotting flesh and all things vile.

Instinct had him reaching in vain for his magic. He glanced behind him. There was no escaping this. He could outrun Marek if they were on equal footing, but they weren't. Marek still had magic.

"Take me to your king," Marek commanded, all his casual politeness gone.

The riders didn't speak but arranged their horses in a wall around Marek and Callen as they made their way to the fort.

Callen didn't want to speak to Marek. He didn't want to hear one more word than necessary from the madman's mouth. He'd betrayed him, let him down, used him, hurt him in ways he'd never thought possible, ruined his chances to pass the magery test, and harmed the girl he loved. But curiosity got the better of him.

"What are they?" he asked.

"Demons," Marek said. "And if you try to trick me, injure me, or escape in any way, I will give you to them. They will make you their slave for eternity."

A portcullis dripping with something red clanked slowly open as they neared. The riders left them at the gate, but they didn't enter alone. A dozen demons, bald as the first, surrounded and herded them between stone walls until they reached a central room. The interior of the fort matched the outside; crumbling black rock and compacted dirt floors. Torches and the ever-constant red glow from the sky for light.

The heat didn't lessen once inside. If anything, it magnified without any windows or open air. There was no décor, no portraits or rugs, nothing but the occasional stone bench. No way out. No mounted weapons or anything that could serve as one. A massive black chair sat at the back of the room. A throne.

A demon twice the size of the others sat sprawled across the throne. Shirtless, his torso was muscled like that of a strong man, but instead of skin, he was covered in small, hard scales as red as the sky in this demon world. His face, though the shape of a man's, had the same scales, with pointed ears and eyes as black as the others. Most menacing were the two black horns jutting back from the top of his head, ending in points sharp enough to impale someone.

Callen trembled. Primal fear awoke in him that he'd never known before. His legs sought to run but wouldn't move. He reached for his magic, but the irons kept it from coming. The demon shifted, revealing a pair of wings folded behind him, black as night. Marek hesitated, then shoved Callen forward. He was a human shield from the evil sitting before them.

"Marek," the demon spoke. "You found a way." The words weren't English, more of a deep guttural rumbling that sent chills up his spine, but Callen understood him all the same.

"King Theron." Marek stopped and lowered himself into a bow until his head touched the floor.

Callen followed half a breath behind, but he didn't remember deciding to bow. As if he had no control over his own body.

Marek rose, but it took several moments before Callen remembered how to move his muscles. This couldn't be real. Except when he focused, a small spark of a feeling came from another world, full of life and energy. It tethered him to reality. Ricci was keeping track of him. How he was able to feel her, he had no idea. Perhaps part of her gift, but he was grateful.

"I have control of one who can create the portals. It's the daughter."

"Where is she?" Anger and disapproval rang in the rumble of his voice.

"In the human world, of course. I couldn't bring her and risk being stranded. The boy's life was sufficient motivation."

The demon king bared his fangs in a rippling snarl.

"I've done all you commanded," Marek said, seemingly unafraid in the face of a monster. Almost aloof.

"She's untouched," the demon king rumbled, looking at Callen now.

The urge to shrink under his scrutiny was nearly unbearable, but Callen lifted his chin—a small act of defiance. Ricci would not be *touched* by this king of hell.

Marek followed his gaze. "Yes."

"Then after the human world, your daughter will come to me as my bride."

"Of course," Marek said quickly.

"No, Marek," Callen said with urgency. "You can't do that to her."

The demon king stood, tilted back his head, and roared. His colossal wings flared wide, and black feathers shimmered in the torchlight. The sound rattled the walls. Dust and debris rained down. Callen clamped his hands over his ears, hunching.

Marek acted as if he didn't notice the outburst. "Forgive my ignorant apprentice. His usefulness is about to run out. I will see that he's punished."

The spark that was Ricci grew stronger. The world around him turned foggy, like being in a cloud. Blissful cool air rushed into their space. The hour had crawled by like an eternity.

Ricci appeared beside them, though more in the human world than in this hell. Still chained in Marek's dungeon, she glanced at the half-crumbling room around them, but the portal didn't extend far. She couldn't see the demon king.

"No reason to delay," Marek said to the demon. "She's in need of instruction."

The demon king growled but stood and paced toward them.

"Ricci, leave! Go now and never come back." Callen pulled against the chains, reaching in vain for his magic. The demon could not be allowed to cross into their world. Callen knew this beyond instinct, beyond any truth to ever exist. He lunged toward the demon. "Go!"

With a hiss, Marek used magic to weigh down the chains as if they were attached to boulders. Callen slammed to the gritty ground, knocking the air from his lungs.

Ricci's gaze swiveled to him and away, eyes wide as the demon king stepped through the outer edge of her portal. He neared, lips pulled back to expose a fang. He towered above her twice over.

"Ricci," Callen gasped out, struggling to regain breath.

She stood paralyzed. Her mouth gaped in wordless fear. The portal shuttered, the human realm winking in and out of sight.

"Keep it steady, young one." The demon's voice seemed calm and reassuring, though the bone-shaking rumble hadn't changed. The contrast shook Callen to his core. The demon was wooing her.

Ricci swallowed. The shuttering ceased.

"Oriana." Marek stepped as far away from the demon as he could. "King Theron has a job to do. You must learn to make the portal big enough and stay open long enough for him to accomplish it."

Ricci's eyes didn't stray from the demon king. "I can't make it any bigger." Her voice trembled.

The demon king stepped closer to her. "I will show you."

Callen pushed to his knees, but his manacled wrists stayed rooted to the ground.

Before she could recoil, the demon placed his palm on her brow. Red light burst from the space between his hand and her skin. Her eyes rolled back in her head.

Callen kicked out, but Marek yanked on the chains, sending him sprawling.

"He's not hurting her," Marek said. "He's giving her a gift. Think of it as a wedding present." He smirked.

A gift? Nothing from the hands of that monster could do anything but harm her. Helplessness devoured Callen from the inside out. What was happening to her?

In a few minutes, it was over. The demon king removed his hand. Ricci slumped against the wall, panting. But the portal stayed open.

The demon king let out a faint chuckle. "Daughter?" He paused. "You've brought me quite the prize." He turned to them, but Marek didn't look surprised. "Take care of my bride. When you return, the army will be waiting." He paced to his throne without a backward glance.

Callen lifted his arms, no longer weighed down. He moved

toward Ricci, and Marek didn't stop him, though he gripped the end of the chain. Callen placed his manacled arms around her, rocking her as she trembled uncontrollably, eyes far away.

"Time to go home, Ricci," Callen said. "Take us home." Concern locked the breath in his chest.

"Home?" she asked, dazed.

"Take us to Lela," Marek said. "Or your family will die."

Ricci didn't seem to hear him—didn't react in any way. Could they somehow leave Marek here?

As if Marek had read his mind, he brandished a knife, sticking the point toward Callen's back. "Tell her to bring us back."

Callen snarled at him, then turned to Ricci. "Close the portal, love," he murmured in her ear. "Take us with you."

Ricci gave the barest of nods, and the blistering demon world disappeared. The dungeon was ice-cold by comparison. Callen had never been so happy to be out of that hell and back to being locked up in a dungeon.

Ricci sat back against the stone wall, looking utterly spent.

Marek tugged on his chains. "Get up."

Callen glared at him. "How could you let this happen? How could you do this to your own daughter?"

"You don't even know what's been done to her. Now get up, back to your spot before I decide you're no longer worth the trouble. Then whatever plan you think might get you all out of this will never come to fruition."

Callen dropped Ricci's hand and allowed Marek to rechain his arms above him. He might have been younger and stronger than the aging mage, able to take him on in any form of hand-to-hand combat, but he'd never best him at magic—Marek had seen to that by not training him properly—even if he could somehow find a way out of the chains. Callen would do no good to Ricci dead.

"Bring them water. And food," Ricci said, voice surprisingly strong as Marek chained her to the wall, leaving one arm free. "Or I'll not help you again."

Marek chuckled, but said, "As you wish." He locked the door behind him.

Lela still slumped in her chains, though it was hard to see her in the dim light.

"Is she... dead?" Callen asked.

"No. Unconscious."

"What happened?" he asked. "Are you okay?"

"That creature showed me things. He showed me how to dig deeper within my magic. They want me to open a portal twenty men wide and hold it open for hours. He showed me how." She shuddered.

"Could you do it?"

"Yes. There's enough in me to do it. I know that now. I know how to control it." Her voice sounded sure, not carrying any of the fear having these new skills should bring, knowing what they would be used for.

"You've been through a lot." Too much. Her face looked pale, and she wouldn't meet his eyes.

"I've never felt anything like it before. The way he connected to me. He tapped right into my magic. He could have taken it all, taken my very soul, but he didn't. I sensed kindness in him." She shook her head like she couldn't believe her own words.

"*It*—not him. The demon king is not a him. And that wasn't kindness. It was a spell to make you see him as he wishes. He's evil. He made Marek promise to give you to him as a part of the deal to get the army."

The servant returned, interrupting whatever she'd planned to say. He brought food and water to Ricci and Callen, but not

Lela, and he didn't unchain Callen's arms. Callen stared at the sloshing cup of clean water.

"How is Callen supposed to eat or drink?" Ricci asked, anger in her tone. "And what about Lela?"

The servant ignored her and left.

"I'm sorry. I didn't think." She glanced at her own food and drink.

Callen licked his dry lips. "You go ahead and eat. I'll be fine." Magic drained energy, and a little bit of food helped a long way. They wouldn't wait just because she'd chosen not to eat. And who knew how much rest they'd allow her before asking the impossible?

"Ricci, what's the demon army's purpose?" he asked as she ate.

"I don't know. I wasn't shown that."

He knew what it was for. Marek wanted to be High Master of the council. He wanted power, and this was how he'd get it. A demon army unleashed on the earth.

CHAPTER 39

R icci sat against the cold, stabbing wall, and lay her head on her completely numb arm. Her head pounded. She rubbed her eyes with her free arm, trying to keep her emotions from spilling out. The demon king, he'd done something to her. Opened her mind to her true depth of power. All with a simple touch. She'd never been so afraid and so intrigued at the same time.

Lela groaned, chains clanging. Ricci sat up in relief.

Lela's eyes fluttered open, then she moaned. "My head. Oh, it hurts."

"You cracked it pretty good when Marek attacked you," Ricci said. "I'm just so glad you're alright. How do you feel?"

"Like I've been run over by a herd of unicorns," she said, eyes clenched against the pain.

"If it's half as bad as these irons, I feel your pain," Callen said, voice scratchy.

"What happened?" Lela asked. "The last thing I remember was—" She gasped and her eyes flashed to Ricci. "Did you do it? Did you open a portal to the demon world?"

Ricci held up her free hand, palm up. "I didn't have a choice. He threatened to kill my family."

"He took me to the demon king," Callen said.

Lela shook her head rapidly back and forth, lips quivering. "I knew the danger for my kind wouldn't come from you, but I never thought it would come from there. You can't imagine what you've done."

"What have I done?" Ricci asked, guilt and fear driving needles into her heart.

"King Theron, ruler of the demon world. It isn't just a fable. What did the wizard want with him?"

"I believe Marek means to take over the mage council," Callen said bitterly. "The demon king... he touched Ricci with his palm. On her forehead. She hasn't been quite the same since we returned." He met Ricci's gaze.

"I haven't?" Ricci had been tired, sure, but that wasn't unusual, given what they were going through.

"Ricci," Lela breathed. The sound was so finite and infinitely sad that Ricci tore her gaze from Callen. "We won't let King Theron have you. I know what he really wants. He wants to destroy my people. It's in our children's stories, but they must be real. The stories say he never found a way to get there. The humans and fae were rightfully too afraid to seek him."

Ricci's heart thundered in her chest. "Are you certain, Lela? How could you really know? A portal hasn't been opened in centuries. Maybe time has twisted what his true intent is? He seemed so kind when we spoke with each other." Time could warp the truth.

Lela and Callen exchanged a glance.

"You didn't speak at all," Callen said, talking slowly. "He invaded your mind without permission after stealing your promise of marriage without asking and guaranteeing a demon army for Marek to attack and overthrow our own people."

"Yes. That's true." Ricci nodded. That didn't sound kind at all.

Callen wasn't wrong, but it didn't feel as bad as he made it seem. King Theron was just trying to help his people leave their horrible world behind. It was so hot there. And who could blame him for wanting to help his people? She blushed, remembering the heat of his palm against her skin.

"Ricci, look at me," Lela said. "You cannot do this. Don't open another portal. Don't let those beasts come here."

"But, my family. Marek will kill them." And what about King Theron?

"If you let them come here, you may as well kill them yourself," Lela said.

Ricci flinched. She'd never hurt her family. How could Lela say that?

"The demons won't be controlled once set loose." Lela rose to the balls of her feet. "Even if the wizard has plans for what to do with them after he's made himself ruler, they won't comply. They will pillage and murder until King Theron tells them otherwise. No one nearby will be safe. No one in the world, if the demons decide that's what they want."

Callen's chains rattled as he leaned forward. "My family lives nearby. My father is high lord." His mouth dropped open with understanding. "Marek will have them killed. My brothers. My sisters."

"Yes," Lela said.

"Then we must stop Marek," Ricci said. Stopping him didn't mean King Theron had to suffer. "But how?"

Silence.

"It has to be you, Ricci," Lela said. "You're the only one he gets close to, the only one who can still access their energies." She jiggled her manacles for emphasis.

Callen fidgeted. "I have an idea that might work, but you won't like it, Lela."

"What?" she asked flatly.

"Ricci will open a portal to the demon world as instructed, pretending compliance. Marek will be with her, of course, to make her do what he asks. Then when she closes the portal, she leaves him stranded in the demon world."

Ricci nodded. Trapping Marek was a good plan, and she'd get to see King Theron again.

"No," Lela said with anger and a tone that brooked no argument. "We can't risk it. Whatever plan we make will be one in which a portal is not opened."

"Look," Callen said. "You know more about this than both of us, but if no demons cross over, what's the harm?"

"No." Lela took a deep breath. "There's a story of King Theron that says long ago, when humans and fae shared worlds, King Theron bewitched a fae princess. He'd been fae himself then. She was heir to the throne, and he wanted to be king, so he tricked her into marrying him. Almost. The princess saw through his plan, and so bewitched him first. He was banished to the demon world. It's said that while he suffered with his anger, he changed. He fought his way to be king of the demons and vowed to return and conquer the fae someday."

Ricci shook her head in the silence. Lela's tale had it all wrong.

"If he's as vengeful as in our story books, you can't open a portal," Lela said.

"Well, no one else has a better idea. Besides, it's up to Ricci," Callen said.

"I like Callen's idea," Ricci said quickly. Marek was the enemy and had to be dealt with.

"Don't do it," Lela pleaded. "King Theron is playing tricks with your mind. He wants you to go to him willingly. He's using you."

"Using me?" There was truth to Lela's words as well, but she couldn't remember what. Her mind was a fog. "Something's wrong."

"Don't trust yourself, Ricci," Lela said. "Trust *me*. Do not open a portal."

Marek entered the room, breaking Ricci's concentration. He held the key to her manacles. She stared up at him. He was the mastermind behind all the evil that had happened in her life. He had to be stranded in the demon world. It was the only way.

"Thank you for eating and keeping up your strength, Oriana. It's time to go."

"Not before you unlock one of Callen's arms, and one of Lela's. And give her food and drink as well." Some things weren't clear, but that was. Her friends needed to be alright. "And no poisoning them."

Marek sighed but looked at her, considering. "For the fiancé of King Theron, it will be done."

He called out and gave the servant instructions.

His words excited her for some reason. *Fiancé.* She looked at Callen and smiled.

"This way, Oriana." Marek unhooked her chain from the wall, then tugged her toward the door.

"Not here?" She twisted to look at Lela and Callen.

They stared back at her, worried.

"Of course not. An entire army couldn't march out of my basement, now could they?" He tugged harder.

When they were almost out the door, Lela called out to her. "When you feel lost or confused, remember who you love and who loves you in return. That is truth. That will lead you out of the dark."

"Quiet," Marek snapped. He rushed them out of the room, slamming the door closed.

When they finally reached outside, it was night. The rolling lawn in front of the estate was lined with burning lanterns. Such a wide-open space at the edge of town. Perfect to begin an assault on the mage council. But that wasn't going to happen. She'd leave Marek stranded before a single demon passed through. She just needed to see King Theron one last time, then she'd close the portal for good.

"Here will do nicely." Marek stopped her at the top of the gently sloping hill. "Now remember what you've been shown and what will happen if you don't do as I wish. Nice and tall and wide."

Ricci reached into her magic. It was easy. There was so much of it, like a fountain continuously fed from a spring of the freshest, purest water. The portal opened in moments, tall and wide as he'd said. The heat was suffocating.

Marek laughed. "My, King Theron's magic works quick."

Ricci looked around the opaque surroundings, the same bright red as before. Her heart went staccato at the sight of King Theron. He stood but ten feet away, arms relaxed at his sides. Bare-chested, a black sword as tall as her was sheathed at his side, all shadows and jagged edges. He watched her like no one else mattered in the world but the two of them. His wings flapped, kicking up sand with a burst of hot wind.

"Well met, Oriana," King Theron said, his thundering demon-speak crystal clear in her mind. More beautiful than she remembered. "Have you come to help me and my people?"

There was something else she was supposed to do. Something important. But, it couldn't be more important than helping save his people.

"Yes," she said.

"Wonderful," Marek said, laughing.

She'd forgotten he was there at all.

He unlocked her remaining manacle. The chains dropped to the ground with a clang. "She's all yours, as promised."

"March," King Theron called out, stepping toward her. The heat of him warmed her even more than the blistering air.

The dark, misshapen forms of the scariest creatures she'd ever beheld entered the outer range of the biggest portal she'd ever opened. Walking death with black, soulless eyes and skeletal hands. She gasped, backing away. The portal flickered.

King Theron unfurled his wings, blocking her view. He placed a massive, clawed hand against her face. It was bigger than her whole head. The ridges of his scales caressed her skin. "No need to be frightened, Oriana. They won't hurt my bride. Keep the portal wide, for as long as you can."

The demon army flanked them, marching on both sides like King Theron was a rock parting water. They squealed and spat, stomping and clanking, row after row after row. Some on skeleton horses, some on foot, but Ricci didn't mind them. She stared into King Theron's eyes the entire time.

Hours passed before he spoke to her again. "When we are wed," he said, "your power will belong to me. You will use it to do my bidding. And we will rule together."

She nodded, staring at his mouth, wishing she could taste him.

The sky lightened, and her eyelids grew heavy. Her limbs shook. She stumbled and King Theron caught her, holding her up in his strong hands. "Your power is impressive. Not much longer."

She held off as long as she could, becoming dead weight in his arms. She felt sick, like a dried husk of a person. "I can't. I must rest," she pleaded.

"You can let go now," King Theron said. "It is done."

The portal closed, and she fell into sweet oblivion.

293

CHAPTER 40

"I'm worried about her, Lela. Will her confusion wear off?" Callen asked not long after Marek took Ricci. Though, *worried* didn't cover it. Scared out of his mind was more accurate.

"King Theron's bewitched her. If it takes root, she won't remember that he's evil and will destroy all she holds dear." Though Callen couldn't see Lela's face from this angle, her voice sounded hollow. She sounded as scared as he was.

"We should have tried harder, said something more to convince her." Would she listen to Lela and not open a portal at all? Or would she try to strand Marek in the demon world?

"I didn't want to push her. If she started on the path of defending King Theron, she'd become his most powerful ally, convincing herself of the lie. You heard how she spoke about him, saying how kind he was."

"Yes." He sighed. "What can we do?"

"There's nothing we can do," she said sadly, detached as if in disbelief. "She has to remember the truth on her own. With luck, she can resist it enough to keep from opening a portal."

"But how can she? If she's under a spell by such a powerful being?"

Lela didn't answer.

The door banged open, and Marek rushed in.

Callen's lips parted. Ricci hadn't trapped him in the demon world. What was happening out there?

Marek sneered at Lela, then hurried over to Callen. With a knife to Callen's throat, he unchained him from the wall. "Time for you to fulfill your usefulness," he said. He turned to Lela. "You're next." He pushed Callen ahead of him.

Callen wouldn't be his tool. He planted his feet and shoved his head backward. His skull connected against Marek's nose with a sickening crunch. Callen turned, reaching to wrap the chains around Marek's throat.

"Watch out!" Lela cried.

Marek lunged with the knife. It stuck deep in Callen's side. Pain exploded, blinding him and blocking all other thoughts. He fell to the ground.

"Bold. Very bold." Marek clutched his broken nose. Blood poured down his face. He grabbed a handkerchief from his robes, and it immediately soaked.

The potion for nosebleeds irrationally sprung to Callen's mind. He pushed manacled hands into his wound, crying out in pain.

"Now you still have to come with me, only you'll do it injured." Marek pointed the knife and used his magic to pull Callen to his feet.

Callen hissed with pain.

Holding a handkerchief to his nose, Marek examined Callen's bloody robes and hands. "This will serve my purpose nicely."

Two demons entered the basement, black armor grinding beneath their lipless, empty-eyed faces. Lela gasped, backing against the wall, but they didn't stop at her. They each took one of Callen's arms, wrenching his hands off the wound where he'd struggled to staunch the flow of blood.

The demons' cold armor bit into Callen's arms as they dragged him away, Marek following. While Marek's nose had stopped bleeding, the cut in Callen's side flowed free. Each step felt like a white-hot poker speared into his guts, again and again. The walls spun, and sweat beaded his upper lip.

All that was forgotten when they reached outside. Ricci stood at the top of Marek's property. An entire army marched through her portal on either side of her—snarling monsters with vacant eyes that made the hair on Callen's arms stand on end. The demon king towered over her, staring down at her like his prized possession. And she stared up at him in a way Callen had only seen her do a few times before. Horror quickly overrode jealousy.

The demons bore torches, streaming through in endless rows. The front of this terrifying parade had already passed through Marek's front gates long ago, with the army trailing out of sight down the road leading toward town.

The whole city, maybe even the world, was at stake, yet she didn't move or blink her gaze from the demon king. She'd truly been bewitched.

"Take him to the carriage." Marek watched the procession with fascinated satisfaction, ignoring Callen and his demon captors.

Once inside, Callen pushed his hands against his bloodied side, hissing with the pressure on the wound. The demons climbed in with him, jolting the wagon side to side. They sat facing him, gauntleted hands on their swords, watching with their black, empty eyes. Marek rode up top with the driver—another demon. The skeleton horses pulled them swiftly away.

CHAPTER 41

Callen's vision swam. It was like a bad dream he'd wake up from any minute. Then he'd know Ricci was okay—and his family, and the mage council.

"You're a fool, Marek," Callen called out loudly, watching the demons' swords. "You can't trust the demon king. You may force your way into being high master, but it will never belong to you."

Marek did not reply.

They bumped swiftly down the road. The pealing of the fire alarm reached them as they neared the main part of town. Everyone was screaming. People emerged from their homes still dressed in night clothes, panicked at the sight of the demons. But the army didn't touch them. This wasn't their purpose. They marched to the mage building. Callen leaned his heavy head against the side of the wagon.

He must have blacked out, because he awoke to the sounds of burning, and screaming, and thunderous magic. He was chained to the door inside the carriage. The demons and Marek were gone. Outside, the army wreaked its chaos. Shops burned.

Villagers fled, clutching their children. The statue in the bubbling fountain lay split in two, as if sliced through with a great sword. Flashes of blue followed by pops and explosions sparked from the mage building windows.

High Master Aldridge rushed by, headed toward the building, followed by town guards and his own personal guards.

"High Master!" Callen yelled. He clanked his chains against the side of the carriage, pulling at his wound. The high master did not hear him.

A company of demons spotted them and chased them to the doors of the mage building. The guards turned and fought, charging with swords raised. They were sticks compared to the demons' weapons, doing little damage to their superior armor. In moments, the guards' courage was rewarded with swift deaths.

Behind them, High Master Aldridge finished conjuring his spell. With a clap of his hands, an invisible force slammed into the demons. The demons' heads turned backward on their shoulders with loud cracks. They dropped to the ground.

"High Master!" Callen yelled again, but no one heard him over the raging fires, screaming townsfolk, and pillaging demons.

Just as the high master was about to enter the mage building, Marek stepped out. He was followed by the most menacing demons yet. In addition to their black armor, they wore red capes, and their helmets were spiked, matching King Theron's horns. They were clearly leaders—demon generals.

High Master Aldridge backed away. His remaining guard trembled before the towering demons.

"I wouldn't bother, Aldridge. Everyone in there is dead." Marek took in the group in front of him.

Grief threatened to crush Callen. Everyone? Even the apprentices? The young scribes?

"You did this," the high master said. "Why?"

"King Theron wills it so." Marek gestured with his arm.

The demon generals—four in all—spread out and attacked. Marek raised his hands, as did the high master. The two masters circled each other in the center of the fighting. A mage duel.

Callen jerked against his chains, but of course, the metal didn't yield. His gash pulled, and warm blood flowed anew. If he could help the high master defeat Marek, then together they could find a way to help Ricci and stop the demon king.

The high master cast first, sending a bolt of lightning flying from his hands. Marek held up his arm, and his magic deflected it. The bolt flew sideways, hitting one of the demon generals in the chest, piercing its armor like a spear. It fell over, writhing. A guard cut off its head.

The two masters traded blows, magic on magic, in a flurry of spells. When one master fired, the other would be ready to deflect or form a shield. Callen had never seen such mastery. No one fought for their lives in ordinary duels.

Marek slowed, and a fireball hit him in the knees, engulfing the bottom of his robes.

"There's a reason I'm head mage and you are not," High Master Aldridge said, buying him time to conjure the next spell. "Today has made that all the more apparent."

Marek managed to extinguish the flames, only to be met with another ball of fire. This one hit him in the chest and burst all over him. Callen leaned out the window. The high master was going to win. Marek's skill couldn't compare.

"Get him!" Marek yelled, beating at the flames with one arm while directing a spell with the other.

"No," Callen breathed. Of course Marek wouldn't fight by the rules of engagement.

The demon generals stood from their dead opponents,

mouths covered in blood. They circled the high master and pointed their massive swords. The high master's eyes went wide. His hands flourished in the air, but it was too late. The demons stuck him through from three sides, pushing against each other.

High Master Aldridge's white robes ran red with blood.

"No!" Callen cried out.

Blood spurted from the high master's mouth. He sagged to the ground as the demons yanked out their swords. Grief wrapped cold hands around Callen's chest, squeezing until he couldn't breathe, overriding the pain from his wound.

High Master Aldridge had been their last hope. More than that, he'd been a friend, building a bond while teaching him these past weeks.

Marek didn't even look triumphant. He stood over the high master's body with a bland expression, almost bored. His goal had been realized, and he didn't care.

He said something to the demon generals, and they left swiftly, stepping over bodies and gore. Marek glanced sharply up at Callen as if just remembering he was there. He returned to the driver's seat with the remaining general, but no one joined Callen inside before they took off.

"You have what you wanted," Callen said, hoping Marek heard him. It hurt to raise his voice. "Let me go. Send the demons back, and let Ricci go."

His pleas went ignored except for a rumbling laugh from the demon general.

Callen drifted in and out, struggling to staunch his wound and ignoring the blood pooled on the seat. He worked to focus his gaze and finally noticed their surroundings. Dove Park with its pond and white wooden bridge. Kolassi's Bakery where the chocolate croissants melted in your mouth.

This was where he grew up before leaving to become a

mage. They headed for his childhood home where many of his siblings still lived. The high lord's home. They were not far now. The land began where Main Street ended.

Callen strained to look behind him. The demon army followed. Marching down the once-beautiful Main Street through town, they filled the space with their black, oozing bodies from one side of the cobbled street to the other, stretching so far back Callen couldn't see the end.

A few minutes later, Callen spotted his father's personal guards and dozens and dozens of citizens standing behind the fence that encircled the property, swords at the ready. They must have assembled as the demons slaughtered the mages.

It was an impressive turnout, but only a temporary obstacle to the single-minded ferociousness of the demon army. Father had a saferoom, and maybe he'd make Mother and the family stay there, but it wouldn't save them. The demons would burn the mansion down around them if ordered.

Father wouldn't hand over the city. Their family had ruled for decades under the direction of the monarchy.

"Please don't do this, Marek. That's my family."

"Things so desperate you're reduced to begging now?" Marek called back, finally answering him. "You hate them anyway. It'll be a relief to watch them die."

Callen shook his head. "You don't need to do this. You've won the mage council, why take the city?"

"You think King Theron and I only want the council?"

Callen paled. The demons had destroyed their biggest obstacle to taking over Timbercross. Human soldiers would be no match against them without the power of the mages.

The carriage stopped at the gates. The demon army spread out behind them, spanning the length of the long wrought-iron fence at the front of the property and beyond. The guards inside glanced uneasily, some even backing up from the fence. But they had nowhere to go. The demons surrounded the estate. Even spread out, they were rows and rows deep, and still coming.

The carriage door opened. A demon general pulled Callen's chain from the wall, cracking the wood in half. The demon hauled Callen out, and he shouted in pain.

Marek paced along the fence. "This is Lord Callen Kealamin. You will tell High Lord Cameron that I have his son, and I wish to speak to him."

The townspeople murmured, shuffling uncomfortably.

In the distance, the guards parted to the barking commands of their lord. Callen's father stepped to the gate, dapper in his tailored shirt and breeches, with a leather cuirass and a red face. Callen might not have been close to his father, but he loved him and didn't want anything bad to happen to him, despite what Marek thought.

But what could he say? Don't fight? The demons would kill no matter what. And once the demons controlled the city, no one was safe.

From behind the gate, Callen's father glanced from Marek to Callen. "Are you well, son?"

Callen clutched his side. "I'm fine." Far, far from the truth.

Marek interrupted. "Give me the city, or I take your son's life."

Father didn't hesitate. "I love my son, but I've always taught him about duty. And my duty is to the people of this city."

Marek chuckled. "No wonder he wanted to leave you." He turned to the demons on either side of Callen. "Kill him."

Callen flinched.

"Now!" Callen's father yelled.

A volley of arrows sailed from behind the fence. Callen

braced to be impaled, but they missed, landing dead-center in the open faceplates of his demons' heads. They dropped to the ground. Marek raised magic to shield himself. The arrows hit and embedded in a sphere around him.

Callen ran for the gate.

"Hurry, son! They're coming!"

The pain in his side bloomed black spots in his vision with every pounding step. The gate opened a crack, and he aimed straight for it.

Marek bellowed behind him. "Attack! Kill them all!"

The demons roared, vibrating rock and metal.

Callen squeezed through the opening just as the first arrows struck the fence. The gate slammed closed, resealing the fence's protective spell. High Master Aldridge had overseen that spell personally, but it wouldn't take Marek long to break through it.

Father caught Callen as he stumbled. His hand came up red with blood. "Physician!" he shouted, leading Callen behind the lines of soldiers waiting for the slaughter.

Callen wanted nothing more than to fall into the oblivion his wound demanded, but that would only lead to death. The physician lifted Callen's robe in front of everyone, leaving him exposed in his undershorts, the clothing hanging from his manacled wrists. Callen got his first look at the damage.

The knife had stabbed into the left side, and not cleanly. It was gaping and still bleeding.

"This was a poisoned blade. An herb derivative. Hemlock, I suspect. See here?" The physician pointed at Callen's skin where tendrils of dark blue branched from the wound. He splashed an ointment which burned like the fifth level of hell, then fished a needle and string out of his bag.

"What in the Gods' names is going on, Callen?" Father demanded.

The demons threw themselves against the fence, swords slashing, lipless teeth gnashing. Callen winced as the sutures went in and out, in and out.

"Marek went to another world. He made a deal with the king of the demons. He destroyed the mage council and now seeks to rule the city."

His father lowered his voice. "Use your magic. Help us out of this."

Callen held up his manacled wrists. "Iron blocks magic. I don't have a way to remove these."

Wait a minute. Maybe he did. "Father, my bags. The innkeeper was supposed to deliver them here. Where are they?"

Father scrubbed his face. "A courier dropped them off. I believe your mother had them taken to your old room."

Callen sighed in relief. "Is the family in the saferoom?"

"Yes."

"The city will fall. I'll lead them away. It's the only way to save them."

The physician bandaged Callen up nice and tight. Callen pulled on his robe, thanking him.

His father's mouth thinned. He clutched Callen by the arm. There were a thousand unsaid things in his eyes as he looked at his son for the last time. Apologies. Wishes. Regrets. "I'm proud of you, son. You've grown into a good man."

The words pierced Callen's soul, sinking in deeply. His father never gave compliments. They hadn't even seen each other in over seven years. "Thank you, Father," he whispered.

His father squeezed and let go, rushing toward the guard. He shouted orders while the demons raged against the fence. Callen hurried inside. Servants jumped from where they watched at the window.

"Get out of here," Callen said. "It's not safe." He didn't wait for their response.

He pounded up the polished stairs and into his old room. All his personal belongings were gone, though the furniture was the same. He snatched his potions bag from the dresser. The bottles clinked as he rifled through them.

"Where is it? Where is it? Ah-ha!" Callen snatched up the bottle.

For Daring Escapes

He would have laughed at the irony if demons weren't roaring outside, a constant reminder to hurry—his failed potion that was supposed to open a portal. He'd brought it in hopes of finding a use for it, to impress Marek.

Awkwardly and as carefully as he could with his hands bound so close together, he unstoppered the tiny vial. He tipped the liquid, letting it run over the hinge of his manacle. Too much spilled out. Drops hit the floor, immediately eating through the Parnuvian carpet and Northland Oak wood floor.

But the manacle was dissolving too. The hinge disappeared, and the metal slipped open. He grinned. The potion worked on iron. What else would it work on? He quickly dissolved the other manacle. His wrists were blistered raw.

With the iron gone, he took a deep breath, then winced at the pain in his side. Magic fizzled back. Sun after months of darkness. Food after dying of starvation.

"Hello, old friend." Callen smiled, grabbed his pack, then hurried downstairs. The saferoom was behind a hidden wall in his parents' bedroom suite. It was a home of its own, with sleeping quarters and food storage. He pounded on the door. "Mother, it's me. Open up."

There was muffled arguing.

"Callen?" his mother asked with a voice like she'd been crying.

"Don't let him in. The enemy might be forcing him." Definitely his oldest sister, Tamri.

"Make him do the secret knock," his favorite brother Brander said.

Callen did the knock, barely remembering it. Four slow raps, four quick, then a series of taps. The door opened, and all his family stood in the doorway, mixed expressions on their aged faces. He hadn't seen them in years. None of them had bothered to write or visit, even his mother. It was as if he'd never been a part of them.

"What is happening, Callen?" his oldest brother Marlo asked, taking control. Marlo would be the new high lord—if he survived.

"We're under attack from a demon army. Father sent me. You must come with me. It's not safe here." He held out his hand, which his mother took automatically.

"No. This is the safest place to be. It was designed against an attack." Marlo sniffed.

"No room is safe when they burn the place to the ground—like I just watched them do to half of the mage community. You stay here, you die." Callen had never spoken to them like that. He was always the little brother, the youngest. But they took notice now, eyes wide.

He guided Mother out, and not one of them argued as he led them down into the basement. Through a grate in the floor, they dropped into an old tunnel that connected all the older estates. With luck, Marek didn't suspect the mansion had an escape tunnel.

Callen used some precious magic to form a ball of light. Since he'd been ignored as a boy, the tunnels were one of his favorite places to practice magic alone. His second-oldest sister, Patience, complained the loudest about the smell but followed as Callen led them further and further down the tunnel. The demon's screaming crescendoed. An ear-splitting crash sounded from above.

"They've breached the fence," Callen said, pulling Mother along. She panted, winded, quiet tears spilling down her cheeks. She wasn't prepared for this, with her fine gown and thin, embroidered shoes.

"That fence is impenetrable," Tamri said.

"Not for them."

When the sound of the fighting could no longer be heard, and they'd traveled far enough, Callen found a grate and climbed. The motion pulled at his stitches. He pushed open the grate. They were in someone else's basement. He climbed out and helped the rest of his family.

"Oh, this is the Tueman's residence," his mother said as they ascended out of the basement.

The house was empty and not far enough away from the fighting for Callen to be comfortable.

He turned to his family. "Find some weapons. When things die down, we're going to the river market."

"Why there?" his mother asked.

"A friend needs my help." *You're not alone, Ricci.*

CHAPTER 42

Lela sat with her back against the wall, head throbbing. The slightest movement sent shooting pain through her skull and chained arm. The food and water had been gone for hours. She hadn't been weak enough to show hunger or thirst as Callen had, but she was eternally grateful when Ricci made the deal to include her.

Ricci had not been herself then, yet she'd remembered her friends. Her cousin. Lela almost smiled. Extended family was rare, and now she had a cousin and an answer for Mata for where Aunt Fenity had gone. And an answer to why she felt so protective of Ricci from the first time they met.

Had Pata felt that same call? Was he truly trying to help them back at the cottage, or was it more lies?

King Theron's hold on Ricci was already taking. She only hoped what the stories said he did to young maidens wasn't true.

The door slammed open, kicked by someone. King Theron ducked through as he carried Ricci in, horns glinting and wings splayed. She was unconscious, hanging limp in his scaled arms. He laid her on the ground. Lela drew up her legs, trying to hide in the shadows.

The movement drew his attention. He sniffed the air, scenting her.

"You're the cousin," King Theron said. His rumbling voice sent her trembling. "Ensure she recovers. There's work yet to be done." He paused at the door, black eyes piercing her. "You can't break my spell, healer. It's useless to try."

She shivered. Healer? How could he know she was an herbalist?

He left without locking the door. He hadn't shackled Ricci either.

"Ricci!" Lela called out. "Ricci, wake up."

She didn't stir, not even a mumble. Her red hair tumbled in every direction over her pale-as-death face. Deep, dark bags sunk each eye. She wasn't well, but she was alive, chest moving up and down with each breath.

Hours passed before Ricci awoke. She groaned, rolling to her side.

"Ricci, are you alright?" Lela asked. She braced for her cousin's answer, who she would be when she spoke. How much of Ricci remained inside?

Ricci blinked and looked around. "I'm back here?" her voice rasped. She looked at her wrists. "I'm not chained."

A dewdrop of relief threatened to raise Lela's hopes. Ricci sounded like her old self.

"The door isn't locked either," Lela said. "It seems King Theron believes you'll stay here." She pointed. "Try the door."

"King Theron wants me to stay here?" Ricci asked, sitting fully up.

"What? Umm, no. He wants you to find the key to my binders." Her brief hope burst into flame and crumbled to ash.

309

Ricci backed to her old spot along the wall. "Why bring me here if he wanted me somewhere else? I'm staying."

Lela sighed. "Do you love King Theron?"

Ricci cocked her head. "Y-yes. Of course."

"Does he love you?"

"Yes. He's going to marry me." Ricci smiled fondly.

Just like the stories. "Then why is he leading an army to attack the city? Why is he putting your family in danger?"

"My family's in danger? That can't be true." Ricci clamped her hands over her ears and rocked back and forth.

"Just listen to me. Ricci?" Ricci ignored her, and eventually Lela left her alone. The more Ricci defended King Theron out loud, the more she'd fall under his spell. The stories in her books told of King Theron's power of enchantment, but in a vague way that offered no useful strategy to counteract it. '*The prince broke the princess's curse using the deep bonds of true love.*'

If Lela couldn't find a way to make Ricci wake up, she'd never get back to her own world. To warn her people. To save Oren.

The crash of the door startled Lela awake. The wizard entered. Blood crusted his scorched robes, and he had dark bruises under his eyes and on his nose. Callen was not with him.

"Did you kill him?" Lela asked, past caring about what he might do to her. "Are you going to kill everyone Ricci loves?"

He smirked. "Not everyone."

King Theron entered, ducking to fit through the door. Lela's mouth clamped shut, and she huddled against the wall.

"The city is won," King Theron rumbled, wordless tone somehow making its meaning known. "I've come for her."

Lela glanced at Ricci, still asleep. What more did the demon king want with her?

"Wait," Marek said. His worried voice had Lela glancing up to study him. He looked scared. "Can't she stay here?"

Did he mean to keep Ricci's ability for himself?

The demon king roared, and it shook the very foundation. Marek cowed. Lela hugged her knees with her free arm. No world wanted to unleash the fury of King Theron, ruler of nightmares and death.

Ricci blinked awake. She raised her head, mouth curling into a love-sick smile for King Theron. Lela's empty stomach churned.

"I will take what you don't give willingly, and you will suffer the consequences." King Theron held out his hand, and Ricci rushed to him.

King Theron, hand-in-hand with Ricci, faced the wizard.

"The fae girl," Marek said. "Take her instead."

Lela shivered.

"What use is she?" King Theron asked, examining Lela's trembling form.

"She's the daughter of General Ashryn, the king's most trusted leader. You can use her as I used the boy. When they open the gate to let her in, their defenses will be weakened."

King Theron truly meant to invade the fae world. It was the prophecy coming true. Ricci might have been innocent, but through her, the demons would be unleashed. Lela bit her cheek until she tasted blood. Her trembling stilled. She would not break down and show fear to this demon king.

King Theron growled. "Are your fae armies so great they could defeat me?"

Lela thought about lying. If the answer was no, then he wouldn't feel the need to bring her. But the stories said he could detect lies and deceit. "Our warriors are very strong."

They'd been preparing for this outcome even before the first portal opened.

"Then I will take both the fae and my bride," King Theron said, flaring his wings and staring Marek down.

Marek's face went blank. He bowed as he produced a key, then he unchained Lela from the wall.

Lela sprinted for the open door. King Theron turned. His black wing slammed into her chest. He roared as she fell to the ground, coughing and sucking in air. Marek was there, and he clasped the golden binder to her other wrist.

King Theron grabbed her upper arm, easily hauling her off the floor. Lela pulled in vain against his unbreakable, claw-tipped hold. Ricci studied Lela and King Theron with a confused and pained expression.

"Ricci, don't do this," Lela said.

Ricci locked eyes with her, confusion still there, but she didn't seem to register Lela's words. She was silent as King Theron led them outside.

Lela blinked in the afternoon sunlight, then gasped and stumbled. Soldiers filled the landscape. The entire valley was covered with roaring black shapes.

"Oriana," King Theron said. "Make a portal to the fae world."

The pulse as Ricci reached into her well of magic shook the air around them. The portal expanded, as wide as a river. Wide enough for an army. Her people would be slaughtered.

Lela gaped in horror. "Close the portal!" she screamed. Her mata. Oren and his family. The demons would burn their farms and kill everyone. Tears stung her eyes and spilled over.

King Theron tugged her chain, rattling her bones. "Silence," he commanded. "Keep it open, Oriana. Your cousin and I have work to do."

King Theron wrapped his scaled hand around Lela's shoulder, guiding her in front of him. They entered the portal. The foggy world turned solid. They stepped onto a grassy knoll with trees behind them. Lela didn't recognize this place. They weren't on her mata's land. But then she scanned the horizon. Familiar castle turrets rose to the sky behind a hill in the distance.

Ricci had brought them straight to where King Theron needed to be, but without him asking. Alberry, where Pata held Oren captive. Where the king and his heir resided.

How much was Ricci in control of her own mind?

The alarms sounded, the gongs ringing furiously. The demon army poured through the portal around them, on foot or with demon horses. They rolled wagons of weapons and supplies, carried great ladders, and pulled catapults. They'd come prepared, and they'd come to conquer.

The demon king was here for revenge after an eternity trapped in a dead world. King Theron would not ruin his second chance.

As the demons marched, King Theron pushed Lela ahead, leaving Ricci to hold the portal open. Lela stumbled, weighed down by the binders blocking her power that seemed to leach her strength. She had hoped the demons would camp while their army assembled, buying time for the fae to organize.

Down the hill and up the next, she trudged, the demon king a dark presence at her back, until they reached the bridge to the king's castle, the same one she and Oren had rowed beneath. The army stopped out of bow range, and the demon king pressed forward without them. Taking her with him.

They crossed the bridge at a steady pace, her nervous gaze on the battlements crowded with fae warriors in glinting silver and black armor, arrows nocked and aimed. They lined up in rows on the thick, gray wall, visible between the slats. Steam rose from hot barrels of tar poised to pour down on the enemy at the gate.

Her ears picked up everything inside, the scrape of swords as warriors rushed into position, the shouts from captains to their troops, the constant ringing of the gong which signaled the portal was still open, demons pouring through. On both sides, catapults clicked back, ready to launch their boulders.

King Theron stopped before reaching the gate.

"The day you've long awaited has come, Fae King. I have the portal opener." King Theron's rumbling voice spread wide and loud, vibrating her bones. "I have one of your own." He shook Lela by the shoulder. "Open the gates, or watch her die."

The warriors above the gate moved aside, and a taller fae clad in regal black armor etched in silver stepped forward. Pata.

He scanned the horizon, surveying the assembling army, then he met Lela's eyes. There was nothing in his expression. But, was that sadness? Or resignation?

"King Sidian will not yield," Pata said, voice strong and carrying. "Your prisoner matters not."

Pain lanced Lela's heart, but she didn't know why. Of course Pata wouldn't yield the kingdom for her. She wouldn't have expected or wanted him to. So why did it still hurt?

Pata stepped back, and the warriors reclaimed their positions. Lela did a double-take at the warrior in front, pained eyes clear even beneath his helmet.

Oren.

Pata had been true to his word. Oren was alive and free.

He didn't nock his arrow like the others. His arms drooped, and he stared at her with lips parted. His gaze fell to the binders on her wrists, the demon's hand on her shoulder.

"Then there is nothing you can do but die." King Theron

turned her away, forcing her to tear her gaze from Oren's as they re-crossed the bridge and joined the front line. "Catapults," he said to one of his generals in a red cape.

The command rang out, followed by the screech of metal and wood. The boulders, black and deadly, soared above her head with a whoosh that overwhelmed all other sounds.

They smashed into stone with deafening crashes that vibrated through the soles of her boots. Some soared over the wall. With cries of anguish, they killed her people.

Oren. She craned her neck. The twang of a thousand arrows sounded from the wall as fae fired arrows back. Oren was gone. Lela's heart raced. Had he been struck? Was he okay?

King Theron pulled her further into the ranks. Fae arrows rained down around them, striking the ground and pinging off armor. They shouldn't have been able to reach this far. They were being magically lifted, and Lela had no armor.

King Theron cursed and slapped away a pair of arrows that would have impaled him. He moved so fast!

Arrows sunk into the ground at her feet. King Theron let go of her shoulder to whack away more arrows.

Lela didn't hesitate. She ran for all she was worth out of the middle of the demon archers, evading them as they loosed arrow after arrow. Her breaths turned to wheezing from what should have been an easy distance. She sprinted past the front line into the open space leading to the bridge.

King Theron roared, but no one chased her. She dodged and weaved as arrows flew past, slow, as if the binders anchored her to the ground. The warriors cheered as she sprinted across the bridge.

Lela slammed into the gate, pounding on the metal bars with her bound fists. "Open up!" She glanced behind her. "Hurry!"

The demons stopped firing at her. The gate did not open.

King Theron sauntered from the ranks, casually deflecting fae arrows. "You think you slipped my notice?" He looked up. "Your father isn't as weak as I'd hoped."

Lela blinked as he approached. He'd let her go on purpose. The arrows had missed on purpose. She'd been bait, to see if they'd open the gate for her. An invitation for the demon army to storm the keep. Her eyes narrowed.

"Yes." King Theron let out a rumbling laugh, seeing the realization on her face.

The cold, metal bars pressed into her back. Lela glanced to the side. There was another way in. The door they used when freeing Ricci. The demons would have difficulty following her. The hill was too steep down to the river, and the path too narrow along the wall. The door was too small for the army to march through. But would her people open it?

It didn't matter. There was no choice. Anything was better than being a prisoner, even an arrow to the back. Lela leaped over the shrubbery that flanked the gate and took off at a sprint down the narrow path along the castle wall. Blood pounded in her ears. If the fae saw her, they were silent, focused on defending against the enemy.

King Theron didn't chase her. Maybe he had decided she wasn't worth it since she held no value as a prisoner. Her pata had made that clear.

Without warning, silence descended over the battlefield. The arrows hitting the wall above her ceased. She glanced across the river to where the demon army spanned endlessly. They'd lowered their bows. They aimed for her. He was taunting her, making her think she stood a chance.

Lela sped, running as fast as she could, gulping in air. There was nowhere to hide, no cover to shelter her, only open air, a wall at her back, and binders blocking her magic. She wasn't halfway to where she remembered the door to be.

Lela stopped, paralyzed. This was it. This was how she'd die. A traitor and a failure. This was all her fault.

King Theron raised his arm, then threw it down. He snatched a bow and arrow from a nearby demon.

"Fire!" a demon general yelled.

CHAPTER 43

Lela raised her chin and took a steadying breath, staring down the demon army with defiance.

"Lela!"

A rope hit Lela's side, then someone dropped down in front of her just as the arrows arrived.

Pata.

Weaponless. Defenseless.

He pinned her against the wall, shielding her.

"No," she said, breath shaky.

Pata grunted as the arrows struck, some pinging off his armor, some not.

"I didn't ask you to do this." She shoved against him, trying to take his place. Like shoving a boulder.

Panic gripped her throat with piercing claws. She *pulled* at her magic. The binders seared her with blinding pain.

Blood splattered Pata's helm. Her tunic. "I'm proud to do it, young one."

"We have to move. We can make it." She nudged them

toward the door, but he didn't budge, continuing to hold her in place. To protect her. "The kingdom needs you. I need you." There was nowhere to go.

"Take care of Mata." The light was slowing draining out of her pata's loving eyes.

Her fault.

Her fault.

Her fault.

Her mata was losing her mate. The kingdom, its general. And Lela, a proud pata who should have lived hundreds of more years.

"I'm so sorry." Tears poured down her cheeks. "I should have listened. I should have obeyed." Her breath came in hiccups.

Arrows streamed around them. Into her pata, again and again.

"It's not your fault," he whispered, breath gurgling. "Never your fault." He coughed once, blood spraying, then slumped against her. Dead.

A scream ripped its way out of her throat. Her limbs went numb under the crush of despair.

Loud splashes came from the river. She risked a look, blinking furiously against her streaming tears. A team of demons advanced to end her. The fae in the battlements targeted them, downing some, but more took their place.

Over the ping of arrows and Lela's sobs came the scraping of a door opening.

"Lela!" Oren. Alive and unharmed. He hurried to her, crouched low and holding a great shield. The demons peppered it with arrows, diverting their attack.

"Oren," she cried. "Pata, he's..."

He reached her, putting the edge of the shield over her

pata's body. "I know. They're coming. We have to move." He held out his arm.

Lela choked on a sob, kissed her pata's cheek, then stepped behind Oren's massive shield. She cried out when Pata's body crumpled to the ground, rolling partway down the hill.

"Don't look, Lela. Just keep moving." Oren held the shield steady, low enough to drag the ground.

Arrows thunked, vibrating the wood as they made their way with agonizing slowness toward the door.

The arrows stopped.

Oren peeked around the shield. He cursed and dropped the shield, grabbing her arm and running.

As soon as Lela left the safety of the shield, she saw them. A dozen demons crested the hill, lipless jaws gritted as they sprinted at full speed. The enemy arrows had stopped so they wouldn't kill their own.

They reached the door just ahead of the demons. It opened, and Oren shoved Lela inside. He turned, sword drawn. Two demons attacked at once. Oren slashed the first across his throat. Black blood spewed as the demon died. Oren turned to the other, too late. The demon stabbed under Oren's upraised arm. The sword met fae armor forged with magic. It struck and glanced off.

Oren brought his sword around and felled the second demon, slicing its head clean off. But more demons quickly followed the first.

"Come on!" the door guard yelled.

Oren jumped into the room. Lela and the guard slammed the door shut behind him, then barricaded it with a large beam. The demons beat against the door, but it was two feet of solid stone. They wouldn't get in easily.

Oren rushed over to her, removing his helmet. "Are you hurt?" His hands fluttered, looking for injury.

"No, I'm okay." Her breath shook. "Pata saved me." The image of him sliding down the embankment, body full of arrows meant for her, flashed in her mind. The binders clanked, trembling as she covered her mouth. "What have I done?"

Oren took her hands. "You can't think like that. You didn't do this. The demon king did." He fished for something around his neck. "I know what will make you feel better." He lifted up a chain, and dangling from the end was a golden key. The key they'd taken from Pata. A special key made for only one purpose.

Unlocking golden binders.

"You kept it." Hope swelled in her breast. Would it fit?

He smiled and stuck the key in the lock of one of the binders. It slid in smoothly and clicked when he turned it. The binder swung open. She gasped. He quickly unlocked the other. The binders fell heavy off her wrists and clanged to the ground.

Instantly, breathing became easier. The crushing weight of the spell that had been constricting everything lifted. Her wrists were rubbed raw, but not so bad as Ricci's had been. Strength returned, and her energies began to refill. Her head had been underwater. Now she was released, air free flowing.

With the clarity came the pain. Pata had never betrayed her. She'd betrayed him. And he'd died for it. Fresh tears welled and dripped over her cheeks.

Lela threw her arms around Oren, awkward with the girth and unyieldingness of his armor. He dipped his head, rubbing his cheek against hers. The smooth, soft slip of his warm skin as it caressed over hers sent pleasant prickles up and down her spine.

He pulled back, gazing down into her eyes with warmth

and tenderness. She looked at his lips, wanting nothing more than to kiss him. When she looked up, she gasped in alarm.

"You've gone pale," she said, startled. "You need to sit down." She'd seen plenty of people right before they passed out while helping Mata.

He nodded, eyes going far away, and then collapsed. Lela reached to catch him, but his armor dragged her down. He hit the ground hard, then gasped in pain, reaching feebly for his side. Lela moved his hand. Blood seeped underneath him.

"He must have been struck," Lela said to the soldier still guarding the door. "Help me remove his armor."

He rushed over, luckily knowing where all the snaps and releases were to unhinge the breastplate from Oren's body. She removed his leathers, too, until he was down to his undershirt, soaked in blood. She pulled that up and saw a bloody gash in his belly, intestines peeking through. Oren's eyes fluttered shut.

"Where did this wound come from?" His armor was intact. She lightly traced the edges and gasped. The leftover energies burned her fingertips. Dark and rumbling. The demon king had done this.

"Bandages," she ordered. "And I'm going to need some echinacea, willow bark, and sladlen syrup." Lela's usually steady hands shook. She'd seen this kind of injury only three times at home with her mata. A farmer gutted by a wild animal, another injured on a tool, and a swordfight gone wrong. None survived.

Oren would. She wouldn't let him die.

The door guard ran to the cabinet and brought back clean bandages and a clear bottle of alcohol. "This is all we have. And this." He handed her a suture kit. "We don't have none of the others you said."

"Nothing?" she asked, incredulous. "Crealt bark? Honey?"

The pool of blood beneath Oren expanded despite staunching the wound. "Where is all this blood coming from?" She rolled him to his side. He didn't even groan. There was another wound in his back bleeding profusely.

"Help me get him to a healer." She took one of his arms.

The door guard didn't move. "The healers are only taking those with a chance to live. I'm sorry, but he's not going to make it."

"You're joking. Get over here and help me!" she yelled. "He's breathing, isn't he? He's alive, but I can't carry him by myself. *Help me.*"

"I'm sorry." He turned his back on her toward the door. "I can't leave my post. If these demons break through, I have to defend the keep and sound the alarm."

Lela screamed. Oren's pulse and breathing slowed. "This can't be happening. I won't let it." Not again. Not another person she loved.

She reached into her energy which had barely trickled back, and pulled with all her might. Her slight gift was to grow. Maybe she could grow his wound closed. It was mad, but it was all she had.

Arms wide, Lela placed a hand on each wound, holding in as much blood as possible. Her energy flowed up from within her. She sent it through her hands and into Oren. *Make him right. Make him whole.*

Her energy had only ever gone through plants, never living beings, but they could be the same. She willed them to be. Lela pushed, focusing. She closed her eyes, feeling the edges of his wounds with blood-coated fingers.

Grow.

Heal.

The energy trickled through her fingertips. She bit off a gasp as the skin started to shift. It was working.

It was working!

She opened her eyes. New skin grew, covering the lesions to seal his body against infection. It siphoned her energies, transferring it directly to the healing. His color returned. Her limbs and eyes grew heavy. Just as she reached the dredges, his breathing leveled out. Her hands slipped away, and she collapsed on top of him.

CHAPTER 44

Ricci dropped to her knees on the fae hillside, exhausted. Even while her strength gave out, the portal around her held strong. King Theron was gone, but his army continued to pour through from Marek's estate. She could hold out, so long as they still came. She wouldn't let King Theron down.

Hours passed, and finally the last few rows of troops crossed through, leaving her alone. Which world was she supposed to stay in? King Theron hadn't said. She was half in the human world, on the empty lawn bathed in morning sunlight, and half on a hill with a smoking castle in the distance.

Her vision blurred, and she blinked. She looked at her wrists. Her manacles were gone. She was free. King Theron had saved her from Marek's dungeon. And he was at the castle. He might need her help to win the war.

What war?

The war against the fae. What a monstrous people. They'd imprisoned and starved her.

But, Lela was fae. And Oren. They were kind and saved her.

Her family, Mama and Papa, they were in the human world. She missed them dearly.

But King Theron was her fiancé. He cared for her. He needed her.

The fae world, then.

Just before Ricci closed the portal, a voice shouted from afar.

"Ricci!"

She knew that voice. Callen. Exhaustion forced her eyes shut as she closed the portal. She fell forward into the thick grass. It tickled and poked her cheek, keeping her from the oblivion she sought in sleep.

"Ricci." Hurried footsteps over the grass, then a warm hand on her back, shaking her. "Ricci, can you hear me?" He shook her again, and she opened her eyes, irritated.

Callen stooped beside her, his handsome face the picture of concern. His onyx hair hung in wisps, and there were deep circles under his blue eyes. She reached up absently to trace them.

"Are you hurt? What happened?" he asked.

She sat up, limbs trembling. She was in the human world. Smoke rose in the far distance where the town was—no castle. Callen didn't have manacles either, just bandages where they'd once been.

"Did King Theron set you free, too?" Ricci asked. The king, he would wonder where she was.

"No," he said slowly. "I escaped. Did he set you free?"

"Yes." She smiled. "I need to get back to him. He's attacking the monstrous fae." She reached for her magic but found only dredges. Not enough to open a portal.

Callen took her hands. "I know it's hard, Ricci, and you're very tired. But the demon king is not your friend."

Ricci jerked her hands back. "You lie."

"Think it through. He put a spell on you. You can't go back there to help him defeat Lela and her people, right? The demon king took her against her will. Your cousin. Your family. Would a friend hurt your family?"

"King Theron wouldn't hurt my family," she snapped. "He loves me."

He took a deep breath. "He took Lela to use against her father in his war. Do you remember that?"

Her gaze drifted downward. Something about that sounded familiar.

Callen slowly reached forward, as if afraid to scare her away. She let him touch her hand. "If you can trust me, I'll make this better."

"Make what better?" Was something wrong? "Why should I trust you?"

"Because." He swallowed. "I love you, Ricci."

The words made her heart speed up and her deep breath quiver, but she couldn't recall why. "King Theron loves me."

Hurt flashed in his eyes. Had she said something wrong? She pressed her palms into the sides of her aching head.

Callen wrapped his arms around her. "I know. We'll sort you out. Somehow."

The embrace was the most comforting thing she'd ever felt.

"Ricci!" a frantic scream called out behind her.

She looked up. Her entire family was running toward her, clambering up Marek's lawn. Callen helped her to her feet.

"Mama! Papa!" Her parents led the charge. Papa in his baggy trousers and big boots, eyes tight with unshed tears. Mama with her homespun dress held aloft in one hand, tears streaming unabashedly. Her brothers and the rest of the family followed close behind with a mixture of giant grins and crinkly-eyed concern.

"I found your family," Callen whispered in her ear. "They were waiting for you at the market. I told them everything—even about your new ears. They helped me and my family come here to find you."

"Your family?" She spared a look but didn't see any others.

"They're in the wagon. We barely escaped King Theron's demon army."

King Theron?

Mama and Papa wrapped their arms around her, taking her weight from Callen. Their tears of joy mixed with Ricci's as she found her own tears flowing, but why was she crying? Because this was her family. She loved them. Her brothers and family joined the pile, then Papa pulled in Callen until they were one big circle of arms and sobbing messes.

"Oh, Ricika," Mama said. "I'm sorry we never told you about your birth mother. She said it wasn't safe for you to know. Your ears look just like hers now."

"We love you so much," Papa said.

"I forgive you. I know you were only protecting me." The words came out sleepily, but no less true.

This wasn't the same as what King Theron offered. This was more.

And it didn't matter that Mama hadn't birthed her. She belonged to them, and they belonged to her. Completely. Unquestionably. Eternally.

This was love.

Callen finding her family and bringing them here, that was love. Mama and Papa raising her and providing for her unconditionally, that was love. Her birth mother fighting for her life and finding the courage to give her up, that was love.

There was a ripping sound, then pain, like something tearing through her brain. Ricci cried out and clutched her head. Her family stepped back, but Callen was right there, holding her.

"It hurts." Ricci sobbed against him.

"Let it go." He pressed his lips to her temple, gently.

The pain spiked, then was gone just as quickly. A stream of red light flowed from her forehead and up. It hung above them for a moment, then broke into a million pieces and disappeared.

Ricci gasped as understanding washed over her. She stared unseeing as the horror of the past days consumed her. The portals. The demons. The fae. *Oh Gods.* "What have I done?" She shook her head. "What have I done?"

Callen scooped her up into his arms. "She needs rest. Marek will be back. It isn't safe here."

Her family exchanged glances, then her brothers fanned around them, wary of any threats.

"Come," Mama said, taking Ricci's hand. "We will leave this place and never return."

"No." Ricci struggled weakly in Callen's arms. They couldn't leave. The fight was not over. "I must go back. I have to fix the mess I made." Fuzziness invaded any plan her mind tried to conjure.

"We will, but not until your strength returns," Callen said.

Ricci shook her head, eyes drooping.

What felt like minutes later, Callen nudged her awake. "I'm sorry for waking you, love."

She smiled at the sound of that. Then the memories of the past few days crashed into her.

She sat up, banging her head on the wagon's ceiling. "Lela. The demon army."

"Yes," he said. "That's why I woke you. You've slept quite a long time."

Afternoon sunlight streamed through the windows. The

wagon swayed and bumped as it traveled. Through the window, more wagons and people on foot shared the road.

What had she done? How many were dying even now because of what the demon king had her do? But, no. The blame wasn't his. It'd been she who'd opened a portal in the first place, and just like the fae said she would, she brought destruction on their people. On her own people, too.

Her dry throat wouldn't allow her to swallow. "Where are we going?" she asked.

"Your family agreed it was best to leave town. My mother and siblings are in the wagons behind us. Marek has taken control of Timbercross with some of the demon army. It's up to the king's army to defend the city, but that will mean more casualties."

"Ack, leave her alone until she's had something to eat," Mama interrupted.

Ricci eased down from her bunk and hugged Mama tight around her thin waist, seeking comfort. Mama kissed the top of her head, then sat her down at the tiny table. Ricci inhaled the smothered chicken with rice and mushroom gravy, sopping up the juices with a hunk of flat bread. Callen ate his meal with a little more refinery.

Mama refilled her plate. She couldn't eat another bite, but she tried. It'd been so long since she'd been home, going from one nightmare to another. She'd never wish away her perfect life again.

When Mama was distracted with the dishes, Ricci turned to Callen and lowered her voice to a whisper. "Leaving town won't save anyone. With the demons on his side, Marek's a threat to everyone, no matter where our families go. And he'll come for me, once he's done burning the world. We have to stop him."

Callen's mouth curved into a knowing smile.

"You have a plan, don't you?" she asked, voice flat.

He grinned. "It's not very detailed, but I have a plan."

"I don't like it," Mama said, banging the dishes around.

Callen's smile vanished. "Truthfully, neither do I, but I can't think of any way around it."

The food turned sour in Ricci's belly. "You mean to take on Marek by yourself?"

"He killed my father." Callen took her hand. "The demon king will be wondering where you've gone by now. He's probably searched the area and is suspicious that his spell has been broken."

"So I will go and stop him," Ricci declared. She was the one who brought him there, and she would be the one to send him back.

A glass hit the floor and shattered, making them jump. "No," Mama said, eyes wide. "You cannot do this thing."

Callen bent to pick up the pieces. Mama tried to help, but Callen waved her away. "No worries. I've cleaned up lots of broken glass in my time." He wiped up the smaller shards with a wet rag.

"I have to do this, Mama." Ricci took her hand. "And I can." She turned to Callen. "I'll say I collapsed, closed the portal while on the wrong side, and only just now awakened. That can be my story." She swallowed her rising panic—she could be brave even in the face of near-crippling fear. "The fae will never defeat him on their own. I'm the only one that can get close to him. I can send him back to the demon world."

Callen took his seat, nodding, and something like pride crinkled his eyes. The intense way he looked at her made heat simmer in her belly and rise to her cheeks.

"I forbid it." Mama crossed her arms, eyes filling with tears.

Ricci wrapped her mama up in a hug. "I love you, but I wasn't asking for permission. You and Papa always said to use my gifts. This is my gift, and I can use it for good." She kissed her on the cheek.

Mama's face crumpled, but she nodded with a shuddering breath, wiping her tears. "You make me very proud, Ricika."

"Just be careful, Ricci," Callen said. "I've met him. I was next to him when he simply touched you and took over your mind."

His words shook her, but resolve steeled her nerves. She'd done unthinkable things, even before the demon king's spell. She was through being afraid all the time. It was time to make it right.

CHAPTER 45

Lela awoke to the blissful feel of callused fingertips stroking her hair. She blinked up at Oren. He was sitting up, and her head was in his lap. He stared at her with complete adoration, a smile on his face. The sound of demons pounding at the door was gone.

"You're okay," she croaked.

"You healed me." He smiled wider.

"I'm not a healer," she replied. "I merely shaped what I already had." And yet, here he was.

"You are. You've come into your energy. It came to you in a time of need."

A most vital need. There was no life without Oren in it.

It hadn't come in time to save her pata.

She sat up, brushing the tears from her eyes and the pain from her heart. Her head spun. "A healer," she whispered. "And you're alright? Everything okay? No more bleeding?" She poked the bare skin where the wound had been on his stomach, then examined the smooth skin of his muscled back. Not even a scar.

He took her hands. "You're amazing."

"I always wanted to be a healer." She marveled at his warm touch.

"I think you always were. Just like I was always an idiot."

"Huh?" She blinked.

"I'm sorry, Lela, that I treated you like a child. It hurt me so much, but I thought it was for the best because of the law about our ages." He pulled her closer to him. "I was wrong. The laws don't matter. I've wanted to be your mate since I first understood the meaning of the word." He put his hands on either side of her face, gentle, loving. She soaked up every word. "I belong to you, and you to me."

He tilted his head and leaned forward. Their lips met, and the world changed. It turned into fire and ice, the taste of his hunger, the intoxicating movement of his mouth, the slipperiness of his tongue meeting hers and what it did to her core.

She wrapped her arms around him, pulling him closer and deepening the connection. More, more, more. This was what she was meant to do with her life. Kiss Oren and love him with her whole heart.

It was everything she'd hoped her real first kiss would be.

He broke away, sighing reluctantly. "We have forever to do that, but we are needed now." He helped her stand. "I'm sure the king's healers would love another addition."

She nodded, pride and hunger competing for attention. "You be safe."

"I'll see you after." He grinned.

"How do I find the healers?"

His smile disappeared. "Follow the stretchers." He kissed her on the nose, then hurried away.

Lela took all of five steps into the empty hall before her back hit the cold, stone wall. *Pata.* Heartache pierced her through, crushing her chest and tightening her throat. She slid down to the floor. Her pata was dead. Sobs racked through her.

How did this pain not swallow her where she sat? How was anyone expected to go on from such a loss?

She buried her face in her hands, but it didn't hide her from what she'd done. The bad decisions that had led to this outcome. Her weakness at not keeping it together when their very world was in jeopardy.

Warm arms encircled her. Holding her. "You don't hide your pain from me," Oren said, lips near her ear. "You don't wait until I'm gone to show what you're truly feeling. I'm with you. I'll carry you. I'll break with you. Whatever you need, it's you and me now."

Lela gripped Oren to her like she'd split in two without the touch of him. "I did this," she gasped.

"No," he said firmly. He pulled back and tilted her chin to him, kissing away her tears. "You don't shoulder the actions of our ancestors. That weight would crush you." He smoothed back her hair. "Your pata is gone, but that's not your fault. He *chose* to save you. It was going to be me. But he stopped me. He sent me one way, knowing he'd take the other."

"He sent you?" Her pata had sent Oren for her. Sent him so that Oren might live, while he died.

"He knew we couldn't live without each other, and he couldn't live without saving you."

Numb, Lela allowed him to help her to her feet. She swallowed hard. "Pata's sacrifice won't be in vain."

Oren held her cheek in a warm and calming caress. "Don't give up the fight now. I'll find you." He gave a small smile and jogged away.

Lela took a deep, hitching breath. There were lives to save. She headed in the opposite direction. The pain of losing her Pata was still just as strong and all-consuming, but Oren had given her a gift. She didn't have to bear it alone. The ground might not swallow her today.

Oren was right. Once she reached the main hall, bodies on stretchers streamed by in a steady line. So many! She followed, passing beneath an archway and entering into organized chaos. Healers and assistants ran from bed to bed, some using magic, some not. Fae warriors screamed and groaned, arrows sticking out of them or sword slashes to their skin. Blood leaving trails to their beds.

Lela finally found someone in charge. "How can I help? I'm a healer."

He cleaned fresh blood from his hands with a cloth. "Which school did you study at?"

Lela's cheeks warmed. "I haven't, but I have the gift."

"Right," he said. "I'll assign you to a healer. They need people to fetch supplies and mop up blood."

Lela frowned, but he didn't give her a second glance. "Fetam," he called. A female looked up from where she sewed a wound together. "I found you a runner."

Fetam nodded and went back to her patient. Lela studied her, but of course couldn't guess her age. Brown hair braided and wound into a bun, matching brown eyes, and a blood-smeared apron over fitted clothes.

"Go to her. Help her in any way she needs. I hope you've slept." The healer walked away.

Lela approached Fetam. A young warrior lay unconscious on the table, blood tricking from a hastily patched-up wound in his side. "Anything you need?"

Fetam didn't look up. "Bandages."

Lela looked around helplessly before spotting a supply cabinet that many others were grabbing from. She rummaged until she found what looked right—what Mata would have wanted—then handed it over. Fetam took it without comment, and Lela smiled.

A loud crash made the walls shake, as if the very castle might collapse.

"Ah," Fetam said, finishing with the bandages. "They restarted the catapults."

Lela shuddered. "How many battles have you seen?"

"Too many. I've been a healer at this castle for 150 years, more or less."

"But you don't use the energies?"

"Of course I do. But not for a simple bandaging. Energy is for the problems our hands can't perform."

Lela nodded, understanding. "I'm going to be a healer one day. I just found my gift." Even saying those words, she couldn't believe it. Mata would be so proud.

An ear-splitting crash slammed just outside the room, rattling the ground. Lela grabbed the table.

Fetam smiled, her ease contrasting with her hurried movements as she continued to treat the patient. "Good for you. This world needs more healers. I see you've already got the basics." She pointed to Lela's wrists.

The skin was pink, newly healed. It should have taken days for the wounds from her binders to heal. She'd done it without realizing.

"How did you know?" Lela asked.

"Training and decades of experience." Fetam put her fists on her hips. "Go ahead and wake him up then."

Lela blinked. "Won't he be in a lot of pain?" Also, how in the valley would she wake him up?

"Yes, but see, he took a good knock to the head, and we need to assess him." She pointed to a bruise and swelling on the side of the warrior's scalp that Lela hadn't noticed. "Now I may seem patient and easy-going, but that is not because our situation is such that we can afford to take our time. I give you an order, you obey."

"You're right. Where are the smelling salts?" Mata used them a lot on their patients at home.

Fetam tsked. "His condition will require energy."

Lela straightened, then quickly turned to the warrior. She placed her hands on his head and called to her energy. The sensation of it without the binders was a familiar comfort.

Wake up.

He didn't budge.

"It's not working," she said.

Fetam stared, as if to say, 'Try harder'.

Lela released the energy, allowing it free range to go where it was needed, instead of where Lela thought best. Slowly, the bruising vanished.

The warrior's eyes fluttered open, then closed in restful sleep.

"You can stop now." Fetam spread his eyelids, checking his pupils. "He's okay." She motioned to someone, and a pair of fae grabbed his pallet and took him away.

Lela swayed, dizzy.

"You have a very powerful and natural gift. I didn't actually expect you to be able to do that. What is your name?"

"Lelana Ashryn. Lela."

Fetam stopped and stood straight. She looked at Lela as if she hadn't really done so before, and then her eyes creased and lips downturned. "I grieve for you. Your pata was a great general. He saved this land from many enemies. It will be a tough loss for us all."

"I'm sorry," Lela said.

"What for?"

Lela shook her head, holding the pain at bay. The apology had come automatically. "He shouldn't have died. Wouldn't have if I had done my duty as a daughter and listened to his wisdom."

He'd been absent a large portion of her life, but that hadn't meant he didn't love her. He'd saved her, paying the ultimate sacrifice to prove that love. Because of her, they'd lost their best chance at victory. What would happen to her people if King Theron won?

Fetam chuckled. "I've raised two daughters. Sometimes it's your duty *not* to listen to his wisdom and to carve your own path." She looked away as a new wounded warrior was placed on their table.

Lela grasped the small comfort with both hands.

They didn't speak as much after that. She assisted Fetam through the night, gathering requested supplies, performing small and large feats of healing when her well refilled, and slowly learning her way around the healing unit. It was the perfect distraction from dwelling on Oren's safety and Ricci's fate, neither of whom she could help right now.

The booms, bangs, screaming, and wailing became background noise. Soon, she barely flinched when a boulder crashed somewhere nearby, just like Fetam. Her mind was too weary and too busy keeping up with the next task to have room to care. If it came for them, at least she'd get to rest.

Somewhere near morning, she fell asleep leaning against the mop handle.

Fetam shook her awake. "Time for a proper rest and a meal." She shooed her. "Go on, you've earned it. I'll have one too, and we'll be good as new for the next go-round."

Lela looked at her skeptically. How much longer could this go on? Surely one side was close to winning.

"You won't miss anything. Have you heard of the Battle of Riverspent?"

Lela nodded, head heavy. It was a hundred years ago

against invading goblins—way before Lela was born, but Fetam would have been there.

"The siege on the castle lasted five months," Fetam said.

Lela gasped. "Five months?"

"We're prepared to hold out for twice that." Fetam nodded. "Now hurry along. Can't save warriors if you're falling asleep."

Lela did as told. After a hot meal of beef stew and thick, crusty bread, she fell onto a lumpy cot and slept the best sleep she'd ever had.

CHAPTER 46

C allen stood beside Ricci in a small clearing just off the side of the road, waiting for her to open the portal. Their families watched from beside the wagons, fidgeting and whispering to one another.

His heart pounded in his chest, but not for himself or what he was about to attempt. Ricci stood there, silent. Nothing happened.

"This is mad, you know," she said. "Maybe I should go with you. We can take Marek on, then find King Theron together."

Callen took her hand and squeezed. She'd been through hell, but she was so incredibly brave. "Every minute we delay, King Theron gains more ground on the fae."

She stared off into the trees, seeing nothing. "I know. And you can't go to the fae world with me, either. If someone sees you, they'll know the spell is broken. We can't risk it." She sighed long and hard, meeting his eyes. "I just wish there was another way."

He pulled her against him, conscious of their watching families and his burning wound. She looked up at him, eyes lingering on his lips. His heart skipped a bit as he leaned down slowly, head tilted.

"How long does this take, Ricika?" her mother shouted to them.

They jumped, and Ricci chuckled. Callen gritted his teeth.

He took a reluctant step back. "Hold still." He took her hands and cupped them together. Concentrating, he called his magic forward and shaped it to his will. Gods, it was good to have his magic back.

Ricci gasped at the glowing ball that floated above her palms. With a little more effort, the ball formed into a flower, losing its glow as the magic settled. The silver bloom landed weighty in her hands—one of many things High Master Aldridge had taught him in their short time together.

"It's beautiful." She examined it, pinching it between two fingers, turning it to and fro.

"I can trace my own spell back to you, so long as you have this," he said. "And I'll know you're okay."

"And I can come back to you, like I did before."

He nodded, and she took his hand. The motion seemed natural, easy. But it sent his veins thrumming. She cared for him, as he cared for her. He never thought he'd find something as important as taking the mage tests. It was more than he knew to hope for.

There was a shift in the wind as Ricci reached for her magic. A staticky buzz drowned out the rustling leaves. The portal opened, and the air around them cooled, like stepping from sun to shadow on a spring day. The checkered floor of the council room mixed with the grass they stood on. The room was empty as far as he could see it—as far as the portal's reach. No one cried out at their sudden appearance, anyway.

"You have gotten better at this," he said, impressed.

She laughed, red hair tumbling over her shoulder. "I wasn't

sure if that would work. I've never opened a portal to another part of the same world before." Her smile vanished. "Be careful. I just found you. I don't want to lose you."

"You be careful, too." He stroked her soft cheek with the back of his hand.

Ricci took it and kissed it, then pushed it back to him. She closed the portal, her on one side, him on the other.

The room came into complete focus, and Callen gasped. Bodies, bleeding and broken, lay strewn over desks and railings and forgotten on the floor. Scorch marks and splintered wood chips everywhere. A few dead demons, but not many. The mages had fought with their lives and lost. Was there anyone left to help?

Callen picked his way out to the hall and was met with more evidence of violence, but not one living soul. He took the stairs, scanning the rooms as he passed. Only bodies. Young and old.

He hurried to his favorite place in the mage building—the potions room. It had been ransacked, vials scattered everywhere. But he was used to finding his way through the chaos. Treading carefully through broken glass and spills, so as not to accidentally melt his leg off or something, he managed to find what he needed—an untouched rack of potions made by the best brewers in the kingdom. These could do some lethal damage if he had to fight an army of demons to get to Marek.

Heart heavy from so much loss, he took to the streets to track down his former master. By now, he would have moved the army to intercept whatever aid King Willmot would send. Callen had to find him and end him in any way possible.

A bloodied band of town guards rode by on horses—a scant three of them. Callen flagged them down.

"A mage? I thought they'd all been killed," one of the guards said, his horse pawing at the cobbled road.

"I'm hunting the demon army," Callen said. "Which way did they travel?"

"You haven't heard?" The guards glanced at each other. "They felled High Lord Kealamin, may the Gods rest his soul, and made camp at his estate. The king marches, but the army is days away."

The air rushed from Callen's lungs, and the blood drained from his face. So it was true. His father was dead. He hadn't realized he'd been holding on to hope. Now it was gone. The blaze in his heart eclipsed the wound in his side.

Callen bid them goodbye and numbly made his way back to his parents' estate. The streets were eerily empty and quiet. Still some distance away, he saw demons moving over the property, still thousands strong. Though the fence had fallen, miraculously, the mansion still stood. At least they hadn't burned it down.

The high lord's mansion was a symbol of power. The ruler of these lands had resided there for as long as the kingdom had required such a position. It was no wonder Marek kept it for his own.

But this was Callen's home. And he knew its secrets.

From the neighbor's cellar, he dropped down into the undiscovered underground tunnel, listening for movement at every turn. When he reached the mansion, he lifted himself into the basement, holding still and listening again. The demons rumbled outside, and hopefully that's where they'd stay.

From the basement, he entered the kitchen and slipped into the servants' stairway. After the first spiderweb to the face, he held his hand in front of him. Callen and his brother Brander spent many hours using the servants' passages to spy on their parents or play tricks on their brothers—until Callen's magic came in. Up one flight of stairs, Callen pressed on the wall, and the door swung soundlessly inward.

Footsteps treaded from up the stairs, heading toward him. He hopped back in and clicked the door shut just before someone passed. Whoever it was paused, listening, then continued on. Marek was still in the house, because the army was still here, and King Theron was not.

Sidestepping through the narrow passage, Callen climbed, winding his way up. Then he heard him. Marek. Callen followed the sound of his former master growling orders to the demon soldiers. It led all the way to his father's study.

Callen barely breathed. Through a knot in the wood, he spotted Marek at Father's desk, counting gold coins beside the open safe. The demons he'd been speaking to were gone.

Callen pulled a vial of potion from his pocket. He slowly uncorked it, but it gave a loud pop. He froze. Marek halted, looking toward the hall. After a minute, his gaze slid over the wall where Callen hid, then back to the coins on the table. Callen released his breath and then dumped the contents of the vial over his head. It tingled on his skin but didn't burn.

He patted his pockets, unnecessarily rechecking his potions.

"I know you're there, Callen."

Marek's words stopped him cold.

CHAPTER 47

Ricci closed the portal, leaving Callen at the mage building. *Gods, please protect him.*

She gave her family a weak smile, hoping to put them at ease, but her hands shook. Callen's family watched her from beside the wagons. Callen had introduced them briefly—just long enough to hear and then immediately forget their names. They seemed nice enough, if she ignored how they peered down their noses at her and her family.

Mama watched her, clutching Papa's arm. There was no doubt if Ricci ran to them now, Mama would wrap her in her arms, and her family would ask no questions. She curled her fingers into fists. That wasn't going to happen.

Ricci summoned her magic, and quick as a flash, opened and closed a portal into the fae world. She stood on the side of the hill, exactly where she'd been before. Where she'd let the true monsters in. She remembered it all.

For a few quick heartbeats, she listened, but the alarms didn't go off. She'd been fast enough. Only the roar of demons and the crash of what sounded like boulders smashing into buildings.

"Where have you been, Oriana?" King Theron's rumbling reverberated through her bones from behind.

Ricci yelped and jumped.

"My king," she said, panicking. How had she acted before when under his spell? Should she swoon? This close up, his armored chest and scaly arms, pointed black horns and enormous flared wings confounded her.

What had he done with Lela?

"Where have you been?" His voice took on an edge of anger.

"I've only just awoken," she said, struggling to keep her voice steady. "I was in the human world, for some reason. I've come to find you."

"Mmm." He watched her.

She thought of Callen and her feelings of tenderness toward him, ignoring the blackness of the demon king's eyes as she stared up at him. She took three deep breaths, pushed her shoulders back, and raised her chin.

Ricci forced her gaze to his red, scaly lips, remembering how she'd longed to taste them. She imagined they were Callen's lips, licking her own and drawing closer to the demon.

King Theron rumbled, pleased. "I have a task for you, my bride."

She didn't speak, simply waited for his command, as any slave would.

"It's proven difficult to storm the castle. You will open a portal inside so that my army may pass through."

Ricci nodded, barely covering the horror that threatened to break through. The wall was likely the only thing saving the fae from annihilation.

"Come." He touched her shoulder, the barest pressure

directing her toward the castle. The heat from his hand sunk into her skin, as hot as the world he came from.

She leaned into the touch, then stopped, sickened with herself. Then leaned more, because clearly that was what he meant her to want to do. Even now, the magic of him—the allure of him—sought its way inside her being.

They trekked across the trodden field. Infatuation drifted over her awareness, like a poisonous fog. But it wasn't real. She took that poison and held it at bay. The love of her family and Callen was real and formed the perfect barrier. From this angle, she could study King Theron's spell. She knew what it wanted her to feel, how it wanted her to act—to trust, lust, and obey without question.

Ricci was an actress. She knew her part. Silence and subservience. She also knew there was no way she'd bring that army into the castle.

At the back of the battlefield, the demon lines stood restless, waiting for their rotation to the front. Ricci struggled not to gag at the scent of rotting flesh. They leered as she passed, black eyes following her until King Theron gave a low, warning growl.

Ricci kept her eyes on the ground because every time her gaze drifted up, she witnessed a new horror. Demons scaled the wall on ladders and ropes. Fae fell to their deaths from atop the high battlements. Burning rock flew from the demons' catapults, exploding somewhere on the other side and wreaking unknown destruction and death.

As they neared the front, a demon with a red cape approached them. It was taller than the others, with horns on its helmet.

"We've breached the door the female revealed," the demon rumbled. "What are your orders?"

"Go. Once the portal is open, I will join you."

The red-caped demon bowed and retreated.

King Theron turned to her. She looked into his eyes adoringly, then stared at his mouth, imagining it was Callen's mouth, longing to kiss him.

He motioned with his hand, and the ranks lined up, ready to file into the castle through her portal and destroy the fae. Her face remained spellbound while her mind raced. *Think, think, think.* How was she going to get around his orders without revealing she wasn't under his spell?

She gasped as an idea tried to take shape. King Theron's gaze drifted down to her, his face still blank, but his scrutiny raked her body.

He lifted his hand to her forehead. She managed not to flinch when his scales touched her skin and his power flowed into her. Her gaze went blurry, then black with a million twinkling stars. *Beautiful.*

You're mine, he said. *Your power is mine. You are devoted to me and will obey only me.*

I'm yours. Callen, her doting brothers, her family. That was true love.

He released her, and the red magic faded from his palm.

She panted, mind clouded.

"Open a portal into the keep," he commanded.

"Of course, my love." Ricci reached into her magical well and opened a narrow portal.

They stood on a faded stone floor, the air cool and stale, but they couldn't see more than a foot in either direction. There was no way to tell what part of the fae castle they were in.

"Wider," he rumbled, irritated. "Let my army pass."

"Yes, Master." She stared at him, adoring him.

But it was all an act.

His spell hadn't touched her. Her mind had been wrapped up in the love of her family and Callen, protected.

He turned to her, sensing something was off. His lip curled, revealing fangs.

She closed the portal, trapping him in the fae dungeon where she'd spent so many days.

As quick as a flash, before the demons could notice, she replaced it with a different portal into the castle's keep, wide and tall—the demon's castle. King Theron's roar of fury shook her, but the demons didn't seem to hear it as she did. The orders came to charge, and row after row, the demon soldiers rushed through her portal and back into their own world.

It wouldn't last long. The general would realize what she'd done, but every demon that crossed back over meant more fae saved.

Shouting grew from the demon world. Orders came to halt the stampede, to turn around and hurry back. The demons stumbled, tripping and running into each other. Before any could cross back to the fae world, Ricci closed the portal. Every demon in the portal's range disappeared, leaving a wide clearing of bodies around her.

At the same time, there came a rending sound, like the earth splitting in two. A spout of flame erupted from inside the castle walls. Something shot up into the air.

King Theron. He hovered, massive wings beating against the pink sky.

Ricci was exposed on an empty field, and he stared right at her.

CHAPTER 48

Callen's breaths came too fast, so loud in the confines of the servants' passage. How had Marek known he was here?

"Whatever you're planning won't work." Marek didn't even look up from the desk, still sorting Callen's father's coins. The father he'd killed.

Callen saw red. He mashed his teeth and kicked open the hidden door. He conjured a sword, quick as he ever had. It glowed blue with flame. "You dare stand there after invading my home, killing my father, threatening my girlfriend?"

Two demons rushed into the room, but Marek waved them off, straightening. "Girlfriend? My daughter, Oriana, is engaged to King Theron. There's no magic in the world that can break the spell she's under." He smirked. "That's the strongest sword you've conjured. This should be fun." He conjured his own sword—a wooden practice one, just like at their lessons. Arrogant bastard.

Callen rushed him. Marek raised his weapon to block.

Their swords connected, and blue flame erupted over the wood, drenching it with dollops of inferno.

Marek's eyes widened. The air zinged as he drew magic to control the blaze.

Callen parried, and again Marek blocked him, but more flames dripped down to catch Marek's robes.

"Enough of this." Marek raised his free hand.

The spell hit Callen square in the chest. And did nothing. The force of the magic should have killed him. The shield potion Callen had dumped over his head worked.

Before Marek could react, Callen thrust upward, slicing into Marek's forearm.

He screamed, dropping his wooden sword to clutch his arm. "Get him!"

Two demons charged into the room, swords brandished. Callen dropped his weapon, dissipating it. He popped open a potion and flung its contents just as the demons reached him.

The amber droplets splattered against them. They turned to solid wood. Their momentum carried them forward, and their forms crashed into Callen at the knees. Pain flared, and he tumbled to the ground. Red seeped through his bandages.

"So you've come to play." Marek pulled at his magic, like a storm sucking the energy from the air.

With no visual warning, the remaining vials in Callen's pockets shattered. The potions mixed together.

Oh, Gods. Still on the ground, Callen ripped off his robes. The moment they left his hand, they exploded. Callen was blown back toward the hallway. Marek crashed into the wall by the window. The center of the room went aflame, with smaller patches scattered from the blast.

Pushing through the pain, Callen struggled to his feet and hurried down the hall to his room.

To the bag of potions he'd left in his haste to find his family. The bag Marek had insisted be brought here from the inn.

Marek's laugh followed him. "You're weak."

Callen burst into his room. The bag was still there. The vials were still intact. He grabbed one, uncorking it as carefully as he could with shaking hands.

For Your Enemies

"You've been a nuisance long enough." Marek's voice was right behind him.

Callen jumped and spun. The contents of the vial flung out. He gasped. Some drops landed on the floor, instantly dissolving through the thick carpet.

The rest splashed over Marek.

"Your potions aren't good for anything. Quit getting in my way and hurry up and die." Marek pulled at his magic, then he glanced at his shoulders and chest where the potion was eating through his robes.

Next would be his body.

All the years his master taught him potions flashed through Callen's mind. He hadn't been horrible the whole time. Kindness had prevailed as he'd shown Callen how to run the shop and given him his independence—taught him how to be his own man. But that didn't matter in the face of what he'd done and what he still might do. Right?

Marek screamed as the potion reached his skin. He grabbed at his chest, swiping. Callen rushed to his potions bag. He dug for anything to counteract the acid. *Anything.*

With the force of a hurricane, Marek pulled at his magic.

The windows exploded out. The vials shattered. Callen flung the bag away before it burst into flames. The furniture splintered, pieces hovering in the air before blasting out in all directions.

Callen ducked, covering his head.

Marek writhed, sending spells rocking through the room. Clouds formed, and rain poured down upon them. The floor bucked beneath them.

Marek fell to the floor. The rain stopped. Magic cleared from the room. He turned to Callen, panting. His breathing slowed.

Callen stood, heart pounding, readying for whatever destruction would come next.

A red light flowed from Marek's forehead and up.

A light, just like with Ricci.

Callen's lungs seized. That meant...

Oh no. He collapsed to his knees. "Master," he gasped.

"Forgive me, my young apprentice. I did all I could to resist. King Theron poisons the mind." His eyes closed.

"What have I done?" Callen pulled at his hair.

"You will make a great mage. Tell Ricci I'm sorry. Poisoning her mother. Thought I was saving the world." His breathing ceased.

Callen leaned over his former master, eyes burning. The demon king, he'd been in control of Marek. All this time? Marek's single-minded ferocity was driven by a being of pure evil with only one power-hungry goal—to conquer the fae. But not always. His real master, the master he should have had all along, had shown through in rare, wonderful glimpses.

He wept for the unfairness of it. But there was no time. Callen grabbed a blanket off his old bed and covered Marek's body. Glancing down at his bloody underclothes, Callen darted across the room to the other bag the innkeeper had delivered.

As he was shrugging on a spare robe, boots pounded up the stairs.

Callen darted across the room, reaching the servants' door in the wall just as more demons burst inside. Their snarls and shrieks and his breaking heart were all he heard as he rushed down the passageway toward the safety of the tunnel.

CHAPTER 49

King Theron was too powerful to contain. Ricci should have known the dungeon couldn't hold him. The putrid demons surrounded her, black depths unseeing, yet somehow boring straight into her soul and darkest nightmares.

He hovered high above her, lips curled into a snarl. "Bring her alive, and dine with me on fae meat."

The frenzied demons charged. Like a red death, King Theron dove toward her.

Her breath stuck in her throat. Where could she go?

Lela.

Ricci opened a portal and closed it just as quickly.

The room was dark. It took a few moments for her eyes to adjust. Her heart hammered in her ears. She hadn't noticed it beating so fast with the noise of battle. The sounds were still there—boulders crashing, screams of the dying, swords clanging—just muffled and far away. Here was whimpering and fitful sleeping, with the musty smell of old castle walls. Torchlight filtered from a stone hallway.

Finally, she made out the forms of sleeping bodies huddled under thin blankets. No one had awoken at her arrival, but Lela had to be here.

"Lela," she whispered. No one stirred. "Lela," she said louder.

A few people stirred, looked at her, and rolled back over. She no longer appeared human, but that didn't stop her instinct to hide.

"Ricci!" Lela sprung from a bedroll in the corner. She hopped over a couple people and launched herself, hugging Ricci tight. Then she pulled away with a worried look. "Did King Theron send you?"

"He bewitched me. I know that now," Ricci said, ashamed.

Lela's brow creased. "He's the most powerful sorcerer in existence. How did you break his spell?"

"He made me feel I was devoted and indebted to him. That I loved him." Ricci spoke slowly, the thoughts forming as she said them aloud. "And I believed him because my birth mom is dead, my birth dad is pure evil, and my parents never told me the truth. But then I realized that doesn't matter. Their love for me is real, and it will always outshine any half-truths." She looked around. "How did you get away from the demon king?"

Lela's lower lip trembled. "My pata saved me." She rubbed at her mouth. "Oren did too, but he was injured. I healed him."

"You healed him?" Ricci whispered. "With your herbs?" They'd healed Ricci too, when she'd been locked up and sick. She lowered her voice. "I tried to trap the demon king in the dungeon, but he escaped."

"It wasn't my herbs." Lela smiled. "I found my power."

There was a sudden roar, and the wall behind them exploded.

Fae awoke with screams, darting for cover.

"You can't hide from me, Oriana," the demon king said

357

above the crash of stone and debris. "I have your scent. Your magic and blood belong to me."

Ricci didn't think. Reacting on instinct, she grabbed Lela and opened a portal. Stone blocks flew toward them, but Ricci closed the portal, and they disappeared unharmed.

His rumbling chuckle followed them to the other side.

They were in another room of the castle, alone, and further away from the battle by the sound of it.

"Ricci!" Lela cried out. "Take me back. Those other healers, they need our help."

Ricci nearly complied with Lela's commanding authority, but hesitated. She gripped her cousin by the arms. "If we don't stop him, more fae will die. I trapped some of his army back in the demon world, but there's still a lot left. They've breached the castle."

Lela's eyes widened. "They'll take the king. Prince Renic—he has no heir."

The flapping of wings sounded outside above them.

"He's found us," Ricci said.

"Come on." Lela grabbed her hand. "We have to find Oren. I have an idea."

Lela led her through empty hallways, taking a few wrong turns and having to backtrack. "Sorry, I don't know exactly where you brought us."

They reached the front of the castle, exiting into a stone courtyard. Demons were everywhere. The fae fought them in bloody one-on-one battles. More fae fought at the doorways, doing everything to prevent the demons from advancing further. Ricci and Lela struggled to find their way around the melee. Blood ran in streams down the cobblestone.

"This way," Lela said, leading them up a stone staircase with a steep drop on one side. "This is where he was stationed.

He's the only one besides me who will trust you. He'll get the king to safety."

Ricci hurried after her, struggling to keep up with Lela's speed and stamina. She strained to hear the beating of wings, but there was too much fighting.

At the top of the stairs, Lela turned a corner and gasped. The thunderous whoosh of flapping, then the tips of monstrous black wings rose from behind the battlements. Lela stopped in her tracks.

Ricci charged ahead. "Lela!" She pulled up her magic, reaching for Lela with both hands.

The demon king smashed his palm onto Lela's forehead. Red light burst from his hand. Lela stilled.

Her face went slack.

"Kill her," he rumbled with the faintest smile.

Lela drew her knife. Quick as Ricci had ever seen her move, she turned and slashed, left-right-left.

Ricci stumbled backward down the stairs. "Stop! It's not real. He doesn't love you." She reached for a portal, but Lela slashed, slicing her arm before she twisted away.

"Lela!" Ricci screamed.

Lela kicked out. Ricci's legs were knocked from beneath her. She was falling.

She rolled down several steps before finally catching herself on the wall. Pain bloomed all over her body. Knife raised, Lela advanced.

Everything had gone so wrong. Ricci could portal away, leave this world to its own fate. It was what she might have done, once. Not anymore. She pulled herself to her feet. "Don't do this, Lela. We're cousins—family," she sobbed. "I love you."

Lela's mouth went slack.

"I love you," Ricci said again. "Your mata loves you. Oren loves you. Your pata died loving you."

The knife slipped from Lela's fingers. It clanked to the stone stairs, falling over the edge.

"End this," the demon king hissed.

Lela shook her head, and her eyes narrowed. She grabbed a discarded crossbow from beside the body of a fae, taking aim.

Ricci backed down a few more steps, hands raised. "Lela, stop. This isn't you. You know who you are." She readied her magic.

Lela released the bolt. It flew true, right toward Ricci's head. The demon king smiled.

"No!" Ricci flung up a portal around her.

The arrow entered the foggy space. With a split-second shift of her magic, the arrow portaled away from her. Right next to the demon king.

His eyes widened. He tried to dodge, but the arrow drove in right above his heart.

He clutched the shaft and yanked it out with a sickening rip and a grin. His magic tinged the air with an electric zing as he healed himself, the wound sealing over.

No! She looked for another crossbow. Lela scrambled for one as well, her angry glare on Ricci.

He dove for Ricci. Air whooshed from his furiously-beating wings. Ricci jumped from halfway up the stairs, his claws grazing her shoulder. She landed hard on the ground, knees popping as she threw her momentum into a roll. Pain vibrated up her body.

King Theron's laugh rumbled through her. He landed on the stairs, descending slowly, Lela trailing behind. "It's the cousin you want, or you'd be gone already. I can release her. Your life for hers. If you simply submit."

Ricci stood straight and clenched her fists, hating how he'd read her so easily.

The demon king's arm shot out, and he grabbed Lela by the

throat. Her eyes flashed with the pain of betrayal as her feet left the ground, but she didn't struggle. His clawed hand engulfed her entire neck.

"Don't hurt her," Ricci yelled, casting about for another weapon. Her eyes landed on a knife, Lela's knife, and she lunged for it.

King Theron laughed again. "You can't defeat me."

Lela emitted choking sounds, yet still didn't fight for her own life. Ricci smothered her panic. There was no time.

"That's where you're wrong." Ricci opened a portal—the smallest she'd ever made—around the knife in her palm. She closed it, and the knife disappeared.

The demon king smirked. "You've tried that trick already." Then his eyes went wide. He dropped Lela, who landed hard on the stairs, coughing. His hands went to his chest, and he roared. The sound sent Ricci to her knees, coving her ears as it rattled her bones.

King Theron coughed, and blood flowed from the corners of his mouth. He ripped into his chest with his claws, through scales and flesh. But he couldn't reach the knife embedded in his heart behind his ribcage. His wings flapped erratically as he took flight. His body flew off-kilter. Blood splattered the ground in gobs, and then his wings stopped moving.

She might have caused the devastation to the fae people, but now they'd learn she could end it. Ricci opened a portal around the demon king, the first time she'd ever opened one without being connected to it herself—he'd opened her eyes to her true capabilities. Concentrating, she opened a new portal high above the battle, just outside the castle gates where the fighting would be thickest.

With a grunt of effort, Ricci sent the king of the demons through the portal. She left it open as he dropped from the sky, a monstrous red mass in the distance. As he fell behind the walls, she lost sight of him, but the crash and rumble as he landed was unmistakable.

The sounds of battle halted for a beat.

Lela cried out, then her eyes cleared. She slumped against the stairs, panting. Clutching her forehead, a red glow streamed out and dissipated into the air. Her eyes sought Ricci. "I nearly killed you." Her voice was a hoarse squeak, and she looked at her hands. "I wasn't strong enough to resist."

Ricci rushed up the stairs and hugged her cousin. The bruises on her throat were already fading. "I'm okay. We're okay."

Lela wore a quiet look of anguish as she channeled her magic into healing Ricci's cut. Some of Ricci's weariness lifted.

They climbed the rest of the way to peer over the battlements. Wings flayed, blood splatted, King Theron was no more.

Relief crashed through Ricci so hard she gripped the wall for support. "He's dead."

Lela grabbed her arm. "You did it."

In the distance, the fae battled the remaining demons, but they were still outnumbered.

"We have to help them," Ricci said. She didn't know how to fight, but she could portal out as many as she could reach.

"Look!" Lela pointed. Crossing the bridge was a squad of fae women on horseback. "Lady Sarafine is leading them."

Ricci squinted, and sure enough, Lady Sarafine led the pack, maybe a dozen in all. At the end of the bridge, they split off, each going a different direction.

"They're going to fight," Ricci said. "We should help them."

Lady Sarafine reached a fae who fought three demons at once. The demons turned hazy, then disappeared.

Ricci gasped, then scanned the battlefield for the other riders. Where they stopped, the demons vanished.

Lela gripped her hand. "They're opening portals. They have the gift."

Pride filled Ricci. "And they aren't afraid to use it." The roar of battle and the clanging of weapons died down as more and more demons were felled or portaled away.

At the base of the castle below them, a crowd gathered around the demon king's body. They turned their gazes upward. One of them wore a silver circlet—Prince Renic. He stared at her with an open mouth—as if he'd never truly seen her until this moment—before racing back toward the castle.

"It's the human." The soldiers pointed.

"But look at her ears. She's not human."

"The portal opener."

"And the general's daughter. They saved us." A great cheer arose from the fae.

Lela squeezed Ricci's arm. "You're a hero. You've changed our history."

Ricci started to protest—she was the cause of all this—but Lela gasped, turning her attention back below.

Oren pushed his way through the crowd. Helm off and blond hair cascading around his dirt-smudged face, he stared up at Lela, grinning. He rushed inside the keep, dodging bodies and debris, and up the staircase to join them.

"Hurray for Ricci!" Oren yelled, wrapping Lela up in his arms. "Woah, your ears." Blood smeared his black armor, but he appeared unharmed. "Are you fae?"

"She's my cousin," Lela said, pride in her voice.

"Then you're family," he said to Ricci, awe and appreciation in his gaze. "You saved us,"

Ricci almost felt satisfaction, but the ugly truth still hung over them, robbing her of her worthiness. "It wasn't enough. I'm still to blame for what's happened here." All these fae, dead because of her.

"That's not true," Lela said, holding Oren's hand. "It was the demon king. And because of what you did, my people—no, our people—never have to live in fear again. You saved us from the prophecy." She hugged Ricci tight. "I'm so sorry for hurting you. I should have been stronger."

Ricci examined her healed arm. "If it's not my fault, then this isn't your fault either."

Oren wrapped his arm around Lela's waist.

Ricci couldn't wait for Callen to hold her like that. She fished in her pocket for the silver flower, praying he was okay. "I have to go, Lela. Callen needs me."

"But you'll come back?" Lela asked. "The people saw what you did. Word will spread. You'll be welcome here, I'm sure of it."

"In time," Oren added, face tilted in apology.

"Nothing could keep me from my cousin." Ricci flashed a wavering smile.

Lela hugged her tight. "Cousin and best friend." She squeezed. "Thank you for saving us."

"You saved me first." Ricci backed away. "Take care of each other."

Thoughts turning to Callen, she opened a portal, took one last look, then closed it.

CHAPTER 50

L ela watched as Ricci opened a portal upon the castle battlements. It closed impressively fast, but the gongs were already raging from the portals Lady Sarafine and her warriors opened across the battlefield.

Lela's heart broke, watching her cousin disappear. "I hope I see her again."

Oren trailed his fingers down her arm, then took her hand. "She saved us. She's a hero."

Lela's skin prickled with heat where his fingers touched. She couldn't believe he took her hand willingly, and not just for friendly comfort. Their first real kiss had stayed with her all night and day. "Will they ever accept her? Or them?" The fear was rooted deep. The portal openers took a big risk revealing their energies.

Oren's jaw clenched. "Truth will win out. Hopefully. It's difficult to change the minds of a millennia of stubborn fae. I mean, look at me. You had trouble convincing me, and I'm your life-long friend."

She turned to him. "Friend?"

His cheeks reddened, but his eyes turned hungry. His gaze flicked to her mouth. "Mate." He drew the word out, each sound deep and annunciated, sending shivers through her body.

Lela licked her lips.

He pulled her hips against his. "I'm sorry I treated you with indifference. I was an idiot—even if our laws wouldn't allow it. Before."

"Before?" What day was it? "Oh!"

"Happy birthday," he said, low and husky. Then he crushed his mouth against hers.

Lela kissed him, meeting his passion. Nothing could make her more complete in this moment. She couldn't wait to get home and tell Mata.

Callen fought against grief as he traveled the underground tunnels, stumbling, sending loose rocks skittering. The demon army still roared outside. Any minute one of them might find him. His father was dead. Marek was dead. Callen had been under his roof and tutelage almost as long as his own parents. How much of that time had Marek been under the demon king's influence? The entire apprenticeship, surely. But there had been good in him, too. A part of him had wanted Callen to succeed, had shown him kindness.

Marek had been a great mage once. Callen vowed to honor his legacy, and his father's, by becoming a great mage too. He'd start at the heart of the mage building.

His steps slowed. He'd already done great things, hadn't he? He'd saved his family, found love, broken the curse that had held Ricci in its grip, and defeated a powerful mage who would have destroyed the world.

Callen's steps landed surer, chin a little higher, as he made it through the rest of the tunnels without being seen. When he emerged from underground, he spotted the king's army in the distance, riding to save them. Leaderless and without the power behind Marek's sorcery, the demons wouldn't hold out for long.

Ricci, where are you? As Callen hurried back to their families, he opened his magic and reached for the silver flower he'd made for her. His magic touched upon it, bobbing and weaving in the other world. She was still alive, fighting for life, it seemed.

Callen was almost at the camp when the connection suddenly disappeared. Callen gasped, coming to a halt. Had someone destroyed it? Destroyed her? He pushed his magic, willing it to find her. *Find Ricci.*

Please, you must be okay. You must.

Static buzzed in the air. Callen swung around. When he looked back, there she was. Ricci stood in front of him, a shy smile on her face.

Ricci hadn't needed the silver flower to find Callen. She'd wanted him, and there he was. She closed the portal, and he stood in front of her, looking wet and haggard. A grin lit up his face. He rushed to her, limping. She threw herself into his arms. Callen spun her in circles, laughing with her. He smelled like burnt metal and felt like coming home.

"You're okay," he said. He put his forehead to hers.

"And you're okay." She chuckled.

"Marek is dead. King Willmott rides to finish off the demon army."

"The demon king is dead." They spoke at the same time.

"We did it," he said. "What about Lela?"

"She's safe. Their world is safe now." Ricci smiled, but her lips trembled.

"You'll see her again," he said, already knowing what troubled her. Callen held her close. His arms eased and warmed her weary soul.

She lay her head on his chest. "I will."

"There's something I've wanted to do for a long time." He lifted her face and leaned down.

She licked her lips, giving permission, and he touched his mouth to hers. Her breath caught. His kiss was warm and silky, inviting her in for more. His hand rested against her cheek, and she wrapped her arms more fully around him as their lips danced. Her entire body pulsed and tingled. Her first kiss. *Their* first kiss.

Too soon, she pulled away. There were still so many unanswered questions. Where were they?

They stood on a dirt road, uneven with numerous wagon ruts and scattered with crackling leaves. Empty market stalls and shops lined the road. Everything was so quiet. A river gurgled in the distance.

"This is the market in Timbercross," Ricci said.

"Yes." He took her hand and smiled. "I know what will complete this moment for you. Come on."

He led her around a bend, and Ricci saw green ahead. She gasped in delight. "You brought me home." Her parents were parked right where they'd been when this journey began.

Ricci and Callen took off at a jog.

"They're here," Mama cried from the back of the wagon.

Her family poured out onto the road while Callen's family went to embrace him.

They gathered her up in a big group hug, laughing, crying, and asking questions all at once. Papa shooed them back, and he and Mama took her hands.

"Ricika, my baby, you're back," Mama said. Tears filled her eyes.

Ricci squeezed her hands. "It feels so good to be home."

She hugged her stubborn, nagging, wouldn't-change-her-for-the-world mama hard around her waist. Papa wiped tears from his face, laughing.

Callen put his arm around his mother's shoulders, smiling at Ricci.

"If we hurry," Nicholas said, "we can make it to Pulton before market is over."

Her family cheered, but Ricci pulled back. Yes, she had control over her magic now, but it still seemed reckless to go back to opening portals on stage. What she needed was time, and a place to learn all she could about the potential consequences of opening portals to foreign worlds.

Her parents and Callen watched her, waiting for her to speak.

"Actually, Mama, Papa. I'm thinking of taking a break from performing to study magic. I need to learn what I'm capable of before I take the stage again." And maybe use the time to right more of the wrong she'd caused.

Her birth mother had died living her whole life hiding her magic from her own people. Ricci could honor her by learning and not hiding from her own gift.

Callen beamed, looking like he might burst with happiness.

Her family lapsed into silence and stillness.

Mama and Papa exchanged glances.

Papa stepped forward. "You do anything you want, my Ricci. Whatever choice you make, you will not disappoint."

Ricci let out a breath and hugged him fiercely. "Thank you, Papa."

He patted her back. "You will always have a place with us."

Her brothers, Nora and Jace, her aunt, uncle, and cousins took turns congratulating her, then Callen wrapped her in a hug and kissed her sweetly on the mouth.

"You'll always have a place with me, too." He kissed her again. "I can't wait to start our next adventure together."

Ricci grinned ear to ear, cheeks hot. She thought she'd known what happiness was. She thought if she just had certain things, her life would be so much better. It took almost losing the things most precious to her for her to value what she already had. And she had a lot. Family and love. They'd taken on new meanings, too.

The End

Did you like this book? Please leave a review!

Scan the QR code or visit kristinlhamblin.com to access Kristin's other books, fun links, and monthly newsletter for updates and giveaways!

Acknowledgments

I'd like to thank my early critique and beta reader team for their help working the kinks out in this story, especially Ann Adams for her insights and feedback.

Thank you to my lovely ARC readers! Your enthusiasm from the start made this such a fun and rewarding process. Angie Marie, Ashley Berry, Jamie Fallowfield, Dianna Britton, Brianna Storti, and so many more! I had the best time as you championed this book. You're all amazing and invaluable!

To my Watchers (newsletter subscribers)! Thank you for letting me into your lives once a month with my author stories, book updates, and pet pictures. Your replies, giveaway participation, and enthusiasm lift me up and give my efforts meaning.

Thank you to my daughters, husband, family, and friends for your unyielding support, excitement, and willingness to always help!

Readers! Thank you for being here. For reading these last words at the end of a piece years in the making. This would be nothing without you, your kind comments, reviews, word of mouth, and enthusiasm.

About the Author

Kristin L. Hamblin writes young adult romantic fantasy stories full of unforgettable friendships, forbidden love, and strong female characters who kick butt on their way to happily ever after. She lives in Oklahoma with her husband, four daughters, and a menagerie of pets including two wiener dogs, Ruby and Sunny. Join her newsletter for exclusive content and connect with her at kristinlhamblin.com

Made in the USA
Columbia, SC
29 October 2024

45026215R00231